BURIED SILENCE

BURIED SILENCE

UNDER THE BIG SKY

A NOVEL BY

SUSAN HEMPHILL

First edition

ISBN 978-0-9972777-1-5

To Toni
Queen of the Valley

PREFACE

I began writing *Buried Silence* after my best friend's friend was killed in an explosion inside her home. She was the Chief Financial Officer of a residential club for the very wealthy who lived behind the private gates of privilege, opulence and excess.

The story takes place in 2012, before television shows brought the attention of the masses to life in Montana. The members of the residential club had moved there for all the things their money could buy, a protected life below the majestic mountains on the banks of the Yellowstone River. Although the characters are fictitious, the lifestyle was not. They lived in an endless swirl of parties and rendezvous, much like the Great Gatsby era. No one thought of it as an unprecedented time, they believed the champagne would flow as freely as the river and their innocence was a God-given gift, as abundant as the surrounding wildlife. I invite you to join me in those days, where Buried Silence twists inside the façade of stillness.

Susan Hemphill

Please check my website, SusanHemphill.com, for more about the characters in *Buried Silence*.

PROLOGUE

The super-rich weren't always a part of Paradise Valley, Montana.

Like the Native Indians who had never encountered the white man before, Montanans had never seen such mansions and ostentatious people move into their state.

The community was the neighbor to protected Yellowstone National Park, with its incredible beauty. Here, home was truly on the range. The deer, antelope, bears and buffalo knew no boundaries, roaming freely through the valley as well as the park.

This had been the land where proud, weather-beaten people stood by their word. Now came residents who stood, not by their word, but indiscreetly on top of their money.

★★★

She felt water and soot oozing inside her black Chanel ballet flats as she tried to tip toe through the wet ashes; her swollen ankle made grace difficult. Katherine wondered why no one was around. Maybe last night's storm had blown away the crime scene tape. Maybe crime scene tape was too urban for Montana.

Part of Stacey's barn had flown into her kitchen area. As Katherine stepped over a piece of tack and doorframe she felt the slight ping of a snag on her pant leg. Another annoyance but small amidst a life ripped to shreds.

Shattered glass and blackened wood were thrown next to wet and dirty clothing. All that was left of a fishing rod was a slender charcoaled stump. Gone were her sketches of birds and wildlife. Katherine bent down to pick up a florescent yellow plastic paper, maybe DuraForm, as it was waterproof but not fireproof. The bottom part had burned off but she could still read the remains of Stacey's fishing license from Montana Fish, Wildlife & Parks, Eyes: Blue, Height: 5'3", Weight: 110, Hair: Blonde.

The explosion four days ago had spared some of Stacey's possessions but not her life. Why wasn't anyone here? The authorities must have had something else to do. They took their time in Montana. Life in this new Wild West was upside down for Katherine. If this had happened in New York, the area would have been swarming with law enforcement. Maybe it was apathy but this was more likely another example of a culture with slower standards. Here, there was no immediacy to anything.

Katherine pushed back the tears, knowing her mascara was running down her cheeks but she didn't care. This moonscape was what was left of Stacey. It gave her the chills. Standing alone, she felt like it was surreal, as if the devastation was worse and stung even more than it would have been on the ambitious and fast East Coast. This was where she had believed life would be safe but Stacey's death made time stand still and for the first time in Montana, she knew that greed, lust and vengeance weren't limited to Wall Street, its roots were even here, under the big blue sky and the enormous ancient mountains.

Local Montanans didn't pay much attention to those associated with the Antelope Club. They didn't care about what went on with the rich or the famous. Years ago, when California's former governor hit the headlines for being the baby daddy of his housekeeper's child, he fled to Montana. In the midst of a paparazzi storm unveiling his life's intimate details, he sat having breakfast at Pinky's, Livingston's small café on Main Street, just down the highway from the Antelope Club. Katherine had been amazed that the locals didn't call TMZ. Maybe they didn't know what TMZ was, just like they couldn't tell a Max Mara from a Michael Kors. But most likely it was because even film-star governors weren't treated much differently than a miner or a railroad worker, where privacy and a populace regarded a good fisherman as more important than a billionaire. This was why the overly affluent came to the southwest corner of the last best place on earth. Montana offered the rare commodity that their money could still buy, an almost invisible freedom amidst wide-open spaces.

As she stepped through the ruins of Stacey's home, she heard her husband's voice in her head. *Katherine, we need to live away from crowds and people. The Antelope Club is tucked away on an endless frontier with infinite trails and its own airstrip. We need to leave the Hamptons, sell the loft in TriBeCa. You can bring your horse from Bridgehampton and ride every day. We'll have privacy and protection from the never-ending shit of everyday life.*

Some protection for Stacey. Her friend, the Club's Chief Financial Officer, had been whisked out of their overly glitzy enclave and mercilessly unceremoniously cremated.

They had taken a trail ride up to Emigrant Peak the morning of the explosion. Stacey wasn't riding the trail as smoothly as usual. She was preoccupied, and her horse was feeling the anxiety. Stacey had pulled her iPad out of her saddlebag when they stopped for a break. The conversation had been minimal.

"There's something I've got to tell you and you're the only person who can help me."

"Sure. What's up?"

Stacey's fingers swished over the screen. "Never mind, I think I can fix it but I've got to go now."

Katherine had tried to stop her, to get more information, but Stacey had run back to her horse and flew down the trail like a barrel racer in the finals. Minutes later, as Katherine had just begun her own descent, she heard what sounded like thunder rolling up from below. Then all the flames and all the smoke.

Here was the shocking evidence pile of what happens when you know too much or fuck the wrong people.

She looked up into the tall granite mountain peaks above her. Quiet. As if one person, more or less, didn't matter.

CHAPTER ONE

It was five days earlier. The invitation for this party, printed on a copy of a Spam label had said, "Bring a chair and a dish to share." Katherine juggled her lawn chair and a pot of bourbon hot dog appetizers as she walked from her car on the gravel and limestone walkway to Marie and Scott's mansion. She could hear the band playing older country, Scott's favorite. "When it comes to brains, he got the short end of the stick." Had to be a cover of Trisha Yearwood's "She's in Love with the Boy."

Stacey was standing ten feet from her in a small pool of light in front of two large French doors leading to the deck large enough to host most of the town's citizens. She wore a tight, black body suit—exactly the kind of thing she could pull off, and that would piss off the Dolls—and was surrounded by several of the Dolls' husbands, the BM of the BS as they were called – the Big Men of the Big Sky. Some cynics referred to them as the BD of the BS – Big Dicks of the Big Shit. Stacey was never invited to Doll parties. Stacey was viewed more as an employee than a member of the community. She was also universally known to be having an affair with Marie's husband, Scott, the Club's CEO and founder, which made her presence in Marie's home even more surprising. Katherine wanted to go up and give her friend a hug, but in the midst of all that attention, she stood back, better to be an observer. Beautiful smart women attracted the BM crew with a lust exceeded only by their greed for a rich deal. Two beautiful women together would create a violent collision of the Wall Street and Silicon Valley bulls fighting over their prey.

Katherine caught Marie as she was telling a rent-a-waiter (actually a Montana State University pre-med student) it was time to put the White Castle sliders into the oven. There was something slightly off about a party in which the help, with their black vests and bow ties, were overdressed compared to the guests, but such was life in the Antelope Club.

"I'm glad you invited Stacey." Katherine said, knowing it might get a rise out of Marie.

"It's a white-trash party. She obviously didn't get the joke and actually came."

"I see my neighbor over there, the celebrity, came as himself." Although he was surrounded by a group of the more liberal of the Antelope Club members, it was nice that he felt comfortable showing up. He had named an album after the area and the locals, both Club members and townspeople had a cool respect to let celebrities just live a normal life without being hounded.

"He said he'd play a couple of tunes at the end of the evening if anyone was interested. As if we weren't going to be. He only brought his acoustic guitar, so it should be intimate," said Marie.

Katherine had been surprised Scott and Marie were hosting a party at all, what with the state of the Club.

Wanton knapweed and cheat grass were beginning to choke the once pristine flowerbeds and the steam room in the clubhouse had been "Closed for Repairs" for months. She'd heard through the Doll grapevine that some of the local labor hadn't been paid. The Club owed working class people money? She wondered how much Stacey knew.

The Antelope Club was a year-round residential club that sat on thousands of acres that backed into national forest land. There was a golf course for the summer and a private ski mountain for winter. The huge clubhouse was full of stuffed animal heads and gorgeous imported furnishings.

It was well known that those living in the town of Livingston thought everything was overdone and not one bit like a native Montanan community. The houses reflected what the rich thought Montana should look like. They were either log or stone homes, or a combination of both, at least ten thousand square feet, with elevators, pools, movie theaters, and bowling alleys. Most had adjacent guesthouses. Each home was nestled in with private views.

Katherine surveyed the room. The Stiles had sliced a polished wooden drift boat in half and mounted it on the wall below the giant stuffed heads of a moose, buffalo and six-point elk. Usually the boat was filled with ice and oysters, but now it was adorned with a pink and black zebra-printed sheet. In place of Blue Points and Olympias were mixing bowls overflowing with Ho-Hos, Ding Dongs, and the latest generation of Twinkies. The music pulsated from surround-sound speakers throughout the house. There was gaiety in the air. It felt forced for Katherine, but the others seemed right at home.

The Dolls of Paradise Valley lived for an endless round of parties. She wondered how they kept finding so much enthusiasm. The bartender was pouring plastic cups of wine out of a Franzia box. The food was on several card tables. Looking at the tinned luncheon ham on toothpicks, the green Jell-O and the microwaved hamburgers, Katherine wished she'd brought something other than bourbon hot dogs. Something she would actually want to eat.

"Oh, fuck it," she said to herself, and picked up a White Castle. She finished it off quickly and caught a glimpse of herself in Marie's mirror. She adjusted her very short denim skirt, tacky but flattering. Although she didn't feel like it, she was forty-three, but her legs still held their shape and her ass could still deliver. Her long, black hair and steel blue eyes matched her irresistible resolve. She knew she was probably the most striking looking woman in the room, even if she was a bit older than the others. Certainly no competition for who she saw sauntering up behind her.

Alissa had a pack of Marlboros tucked into her overly amped cleavage. At twenty-four, she was the youngest of the Dolls. She had curly blonde hair that she spent hours getting straightened. Her dark bottled tan along with her platinum white-blonde streaks made her look shoot up into the unnatural zone. Most of the time, except tonight, she could

4

pull it off. Tonight didn't really count, but Katherine thought Alissa looked almost natural in her version of the party theme. Her bright red lipstick had overshot the confines of her lips and was bleeding up into her cheek. Her dress was very tight, barely covering her long legs. She held a baby doll dressed in a dirty romper.

"I'm trying to figure out who's my baby daddy," she said. "All my options seem to be enchanted by Stacey over there. What's she doing here anyway?"

"Marie said it was a joke," Katherine replied with a grimace. A part of Katherine wanted to defend Stacey to these women, but the smarter part of her told her it was better to shut up and blend. She was among them but not of them.

Alissa paid no attention. "She's such a slut," Alissa said with a slight slur, still staring at Stacey. "Look at her. She doesn't care how she gets it or who she gets it from."

It was clear she had already downed a few drinks, as had most of the guests, although it was still early. No one was in their right mind and no one was dressed as themselves, although Katherine thought it was a fine exhibit of some hidden inner character traits. Hell, several of the BM of the BS, especially Scott, Stacey had told her, came from the poor side of their hometowns and had clawed their way to the top of the top with whatever it took. It was like reliving their past, with no one saying a word about it.

As she started to look for less pitiful conversation, maybe a bored husband who would talk finance, an unidentifiable man covered in a white plastic bag with cut outs for his eyes and mouth came up and grabbed Alissa's doll.

"I'm your baby daddy!" he said.

Katherine smirked at his very literal take on white trash and walked away, wondering what Alissa's husband, Brad, would think of the tableau. Katherine knew Brad was away, which was why she was comfortable being there. As she had never attended one of these parties before, she had asked Marie what people usually wore. She said, "We all used to go down and sit in front of Pamida to get inspiration." Katherine felt it totally wrong to make fun of the locals, but here she was, embarrassed for herself at this class insensitive party.

Katherine was heading in Michael's direction when she was intercepted by Lyn, who was dressed as an unkempt beauty queen. Her black bra was hanging out of her opaque white dress showing her abundance of cleavage. Her crown was lopsided over some version of teased pageant blonde hair. Her eyes were glossy and her pupils dilated. She had a pill bottle in her hands. Lyn had a reputation for going into handbags in search of "medication." Perhaps she was openly acknowledging her little secret or maybe she was trying to make everyone think it was a joke.

"Hey, see our star over there? Always so polite, very cute. Didn't you think it was amazing watching him with that guitar performing for the whole town? It's his home here now. The thing about him is that he's open to the whole of Livingston. He doesn't hang up here all the time where he lives."

"Who'd he bring with him? He's good looking too," said Lyn.

"That one is Will. He's a hunting-fishing guide and my neighbor, Jean's son. He's a fourth generation Montanan. He usually doesn't show up at these kind of things. Will is a guys' guy. I bet those two started out at The Murray then stopped to see more friends and ended up here. Shakes it up to have different types at these parties."

"Katherine, I just love your outfit. The pink gloves are such a good touch." As Lyn spoke she lost her balance and almost fell straight to the floor.

Scott came up from behind to catch her. Scott was five eleven and had slicked his brownish hair straight back trying to cover his bald spots. He kept in firm shape, like a hard bullet, wearing camouflage shorts with black lace-up boots and a sleeveless t-shirt showing a picture of toilet paper saying, "That's How I Roll."

"Hey, time to shake it, baby." As Scott spoke he grabbed Lyn by the hips and pulled her in so closely they were almost touching lips. "I like to keep the fucking within the family, but since I can't find my sister tonight, can I have you?" He tried for a straight face but burst into laughter. Lyn managed to hang onto him as he pulled her to join the others who were grinding like high school kids on the dance floor.

Katherine noticed her husband, Michael, talking to a young male waiter in a corner. She was glad to see him; he wasn't tall but he was handsome, on the cusp of gorgeous, with his thick head of salt and pepper hair. If James Dean had lived to make it into his forties, Katherine thought he would have looked like Michael: thick eyebrows and full lips. He was small in stature but huge in demeanor. His eyes could be a mesmerizing blue and his nose fit his face perfectly. He was only two years older than Katherine but sometimes, like now, his beautiful smile looked as young and innocent as a child's.

It had been a week since he'd been home. He was usually too wrapped up in his work to waste his time with these parties. But tonight, somehow, he had come up with a pair of black leather pants, steel-toed boots, and a studded leather jacket that made him look passably like a biker.

At the entrance to the home theater, Sophia was talking to a small cluster of Dolls. She wore a leopard coat topped with gobs of jewelry, a blackened eye and fake tattoos across her chest. Katherine smiled as she scanned the ensemble.

"Another party, another outfit," said Sophia with a sigh. Of all the Dolls, Katherine preferred Sophia's company. Neither minced words.

"You look kind of sick, or are you just tired?" asked Katherine.

"Both," said Sophia. "John just got in a heated conversation with Scott. He told him he wanted out of the World Club Italy. We haven't even seen a photo of our new estate and John gave him twelve million up front. Scott had the audacity to tell him he was welcome to sell it. How can you sell something that doesn't seem to exist? John and I want to buy a home in Venice, instead of Tuscany. I'm beginning to believe Scott is nothing more than smoke and cracked mirrors. And then to top it off, this morning John was on the phone with our broker and that wasn't pretty either. John said the guy sounded really shaken, saying things like he couldn't predict the stock markets anymore. "

"Where is John?"

"He's about to leave. He said he's going home to calm down and get back to doing something worthwhile. He's organizing an outing for wounded Vets, taking a group up to the Diamond Bar dude ranch."

Katherine smiled. "You married a saint."

"I did," said Sophia. "But I've never seen him like this. He has a lot invested with Scott and in the markets. I mean, he's so sweet, telling me that it's only money. But it's given me a bad headache. What do you think?"

John came up to them. His genuine smile was refreshing. In his forties and a bit rotund, he was still handsome even with a thinning head of charcoal gray hair. Wearing tan khakis and a golf shirt, he always dressed the same—theme party be damned. He squeezed Sophia's hand then softly kissed her on the lips.

Katherine heard his whisper. "Don't worry, honey, we'll be fine. I'll have a little surprise for you when you get home. I'm sure you won't eat a thing here tonight."

"Thank you, darling," said Sophia.

They watched John as he headed to the front door.

Katherine and Sophia gazed out into the sea of partygoers and saw Scott dancing with Lyn. She was doing a version of the twist and was practically on her knees when she fell into Scott's crotch and laid a messy kiss.

Katherine was nursing the scotch she had brought from home in her silver flask. This was not what she had expected to be doing in early retirement. She scanned the room for Michael, but he had vanished, so she just stood watching the denizens of the Antelope Club amuse themselves.

The drinks used to be on her.

She was glad that she'd be out in the fresh air tomorrow, on a trail ride through the mountains with Stacey.

CHAPTER TWO

Katherine's horse knew the narrow trail well, so well she dropped the reins to lean over the cliff and snap photos of the expansive valley below. She tucked her phone away and looked at Stacey in front of her. Her mare had a huge rear end, quite unlike Stacey herself, who looked great in jeans. She never dressed flashily, especially on the trail. Her worn-in jeans complimented a turquoise, white, and gray plaid blouse, the kind with snap buttons. It was likely from the feed store, nothing expensive. She knew why she wore long sleeves: protection from a fall or a wayward tree.

Of course she had on those boots. Katherine remembered when Stacey had the boots custom made at Wilson's in Livingston. They had gone together and Stacey had been very specific about the color combo. They weren't the fancy kind like many of the Dolls and the Big Men of the Big Sky had made over in Dillon. They were two-tone, green over brown, with a rounded toe and a two-and-a-quarter-inch riding heel.

Neither Katherine nor Stacey had said a word about the party. They'd barely gotten a chance to talk to each other the night before, what with every BM of the BS trying to take up all of Stacey's time. There was something about Stacey that drew in these men—maybe the simple fact that she didn't "need" any of them in the way their wives did. Sex with these married men was fun for her, not complicated and messy—perhaps that's what made her and Katherine such good friends; they were objective and resourceful.

It was a surprisingly warm fall day. As the wind kicked up, Katherine sealed her lips and closed her mouth. After learning to trail ride, she understood the literal meaning of "eat my dust." She held her breath until the grimy swirls dissipated and then swatted a fly out of her horse's ear.

Always a sure horsewoman, Stacey was riding uneasily today. Maybe it was because the Club was showing signs of neglect. Construction on the new super quad that promised to take skiers above the timberline in record time had halted mid-mountain. The garbage pick-up schedule had become erratic and the remodel of the clubhouse had recently ceased after the wrap of Tyvek paper. This wasn't the way a world-class, über-rich community operated. Stacey was CFO of this shit show and she needed to get it together.

Katherine had been a stock market power broker and then ran a huge sub-prime mortgage company back on Wall Street. She planned on telling Stacey that whatever it was, she would help her straighten up the problem. After dealing with the Street, there wasn't anything Katherine couldn't face head-on and she was ready to give Stacey any support she needed. Everything could be negotiated, renamed as something else, or covered up. You just needed to know how.

"Let's stop up here, I'm ready for an early lunch," said Stacey. "That Franzia kicked my ass last night. I probably should have brought my own booze—that's your style, right K?"

"You know I love my scotch," Katherine replied, with an easy smile.

Katherine dug iced teas and sandwiches out of her saddlebag, then turned to find Stacey pulling out her iPad.

Moments later, after a brief exchange, Stacey was back in the saddle.

"I'll call you later, K," she yelled over her shoulder as her horse set off at a

full-blown gallop, kicking like she was in the finals.

Katherine was left with an iced tea in one hand and turkey sandwich in the other. Some Wall Street Queen of the Universe she had become. She sat overlooking the valley and feeling useless. Katherine and Stacey had a bond, like veterans who had fought side-by side. Both of them had proved they could succeed in the minefields of the financial world. Even though Stacey had rushed off without mentioning any details, Katherine's financial hormones had awakened and were streaming in problem-solving, deal-making mode to solve the puzzle.

Mustard stuck to the cellophane as she rewrapped the sandwich and stowed her iced tea, hopping back on her horse, Triumph. They headed back down the mountain, slower than Stacey, but still at a good clip. She wished her neighbor, Jean, a true western cowgirl, had ridden with them. She could have convinced Stacey to stop rushing.

Then she heard it. An explosion, like the bursting of a huge bomb. The roar rolled up from the valley floor and echoed among the cliffs. Triumph reared. Katherine had been riding this same gelding for years. She didn't need verbal commands. She could think a thought and give the slightest pressure and he would obey. She tightened the reins, but he reared again. She pulled back with every ounce of strength in her body, but she couldn't control him. He was out of his mind with terror.

On her right side was a steep embankment running straight up the mountainside. On her left was slippery, moss-covered shale covering a slanted cliff. In a split second she knew she had to bail off Triumph or they were both going over the edge. If they went down together, he could roll on top of her.

This was not going to be an easy tuck and roll, as there was nowhere to go except into the unstable shale. She jumped, pulling her body into a ball, hoping she wouldn't fall too far or break a bone. She hit the shale and rolled and rolled, not stopping until her feet slid into a tree. For an instant she saw Triumph, still on the trail, now in a full gallop, his reins and saddle falling lopsided from his body. When she regained her footing she looked back. The horse was gone.

CHAPTER THREE

Dan Bentley could fill a cinematic frame with his ominous presence. At six feet two inches, he wore Stetson hats, Wrangler jeans, denim shirts and big buckles that drew female eyes to what lay beneath the sterling silver ovals. At forty-five, he was the elected Sheriff of Park County, commanding attention wherever he went. He was vaguely aware that women thought of him as a cross between John Wayne and Rhett Butler: upright, unflinching, and frankly, my dear, not giving a damn. But he did give a damn, sometimes way too big of a damn. He'd just learned the power of not letting it show.

Today was a rare occurrence, a day off on a Saturday. He had meticulously straightened and cleaned his small cabin, and now he turned to the carcass. A buddy who'd worked for him when he'd had his outfitting and guide business had given him an elk that a client had shot back in the Suce Creek drainage. The client, some kind of Hollywood big shot, had only wanted the antlers. Now the three hundred and fifty-pound, field-dressed mass was hanging from the gambrel attached to the chain hoist in his barn. Too much time had passed and the hide had set up, so it was going to take some work to get the job done.

Dan made a V with his index and third finger and pulled the hide away from the flesh. He placed the knife between his two fingers and, starting between the legs, cut up the limb to remove the skin. Once the hindquarters were skinned, he peeled the hide down to the front shoulders. This wasn't as easy as skinning his own fresh kills, when the hides slipped off like socks. It was second nature for him to cut and block out the meat into muscle groups. Raw fat and connective tissue flew into little piles as he flipped them away. The sounds of slicing and chopping continued until nothing was left hanging but the bones of the carcass. Mounds of red, raw game were heaped onto his old, blackened cookie sheets.

He barely washed the crimson, gooey moisture off his hands but was sure to cover each cut of meat with plastic wrap and butcher paper. Then everything was labeled. The entire procedure had taken a few hours, but it would provide a good portion of his year's wild game meals. As he shut the lid to his old chest freezer, he muttered a caustic thanks to the rich egotist who thought killing something permitted wastefulness. But now Dan had a lot of free meat.

Dan was in his car heading for Livingston when he thought he heard something: a deep roar-like boom or an avalanche. A few minutes later, his phone rang. It was Duane, one of his deputies. There had been an explosion. Stacey Olsen's house was on fire. Antelope Club Security was on the scene. Emergency crews were on their way.

As he drove down the valley, he noticed his adrenaline was pumping. Explosions in residential areas weren't business as usual in Paradise Valley. Business was never usual underneath Emigrant Peak but that was why the locals renamed the place Diamond Peak. But to the "exclusive" residents who lived there, it was their coveted and private domain, the Antelope Club.

Stacey; he liked her. Sure, she had a reputation for being a little too free in her private life, but he respected her both as a successful businesswoman and a damn good fisherman. Besides, she was a native Montanan. And there were fewer of them all the time.

Stacey used to book his fishing guides when he was an outfitter. He'd heard some stories that would rock any guy's boat, but she was close mouthed, smart and level headed, and he knew she trusted his advice. They'd been talking about meeting for coffee.

The residents of the Antelope Club would never know Stacey's father had been one of Montana's largest landowners. As she was an only child, with both of her parents deceased, Stacey was probably as well off as most of the members. Like a true Montanan, she kept on working and never flashed her wealth. She must have been quietly laughing at the members thinking they were so superior with all their shiny coin. Hell, she'd been driving the same truck for years. It befuddled him why Stacey lived inside the gates when she could own a home anywhere she chose. Maybe it was because her Aunt Jean lived there in what Dan thought was a humble and great anti-Antelope Club home.

He turned onto the wide, smooth drive to the Club's front gate. Once the only paved roads in Paradise Valley had been the main highways, and the only gates had cattle guards. Now he was slowing down to a set of tall steel bars flanked by river rock and stucco walls that ran for a good thirty feet, surmounted by an enormous log decorated with antlers. Along the top of the log ran hundreds of tiny lights, so that even at night the gate carved territory out of the darkness and marked it as off limits. Dan had read a brochure describing the "rustic majesty" of the gate, but to him it looked like a Vegas rendition of the Wild West.

"Name and identification, please," said the security guard, even though he knew damn well who Dan was and why he was there. Even in an emergency they tried to run the place like the Club was above the law. Or maybe somebody wanted to tamper with some evidence before he got there.

"Dan Bentley." He showed him his badge.

Instead of waving him through, the guard said, "Just a moment please."

The gate didn't move. The guard turned to his computer, typing. Dan put the car in gear and held the badge up to the window.

"Sheriff Dan Bentley. Open the gate or I'm driving right through."

No one would ever believe the Durango could bust through that gate, but the guard gave in with a sneer.

He quickly rounded the first hole of the golf course. Dispatch was on the radio.

"Fire crews and Mark are on their way. What's it like up there now?"

"Can't see her house yet, just a damned big smoke column. But the wind is fierce. That can't be helping any."

Dan smirked, remembering Antelope Club members he'd heard complaining about how hard it was to play golf against the wind. That was one thing they hadn't been able to buy off, the Montana weather. And this open valley floor was totally unprotected. Before the big money came in to transform the place, the land under the golf course and its surrounding mansions was considered wasteland. In fact, it had once been a dumping site. Dan liked the thought that underneath those mansions were tracts of buried garbage. It should have been called Dumpville Estates.

"The Olsen home is right off the second hole. Let them know I'm just about...."

It was rare that Dan Bentley was stunned. But turning at the second hole and seeing the property before him, he could do nothing for a moment but stare. It was as if some old photo of World War II bombing wreckage had filled the space where Stacey's house had been. He'd been prepared to see a house on fire, maybe with a wall or two blown out by an explosion, but there lay nothing but unrecognizable piles of fiery debris.

Even before his conscious mind had absorbed it all, Dan went to work. He swung from his SUV and walked toward the fire, scanning the scene, operating almost routinely from a familiar source deep inside. He ascertained that only Stacey's property had been damaged, as if it had been hit by a very selective volcano. That meant he could focus on just this one site. First, the fire had to be contained. Second, anyone who might still be alive in the house had to be found—although from what he saw, that was hard to imagine. He just hoped the owner herself was off, as usual, doing her job, even on a Saturday. Third, once the fires were out, the whole scene became evidence. He could already imagine the officers of the Club planning to sneak in their contractors and fix things so no one would discover the substandard furnace or badly laid gas line that had caused this. His job was to take control of the scene.

The Antelope Security car was parked nearby, but the two guards inside just sat there watching. Dan ordered them off the premises. They scowled at him, and the driver immediately got on his radio. Dan turned his back on them.

Fire crews arrived. Dan shouted the protocol norm, "Cut off and secure all utilities."

They opened their hoses and beat the fire down. The destruction was already so complete that it looked as though it wouldn't take long.

When two deputies arrived, he had them cordon off an area four times the size of the scene. He doubted the fierce winds of the valley would keep the yellow tape in place but the premises would be in his possession until he was ready to release them. He kept Antelope Security there by telling them to patrol the perimeter and keep the curious out. Then he sent his deputies to locate witnesses.

Dan was pleased to see Park County Fire Chief Mark Adams arrive. They had worked countless fires and investigations together, and Mark had been the county fire chief for years. With a full head of white hair, he'd heard women thought of him as their white knight in shining armor. He was always available, for any tiny problem they seemed to dream up as an emergency, but Dan liked the way Mark worked: authoritative, unrelenting, and efficient. He was also a trained arson investigator, and Dan knew he would do his best to make sure the fire fighters didn't destroy any more evidence than they could help.

"Find anything to suggest a cause?" Mark asked.

Dan shook his head. "We're looking for witnesses."

"Oh my god, my god!" came a voice.

Dan turned to see a woman standing behind the barrier. As he trudged toward her, a Mercedes screeched up, followed by an Escalade. From each of the cars jumped a woman, hurrying frantically to the barrier.

Dan knew who he was looking at. Here were the infamous "Dolls," each beautiful and overdressed. The prized possessions of the BM of the BS, the most expensive pussy on earth. There were too many of them to keep straight, so Dan had made up what he called his "Doll List" to remember a few of their names. It was sort of juvenile for these high maintenance females, but it worked.

Sophia, the Italian-looking one with the dark hair and overly ample chest, was easy. She oozed sensuality like the movie-star legend with the same name. Alissa was like a list of qualities in "arm candy." She was sweet and younger than the rest. Marie was repulsive. His deputies called her "Fruit Loop." She was notorious for filing complaints. Whenever she fired anyone she claimed the former employee had stolen from her. There was a good chance she'd also slept with whomever she was accusing, although that was never in the complaints, so Dan thought of "mare" and "marry." As in, the greatest nightmare imaginable was to marry Marie, but that was Scott's problem.

There were other mnemonics, too, for a couple of the Valley Vixens who weren't there. Thanks to his love of The History Channel he remembered Katherine. She was powerful, like Catherine the Great, the longest ruling female in Russia.

Then there was Lyn, as in linseed oil, which was spontaneously combustible. He was glad she wasn't among them now, though there was a part of him that always wanted to see her face, kiss her breasts, and squeeze her perfectly round ass. He couldn't help it.

Sophia pushed forward, stretching the yellow barrier, and started speaking at high speed. "Dan, Katherine took a trail ride with Stacey this afternoon up to Emigrant Peak. I called Katherine's cell and she answered but then the signal cut out. When I called back it kept going to voice mail. Do you think they might be still up there?"

"I hope so," Dan said. "Better up there than here." He wasn't surprised Sophia knew everyone's whereabouts. She missed very little gossip.

Then Alissa spoke, almost as if afraid to. "No. Look over there in the pasture. Stacey's horses are home."

"Her burned out truck is in what used to be her garage and barn," added Sophia.

They all knew what that meant.

Dan scanned their faces. Sophia and Alissa looked troubled, or at least as though they were *trying* to look troubled, but Marie was smiling. Or maybe it was all that plastic surgery. It was hard to read emotion on a face that looked like it had been stretched by a bad taxidermist.

"Did any of you see what happened?" he asked.

Their voices tumbled over each other as they all answered at once. Dan couldn't follow everything, but clearly they'd all been at their homes, engaging in various pursuits—shopping online, arranging flowers, booking reservations—when they'd heard the blast and had come running, well, driving. He handed them his card and told them to call if they remembered anything.

By now several other onlookers had gathered around the yellow barrier. Dan questioned them all, but none had seen anything. Then he noticed an older couple, probably in their sixties, standing in front of their house across the street. He strolled over and questioned them. The man hadn't seen anything, but the woman had.

"I was doing dishes in my kitchen." She spoke rapidly. "My window looks right into Stacey's front yard. The explosion shook our house something terrible and when I looked up, Stacey's entire house lifted up and just burst into flames. Then came the tiny little pieces and then in a bit, even more smoke from her barn. A lot of the stuff landed right in our front yard. See?" She gestured to their now dusted grass.

"That's when I called 911," her husband said. It seemed to matter to him that he got the credit.

Not in uniform, Dan had on well-worn jeans, that big silver and gold belt buckle he'd won at a bye-gone national rodeo and an old plaid shirt that was fraying at the collar. In addition to his rodeo years he had been a middle linebacker at Park High School in Livingston, big, but not overweight, able to cover the entire field. He dressed so casually he radiated pure cowboy, rugged and ready. As the weather was still nice he wore a straw Stetson hat with a cattleman's crease covering his thick ash blonde hair. He loved his Stetson hats and his comfortable low-heeled black Tony Lama cowboy boots that he'd bought on sale down at Murdoch's. Out of his front shirt pocket Dan had taken a small tablet, writing down everything they said. He kept everything in that pocket. No one ever saw Dan Bentley in a shirt without a front pocket. It bulged and looked unorganized but it held both the scope and the nucleus of the man and his work.

"Have either of you seen any unusual activity in this area lately? Have you seen any people you didn't know, or anyone acting suspiciously?" They kept shaking their heads. "What about unfamiliar vehicles at her house recently?"

"Just Stacey's truck," she said. "And sometimes the Denali."

"The Denali," said Dan, looking at her. "Do you know whose it is?"

The woman didn't seem to want to answer, but

after an awkward pause, her husband said, "I believe it's Scott Stiles'."

"Do you know why Mr. Stiles would be here so often?" Dan asked.

The man opened his mouth, but his wife said, "Absolutely not."

Further questions brought nothing.

Duane was just coming back from his sweep through the area. "No witnesses," he said.

Dan nodded. He thought for a while and then said, "When we're done here, remind me to give Scott Stiles a call."

He walked toward the ruins of the house. The heat was dropping as the fire died. This was going to be a hard investigation. The fire had been like a wild animal, rending and consuming everything in its path. Yet somehow from this rubble he had to find the cause of the explosion. More than that; he had to find Stacey Olsen. He just hoped it wouldn't be in there.

CHAPTER FOUR

Katherine did not hike nor did she camp. She enjoyed being outdoors but she didn't like to sweat. Riding her horse kept her relatively distant from dirt, grime, and perspiration. Now she was sweating. She was a horseless rider stuck on the slippery side of a mountain. She was disoriented. She tried to walk up the shale but her boots slid on the moss. Her leg hurt and her left ankle felt swollen. Normally she would have cared about her ripped top. Now she only cared about finding her horse—and about what had happened to Stacey.

She rode with pepper spray and her cell phone on her belt. She pulled her phone out of the leather holder and tried calling but she couldn't get a signal. Jean was probably working in her garden and didn't even have a cell phone. Higher up she knew she might get reception, but the only way she could keep her balance and climb was on her hands and knees. She started to pull herself up by gripping weeds. Soon enough she was bushwhacking, with twigs whipping her face.

A little farther up the embankment she tried Michael. It went to voicemail. Maybe he had gone to the Cave, or maybe he was at the shooting range or doing whatever else he did on weekends. Katherine left a short message but didn't expect him to listen to it immediately. She hated herself for calling him. She didn't like to be needy. In any case, what could he do? Whenever anything physical needed doing, Michael dispatched an employee, so she called the man whom Michael probably would have called anyway: Clint, who ran the Antelope Club's equestrian center. He always seemed to be around when you called.

"Darlin', I'll be right up," was all he said, and he'd hung up before she could ask him about Stacey.

For a while she lay breathing hard, eyes closed. Then she noticed a throbbing pain in her hand and pulled off her right riding glove. Her thumbnail had been sliced to the back cuticle, severing a good-sized chip. She shook her soft, golden elk skin glove until the huge chunk of nail dropped to the trail. She picked it up, but remembered that her super glue was in her saddlebag. She tucked the nail fragment into her side front pocket of her jeans wishing she at least had a Band-Aid. Time consuming to get only one nail fixed. At the same moment she thought it, she wondered how in hell she could even care about such trivial problems under the circumstances. Then she must have passed out, because the next thing she knew she was looking up at Clint.

There could hardly have been a sight more reassuring at that moment. Clint was a fifth-generation Montanan, and horses had been a big part of every one of those generations. He looked like a cowboy, and like the cowboys that vacationing women hoped to meet in Montana, he radiated sincerity, simplicity and strength. He was tall and thin with strong shoulders and bulging triceps. She was sure a six-pack rumbled underneath his somewhat dirty white t-shirt. Sometimes he wore cowboy hats but today he had on a baseball cap to keep the sun off his tanned and weathered thirty-something face.

Clint helped Katherine up without a word. That's when she noticed the other horse. Clint was ponying her gelding with a rope tied around his saddle horn.

"You found Triumph," she said. "Thank you."

"Pleasure," was all he said.

"The explosion," she blurted. "Stacey was riding home just before. She wasn't there when it happened, was she?"

For a long moment he was silent, and she wondered if he was going to say anything at all. He looked away from her, but she saw the faintest pain in his eyes. Then he said, "Think so."

"God. Clint. What have you heard? Was she hurt... or..."

"We'd better get you home, darlin'."

He pulled Triumph's lead rope from his saddle horn and held it out for her. Obviously he knew it would be too painful for her to ride and intended to walk with her.

She watched him as they made their way slowly down the trail. He seemed just as self-contained as ever, but she knew he must be feeling more than he showed. Stacey was his boss at the Club, and she'd seen how they worked together. Clearly he was among her admirers.

She broke the silence. "Clint. Have they said how

it happened?"

"Told me it was an accident," he said. Then, after another long pause, he added, "Yep. That's what they told me."

She heard an implication in Clint's repetition. "You know it wasn't an accident?"

"She was awful smart," he said. A pause again. "Maybe too smart."

"What are you saying?"

"She was smart, but she was in bed with some bad customers."

It was clear what "in bed" meant. "You're talking about Scott Stiles, aren't you?"

"It's not my place to say anything derogatory about the founder of the company I work for," he replied.

She gave him her most reassuring smile. "No one else will know."

For several more paces it looked as though he was going to be true to his word. Then he started to speak. "A conservationist. That's how Scott shows himself to members and guests and politicians and the press. But I know men in the company who've dumped raw sewage into the Yellowstone River on his orders."

These were more words than Katherine had ever heard from this silent cowboy, and he wasn't finished. "He runs this place like it's his kingdom. I've seen him with the government officials he brings up here on pack and huntin' trips. I've never seen him bribe a man, but I can tell that somethin's going on, just the way they act with him."

Clint's voice began to rise, as if his personal dam

of resentment had finally burst. "He pays fines sometimes, but they're nothin' to him. And nothin' compared to the destruction he's caused, divertin' streams, drainin' ponds, dumpin' dredge, killin' trout. Then he just pays everybody off, as if it's his right. He'll do anything to have it his way. Anything. Stacey knew it, too. Stacey knew it and she was on him to stop."

Katherine waited for him to continue, but the flood of words dried up as quickly as it had started. "Clint," she said at last. "You're telling me you think Scott had something to do with the explosion?"

"Billionaires," he said. "Nothin' matters to them but their money."

"What do you mean?"

But this time he stayed quiet.

Katherine had run into this before in Montana: the mountain man's paranoia about the outside world, the conviction that everything was run by a conspiracy of rich men and corrupt politicians.

"Scott hurting Stacey," she said out loud, but mainly for her own benefit. She wanted to add something about how crazy Scott had been about her, but she knew that with men like Scott, lust didn't necessarily have anything to do with affection.

She wasn't surprised when she pulled up into her driveway and saw Jean standing by her fence. Most of the Antelope homes weren't so close together but Katherine was happy to live next to Jean. She gestured for Katherine to come over. She rolled down the window and yelled, "Come to the car. I've hurt my ankle." And there went Jean hopping over the fence. She'd never seen Jean use a gate but with all that cowgirl strength in her she was quite the sight, climbing the fence and landing lightly as she had probably done all her life. Jean was in her mid-sixties, average height but super fit and amazingly thin. Her hair was auburn with a natural widow's peak. She had curves but she wasn't aware that she still looked good. Her face showed years of working outside, but in a pleasant way. Her riding boots were her work boots, the same, she had told Katherine, as she wore as a child. She never wore makeup. Dressing up meant a good pair of jeans, a crisp, clean shirt with a nice scarf around her neck. Katherine wondered how she managed to do such physical work. Jean hunted elk and deer and occasionally shot game birds but only enough for her to eat. Jean was perfectly capable of doing any job a man could do with perhaps a little more precision.

Katherine admired Jean because she was an authentic, genuine and strong Montanan who had brains and held her power. She had never really wanted to be like anyone else, but secretly she wished she could be more like Jean. No Antelope members knew, but Jean took Katherine on incredible trail rides that lasted at least eight hours or more with her riding group, the Wednesday Pine Riders. Those days were the highlights of Katherine's life in Montana. Antelope members weren't allowed but since Jean was a founding member, no one said a word when she broke the rule with Katherine.

When Scott conceived the Antelope Club he wanted to buy Jean's property. Her family had owned sections upon sections of land for generations adjacent to what Scott purchased. Katherine had heard they offered her an outstanding amount of money for just a piece of her property but she wouldn't budge. So here was this opulent neighborhood with exorbitant homes next to Jean's house, which looked like the groundskeeper's home. It was built by her great-grandfather with hand-hewn logs and she would never, ever think of leaving. It looked very much like the dozens of old homesteaders' dark log shelters that stand in Montana ranch country. Jean's rectangular, one level, small home was a reminder of humbler roots and struggling earlier generations. The logs were dark and there was only one bedroom which had been an add-on many years ago. Her heating came from her log fire. Jean found no use for modern kitchen appliances that Katherine thought were normal. There was no dishwasher, no garbage disposal, and a stove that looked like her great-grandmother had used it.

The black and white photos on the walls showed family, revealing a hard looking reality and not too many smiles. Life was tough on the range and it showed in their worn faces. But Katherine knew her art and she was sure the home was as authentic as the original C.M. Russell painting that centered the wall. This one was dated 1912. It was worth a fortune, but you'd never hear about it from Jean.

Katherine admired the fact that no one could change the way Jean ran her life. Not even Scott could push her around. Jean did it her way.

"What happened to you? And what about all that fire and smoke? Did some Club members get into an overheated domestic fight?" It was a known fact that she didn't like the newcomers and all their flash but for some reason she liked Katherine, probably because she was Stacey's friend and Stacey was Jean's niece. She had told Katherine how she had remembered Stacey as the young child who liked to come over and help her with her garden and was delighted to bring home ears of corn or fresh tomatoes.

"I was riding with Stacey and when we stopped for lunch, she took off and raced down the mountain. Had you been with us you could have been the only person who may have been able to stop her. Then I saw her house was on fire."

"It's these goddam Club members. I'm not counting you, but she should have never worked with them. I tried to talk sense into the girl. She went to the University of Montana, got her degree in finance, went East for a few years and then came back and didn't want to leave our state. This CFO thing was the best paying job around. In fact, I believe she was overpaid. Not that I didn't want her to do well, but I always had this feeling she was messing with big guns with bigger agendas and she was too honest."

Jean never showed a lot of emotion but Katherine could tell she was thinking the worst. "Stacey is the only girl in the family. I'd better get going over there to see for myself." Katherine wished she would have stayed a little longer but she hopped over the fence again without saying good-bye. Jean didn't even say good-bye when she talked on the phone. She was simply direct and to the point, and Katherine never knew when she would end a conversation. She always felt more grounded around her neighbor. She made the big sky bigger and the sun shine brighter. Katherine knew this would be very hard on Jean.

CHAPTER FIVE

He was lightheaded enough to believe his cock would surge to the size of his wealth. He was lucid and floating. The rush and danger, so much like his work, like playing the variations of volatility in the marketplace—he had to have this.

Michael could be the straight man, but inside he was perpetually torn as he craved virile excitement from the male species. He was shrewdly aware of the risks he was running. He thrived on the thrill of the margin between success and failure. Amassing instant fortunes through his own brilliant algorithms, his computers changing the world's markets faster than even he could think, getting out in the instant before the flags were raised. Flying across the world in his Cessna Citation X, flying back and forth between Livingston and the Cave at Lolo Pass in his Bell 230, sleeping in two-hour intervals, never stopping work. The weekends were a letdown. Except for this. This was the high that eclipsed all. This was the other way to ride the edge of fatal vulnerability.

The man-boy had tied him in the running noose. He didn't use nitrates anymore. The orgasm was more intense when his blood and oxygen supplies were cut off. This boy was good, just the right pressure from his hand, just the right rhythm in his arm, working Michael's cock faster and faster as he lifted out of the world into intoxicated delirium. He was wasting his time as a waiter at asinine private parties. He could make so much more as a personal slave. He was a part-time waiter, on the football team at Montana State University and had modeled for Calvin Klein undergarments before coming to Montana. He had the perfect butt and a perfectly sculpted body, a male model stepping out of the pages of GQ, just for him.

Michael saw himself for an instant, a naked small-framed but muscled body that he kept in perfect condition, even to the point of making sure all of his body hair was shaved off. Here he was, strung up on a beam in a secluded cabin, an image of absolute helplessness to anyone who didn't know who he was, but in fact a man of absolute power, a man who made billions while others were losing them, a man who used his brilliance to snatch fortunes greater than any old-school investors would ever see, grab them and disappear before anyone even knew what had happened. Today had been another triumph. Today he was celebrating.

The ligature tightened. He bit his slightly protruding tongue. It was coming. He was ready. Then the slave boy pulled the noose tight, just as he was told, just as the orgasm began to build from Michael's loins. Michael felt himself soaring, felt the explosion in his cock and the flashing eruption, felt himself almost going out, almost going down, floating into death but released just in time. His thoughts drifted to the day when his real life would be as intense as his secret life, playing real-world games as scary as this game, building to the biggest orgasm of all.

As Michael glided through the bliss of semi-consciousness, he heard a ringing, a very familiar and distinct ringing. He came up into awareness, sooner than he wanted to, recognizing his cell phone, recognizing the sound of a marimba, Katherine's ring tone. Katherine calling, as ever, at the worst possible time. Katherine no doubt calling with one of her boring questions. "Why did you schedule the new landscaper without telling me?" "What did you do with the spare key to the Tahoe?" Or nothing that ever, ever mattered. "I'm sure you won't mind that we are going out tonight with Lyn and Eric."

He refused to be interrupted. He'd had his turn and now it was time for him to play with today's young man.

"Your turn, Justin," he said, sliding the noose from his own neck. Then he wondered if he even had the guy's name right. Maybe it was Jason. It didn't matter what his name was, but Michael hated to make mistakes, like forgetting to silence his phone! Katherine's call had him rattled. He was about to tie this beautiful man-boy up, tease him, bring him to his own explosive frenzy at the edge of fatality. He didn't want to be wondering what his fucking name was.

Then another shrill alert from the phone; Katherine had left a voicemail. That meant he had to call her back soon so she wouldn't start to ask herself where he was, wouldn't start to ask questions. He didn't want to be standing naked in front of this beautiful slave, calling his wife and trying to sound like an ordinary man, like any other husband. He couldn't decide what he wanted to do. His thoughts were pierced with anxiety.

Michael picked up his bag, the one where he kept his street clothes. He pulled his wallet out of his dark blue slacks, dug out five one-hundred-dollar bills, and tossed them at the naked waiter without even looking at him. He got dressed, facing the closed door.

He still felt a noose around his neck. But the hand at the other end of this one was Katherine's.

CHAPTER SIX

"Like the aftermath of a bombing mission," Dan said to Mark as they walked the perimeter. They'd spent all morning at the site, sifting through ashes, trying to make sense of what remained. "You know this place must have flattened in seconds."

"Never seen anything like it," Mark replied. "Foundation cracked, stonework shattered, even the frame timbers are reduced to ashes. Just that one wall left intact."

"Not sure I'd call that 'intact,'" Dan said. He and the fire chief were walking toward the far side of the property, where most of the back wall of Stacey's bedroom hung from the limbs of the tall pines. It was almost comical, that one fragment of the house being flung through the air in a piece, landing in the trees like a monster-sized kite. Dan could even make out a light fixture and a row of iron hooks still attached to the wall, and on the branches below it, the dull glisten of leather and the glitter of steel buckles.

"Horse tack," Mark said.

Dan thought it was strange for Stacey to have had so much horse tack hung up in her bedroom, since she was one of the few residents in the Antelope Club who didn't keep her horses in the equestrian center. She actually used her barn for livestock instead of making it into another western-style party palace.

"Let's get the pictures started," Mark said, turning back toward the remains of the house. "Then we'll get it all bagged."

The heat had dropped and the smoke had cleared enough for Dan to send his deputies around the perimeter of the ruins, at least, to photograph every item on the site. Once they'd captured and recorded the relative positions of every object and the conditions of the grounds in five or six or seven hundred photos, every surviving portable item would be marked and sealed in plastic bags to be sent to the county lab.

"And look for V patterns," Mark added.

"Yep," Dan said. The force of the blast would have sent things flying out from it in a V formation. The bottom of the V would be the point of origin.

Mark took a moment before speaking. "With this kind of devastation it could take days, even weeks, to find a body part. There may be nothing left bigger than teeth or bone fragments, and the ashes are probably five or six feet deep over there."

Dan sighed. "What could have done this?" he asked.

Mark shook his head. "We'll have to dig down through the basement and see what the propane lines look like."

"You think this was propane lines?"

"Seismic activity could have cracked some lines. You remember that rumble last week?"

"How much propane would it take to demolish a house like this?"

"Volcanic gases, maybe," Mark said. "Hell, we're near Yellowstone."

The wind came up in a strong gust, blowing ashes into Dan's face. He slowed his pace, letting Mark stride ahead. When he brushed the ashes from his eyes, he found himself looking at a twisted mass of blackened and partly melted metal. Stacey's bed.

He felt a chill roll through his body. He remembered a fishing buddy of his calling Stacey the "hottest chick in Montana," and the fact that he almost wanted to make a joke out of that now made him slightly sick to his stomach. Those stories had carved a place in Dan's mind. He'd wanted her, fantasized about her, resented her for being always out of reach. Now he was looking for her in the ashes, and he couldn't stop thinking that somehow the heat she had generated in that bed and the heat of the explosion were the same.

Dan never liked to admit how often he relied on intuition. He liked to line up his evidence before he voiced a hypothesis, as if he'd worked his way there by sheer logic and analysis. Only he knew how many of those hypotheses had started as feelings in his gut. Standing in the wind now, stung by flying cinders, scanning the dark and smoking wreckage around him, he had one of those feelings. Asking himself if this could have been caused by an accident, his gut came back with an answer: anxious, jumpy, a little sick.

He circled inward toward the middle of the blast. He didn't know why. There was an eerie quiet between the blowing gusts. He dug the digital camera out of his pocket and started taking pictures of the ruins. Slowly he circled toward where the stairwell to the basement lay filled with ash and rubble. His boots sunk into a couple of feet of ashes. He backed out very carefully. He followed the circle back in the opposite direction.

His boot hit something. He bent down and dug with his gloved hand into the deep debris.

He picked it up. It was the thick, charred heel of a boot. A riding boot. He dug deeper and found the burnt remnants of the boot itself, green leather over brown, a rounded toe. He looked at it as if it could tell him what he needed to know. When he realized that someone was saying his name, he was shaken out of his contemplation.

"Dan?" the voice asked again.

He looked up. She stood there against the afternoon sky, her hair dancing in the wind. She looked at him, a bit impatiently, apparently not noticing what he had in his hand. In front of her, she held a tray covered with a linen towel.

"Lyn," he said.

She held the tray out to him, as if demanding he take it. She said, "I thought you might like some of my chocolate chip cookies."

CHAPTER SEVEN

Lyn was not used to taking "no" for an answer, especially from someone she was sleeping with. She had often wondered if Dan was having a fling with Stacey—after all, wasn't every other man in the valley?—and now she was almost sure of it. Why else would he be so rude when she offered him her very own, homemade chocolate chip cookies?

Or was she supposed to take his rudeness because she didn't count as a real girlfriend? She remembered what he had told her when she asked if he was afraid of dating a married woman. "Nope," he'd said. "It's easier: no commitment, no hassle."

She stomped to her massive SUV, her hips swinging back and forth as she struggled to find her stiletto-heeled footing in the ashes. At least she'd secretly snapped some good photos before Dan threw her out of the crime scene. Everyone said she took the best pictures.

She looked back as she climbed into her Range Rover to see if he was watching her go. He wasn't. That stung too. Surely he knew that she would look, and by turning his back on her and acting as though he was preoccupied with whatever it was he was holding in his hand, he had shown her up. She had been outmaneuvered by a lunk of a man—and just a county employee at that—and that made her even angrier. Two of the firemen and at least one of the deputies had been looking at her, she was very sure about that. Still, as she gazed at his broad back and watched him move with that manly deliberation, she remembered why she was willing to put up with him. Plus, she knew he loved her looks, blonde shoulder length hair, an ample chest with a small waist and full willing, curvaceous hips. Somehow he noticed none of it today. Maybe her hair was too blonde. True, she was getting to like the look of living on the edge.

Dan had been a fun diversion for Lyn. She'd had affairs before, anything to lessen her isolation from a husband who had seemingly been on a decade-long hunting trip. Eric and his parents owned one of the world's largest international engineering and construction companies, founded by his family a hundred-and-something years ago. They built large corporate communities, even entire foreign cities. Eric had grown up accustomed to a life of private jets, opulent homes scattered around the globe and obligatory engagements with international dignitaries.

During their courtship in college, and after they had married, their life in San Francisco had been idyllic. Eric seemed to like that she always knew what to do and how to plan. He had been a mama's boy and she stepped in as his new decision maker. They had been the young *It Couple* from Pacific Heights, front and center opening night at the San Francisco Opera's gala and throughout the philanthropic season.

She couldn't believe her good fortune. Eric was always up for sex, whenever she suggested, to the point she thought she was living inside her own private film of non-stop erotica. When she couldn't conceive, she was perplexed and depressed. She began to drink, but not for fun, like her sorority days.

It still made her skin crawl now: Eric watching her buy all those pregnancy tests. One by one, every month, she threw the one-lined tests into the trash. And all the while, he insisted they move to the Antelope Club full time. She agreed because raising children in safe and beautiful Paradise Valley sounded like a dream.

If he'd just told her sooner, she probably wouldn't have started the Ativan. But that bastard had gotten a vasectomy soon after they married telling her later that it was because he wanted to be her "only number one." He said she could have anything in the world she wanted, just not a child. How like a child to insist on such a thing! Their marriage became as empty as his sterility.

Lyn originally thought she could cope. Money could be an amazing distraction when used properly, and she spent hours on the phone with Stephan, her personal shopper at Saks in San Francisco, bemoaning her marriage while deciding which color Céline bag to purchase ("Just get both!"). But her boredom without a baby escalated. There was no place in the "Treasure State" with the sophistication of Union Square, where she could shop to make her unhappiness go away.

She became increasingly cold to Eric. A normal Sunday of rumpled sheets and naked pancakes had turned into an hour in their private gym followed by hours at Chico's spa and pool (for her) and a day of fishing or hunting (for him). They avoided each other, which was easy to do in the fifteen thousand square foot home.

She threatened him with everything she could think of—she'd even told him she'd had affairs—but he made it clear that he was only putting up with her because his family would never accept a divorce. She could do whatever she wanted.

She sometimes thought back to the people they were in The City by the Bay and wondered if it was the Big Sky that had poisoned them against each other. If she had been clear about her need for a family before they married, would he have still asked her?

So, she developed an appetite for the wild side of the Rockies, and collected other men to keep her company, men who would be much easier to manage. She had tried to conceive with several of her male lovers. That plan would have certainly kept Eric under wraps, but she never became pregnant. She had promised herself that her first missed period would signal her first missed alcoholic drink. That day had never come. Her doctor told her it could have been from complications from an abortion in her senior year in college. Eric's unknown, unborn child. She had always believed she could control life but it was all too horrible to think about. It was maddening to realize she had willingly given up what she had wanted the most. Timing was a bitch. Now her only solace was between the smooth sheets of Ativan induced sex.

The Sheriff had been her biggest challenge so far. The ordinary man could be snared with little presents, shows of emotion and innocent-seeming gestures like baking his favorite cookies. Dan hadn't been as eager as the rest. Eventually, though, she enticed him to her home and then out to her playhouse, an upgraded and over-decorated sheepherder's wagon. He'd made fun of it, but he'd also ended up in its narrow, nailed-to-the-wagon board bed.

That first afternoon had only been several months ago. They made love a few times a week, but lately Dan had been changing toward her. One day he'd be so close, the next she felt as if she hardly knew him. Sometimes he'd be suspicious of things she did, even the most innocent things. And now, this afternoon, she'd bothered to go all the way out to him over that sooty ground, through smoky air, to bring him cookies she made herself, even knowing that he had probably been sleeping with Stacey. If he *were* sleeping with her, then that made her gesture even more selfless. But he'd snapped at her as if she was an idiot and told her to get back on the other side of the yellow tape like some Montana lowlife.

Then, as she turned into her driveway, the thought struck; maybe he was about to break up with her. She felt her stomach lurch. She didn't want to lose this relationship. She was acutely aware that she was in the category of the "available unavailable." There were limitations to finding a decent lover. She simply couldn't stand the thought of being left. She never broke off a relationship without having a new guy in line. All her previous affairs had ended when she wanted them to.

She looked at herself reflected in the glass of her front door. No one would have called her slender but she had always thought her curves were in the right places. Now she saw heavy make-up, overly bleached blonde hair, sweater pulled taut over areas that bordered on bulges, V-neck showing overflowing cleavage, and a plate of cookies in her arms. Somehow she looked years older than when she had checked her reflection less than an hour ago, before going out. She snarled and threw the plate against the glass. Eric wasn't home, of course. The housekeeper would take care of the mess in the morning. Lyn started upstairs.

She needed something to lighten her mood. She stepped into her bathroom and opened the prescription bottle of little white pills. There were only a few left. She checked the prescription date. It would be another week before she could get a refill. She took two, thinking she'd have to tell her doctor she lost the bottle again.

Within ten minutes, she felt infinitely more relaxed and optimistic. She reviewed her photos from Stacey's former house. One had Dan and Mark walking together in the soot, another showed the yellow tape against a blown-out wall. She got a close-up of a fragmented piece of what she was sure would mean nothing to Dan and his fire chief, vintage Wedgewood china. She had never thought of Stacey as classy enough for Wedgewood. She uploaded the new photos on her Instagram.

CHAPTER EIGHT

Katherine was trying to sip asparagus soup but she wasn't hungry. There weren't any restaurants that delivered, so her lunch was often the same bland choice. The frozen vegetable medley had reduced the swelling of her ankle and leg, but nothing could put the chill on Katherine's thoughts about what happened to Stacey. She'd gotten voicemails from a few of the Dolls, making sure she knew. They all said it seemed likely that Stacey was dead, some sounding gleeful and some simply horrified, although so far no one knew for sure.

The peas and carrots began to get mushy as she sat on her bed watching the Yellowstone River. She and Michael lived in a muti-story log home with western furnishings. Lots of Native American rugs and antique relics of Montanan days gone by, like huge snow shoes, hung with feathers, old wooden skis and vintage wicker fishing creels. When she first moved to Montana she was so excited to decorate in pure western cowboy-Native American style, but if she were honest with herself, she realized she'd probably overdone it. Not that it was over-the-top by Doll standards, but it was far past simplicity.

Focusing on the water was a form of meditation for her. It usually brought some serenity, but today that serenity was only relative. The river never stopped flowing, nor did it ever look the same. It was windy outside and little white caps crested, as if to remind her that she was no longer in peaceful waters.

Michael had come home in an angry, almost frantic mood and headed straight into his office. Katherine wasn't sure he even noticed she was home. She heard him stomping around and slamming drawers. This was what he always did when he came home. Today he was louder and more frantic than usual.

When he came out, he barely looked up from his copy of *The Economist*. "What is it, Katherine?" He almost sneered as he asked it. "What did you do to your leg?"

"Are you fucking serious? Didn't you listen to my voicemail? I thought that was why you came home."

"No, I didn't listen to it; I was too busy but I saw fire trucks leaving when I came through the gate."

"There was a huge explosion at Stacey's home. I was with her before it happened. I think I may have been the last person to see her."

"So why the peas on your leg?" His tone softened a bit.

"Triumph reared and threw me. Stacey and I had been riding. Then she just got some message on her iPad and went home at a gallop."

Michael read while she was talking. Without looking up, he asked, "Did you find your horse? Are we getting a huge vet bill?"

She was stunned. "Michael," she said. "I don't know what I find more appalling. Your complete lack of concern for Stacey. Your complete lack of concern for me. Or the fact that a man worth billions of dollars is worrying about a fucking vet bill."

Now he looked straight at her. And what she saw in his eyes was contempt. "I know about the explosion," he said coldly. "I've talked with a few of the Club's board members. Until we know more about what happened and why, I don't see the point of wasting any emotion on it. As for you, I would certainly be concerned if anything truly serious were wrong with you. But my experience has been that any injury treatable with a bag of frozen peas is probably not one to worry much about."

He snorted a laugh at that, as if he found himself very witty. Then he turned his eyes back to the pages of *The Economist* and left the room.

Katherine could only sit and look at the river. She turned the vegetable bag over and pressed it into her ankle. She pressed hard, as if feeling the pinch would dull the pain elsewhere.

Michael could be as icy as a number on a P&L statement, but Katherine always thought she saw another Michael, a softer Michael, inside. They had met at an NYU alumni fundraiser. He was shy and had come on a dare from a former mathematics classmate. Katherine had seen through his brainy camouflage of wrinkled shirts, pants that needed to be shortened, and his patchy stubble of a beard. She was shocked that he'd never been married. Little by little he had agreed to her grooming suggestions and now he took pride in his immaculate, if not obsessive, personal appearance.

Michael was fast, just like his trades, his cars, his jets and his helicopters, but with her he'd been cautiously slow, respectful, and understanding. She thought she'd met her match of brains, beauty and talent. He was generous during the first years of their marriage. He had sent floral arrangements almost every week: white orchids, white lilies and moonflowers or deep-red, long-stemmed roses, Black Magic, and Red Masterpiece. Sometimes the theme was tropical, yellow pincushion protea and Birds of Paradise. They all came with complimentary, endearing notes to her office. She still had them all in a shoebox somewhere, those tiny mementos of their once passionate marriage. She had appreciated the thought behind the quality jewelry. Even though his taste was sometimes overly pretentious for a bland quant, he made big efforts. He'd bought her a silver Lamborghini. That should have been an early warning of his narcissism, as Michael was always the one driving the sleek oversized toy. But its speed made the long weekend drives to his home in Bridgehampton exhilarating.

Everything about him used to scream sex, like they were the very first people to discover marital bliss. She was sure they'd both been living in a drought before they met. She'd barely be home from work before he'd unzip her pencil skirt, throw her up on the kitchen island and lustfully take her into realms of multiple climatic ecstasies.

In business and sex she had always sported her A game. She loved the challenge of topping Michael's desires, overshooting his expectations and watching him become engulfed and mesmerized by her skills. Plus, he fit her body so perfectly. She had secretly feared she would never get enough of him. But something began to change after he'd persuaded her to move full time to their vacation home in Montana.

Montana had seemed like the perfect solution for Katherine. She had been an architect of the finance superstructure that created the subprime mortgage boom. She had risen above most everyone on Wall Street, a power broker that operated by her own rules. When the SEC cornered her for questioning about substandard practices, she played it her way, using influence and common sense to save both herself and her company. And now, what seemed like many years after the sub-prime crash, she rarely looked back at the fact that she was a facilitator of the liar loans that helped create the devastation of the American economy. She wasn't alone in believing real estate prices would continue to soar and borrowers wouldn't need verified credit to back their loans.

Instead she was smug about the power she had to keep the probing SEC lawyer quiet. She hadn't ratted out her associates. And when that lawyer had tried to turn on her she had made sure he'd never utter a word. Perhaps they were all guilty in some ways, but she hadn't provided the Feds with the intel to take anyone down.

Michael had always seen the fallacy in the sub-prime markets. He had bet against the very bonds she had created. He had told her to pull out before she lost everything. Michael had never known what she had done and she'd never tell him how she got away with it. She had taken his advice, exited the markets and moved to Montana. Michael's persuasion that she pull out was right after the SEC's questioning, even though he'd not known about their probe. She had forced herself into early retirement without earning the watch. She could have purchased her own gold-diamond Rolex, but time stood still in Montana.

Katherine waited for Wednesdays like the Dolls waited for a party invitation. If she got to ride with the Pine Riders her life turned into pure glee. Her dream had come true of riding through rough territory and the many forests and mountains. Each time was a new adventure. No kids, husbands or dogs were allowed. And they always rode making a giant loop, never taking the same way back. She knew why only ranch women who'd lived in the valley for their entire lives didn't want newcomers, they wanted proficiency in their riders and frankly they didn't want to waste time with helicopter rescues. Katherine barely uttered a word on the rides although Jean always rode in front of her. Thank goodness Katherine had a seasoned horse because they rode the unexplored country, not trails. Most of the time Katherine held on thinking she was going to die but Triumph seemed to love it.

She had thought about becoming more involved with the mortgage fund charity she'd founded in New York, but it seemed to be running smoothly without her, and now that seemed so boring compared to the Pine Riders. She knew her former colleague Jack, an ace with anything technical, also had a business head and he handled their charity so well it had even grown beyond her expectations. She had originally believed Montana would bring her husband, Michael, closer to her, but he always seemed to be on the other side of her fading rainbow.

Because of her success, men had always been easy for her to attract, so when Michael didn't pay much attention to her business accomplishments, she had believed he had loved her for whom she truly was, not just because she was some Wall Street hot shot. Back then no one had ever heard of high frequency trading. She thought they were equals, and Katherine had secretly loved the fact that Michael had begun to outsmart the smartest of her peers.

For a long time, she waited for him to take her into his confidence and treat her as a true partner, but he had never pulled aside the curtains of his secrecy, keeping her out of his vast empire of buying and selling. Michael was still her challenge.

After her move, the sex slowed and then stopped. Katherine hadn't been too worried, as there was someone else who took care of her needs when Michael wasn't around (not that Michael had any clue).

When she thought about the last time they'd had sex she realized it had been months. His whining excuses had always made sense. Headaches, lack of sleep, anxiety about the markets. In Montana, he had become a touchy work robot that couldn't be distracted.

She thought that with having enough money for

generations of lifetimes Michael would start to live a simple life with her in the Rockies. She had believed that by leaving their kinetic life behind they'd slow down and find more to share with each other. She had wanted him to help her with her foundation. She knew her charity was a drop in the bucket in comparison to what she had reaped from the system but still he should have given to help others, especially with a foundation co-founded by his wife. She'd encouraged him to give back, but Michael's checkbook remained shut.

Instead, his cheapness began to show itself, a cheapness that was outright bizarre for a man with his kind of money. He was constantly siphoning favors from the other Club members' hired help. He made deals with Scott's pilots to fly his helicopters and jet planes during their time off so that he didn't have to keep them on his own payroll. It was embarrassing. She suggested that she could foot the bills. She didn't have Michael's kind of money but there was a point when rich was rich enough. He dismissed her offers thinking it was somehow more brilliant to be cheap.

Although this was Michael's first marriage, Katherine had been married before. She'd been young, just graduating from NYU, when she'd met her former husband, James McIntire, who was getting his PhD in mechanical engineering at Columbia. The marriage to JM lasted a little over a year, enough time for Katherine to realize that he was a boring slob. He wasn't of her stature and he did nothing but face the television and search for the remote. She simply purchased her freedom. She'd written a check that finally made sure Jimmy Mack understood he'd never be coming back.

Michael's coldness after her accident made her wonder if she had somehow chosen another loser, only this round, a richer and more handsome one. Maybe she had married Michael too quickly. It had only been four months and they'd tied the knot. It was naïve to think it was a long enough period to assume a certificate could be the solidifying bond. And now, ten years later, they were merely drifting through routine.

When he began to make excuses to skip social events she thought she saw a sign of hope. She was unrealistic to think they both would stay home by the fire and truly get to know each other better. The secrecy that already cloaked his work drew increasingly around his schedule, his whereabouts and his feelings.

Today, though. Today was beyond humiliating. Today he had been so awful that she found herself asking—for the first time, seriously found herself asking—how long she would put up with this.

Her phone rang. She was grateful for the interruption, less grateful to hear Lyn's voice. "Did you see my post yet? I put up some pictures I took of Stacey's bombed-out house. They're amazing. Take a look. Maybe you can help me tweak them like you did with Sophia's last tiara party photos. I heard you were up there with Stacey, on the trail. What did she have to say?"

Word traveled quickly among the Dolls. Katherine

couldn't remember who she had told about going riding with Stacey or how Lyn could have found out, but it really didn't matter. Katherine knew how to use her to spread information, and she knew how to shut her down when she needed to avoid unnecessary damage.

"Lyn, you shouldn't be posting those pictures," Katherine said. "Hasn't the sheriff's office locked it down? You're asking for trouble."

"Oh, I don't think I'm going to get into trouble with the Sheriff," Lyn giggled. Somehow in trying to sound knowing, she only managed to sound juvenile.

"Dan needs a little jolt now and then," Lyn continued. "So what happened on the trail? Is it true that Stacey rushed home right before the explosion?"

"I've got to go. Bye now." Katherine hung up.

In the silence that followed, she heard Michael's voice. It came from the hall. He was speaking levelly, cordially. She started her awkward limp toward it.

"I agree completely. It's a blow to us all and a terrible loss to the Club. She was such a wonderful, bright woman, always there for all of us. Yes, please keep me apprised of whatever happens. Thanks, Scott."

Katherine rounded the corner and found Michael standing in the doorway to his office, his phone in hand, gazing at the floor. His eyes were nearly expressionless, but there was something in them, some ghost of emotion that she couldn't name. She opened her mouth to speak, but no words came out.

Then he looked up at her. There was an openness in them she hadn't seen for a long time, a reaching out for contact.

"They believe she was in the house," he said. "They're still searching for evidence, but they think it's very likely."

"Oh, god."

"Yes," he said softly. Then she saw something she could never remember seeing before: Michael's eyes being misted by tears. "Katherine," he said. There was a quaver in his voice. "Katherine, I'm sorry for how I spoke to you. I think I didn't want to admit the possibility that she was truly dead. It wasn't fair of me to take that out on you."

"I understand," she sighed. "Thank you. Oh god, Stacey." She stepped toward him. He turned away and then changed his mind and gave her an automated hug. He didn't end it with a kiss on the lips with his hands cradling her face, like he used to do.

"I need a drink," he said.

"It's just after lunchtime," she said, knowing he had already tuned her out.

She watched him hurry away from her. She wanted to run after him, grab him, shake out some emotion. But his hunched shoulders and rapid steps warned her that he wasn't ready for that.

That's when she realized that she was standing in front of his office door. And the door was open. The door that he disappeared behind every night he was home. The door that hid so much of his life from her. She stared at the desk directly across the room from her.

It had never even occurred to Katherine to dig into

his private business. She was a professional woman, not some snooping wife. She respected his boundaries as she expected him to respect hers. Whatever he wanted her to know, he would tell. What he didn't tell her wasn't her business and what she didn't tell him, he would never know. But standing in that open doorway, facing that desk, she could not help wondering if what she needed to find out was right there, if she were just a few minutes of searching away from understanding what was wrong and how to change it. Just one discovery away from regaining the life she thought she wanted. She took a step into the office. Then another.

A phone rang. It was the landline, on the other side of the house. She always ignored that phone, caught too many times by telemarketers and political robocalls, but she heard Michael answer. A few words too distant to hear, then silence. She waited a moment but then it hit her; he was coming to find her.

She stepped back into the hall just as he stepped around the corner.

"Phone's for you," he said. Then he turned away, lost in his personal fog again.

She collected herself as she approached the phone receiver lying on the kitchen counter. No one she knew well called her on the house phone.

"Katherine, this is Sheriff Bentley. I understand you were with Stacey Olsen on a trail ride before the explosion. I'd like to speak with you. May I come over this afternoon or would you like to meet me in town?"

CHAPTER NINE

Dan Bentley had suggested the Murray Bar on Park Street. She was going to meet him only for Stacey. As usual, downtown Livingston looked as though former resident, Calamity Jane, could be walking down the sidewalk holding her Winchester. It hadn't changed since frontier days; Livingston was just like a wild-west movie set, with original brick buildings that had been built when The Northern Pacific Railroad established the town in 1882.

Now the stores were a combination of looking like the old west but carrying items the area needed, like Catherine Lane Interiors. She carried the most gorgeous furniture plus the perfect gift that anyone would appreciate, from small picture frames, hand-made necklaces, pewter serving platters or Katherine's favorite, an incredible assortment of scented candles. And the Bistro and Gils were great places to eat and hang out.

The place was overly filled with bars but she'd heard back in the day, the town had many more. The narrow and deep downtown spaces now also held art galleries and antique shops. All the stores still had the small-town friendliness of a bygone era. Most everyone was recognized by name and outsiders were welcomed with genuine hospitality.

Jean had told her that although the locals might

be laughing behind the Dolls' backs, they were too courteous to treat them any differently than the families that had shopped there for generations. Katherine loved that Livingston was still a town where a smile, your word, and a handshake mattered. She tried calling Jean and after about eight rings she was about to give up when she answered.

"I have to meet with Sheriff Dan Bentley about Stacey and I'm kind of scared."

Jean's voice sounded heavy, like she guessed what had happened to her niece. "Dan's a good guy. Tell him the truth, anything you remember. You'll be fine."

It was fortunate that it was her left and not right ankle that had been injured; driving wasn't a problem. As many times as she'd passed by the Murray, she'd never been inside. It was the watering hole for fishing guides and hunters, an unkempt class of men who she ignored on the streets. And Sheriff Dan, she'd seen him around. He was as big as a lumberjack, and seemed as simple as the rural county he protected.

The afternoon sun was still glowing outside, but inside the bar was dark. The place had a reputation for wildness, but it was quiet now. It smelled like the floors had been mopped with stale beer. She drew her sleeve to her nose to cover the stench. She saw Dan sitting at a far table, working two beverages at once, sipping something brown, like VO, and chasing it with a beer. She'd heard that the Murray had been his hangout out for decades, that he'd gotten his first job there, in seventh grade, swamping the bar. He removed his hat with a slight nod, just like a cowboy. She noticed he wasn't like a lot of rodeo types who looked better in their hats, covering up balding domes. As she watched Dan run his fingers through his thick head of ash-blonde hair she noticed his huge hands were covered with red spots.

"What would you like to drink?" he asked.

"What's that on your hands?"

He looked down. "Oh, nothin'. Skinned an elk earlier today. Guess it didn't all come off. Like I said, "What are you drinkin'?"

Katherine cleared her throat.

"Scotch, on the rocks."

"Sure you don't want something stronger? It's getting close to a Livingston Saturday night, five o'clock somewhere."

Was he trying to be funny? "Wouldn't have pegged you as a Buffet fan," she said.

He picked up his now empty beer can and spit a large wad of chewing tobacco onto the top. Katherine had never seen someone spit up a brown mound right in front of her face. Holding up her chin, she pulled her head back.

He seemed amused by her reaction but his hazel eyes remained hardened. He called her order to the bartender. She was surprised to catch a scent of cologne, some very masculine scent, maybe Lucchese. She wouldn't have thought of him as the cologne-wearing type.

He looked at her for a moment before he spoke again. "I understand you were pretty good friends with Stacey Olsen."

"I knew her, yes. She was a big asset to the Antelope Club," Katherine said.

"Not many of the women in the Club seemed to feel the same."

That was obviously common knowledge, but under the Sheriff's gaze she felt a protectiveness for the trivial Dolls. "I can't really speak for them," she said.

That brought an actual smirk to his face.

"What?" she asked.

"I've never found those ladies unwilling to speak for each other," he said. "Or about each other."

She tilted her head with a cynical smile. "Maybe."

The bartender delivered her drink. Dan let her buy it herself.

He hadn't taken his eyes off her but it wasn't in admiration. "Sometimes I get the feeling that you're the worst of them but then I think you're different from them—and that has a lot to do with your friendship with Stacey and Jean."

"You could explain that," she said. She consciously gave her tone a bit of push-back.

"It's just that most of the women there don't have a lot of...." He acted as though he was searching for a word, but she had a feeling he'd chosen it long before, along with the dramatic pause—real-life experience, let's call it. I get the sense that a lot of them grew up in gated communities, got shipped off to boarding school, landed a rich guy in college, and have never had to take care of anything themselves."

To Katherine that sounded like a direct jab at Lyn,

and it had an unmistakably sharp edge. "I did have my own career, if that's what you mean."

"Wall Street," he said. "So how did you get here?"

"Just knew it was time for change. Pulled out before things got really bad. Eventually followed my husband to his 'cave,' so to speak."

Katherine usually let that stand as the presumptive explanation for her transformation into a Paradise Valley wife. It was easy for the Dolls to understand and should have been enough for the Sheriff.

She took a long sip of her scotch, not looking at Dan. "I thought a break from finance would be nice."

When she turned toward him again, she found his eyes, for once, not fixed on her. He was looking down at the note pad he was opening, with a great show of casualness, on the table. "I hear your husband is a trader also," he said.

"What my husband does is different. I hardly think it has anything to do with Stacey."

Dan had a confident grin on his face as if she were mildly amusing. "I'm sure you and Stacey had things to talk about that neither of you could share with the other women," he said. "I can't see you talking to many of them about business or finance."

Was he trying to butter her up to get information? "We had some good conversations," Katherine said.

"I can imagine." Then he looked into her eyes again and asked, almost offhandedly, "Do you remember what Stacey was wearing on the ride?"

"Yes. She almost always wore the same thing or a version of the same thing. Wrangler jeans, a long sleeve plaid blouse. It was turquoise plaid this time. And those boots. The ones she always wears. The green and brown ones she had Wilson's make for her."

Dan took a deep breath. His face hardened.

"Why? Did you find her boots?" she asked. "You have her boots don't you?"

He shook his head like he was tossing away what he'd just heard.

"Do you?"

He looked away from her. He was obviously too coy to reveal his findings to her, but his body language told her what she expected. Stacey's boots, and therefore Stacey must have been in her home. Katherine felt her lungs tighten.

He changed the subject. "What were you talking about this morning, on your trail ride?"

"So you're not going to tell me." Katherine got up to go and the Sheriff grabbed her arm to sit her down. She brushed him away.

"I'm sorry if you don't like my questions. I'm looking for any kind of information to figure out what happened. Please."

Everything about him told her to leave.

"You were the last person I know who was with her. I'll let you go in a second. Think about Stacey. I know you have to feel *something*."

Was she that cold? She was grateful for all Stacey had done for her in the Rockies, little things like showing her how to put the skis on top of the car, how to bust snow drifts, even how to layer Dermatone over her face so the sub-zero cold didn't destroy her skin.

It didn't matter what they did together, trail riding, fishing the Yellowstone, getting drinks at the Old Saloon, they were always laughing, whether it was about guys or Katherine's latest fuck-up learning to live in the wilds of the West. Stacey even came over with Jean to show her how to blow the sprinklers out so the lines didn't freeze up when her lawn guy was sick. Stacey had always dropped everything for her. Maybe she should try to talk. It couldn't hurt.

"Well, there was definitely something on her mind. She said it was huge, bigger than I could imagine." She recounted, as best she could, what Stacey had said and how anxious she had been. "When she got the message on her iPad, she rushed home. I've never seen her that shaken."

"She didn't say anything about the content of the message?" asked the Sheriff.

"Yes, she did. She thought she could work it out, whatever that meant. She said she'd tell me later."

"The timing," she continued after a moment. "I can't help thinking that the message was intended to make her rush back. So she'd be there...when it happened."

"But you have no idea who it might have been from?"

"No," Katherine said. "I just...I just wish I'd stopped her."

He fell silent then, and so did she. He moved his hand up to the tabletop. She looked at his hand, so broad and weathered but so rough and bloody. So different from Michael's hands, smooth as a young boy's and always in anxious motion.

After a long pause he asked, "Do you have any reason to think anyone might have wanted to harm her?"

She looked at him sharply. "Then you do think she was murdered."

"Now, I didn't say that." Katherine thought she heard condescension in his voice, slight but annoying. "We just have to look at every possibility, that's all."

Katherine straightened up and sipped her scotch. It was easing her into talking. She told Dan what she'd heard about financial irregularities at the Club, but he didn't take notes. She had no doubt he'd heard it all before.

"Do you even know what caused the explosion?" she asked.

"Not yet," Dan said. He considered for a moment, then continued, "But I can tell you this. No ordinary propane explosion could do that."

"Well, you do have your work cut out for you, Sheriff."

He nodded, but he also shifted his weight to signal that he was about to stand up. "I'd like to take a ride with you up to Emigrant Peak," he said. "Often things we've forgotten come back when we go back to where they happened."

She didn't like the idea of reliving the ride. "I'll have to think about that one. I'd like my ankle to be in better shape."

"Understood. Rest up. I'll check my calendar and give you a call," he said. "Now I've gotta head 'em up and move on outta here." Somehow in that use of cowboy slang he managed to make fun of himself and of the impression he no doubt thought people like her harbored about him.

"Make time for it," he said with a smug smile.

She did her best to smile back.

Then, as Dan stood up, looming over her and swinging his hat to his head with a graceful strength, Katherine found her mind flooded by the incongruous—not to mention ridiculous and somewhat repellent—image of Dan in bed with Lyn. She couldn't imagine what this man could see in that sad, desperate, and often drugged up woman. The mere fact she was having the thought made her disgusted, and she jumped to her feet, trying to keep more weight on her right foot. Who was she to make judgment about a married woman having an affair? She reminded herself that it was none of her goddamned business.

"Thanks, Mrs. Hawthorne," Dan said.

She stuck out her hand as quick and forceful as if she were in a business meeting back on the Street.

Then she turned and did her best not to limp as she walked out of the Murray Bar, wondering if it was Lyn who'd bought Dan the Lucchese.

CHAPTER TEN

Alissa had been home all day after meeting the Dolls at what was once Stacey's house. She made a quick call to Katherine. It went to voicemail.

"Hi Katherine," she said. "I heard you were on the trail with Stacey and you fell. I hope you're not hurt badly. If there's anything I can do, please give me a call. I'm just home waiting for the dryer repairman."

Her housekeeper-nanny had left for the weekend, which was bad news for any mother of a two-year old, but especially for Alissa. She loved her son dearly but she wasn't accustomed to not having her freedom. Of course, nothing changed for her husband; Brad was out hunting with the guys. Alissa always hated to be left alone with little Tyler on weekends, and to make matters worse, this one included a broken dryer. She didn't understand why Carmen couldn't have gotten it fixed before she left. What else was a housekeeper for if not to make sure Alissa didn't have to deal with things like this?

But then, she knew she was lucky just to have a full-time housekeeper. She panicked whenever she thought about the possibility of Carmen leaving her. Like all the Dolls, she found it amazing that Montana lacked a class of people to provide round-the-clock domestic help. There just wasn't any immigrant work force, either because it was too far north and too cold or because there wasn't enough farming work to bring in outside labor. The ranchers used the same help they had for years.

Thus, Alissa had to import Carmen from Scottsdale, and it was becoming increasingly, painfully difficult to keep her happy in the mountainous surroundings. Carmen couldn't find Spanish-speaking friends, and there were few other Latina housekeepers with whom she could socialize. Alissa had heard horror stories of how some of the Dolls had lost their housekeepers when relatives had driven all the way from places like Florida and California to take them home. They would flee in the middle of the night.

Dolls could be tough negotiators, and she couldn't risk losing Carmen. She paid her handsomely. No amount of money, however, would persuade Carmen to work weekends. Because Alissa had a toddler she could rarely put off the laundry from Friday to Monday, and it was nearly impossible to get out of cooking and doing dishes, especially with Tyler being so finicky. In Scottsdale, she'd had a weekend housekeeper to cover Carmen's days off. Now that seemed almost impossibly luxurious. This wasn't what she had signed up for when she had married Brad, and at times like this she could become quite irritated, especially when the repairman should have been there hours ago.

Alissa poured herself a glass of champagne. Perrier-Jouët, her favorite. She loved the flowers on the bottle. The hour she began to drink seemed to get earlier and earlier, especially when Brad was out of town. She just felt so isolated and lonely in Montana. She liked her other Doll friends well enough, but she didn't have much to say to most of them as they were so much older. She admired Katherine the most. Brad had known Katherine for years, from way back in New York, but he was always telling her not to trust Katherine. So funny. Brad was the one she couldn't trust.

She felt a guilty pang. Those things she'd heard from Brad about Katherine's husband's business but she'd promised not to tell. She hated keeping secrets and she would have told Katherine everything if it were up to her, but that was the trouble with being the wife of a former SEC advisor and your friend being the wife of a high-frequency trader. She was sure Katherine would sympathize if she knew.

Alissa couldn't understand why everything had to take so long in the Rockies. She knew everything was big and far apart, but couldn't they just build more? So many things had to be ordered in advance. She couldn't pop into her car and go buy what she needed. Even if she could, the grocery store was half an hour away, in town.

The Antelope Club was full of amenities, but the one thing it had no solution for was "Montana Time." In Scottsdale, scheduled appointments, service calls, meetings, anything with a designated schedule ran on time, or pretty close to it. In Montana nothing seemed to run on schedule. This quaint custom was one of the prime topics of complaints among the Dolls, because they did not like to wait for anyone.

The repairman had to be at least two hours late by now, maybe three, and she had piles of her toddler's disgusting dirty laundry. Thank goodness she hadn't opted for natural cloth diapers like so many of her "green" friends in Scottsdale. The Club had a valet pick-up service, but they picked up on Friday and didn't deliver until Monday. It was times like this when she thought she should go check into Chico Hot Springs. Chico was the exact opposite of the opulent Antelope Club, a rustic resort with a real cowboy flair. Sometimes, when her husband was gone, if she could get a babysitter, she'd stay there. She'd get a massage and enjoy cocktails in the pool.

Brad was a captain of the banking industry. He had formerly been a legal counsel for the SEC but left for a lucrative career in the private sector and rose to become chairman of the board of one of the nation's most well respected banks. The SEC couldn't seem to get along without his advice so they eventually got him to stay on as an advisor. She was not exactly sure what her husband did but she knew he specialized in loans. He was twenty years older than Alissa. Lately it seemed they were more than decades apart. They say an age gap matters less as you get older, but it was the opposite with Brad and her. In the beginning their ages hadn't made any difference, but now he was boring and middle-aged and she was still so young.

Alissa was constantly preoccupied with Brad's whereabouts. He had proved his unfaithfulness a few too many times. She didn't understand why her youth, beauty, and devotion weren't enough for him.

A couple of months ago she had discovered he'd been having an affair with a cocktail waitress at the Antelope golf course, which was officially forbidden, but not by her husband's standards. She enjoyed having the girl fired, but she knew it didn't solve the real problem.

Before she was married she could have easily moved on to the next guy, but now she felt she had to stay with Brad for Tyler's sake. She doubted Brad ever gave parenthood a thought even though he had told her he was so delighted to be a late-in-life father. And now that he did have a son, he never spent time with Tyler.

Alissa turned heads wherever she went. She was used to attention, men doing anything she wanted. She had thought Brad was quite the stolen catch, with a high-dollar tan and a lean golfer's body, but now she had come to realize he was completely self-absorbed. Life would always be about Brad, and she was just another one of his possessions. She was depressed and this was going to be another endless weekend. Most of the Dolls would be going out with their husbands, and even the ones whose spouses were hunting weren't stuck at home while their toddler slept.

Brad finally called. He was hunting at one of the Club's auxiliary ranches in eastern Montana. He sounded like he'd had a good start on his usual string of bottles of Stella Artois. She wondered if the Club's private jets had flown in female fauna for their notorious "after hours" pursuits. Alissa thought she heard female voices in the background but decided to let it go. There wasn't much she could do at the moment except become upset. She was focusing on learning how to control her emotions and pick her battles.

Alissa had met Brad at a PGA tournament in San Diego when he was married to "the ice queen." They had hired local models to serve refreshments on the golf course and because Alissa had modeled since she was named Miss Teen San Diego, the job was a natural fit. The money was great, so she spent most of her weekends while at San Diego State University flirting with golf pros, chauffeuring millionaires around in golf carts, and sneaking champagne while on the job. Brad was a big player, such a smart lawyer, and smitten by her. After the tournament, he found plenty of opportunities to come back to San Diego. Alissa loved being taken care of by an older man—the college guys she'd dated were all about keg parties and their fraternity brothers, but Brad hadn't wanted any of that for twenty years. He was interested in taking her out and showing her off.

She'd gotten pregnant the first time they were together, which had frightened her until Brad proved his intentions were long term. The ice queen had never wanted stretch marks and Brad had always wanted a son.

Brad had done the right thing. The ice queen got a good chunk of his assets, but not enough to make him uncomfortable. After the divorce was final, Brad and Alissa eloped. The Four Seasons on Maui had been a dream. She was over her morning sickness by then and was able to don her baby bump in a bikini and still look hot.

Graduating from college had been her parent's hope, but becoming Mrs. Brad Fairbanks meant moving to his home in Scottsdale. Soon after they settled, he'd changed his mind about Scottsdale. Brad wanted to be where people weren't just rich, but where the elite and powerful had homes. He followed his buddy, the former Chairman of the Senate Committee on Finance, to life behind the Antelope gates of wealth and privilege.

She had been too young to notice that he acted like a bachelor when he was married to the ice queen, and she eventually realized nothing had changed. She had just been one pearl on the string he was collecting. But the perks were great, like the push present when Tyler was born, a brand new Escalade and her very own beauty salon in their home. Every two weeks Sophia would join her. Alissa would get her hair done while Sophia got a pedicure and fill. It took hours to get Alissa's hair the perfect beachy blonde but with Sophia there, the time would fly.

But now, no matter what she tried to do to get Brad's attention, she was left with an empty scorecard. What did they say, that one should choose a husband by how good they'd be at taking care of your children every other week? Brad would make a terrible babysitter.

It was getting late and she was giving up on the repairman. She had probably been naïve to think they would even make a service call on a Saturday. She fed Tyler, gave him a bath, and put him to bed early. He was fussy and cried awhile before she heard the glorious silence. She loved her son, but she also loved it when no one needed anything from her. Now she had the evening to do as she pleased. She went downstairs and picked up her bottle of champagne. There wasn't much left. She finished it off and uncorked a new one.

A call came in from the guardhouse. The dryer guy had made it at last. In a few minutes she heard the truck in the driveway. Alissa opened the door to find not one but two repairmen. They looked like they could be brothers. They both had sandy blonde hair and were probably in their mid-twenties. They wore identical tan Carhartt pants and white shirts. She couldn't help noticing how those shirts bulged with the thick curvature of finely-toned muscles. They dipped their heads deferentially as she led them into her oversized laundry room.

"I'm so grateful to you for coming!" she said. "I can't believe you actually came way out here this late at night!" She had learned that being smug or critical to the local help never worked. Some of her Doll friends, like Lyn, still hadn't mastered rural politeness, and it always made everything take twice as long.

"We would have been here sooner but we had to go all the way back to the warehouse for parts for another customer here in the Antelope Club. It takes more than an hour each way and then we had to stop for lunch."

"And that customer was demanding alright."

They looked at each other. "We didn't expect to be with her so long. She wanted all *sorts* of stuff done."

They both laughed as if it was a private joke.

"It's been one of those days," the other said. "When we got here this morning we saw the FedEx guy had broken down so we stopped to give him a hand. When we came back there'd been a huge explosion and fire and all, and it was hard to get through. We've been running behind ever since."

"Did you see that house? Man it was demolished. Sorry we're late."

"Well, you're here now," said Alissa with her most honest smile, although she didn't buy their excuses. The FedEx guy? Seriously?

Her state-of-the-art Samsung dryer sat there like a dead beast. She showed the more talkative one how she couldn't even turn the thing on. Push the button, nothing happens.

"I've learned how to check the breakers," she said, "and they're fine. So it must be something inside," said Alissa.

"Don't worry, ma'am, we'll get it running in a jiffy."

The way he said *ma'am*, with that country twang, nodding his head and touching the tip of his hat, was so charming. She didn't expect two adorable boys to fall right out of the sky on this lonely night. As she watched them start working, she felt a little perplexed by her own reaction. Normally she didn't give the time of day to blue-collar guys. Her skin crawled at their constant whistles and catcalls. But here in her home they seemed so...harmless. Cute farm boys delivered especially for her entertainment.

She went upstairs to check on her son. He was

sleeping soundly. It looked as if she had quite a bit of time on her hands. It seemed like a good idea to change into something more comfortable, since there was no telling how long those boys would have to keep working. That short, black cashmere lounge-dress was just the thing.

When she came back down she was surprised to find them waiting for her in the foyer. The dryer had blown an internal fuse, that's all. They had replaced it and were getting ready to leave.

"Thank you so much for fixing it so quickly." She didn't want them to leave yet. "Where do you guys live?"

"Belgrade, so we'd better be going. It's getting late. It'll take some time to get home."

Belgrade. She should have guessed. Belgrade was a suburb just west of Bozeman, the fastest growing town in Montana, its cookie-cutter houses lining Interstate 90. Just the kind of place these guys would live. A long way from the Antelope Club in so many ways.

"How about something to drink?" she asked. She caught the eye of the cuter one, the one who didn't say as much. "Come on, it'll perk you up for the ride. I have Coke, cranberry juice, lemonade, beer, vodka, you name it."

Alissa liked the sound of their names, Graham and Cody. She told them they looked like brothers and they laughed. She thought Cody was giving her that "come-and-get-it" look, but Graham's shyness appealed to her more. She had a sudden urge to ask them to bend down and turn around. She loved the way their workman's pants cupped their little tight butts.

"Are you guys always like this?" she asked.

"Like what?" asked Cody.

They were so normal, everyday, innocent, and cute. She couldn't tell them that, so she said, "So helpful."

"It's just part of the job."

"What we do, ma'am."

Their politeness made her smile "Why don't you guys have a drink, sit back and take a rest."

As she filled their glasses she refreshed her own. And then as if prompted by an inner demon she said, "Have you guys ever done a threesome?" Alissa saw them looking at each other in disbelief, almost laughing, as if they couldn't believe their good fortune in finding a beautiful woman who gave them drinks, thought they were fix-it geniuses, and was about to give them way more than a signed repair order.

She took another drink and set her glass down with a clink. She looked from Graham to Cody, from Cody to Graham.

"So? Whadda you boys think?" They froze, watching her. She could tell the champagne was working and refreshed their beverages to hopefully ease them into the mood. She deserved some excitement in her life, and so did these dryer repairmen.

Alissa loved to dance. In their early days, Brad had liked to watch her. She'd decided once to be his own private stripper. She watched movies and went online, soaking up every bit of dancer lore she could find, then practiced her moves in her mirrored bathroom nearly every day. This was before Brad decided he preferred the talents of girls who would work for green stuffed into their G-strings.

She led Graham and Cody into the perfectly staged guest quarters she had once decorated as an alternate boudoir to seduce Brad. She tried not to think about the time Brad had actually removed her hand from his cock in this very room. *Fuck Brad*. Wow. She didn't usually talk like that, even to herself. The champagne was empowering.

Cody said, "I cannot believe this day. No way."

Graham was shaking his head like he was the luckiest guy on earth.

Alissa dimmed the lights. She changed the music on her phone from the spa-type soundtrack she preferred in the evenings to the same sexy playlist she'd practiced dancing to years ago. She knew the sequence by heart. Of course she started with Def Leppard "Pour Some Sugar on Me." She was going to fire these boys up.

She was a pro at dancing this routine, hitting each beat with a tease, flipping her hair, sticking her finger slowly into her mouth, then getting on her knees, rolling over and spreading her legs apart. Hopping up with a twirling thrust of her hips she motioned for a mesmerized Graham to have a seat on a chair without arms in front of a vanity dresser.

Alissa leaned down and softly brushed his lips while straddling him between the knees, her hips moving back and forth as she undulated to the lyrics, "I'm hot sticky sweet, from my head to my feet."

Then she led Cody to the king-sized bed, threw back the burgundy and gold brocade bedspread, and bent from the waist down touching her heels. Very slowly she removed his boots. They were filthy but she wouldn't concentrate on that now.

Alissa grabbed her champagne glass and let the bubbles amplify her courage. Her stage was set. Using the "catwalk," combined with the "sashay," she moved slowly over to a backlight screen from her tiffany lamp, placing one foot so it just crossed the other, moving her hips with a little back motion to the soundtrack, while keeping eye contact with her boys. She was full-on into it now. She swept her hands over her body and raised them above her head, crossing them and pulling off a rotating turn as she moved behind the screen.

She knew they could see her in silhouette as she was moving, pulling her short cashmere dress off from the hem up in an slow tease. She played it with bulletproof confidence, surprising even herself. She threw her dress over the top of the screen. It landed on the floor right to the beat of a new song, Billy Idol's "Rebel Yell." *In the midnight hour she calls more, more, more...*

The rhythm was quickening and Alissa was right with it, now rubbing her hands in a circular motion on top of her chest, then bringing them back to play with the snap on the back of her bra. With one fling it flew over the screen and landed near Graham, who grabbed it. "Baby," she said, as she came out from behind the screen holding her eyes on Graham, "This is just the beginning. You are about to get *sooo* much more."

Cody began to laugh. Then Graham started laughing too. This wasn't what Alissa was expecting.

"Pardon me ma'am, I don't mean to be disrespectful," said Cody.

"What?" asked Alissa. The moment was ruined. Suddenly self-conscious, she covered her breasts and snatched the bra back from Graham.

"We like you," Graham said. "Please keep going."

"You're not like that other lady at all."

"What other lady?" She grabbed her phone, turned off the music, and slipped on the cashmere dress to cover herself.

Cody was trying to shake his chest like he had fake boobs. Graham was cracking up. Cody looked at Graham but couldn't keep a straight face.

"*What* other woman?"

Graham stopped laughing and pointed at Cody. "You tell!"

"Mrs. Stiles," said Cody. "The lady who lives in that big mansion. She got us cornered when we came back with the parts. She said she needed strong, buff men to help ease her womanly desires or something corny like that."

"Yeah," Graham laughed, "and we were the lucky ones."

"That's what she said, we were the lucky ones." Cody grinned and shook his head. "She wasn't a class act like you. Or half as pretty."

"Or young," Graham said, and broke up again.

"Mrs. Stiles," said Alissa, squinting her eyes and tightly crossing her arms over her chest. She couldn't think of what else to say.

"Oh, she's a bitch with a twitch, all right," said Cody. "I've been to her castle before. She's totally lost her grip on reality, that's what I think. You know, she was telling us it was her husband's lover's house that went up in flames."

"I wouldn't be surprised if she'd did it herself," said Graham, getting himself under control again.

"We told her we had to leave to get another part, but we sure as hell aren't going back there," said Cody. "We're letting our boss deal with that one from now on."

Alissa sank back against the wall. She had been angry for a moment, but now she didn't know what she was feeling.

"So please don't stop," said Graham. "You're different. We like you. Come on. Turn the music back on."

Her head was spinning. The alcohol that had been giving her so much focus and courage was suddenly just clouding her thoughts. "No, I think the show's over here."

"Aw, please, ma'am!"

"You need to gather your things and get going."

The repair boys got to their feet but hesitated. Alissa pushed them out of the room. She felt humiliated, then furious at herself, then furious at Brad. Why couldn't he meet her needs like a husband should?

Why did he leave her alone to do a thing like this?

When she heard the front door close, she climbed the stairs, threw off her dress and slumped into her bed. She drained her champagne glass and dropped her arm, letting the glass fall from her limp fingers. She watched it roll across the floor until it hit the wall. She closed her eyes. The anger was draining rapidly, and in its place was only shame and depression and a greater loneliness than ever.

Then a thought swirled up to her out of the darkness and a smile started in her lips. What was Katherine going to say when she heard about *this?*

CHAPTER ELEVEN

The day after the explosion Katherine awakened to an empty house, a semi-swollen ankle, a throbbing thumb, and a deep sadness at the loss of her friend.

Michael hadn't said where he was going, but that was common. With everything she'd been through yesterday she thought he'd stay for at least another night, but knowing him, he was already back at the Cave.

When he built the Cave he had been eager to share everything with her. They'd flown into Missoula. From there he had wanted her to savor the scenery of the perfect wilderness, so he had driven her up to the compound high in the Bitterroot Mountains on the border of Montana and Idaho. It was secluded and remote, impossible to imagine that it hid a fortress of super-computers and the living quarters for super-quants. He had purchased the land long before they'd moved to Montana, when the government was selling off vast tracts of former forestry land to private investors.

Built into the mountain, his compound was entirely hidden from sight. Other than the helicopter pad, it looked as though there was nothing but an old trailer on the property. He had designed the entire compound in an underground cylinder module attached to a larger truss of a dozen segments for his employees. Michael likened it to the international space station.

For maintenance and security, he hired locals, the loners and survivalist nuts who drifted into the Montana wilderness, willing to do anything for part-time work and utterly uninterested in what happened inside. The other employees, his brilliant and obsessive quants, worked in six-month stretches, developing new technologies for global-trading markets. They spoke very little, mainly hovering in front of the computer screens inside their tech-station work capsules. Most were foreigners, siphoned out of low-paying jobs, pledging secrecy in exchange for salaries that supported way more than their extended families back home.

Michael had originally flown in gourmet fare, but soon realized his staff was hardly interested in cilantro and white bean bruschetta, steak tartare or pansy petit fours, so he siphoned a live-in chef from a dude ranch in the Crazy Mountains who cooked camp cuisine. These were techies, not foodies; steak, chicken, and ribs fueled his staff who seemed to be fine with the basics of the American West.

The first day he'd taken Katherine there she knew he wanted to impress her. Standing on his mountaintop, he said he felt financially invincible. Like a golden eagle soaring above the peaks, scanning the whole earth for his next prize. Yes, she knew it was a nerd's fantasy but he'd earned it.

The house was silent, but she still felt his strange energy hovering in the rooms. She lit a lavender candle to help her feel better but the gentle scent brought no relief.

She pinched out the candle and crept into Michael's office. He hadn't taken his laptop so he might not have gone to the Cave. He could be out on the golf course or shooting clay pigeons.

She looked around as if she expected the reason for his recent behavior to pop up like a Google search result. On top of a shuffled pile of papers on his desk was a Nanex newsletter he must've printed off. She didn't know much about Nanex except that it was a company that supplied information and charts to high frequency trading, HFT, groups.

"The reality is that machines have taken over," she read. "When you buy or sell a security, the odds are extremely high the other side of the trade is being placed by an algorithm." That wasn't exactly news, but she wondered if learning more about what Michael was reading and thinking would help her understand what was happening with him. She kept reading.

The only article she found interesting was one about a bizarre anomaly that had occurred in the trading of Yahoo! shares. They discussed the glitch in the timestamps that had resulted in executions being dated 190 milliseconds before they actually occurred, which meant that, as far as the algorithms were concerned, trades had been executed in the future. In the unreal reality of HFT, the speed of money had effectively exceeded the speed of light and broken through the time barrier. To explain it, the analysts coined a new unit of time measurement: "fantaseconds."

Katherine smirked to herself. In a weird way that summed up what she'd been feeling about her marriage; Michael had disappeared more and more into his own world, with its own incomprehensible tempos and laws. Ultimately they weren't even in the same place in the space-time continuum. While she increasingly lived on Mountain Time, he vanished into fantaseconds.

She'd been so busy in New York that she'd rarely thought about Michael's comings and goings. Maybe she and Michael had always been on different trajectories.

She called Sophia who immediately heard it in her voice. "What's wrong? Is your ankle bothering you?"

"Just a little sore still, but it'll heal. It's my damn thumbnail that's giving me hell and Michael is problematic."

"Michael is always going to be Michael. Period. Manic is his norm. You're thinking too much."

"It isn't the norm, Sophia. That's the point. It feels worse. And it's escalating."

"It's probably from what you've been through with Stacey. It's the trauma working through you and you're projecting it on Michael."

Katherine was quiet. She swiveled in his desk chair.

"So you don't like my suggestions. What are you saying? You know Michael is complex. He's like one of his own algorithms—you know it adds up to something amazing but you'll never understand it. Maybe he's so smart it's even too much for him."

"You're probably right. I just don't know."

"You think he's having an affair? Come on. He knows he has the greatest wife."

Affair. Fair. Unfair. "I don't know. It's not like I can go to work and forget about it."

"Have you checked his computers?"

"So I'm supposed to perform some kind of high-tech espionage on a man who specializes in supercomputers? Right."

"As I recall you worked in the business yourself, Katherine. You were a trader and then a mortgage genius."

"Very funny. But what I did was different. Michael's a quant, a quantitative analyst. I could never hack his 'ninja' defenses."

"I'm talking about his personal computer," said Sophia. "What about installing some sort of spyware?"

"*Spyware*," said Katherine. "Right. Your private eye background is showing. But he'd notice."

For a while, when she was young and working as a paralegal and model in New York, Sophia had dated a private detective. Sophia had street smarts unlike most of the Dolls. She'd helped him in his business. He was supposed to be extremely good at what he did, too. Unfortunately, he turned out to have some very shady connections, enough to send Sophia running back to Texas, where she'd met her husband.

"This has nothing to do with that," Sophia said. "For god's sake, Katherine. You might want to check his temporary Internet files first. That would be the easiest."

"It seems like a violation to try to get into his

computer." Even as she said it, Katherine opened the MacBook on the center of Michael's desk.

"What's the bigger violation, looking or cheating?"

Katherine always did what it took, without remorse, and she could see herself trying to believe that things were basically all right. He'd been sympathetic about Stacey—after he'd been an asshole. A quick browse of his computer could set her mind at ease.

"Okay," she said slowly. "I'll give it a hack. I hope you'll be around."

"Have I ever let you down?"

Sophia never failed to forge through the rapids by Katherine's side.

"Do you still want to get lunch today?"

"Sure, I'll see you at noon. The regular spot?"

"Of course."

Unlike most Dolls who preferred the glitz of the Antelope Clubhouse restaurant, Katherine and Sophia liked getting away from everyone and going to the Rib and Chop House in downtown Livingston.

Katherine stared at the open laptop. The screen was dark so she touched the power button to wake it. The screen lit up immediately, open to his desktop.

This was too easy. But brilliant people were also stupid. It had to be negligence. She saw a folder labeled "Hangman Game," and opened it.

It was a collection of jpegs. Photos. Taking pictures was *her* hobby. Click, click. She could feel her heart pounding and her pulse quickening.

Katherine froze. She was staring at a very pornographic scene. Not the kind of photos of nature that she liked to take. And not just normal sex, but BDSM. She clicked on another jpeg. More leather and sex. She hit about ten or twelve other shots. There were more photos of men and women, men with men and women with women. She slammed the computer shut before the screen could slap her face again.

She was in a haze. There was something highly shameful about what she felt. Like she had caused him to do it. Her first reaction was to keep the personal atrocity to herself.

She could sit there and let it fester or do the smart thing and bleed the wound. She picked up her phone.

"He's into full-on porno."

"He and every other guy on the planet," said Sophia.

She knew porno was mainstream. But not in her world with Michael.

"I had no clue that he got off on porno, but there are so many photos. I thought he was too nerdy to be into anything like this. He's a twenty-four seven quant farmer. Maybe I did this to him."

"Katherine, you caused him to do it? Wrong," said Sophia. "It's probably just a phase."

"A phase? There are thousands of pics in there. Men with men too. Every minute he is focused on making his billions. How does he have time for porno grazing? He couldn't be peaking in nano-flashes, because there is too much of it. It takes time to download all this crap. I wonder how long it's been going on."

"It's bad and upsetting, but more normal than you think."

"Not the kind of photos I'm looking at Sophia," said Katherine.

"Well, look at it like pure Michael then, pleasing himself and being emotionally unattached. Do you want me to come over?"

"No," She was quiet for a couple of beats. "I don't want to talk about it anymore."

"OK then, put it out of your mind. I'll see you for lunch."

Katherine walked outside. There was Jean in her garden. Of course she had her boots on with jeans. She wore a straw hat covering her golden hair, a neatly tied cowgirl scarf on her neck and a denim shirt.

"Hi Jean."

"Come on over."

Maybe Jean was what she needed. "Did you hear anything about Stacey?"

"Nope, not a word. Guess we're going to have to wait for the authorities to sort it out. I don't think it was any kind of accident. And I think she would have called or got word to me somehow by now."

"Oh Jean, I'm so sorry."

"You don't look very good yourself. Is it Stacey or something else?

"It's Michael. "

"What did I tell you about him? Do you remember? You don't, do you?"

"Yes, I do. 'Be like a duck and let the water roll off your back.' You're right, except he's thrown me a big one this time." Jean had enough on her mind with her niece to worry about her problems. "Ok. I'll

93

remember," said Katherine as she walked back to her house. "Take care, Jean."

"You too."

Katherine sat outside on their bedroom deck looking at the Yellowstone River. A blue heron was quietly sitting on the other side of the river's shore. With a quick thrash the heron found a fish and swallowed it whole. Was this just tit for tat? Had he figured out the secret she's been carrying for several years now? That couldn't be it. It was easy to hide the affair from Michael. He never questioned her whereabouts in New York; he knew she was always at work. Now they were in Montana and he was never around to notice when she did sneak away. The one thing she knew; she wasn't going to confront him until she figured out what to do.

She went back inside and copied the files onto a flash drive. When she came out she tried to clear her head. The heron had disappeared, and she found herself drawn back into Michael's office again. So he was a smut miner. Out of habit she called him just to see where he was.

Michael answered on the first ring. "Hi, what's up?" It was his cheerful voice, the one she rarely heard anymore.

What's up? She didn't let on. "Just wondered if you were going to be around tonight, do you want to go to the Club?" There. She sounded normal.

Michael was clearly in a great mood. The manic yo-yo was spinning upward. "I'm headed to the golf course later. If you want, come down and meet me after."

"Okay. I'll come to the dining room. What time? Six?"

"Sure. See you then." He rung off.

That was the norm for them recently. No "I love yous." No confrontations. She had thought his disinterest in her had been from work, but trading *them for her*? These people didn't talk back! She thought he'd enjoyed her assertive nature. Truth was, she hadn't thought much about their sex life because she had the perfect distraction, but it gave her a chill to think that her husband preferred the cool screen to her warm body.

CHAPTER TWELVE

Michael looked down at his black calfskin shoes. The sides were covered in mud and caked with straw. Why hadn't he worn his mud boots to the clay pigeon course? Why, because he couldn't simply think about all the stupid little things he was supposed to do in Montana. As he tried to scrape off one shoe with the other, the mud and straw spread and stuck like paste. He grimaced. No shoeshine guy around the corner. He could picture Phillip trying to save his shoes. He'd wet his white handkerchief with ample spit to wipe off the grime, but deem them ruined forever, while pounding the speed dial for his stylist to get them immediately replaced.

When he and Katherine had lived in New York, he had endured a long affair with Phillip, who, year by year, had become increasingly jealous. In the beginning, he had taken him to the heights of ecstasy. Michael had thought he had finally met someone who could understand him, his work schedule, his moods, his need for thrill-seeking edgy sex, but in the end Phillip led him into maddening frustration, always wanting more than Michael could give. He made him crazy, and spun him into an irrational person. When things were good with Phillip, Michael was calm and happy, but when Phillip got into one of his moods Michael became mean and angry with everyone.

Katherine complained she never knew what started his moodiness and unkind behavior. Michael hid his life, making sure she'd never know.

Phillip threw enormous fits when Michael couldn't spend enough time with him. Michael had known the only way out was to move as far away as possible. Phillip needed access to twenty-four seven civilization. He hated anything slightly dusty, not to mention dirt roads. He would die without same-day dry cleaning services and fine stores for shopping. Phillip was paranoid of getting lost in wide-open spaces without cell service and GPS. He wanted streetlights, crosswalks, superb restaurants, bars and Broadway.

The Antelope Club was the perfect haven and Katherine would never know why they moved full time to Montana. Michael supposed he was bisexual, but he preferred men, and he couldn't bring himself to come out. He was living in high altitudes on the well-known down-low. As much as Michael needed a gay life, as much as he wished he could show the world who he really was, he was engrained in the past, afraid of what others would think of the successfully married man, the international mega trader.

No matter how great his accomplishments, he couldn't shake the shame he felt as a teenager when his parents suspected he was gay. That was when he learned the consequences of telling the truth. His father beat him while his mother stoically watched.

If only he could be as astute with his personal life as he was with his professional life. It was a constant conflict to surge through sexually elating afternoons with his lovers and then hours, even minutes later, prove he was a good and respectable heterosexual husband.

Living away from Phillip had helped, but his anxiety was becoming increasingly severe, even the Xanax had stopped working. He was plagued with constant anger, anger at Phillip for making him feel so erratic he had to flee, and anger at Katherine for making him pretend to be who he wasn't. At times, Michael had enjoyed other women, even Katherine. But now, not in the way anyone would ever imagine.

He was glad Phillip wasn't here to complain. As he tossed his shoes into the side of his golf bag he smiled. Why hadn't he ever really thought about what Phillip had done for him? Escaping his ass had turned into a gift. Because it was here, away from the distractions of New York, that had he conceived his truly great plan.

CHAPTER THIRTEEN

Sophia was waiting at the Rib and Chop when Katherine arrived. The formidable brick building was once the railroad's warehouse where they dispersed materials out of boxcars. Old timers who had ordered their homes through a catalogue had watched their new houses arrive by rail and off loaded into the storage facility. Now with brand new red bricks, it was a favorite of locals and tourists. The restaurant sat adjacent to the tracks of Montana Rail Link. The parking lot was usually full, but there would never be valet service in a town whose only elevators held grain. There weren't any fabulous over-the-top restaurants in Montana, but the food at the Rib and Chop was reliable and they always got their favorite table near the Park Street window.

The instant they saw each other, the two friends inspected their outfits and demeanor.

"Hi, Sophia. Love the new necklace." Only Sophia could pull off what Katherine considered flash-to-the-extreme, this time rhinestones and big pieces of turquoise. On Sophia, it looked regal. "Where did you get it?"

"Emma sent it to me. She made it in an extracurricular art class at the Hockaday School. The teacher told her she didn't like it but Emma said I would love it. "

"Well, she's an artist and knows what looks good on

her mom," said Katherine.

"Emma's coming home from Dallas for Thanksgiving but it seems like November is so far away. Enough about me, though. Did you find anything else on Michael's computer?"

"Fuck. I went back to look again and I hit some button and I was instantly connected to a video chat with a live woman fingering herself. "

Katherine and Sophia both started to laugh.

"Do you think she saw you?"

"I have no idea. Technology. I'm suddenly inside a chat room with a naked girl."

"It wasn't just some sort of enticement? She was really there?"

"Yes! Was she going to ask for my credit card? It was bizarre."

Katherine glanced down at the table. Laid out before Sophia was the front page of the Sunday edition of the *Bozeman Chronicle*, a painful picture, but in another way. The color photo of Stacey, with vibrant blue eyes and gleaming blonde hair, beside a large picture of the remnants of her charred house, was a grim departure.

Katherine took a deep breath and exhaled, staring at the photo. "What do you think happened?"

"Well, according to the story they're still saying accident, missing person, possible homicide. Her name has always been synonymous with some sort of scandal. I'm surprised it took this long for something to happen. Who do you think did it?"

Katherine shook her head. She didn't like Sophia

saying anything derogatory about Stacey. "I don't know what to think." She wanted to focus on nothing but Stacey, but all she could see were the images from Michael's computer, swirling in her head.

"The thing is, we know so many women who hated Stacey. With good reason, if you ask me. She was aloof and smug. Thought she was way too smart for the rest. Only the men were important to her. Except you, of course."

Katherine opened her mouth to protest, but Sophia kept talking.

"Who didn't she sleep with, Katherine? I know you liked her, but really. Nearly every woman in the Club had a motive to kill her. Of course, the list has to start with Marie."

"You can't actually think Marie would be capable of doing a thing like this," said Katherine.

"Because she's so kind-hearted?" asked Sophia.

"No. Because she's so...Marie," said Katherine.

"Then how about Scott? He's certainly capable, both psychologically and morally."

"You really are going back to your detective days, aren't you?"

"Hardly," said Sophia. "I mean, sure, I did love being Nick's front woman; I felt like a character in a movie. He was Sicilian, like me, and made me realize things about my culture. We don't stand for bullshit from anyone."

Sophia was normally more guarded about her background.

"So, what made you leave?"

"Ha. Well, he brought in other aspects of that tough Sicilian culture. He had too many clients who talked about their 'family business,' and they didn't mean the little grocery down the street." She got quiet, then moved in toward Katherine, dropping her voice. "The final straw was when I found the body of one of our best informants with a canary stuffed in her mouth. It turned out she'd been informing others, too."

"Holy shit."

"I like it a lot better where I am now. You know, John is such a good guy. Everything feels more stable here, besides Michael's propensity for sadistic porn and Stacey's murder."

"So you do believe someone killed her," said Katherine.

"You think her house blew up because she left on the gas stove? Nope. Bang. Someone wanted her dead." Sophia plunked her water glass down decisively. "I think it's time to gather."

"Meaning what?"

"Meaning it's time for an event to bring all the Dolls together and get them talking about Stacey and her untimely demise."

"Oh. Right," said Katherine. Despite her distaste for many of the Dolls, one of them could lead them closer to figuring out what happened to Stacey.

"We need something that none of them will blow off. A royal gathering. This is the perfect occasion for a tiara party."

"A tiara party? But you always give yourself a month's lead time for those. By that time..."

"Forget the lead time. Everyone must be dying to see each other and hear all the gossip. The day after tomorrow, at my house. I can have invitations hand-delivered this afternoon.

"How are you going to get everything together by then?"

"Katherine, I've done so many tiara parties. It'll be simple. I'll get Zac to cater one of his fabulous luncheon creations. He's always happy to drop everything for me."

"And you're inviting everyone?"

"All thirty of them. Of course, Marie won't come because she knows I can read her botched-up face like no one else."

"Maybe she'll try to fool you."

Sophia arched an eyebrow in one of her superior, all-knowing looks. Katherine laughed. No one ever put anything over on Sophia, least of all Marie.

"I think this is the first tiara party you've hosted that everyone was invited to," Katherine chuckled.

"I remember when you were trying to figure out if there were criteria for who was invited. I think you really didn't get it."

"I'd only lived here for a month. I thought perhaps there was something profoundly serious about the selection process to all these parties."

Sophia laughed and shook her head. "It's simple and I'll repeat myself. Boring, boring, boring will always be cause for exclusion. Except at this party I'm going to include some dormice. Even in their self-absorbed stupor they might have seen something."

CHAPTER FOURTEEN

Marie had been looking forward to the day Stacey was no longer in her life, and now it had come. Now no one would be tantalizing her husband or scrutinizing her moves.

Unlike Scott, Marie didn't fall in love with her lovers. She hated that Scott had been so blatantly obvious with his long-term affair with Stacey. Hated it more that the affair bothered her so much. Stacey wasn't a dumb little plaything like the models and strippers had been. She was smart and real. She could hold a conversation and be as cutting as the meanest Doll. As far as Marie was concerned, their circus of a marriage was over. Scott's unfaithful actions had, little by little, pushed her into making sure she could protect herself without him.

Scott had told Marie they were made for each other. They were married in Las Vegas, counting their lucky cards. He knew her con—it was his also: optimistic deceit. Marie looked at it more like little fibs that became god's honest truth. So what if they lied and falsified their education backgrounds? Did it really matter that they'd fabricated their enviable childhood lives? Their money made it better for others, too. They donated to all sorts of charities to make people believe they cared, to show they had heart. It was so simple, like buying plastic surgery for the soul.

In the past she had believed she'd get back at Scott for all of his cheating with her open-legged strategy, but he was merely amused by her attempts. She had believed Scott when he said they were the same. But that was bullshit and she knew it now.

Marie had responded immediately to Sophia's RSVP on Sunday. Yes, she would be there and was delighted to attend. But she had no intention of going to this tiara party. She acted as if nothing was out of the ordinary and then cancelled Monday night, saying she needed to leave for Paris immediately due to problems with a large antique purchase. To congratulate herself on her brilliant plan, she lay on the couch with a rather large vodka soda. Marie awakened, miraculously sober, at 4:00 a.m., Tuesday morning.

The house was quiet and dark. She sat up and her mind immediately went to the Dolls. Dishonest and manipulative, all of them. She knew they had to accept her because she was married to Scott, the leader and founder of the "Antelope Empire." Scott had made it clear that they had to present a united image, no matter how she felt about him or his meandering. No one else in the Club had their kind of clout; collectively they owned fifty-one percent, the controlling share. If she had any thoughts of ever leaving him, they'd lose their power and status. She needed to play the role. But like the run of all theatrical productions, she was smart enough to realize their life in the limelight might be limited.

Her husband complained she never made lasting

friendships with the people important to him in his inner circles, the wives of politicians and captains of industry. Well, she couldn't afford to! Marie had to take care of Marie alone. She had a plan and a reason for everything she did. She removed people who didn't go along with her wishes or tried to block her plans.

After what happened to Stacey, she knew there would be questions. She had rehearsed and internalized her answers until she very nearly believed them to be true. Honestly, she should have been an actress. She could see herself like Grace Kelly, on the screen until she became a real-life, reigning princess or like Vivien Leigh, swearing that she would never be hungry again.

Checking her email on her phone, she suddenly realized what she had originally thought would be a white lie was now close to being alarmingly true. She had to get to Paris.

A shipment of antiques for the Club was stuck in France due to some kind of mix-up with a letter of credit between her bank in Montana and the bank in France. Although her antique broker was capable of handling it, she wanted to fly to Paris personally, as it was the perfect excuse to avoid Sophia's party, plus she had someone to make her trip to Paris enjoyable: *Trevor*, her new horse trainer. He was young, athletic, eager to please, and totally financially dependent. She had a plan to make sure he'd never forget this trip or her.

Marie had perfected a system for drawing young

men into her web. First she gave them a job and paid them more than they were worth. Then she bought them lots of gifts, gifts they could never, ever afford: watches, designer clothing, even trucks if she really liked them. Rich men always did this kind of thing, so why shouldn't rich women? This was why she could never stop weaving and spinning to hold all her ingenious schemes together. She sensed clouds were gathering, and even the most skillful of spiders lose their webs in a downpour.

CHAPTER FIFTEEN

Sophia's master calligraphy was evident from the invitation. The parchment paper was adorned at the top with red, gold, and purple crystals. She tied them with gold brocade ribbon and sent them out with her houseboy. They were probably the quickest invitations she'd ever produced.

It was high noon on Tuesday and the invite sat next to Katherine in the passenger seat. She looked over at it, taking a deep breath before opening the car door and heading inside to Sophia's.

Katherine looked down at her Chanel flats as she stepped out. They still had a bit of soot on them, so she grabbed a tissue from the glove compartment, wiping methodically as she thought about the scene at what was once Stacey's home. She hadn't visited the site since the explosion happened, but this morning she felt she was finally prepared to see for herself. Sifting through the ashes she came to believe what she'd not wanted to before; Stacey was dead.

The valet handed Katherine a rhinestone-encrusted program as she walked slowly toward Sophia's grand double doors. Katherine's black jumpsuit had seemed like a good choice at home, but when Sophia greeted her in a full-length Oscar de la Renta indigo gown, she realized she was completely underdressed. Her crown was small compared to Sophia's. The understated tiara, made of rhinestones in cascades of hearts, was lopsided and wouldn't stay on her head. Katherine stood in front of the mirror in Sophia's foyer and tried to straighten it. "God damn it," she said as she pushed it back on top of her head.

"Nice to see you, too. It should have little combs underneath. Push down on them," said Sophia. "Here, let me do it," said Sophia.

"I can't fucking believe this is for real."

"It's that hardened Wall Street broad inside of you that thinks you have to be tough. Relax."

"That's not it. I was just at Stacey's. I mean, what was Stacey's. Seeing it in person felt very final. Isn't this just a tiny bit disturbing? A tiara party for grown women? I thought I was getting used to it, but when I look at myself—coming to a party in the middle of the day at the edge of the Montana wilderness, dressed up and wearing a crown, it makes me wonder.. And you know that some of these women are going to be here in their second wedding dresses, or squeezed into their daughters' over-priced prom gowns."

Sophia turned to the mirror and admired herself as she spoke. "We are royalty, in our own strange way. It's lonely at the top. That's why we need to show up for each other. And I'm only telling you, but I have a superstar coming to entertain us all instead of the usual present swap game. He'll for sure lift everyone's spirits. I was very lucky because his agent had said that he was already in the Rockies. You pay the price," Sophia snapped her fingers, "And you get the best. He's coming here to perform for all of us. I sent our jet and he'll arrive after lunch, just before we usually do the present swap game."

"I wondered why 'Bring a wrapped present' wasn't on the invitation but I figured you were in a hurry. "Oh come on, tell me who it is."

"No," Sophia paused. "Go around to as many guests as you can and ask them what they know about Stacey and if they tell you, you'll tell them about a secret star appearance toward the end of the party. One hint— he used to be the lead singer in a 'boy band.' He's been on his own for a while with his own hits and he's an actor."

Katherine sighed. "I'm saying this is getting more bizarre all the time." Katherine practiced her line and whispered in Sophia's ear. "Star performances are nothing new to parties around here but this guy will send everyone spinning."

"You got it!"

"I can't believe you're pulling this off. I want to know more about what happened to Stacey. There's never a shortage of information with these women and I know they'll say some things that will *never* be said around the men."

"That's one thing good about these tiara parties, everyone being themselves without worrying about some man overhearing or deciding to take over the conversation. Just appreciate it for what it is, Katherine, and go get the Stacey details."

"Okay, okay." She gave Sophia a smile.

"Oh, your nails look nice. Alissa's manicurist did a great job with that thumb nail."

"Thanks. It hurts less than it did when we had our lunch, and this color seems to be camouflaging the actual nail color."

"Speaking of, you've got to see her new crown. Brad gave her an incredible tiara for her birthday. It has one hundred and fifty brilliant colorless and pink diamonds."

If Alissa ever discovered her affair with Brad she wondered what kind of over-the-top present his guilt would bring. "Didn't know he had it in him. Nice," said Katherine sarcastically.

Sophia smiled with a bit of bewilderment and moved on to greet the next guests. Her butler was ushering one Doll after another into her drawing room, which in Montana was termed "the great room." Sophia and John's home looked like a castle from the Italian Alps, with tall marble pillars and turrets. The views were panoramic, looking all the way into the Crazy Mountain range, which jutted up beyond the north end of Livingston.

Almost all the Queen-Dolls had arrived, some wearing floor-length dresses, others in dressy cocktail attire. Katherine thought of a quote that seemed to define the Dolls:; "Women dress for women and undress for men." She looked at Sophia's hand-printed menu for the day: champagne followed by hors d'oeuvres, a buffet lunch, and desserts, ending with strong coffee. She saw Alissa and Lyn talking and walked up to them, hoping to get a glance at the rumored tiara.

"Alissa, let me see your crown more closely," said

Katherine. Maybe she should have been jealous, but the absurdity of the crown made it impossible.

Alissa, normally a great show woman, was almost embarrassed. "When I think of *why* Brad probably bought me this, it makes me sick," she said. "It was right after I discovered his AmEx statement. He thought he'd secretly changed access to it online, but I still found it...and there was a $30,000 charge to Pole Chasers in Dallas. I went nuts. He tried to say that it was entertainment for his clients. Thirty thousand dollars is quite a lot of entertainment. I didn't speak to him for days. And then the next week, on my birthday, I get this. As if this crown can actually make up for everything he's done. I mean, yes, I had a baby two years ago, but I bounced back like that!" she said, snapping her fingers. "Who could possibly resist this?" She did a little shimmy that let Katherine know the champagne was working.

Katherine knew very well who never gave his wife a thought when he was getting what he wanted. Katherine jokingly called their sessions "birds of play." They would hop into the back seat of Brad's GMC truck at fishing access landings on the river, from Grey Owl to Mallard's Rest. Katherine had Alissa's husband eating out of more than her hand. Always. And awhile back, when he started to back off their relationship, Katherine had made sure he understood that she would ruin his life. She had reminded him how she still had other friends at the SEC who would be happy to hear that Brad had been negligent in his reports about the background checks of subprime mortgage loans.

"Too bad Brad can be such a prick," said Katherine with a wise smile. It was almost creepy that she knew so much about Alissa and her husband. "I knew so many guys like him back on the Street." Katherine continued, "All the power goes to their heads and they believe that everything they do is justified." She was sure swift at calling the kettle black.

"All he thinks about is being the coolest of guys' guys, and he forgets he's married, and has a baby," said Alissa. "It hurts."

Finally, Lyn piped up. "For now, that crown is gorgeous. Just order the bracelet and necklace to match. In fact, I'll make sure you do. You deserve it, kid."

Alissa forced herself to laugh. "I wish I didn't let it bother me so much."

"It's not worth it," said Katherine. Then she added with a wink, "At least you don't have to worry about a broken dryer anymore. Hey, come over here. I've got an ask-and-tell game going on thanks to our Sophia, the grand hostess. If you can tell me something you know about Stacey that you think no one else knows, I'll give you a hint of what super star Sophia has hired for the entertainment today."

"Super star? We never have them to tiara parties. Sounds like a very different game!" Alissa touched her crown like Tinkerbell about ready to fly. She leaned into Katherine, speaking in a whisper. "Brad and Stacey always had conversations on the phone. Our house phone. Brad was worried about some loans and

Stacey was worried about Scott finding out she knew. I don't think Brad was too happy about it."

Bingo. That was quite a bit more than Katherine had expected.

"Anything more?"

"That's the only thing I can think off the top of my head," said Alissa as her crown slipped and she straightened it. "No, wait a minute. She told my husband she was scared for her life. I thought that was her little ploy to get him to sleep with her. I'm sure Brad had no problem being her savior."

Afraid for her life? That didn't sound like a "come on" line to Katherine. The problem with Alissa was the way she interpreted things. She was literal—like when she first told her about the tiara party she actually thought true royalty was attending. A Countess from Spain had come a couple of times but she was very quiet about her status and Katherine wasn't even sure if Alissa knew who she was.

"So tell me who's coming today!"

"I can only give you hints. Star of a boyband, been on his own for a while. Think about that Trolls movie."

"Oh! Oh! I know who it is. It's…" Alissa had guessed his name quickly.

"Ok, you're right but do not tell anyone a word. Ask others about Stacey and what they knew about her. They have to give you good information or no hints and you need to come back to me with the details."

"Got it. I like this game," and off went Alissa.

Only it wasn't a game and Katherine desperately

wanted to know what had happened to her good friend. But for this type of over-the-top event, she just might come up with some worthy leads.

Lyn gave them a puzzled look and Alissa went right over. "I have some photos I want to show you of my trip to the Caribbean!" She pulled out her phone from her butterfly Judith Leiber.

"Oh fun! You take the best photos," Alissa squealed.

"But first, I have to ask you a question. If you tell me something about Stacey, I'll give you a hint. This isn't just a regular tiara party. A superstar is coming later on. Not just the usual but one you love."

"So I have to tell you something about Stacey."

"Yes."

"Hmmm. Pretty sure she went bone fishing with Eric down in Cuba. Eric mentioned that she came along with all the guys. It was organized by that older fly fishing guy married to the young Cuban girl. So I'm not sure if it was Eric who she was interested in that week. Does that count? "

"Of course it does. So here's the hint, think of that song in the Troll movie," said Alissa.

"I don't go to kids' movies Alissa. That's not fair."

"Okaaaay. He was probably one of your boy band idols, and he can dance."

Lyn looked like she had no idea.

Lyn brushed Alissa off and came directly over to Katherine who had to brace herself for at least fifteen minutes of time spent admiring Lyn's first-class vacation, but instead, found something to occupy her peripheral vision; a very handsome, dark-haired, tanned, and sleek man in his early fifties walked through the double doors and was immediately ushered to the kitchen by one of Sophia's staff. This wasn't the star, but who was he?

Katherine watched Sophia grab a glass of champagne from her butler and down it. She walked purposefully into the kitchen and Katherine excused herself from Lyn's slide show, saying she needed to use the ladies'.

There was something about the way this man carried himself that had her questioning. Yes, the place was buzzing with Dolls and Sophia's staff, but that wouldn't always prevent something terrible from happening.

Katherine stood near the swinging kitchen door and as appetizers came into the great room, she positioned herself to see Sophia, stepping toward this man and kissing him European-style on both cheeks. He looked her up and down, making it clear that they had been more than just friends.

"Nick," she could hear Sophia say, "What brings you here? It couldn't be the warm weather." So here was the infamous Nick, the man who made Sophia run back to Texas.

"Time has given you an extra stroke of beauty," Katherine heard him reply. "I didn't think it was possible. Although I'm hardly surprised. The Antelope Club Board and Scott Stiles have hired my firm to take a look into Stacey Olsen's death."

Katherine felt her gut clench.

"And why would they bring you in all the way from the East Coast? Aren't the 'Boys' keeping you busy enough?"

"It's been a long time, Sophia. I've expanded. Come up in the world. I handle mostly white-collar crime now. It's a lot different from what I did when...you knew me."

"Katherine! I'm not finished." Lyn was at her elbow. "I forgot to show you this photo of our bungalow. Amazing! We had our own masseuse on staff and, plus a macrobiotic chef and...Oooh. Who's that?" The kitchen door had swung back open as two of the waiters were bringing out petit fours in the shape of tiaras. Pink and white pastries on silver trays were presented in front of the women, but Lyn was nearly forcing her way into the kitchen to be introduced to Sophia's friend.

Katherine could see the look of shock and then composure on Sophia's face as she watched Lyn push through the doors.

"Hi Lyn! We were just coming out." Sophia's tone sounded forcibly light as she guided Nick through the doors and into the great room where conversation ceased and thirty pairs of eyes locked on to the only man in their midst.

"Ladies, may I introduce Nick Conti. Nick is a private investigator who's here to help look into Stacey's death. He's an old friend of mine, and I'm sure he'll be happy to speak with you all in the coming days as he tries to put the pieces together the tragedy. But for now, he was just leaving." Sophia's body and tone moved Nick toward the double-doors, but he had zoned in on Lyn and swiftly had her hand in his, taking it to his lips.

"Niiiice," cooed Lyn. "I'm Lyn and I knew Stacey so, so well. We should definitely talk soon."

"Excellent. Here's my card. Please give me a ring; we can set up a private appointment this week. I'm staying at Chico Hot Springs."

Katherine was already disgusted by his slick ways and Lyn's ridiculously over-the-top flirtation.

Katherine could sense Sophia's irritation as Nick slowly handed out his cards to the roomful of women. Katherine looked down at his color photo placed smack in the center, revealing a tacky gold chain around his neck under a black shirt with a black jacket. She watched as he took time to speak to every Doll. When he reached Alissa, she grabbed his elbow and pulled him to Sophia's overstuffed white couch. The two sat drinking champagne, speaking softly with knees touching for almost a half an hour before Sophia intervened, pointing Nick toward the door.

"This party is ladies only and I don't remember sending you an invitation." Sophia said with the kindest smile. Someone who didn't know her would suspect she was making a friendly joking gesture. Thank god he was leaving; Katherine was in no mood to relay any of the information she had already given Dan; if Nick wanted details from her, he could speak to the Sheriff.

★★★

As Nick walked out with a champagne glass in his hand he noticed a younger man sitting in the shade against one of the cars looking a bit hung over.

"Hey, aren't you…"

"Yeah."

"What in hell are you doing sitting over here. Have a glass of champagne."

"What time is it? It's been a long night. The limo dropped me off but I had to take another little break. Looks like the place is jammed full of women."

"You got that one right. It's 1:45," said Nick.

"I'm fifteen minutes late. Hey, thanks for the champagne, man."

He straightened up and walked around back to the barn. Nick sat in his car writing down as many notes in his phone as he could remember. Some women had given him their calling cards, so proper in the middle of nowhere.

Soon he heard screams of laughter and delight to loud music. The super star had an incredible ability to recover quickly.

CHAPTER SIXTEEN

When Katherine drove home from the tiara party, she quickly took off her crown as she didn't want Jean to see her so dressed up. Jean wasn't outside. Maybe she was in her barn tending to the horses or canning something wonderful from her garden.

The house was empty. No telling exactly where Michael was, but he had probably fled up to Lolo.

She took a look at herself in her bedroom mirror. The tiara party was interesting but if she were truly honest with herself, she'd rather have been out riding with Jean or better yet, the Wednesday Pine Riders. These ranch women were the real people as far as Katherine was concerned. They were unpretentious, honest women. They were skilled and they followed a strict set of rules, primarily for safety and courtesy. They wouldn't let just anyone into their tight group. You had to be asked and you had to qualify, two rides in a row and not in the summer, when the riding was easy, but in late fall or early spring.

She remembered two rides last spring. The first one was where she probably had blown it. You had to be ready promptly at nine and she and Jean were there on time as the WPR didn't wait for anyone. This day they had trailered their horses a good three hours from the valley. Then they'd ridden on a very thin trail that if you looked down into the alpine lake and your horse missed a step you'd be over the edge and gone. That's why Katherine never talked. She couldn't believe what she was doing. She was scared and thrilled at the same time. She never let anyone know and trusted Triumph as they headed up the steep grade around some large boulders. They had ridden about four hours straight up beyond the timberline. To Katherine it felt miraculous that they had made it, but to these women it was just another Wednesday ride. They were in what looked like "Sound of Music" country. When everyone found a spot to sit for lunch, Katherine looked at her watch. When she added up the hours she realized it was going to be a long day. She went up to the trail boss and said, "Do you have an idea when we'll be back? I'd told my husband I'd be home for dinner."

That's when the trail boss looked her sternly in the eyes and said, "You tell your husband you'll be home when he sees the rig coming up the driveway."

Katherine felt embarrassed, no one had ever talked like that to her before and she was well aware she was a true novice. Jean had told her the rules: no husbands, no children, no dogs, no cooking or cleaning on Wednesdays. They packed their guns for emergencies and didn't want to deal with inexperienced riders who didn't ride safely or couldn't control their horses. The local paper called them "The Pistol Packin' Mamas," copying the name after the legendary Thursday Sage Riders of Twin Falls, Idaho.

Then there was the time when it snowed all day as they rode in Yellowstone Park up to Swan Lake. They had to stop every so often and scrape the snow that had balled up under their horses' hooves. They all rode with long slickers and hats. It was a nice day when they had started and Katherine had her yellow slicker on but not enough layers to really keep her warm in the freezing weather. The Pine Riders just chattered along as usual but it was slippery and dangerous. All Jean said as turned her back in the saddle was, "I want you to know this is one bonafide ride." Katherine didn't care that she was cold, she was just delighted to be able to ride with them and survive the challenge of the trail. If she were really honest with herself the thing she wanted most, more than any position she had on Wall Street, was to become a member of The Wednesday Pine Riders. But she knew that would never happen because she was on the opposing team, living below what they called Diamond Peak.

She knew the WPR had no time for Antelope Club types. They were looked upon as a plague of locusts destroying their pristine land. Katherine couldn't argue otherwise, because she understood the encroachment.

CHAPTER SEVENTEEN

Michael sat before his four walls of computer screens in his office, tapping from one window to the next, checking a string of fallouts from what he had manipulated, lost, and recouped. Flying from screen to screen, from world to world, was a thrill, an addiction. His genius quants monitored every second of activity and made sure BotDom Technologies would never be thrown off its axis by algos-gone-wrong like Knight Capital. Every day was a race he had to win. But, no matter what he did, he wasn't winning at home.

So much pressure required so much release. He was in the mood for something other than his subscription live-screen sessions.

He could hire anyone to do anything except for what he was doing now. Only he could organize his folders, because this was his private domain. They were all there waiting for him. There were thousands and he was constantly organizing. They all had their own categories but it was imperative that he continually updated and sorted. It was easier to file his algos than these jpegs and videos, and if he didn't check on them all the time he would forget where they were. He was a collector and they were his art. Drag and drop, new photo folder, new name. What was it he was looking for? It was exhausting, keeping the file names in his head. He would build a table of contents soon. What he really needed to do was create a software program for organizing them, but it would take too much time. There was probably an app that would help him keep it straight.

He couldn't sort any longer. He felt the swell. He had to have them now. What was that new category? It wasn't just "slapping." It wasn't "mothers and daughters." It was a flip on those; fathers slapping sons. He unzipped his pants and took a well-practiced mental leap. There was no place like the home screen. Yes, a picture could be worth a thousand wanks. He was the cum master and it was damn fucking great.

Michael was momentarily content. He could switch back to his algorithms almost as fast as he could come. He sent an upbeat message to his staff, who were mostly in New York now, although he had a skeleton crew still in Lolo and a few other pawn locations. Most of them were PhDs, mathematicians, software engineers, researchers, logicians. They designed high-frequency trading algos for a vastly complex network of software that spread across hundreds of computers on hundreds of Linux servers. Those algos scoured the world's financial markets looking for patterns and inconsistencies, saw trends in milliseconds and made profits with an uncountable number of trades. Michael's company worked on slivers of pennies, but operated on such a huge scale that it could accumulate millions before a human thought could register. The algos were his silent key that opened the door to the financial universe, for which he was the master.

He had greased his inside connections within the

exchanges. His orders were given priority and placed so they were filled ahead of other orders submitted earlier. The coding of orders was especially important. He had mastered twists on the "Hide not Slide" move within all of the exchanges. If there was any potential for getting kicked out of the systems by bans on locked markets, BotDom's orders were hidden and slid in front of any other traders. He always jumped the queue. "Negative Alpha" never appeared in his normal day limits.

They thought they could stop him, those cowards in the SEC, like Brad Fairbanks. Oh, he knew what they were up to, he knew the legislation that was being cooked up in the back rooms of the FBI and the Justice Department. They were sniffing closer to him all the time. When they sniffed close enough, he would pull the trigger.

Today he was testing a particularly complex algorithm that determined the parameters of his trading: where it stretched, divided and conquered, and where it stopped. It was a precise sequence of steps performed in exponential increments, rising and expanding at rates equal unto themselves. The beauty was that it happened not in milliseconds but in microseconds. In less than the time it took to tap a key, his new toy spun the global markets to play in his favor. It enabled his super-powered computers to do their work and pulled out before they could raise any red flags. This was faster and more complex than anything ever written or tested before. Einstein redefined space and time. He conquered them both in ways even Einstein probably wouldn't understand. The algos redefined faith. God was a supernerd, and Michael became the real archangel.

Michael sighed and slapped his desk. He loved the rush, the gamble, and the sweat of the margin. As he looked outside of the only window in his home office, his thoughts began to drift. Here he was, sitting in his private domain of flashing screens, like a one-man mission control center, feeling the power flow through his fingertips, outsmarting the smartest financial minds in the world. It had him almost forget how his wife had made him feel like crap before she'd gone to her little tiara party earlier. Almost.

Her nose had been a little too high when she had left for Sophia's. The ridiculous crown on her head was symbolic of everything he had grown to hate about her. It had been a long time since she'd treated him civilly, the way she used to, and Montana seemed to have wiped away her desire for carnivorous sex. In New York she'd work all day and then tear into him at night. This used to be a woman who had to have sex, like a guy. It was the manly part of her that he had liked. He was tired of painting the mirage of marriage. If only she had known his thoughts, like wishing she could have been a man or stringing her up right after she had fucked him with her strap on dildo. But that fantasy was far from reality because in the wild, she was tame.

He had believed she'd be the perfect well-groomed beard for his varied proclivities. She was too self-absorbed with her own career to notice him. She simply hadn't cared that much about his whereabouts. He had enjoyed playing the good husband back in New York. He had admired her intelligence and culture. Although he preferred rock and roll, he didn't mind going to the opera and ballet. She'd never noticed how enthralled he was with the anatomy of the male dancers.

Katherine would never know how much he missed Paddles, his favorite club in Chelsea. He had been testing her for ages. Just like anyone in theory could swim, anyone could be trained to "suspend." He left receipts lying around, even left his computer open with engaging photos to string her up into his world. But she'd never tapped his screen. There was a part of him that wanted her to join him. He had thought he'd seen dominatrix traits in her, but she was only a domina about work.

Before she left this morning, Katherine harped at him to take out the trash, to clean up the boxes of computer miscellany in the garage. Then she dug into him about being a recluse. He didn't have time to listen to her shit, so he just shut the door to his office right in her face.

He listened as she stomped down the hall. Something clattered to the floor—no doubt the hand-painted Herend he had picked up in Budapest as a gift for her. Footsteps again and then the unmistakable sound of glass breaking: their Waterford flutes? He heard her slam the front door so hard the entryway mirror fell off the wall and shattered.

He should have followed her out and slapped her

right then. How would she react to that? It was time for her to remember that she was supposed to be grateful to him. Why had he bothered to save her? She had become his Hellbitch, an uncooperative, wayward, stubborn mare who managed to shove him and keep him in the corral. If only he could devise a formula to take Katherine out of his complex equation.

Why had he ever thought he needed her? Truth was, he had fucked the intriguing out of her.

CHAPTER EIGHTEEN

It was time to review the last few days' complaints. Little three-by-eight-and-a-half sheets with triplicate copies gave him the summary of what his deputies had seen. Most were the usual run down of neighbors complaining about dogs barking, domestic disputes, and disorderly conduct from the town's many bars.

Dan dipped a stale donut into his coffee. Lyn's cookies would have been great right about now, but the aftertaste wasn't worth it. After a failed romance with his former high school flame, he vowed to never let his heart get ripped to shreds again. He had mixed emotions regarding Lyn; he was possessive of her, but knew she wasn't his and was disgusted that he'd let their relationship go this far. He had thought he would stop it after that first carnal rodeo. But here he was, deep in an affair with a manipulative married woman. Sex with her somehow managed to trump all the things he despised: arrogance and gaudy shows of flesh and wealth. He believed his drinking was altering his judgment but he wasn't doing much about that either. He had thought a relationship with a married woman would be easy but there was no free milk, even without the hassle of the cow.

His deputy, Duane, walked in. "Did you see the one I filed last night about the john?"

"Nope, haven't come to it yet."

"Find it."

Dan sorted through the remaining pile. "Okay. Here it is." He skimmed it quickly and laughed. He pushed back his chair and put his feet up on his desk. "You aren't serious."

"Yep. Got a call from a Kyle Hansen down on B Street. Said he hired a hooker, who must have been somewhat of an amateur." His deputy couldn't stop laughing. "He filed a complaint saying she didn't let him finish!"

It felt good to laugh. "Get out of here. Are we talking stupid or what?"

"Exactly. So I booked him on solicitation and her for prostitution." He paused. "She said something interesting I thought you oughta hear. She wondered why we don't ever look into all the S&M activity going on. Said she'd seen some pretty awful beatings. Guys asking her to do bad stuff, thinking she was going to like it."

"I know Gallatin County has had some problems with that," Dan said.

"Probably should have kept her here longer last night. Another john type posted her bail. I thought about it too late and realized you may have wanted to talk to her. Now no one seems to have seen her. Then again, maybe she's making it all up. But she'll have to be back for court."

Dan was still chuckling. "Can't believe the guy filed a complaint for not finishing. But maybe you should follow up on what she said. Just remember she's a hooker. Probably couldn't tell the whole truth if you paid her. Maybe the *only* thing she couldn't do if you paid her." They both laughed.

Dan shifted his focus to the last bite of donut. He was annoyed he wouldn't be working Stacey's case on his own, that he was forced to deal with the big-time, East Coast, private investigator sent in by the Antelope Board.

So far he couldn't sense a clear-cut reason for the explosion. But he reminded himself it occurred inside the Antelope Club. Whether they called them antelope, pronghorn, or speed goats, they were undeniably North America's fastest animals. Thirteen different gaits. These human antelopes, these RFs—rich fuckers—could be pretty quick too. They were also the types who believed money covered up their manure. Which is probably why they'd hired this PI, Nick Conti.

He pulled out the little metal brown can from his front pants pocket. His index finger scooped up a big, brown, chewy wad of tobacco that he folded into his cheek. It was insulting to have to deal with an outsider. Not to mention time consuming. Every minute he had to deal with the PI was time he could use to further *his* investigation, *his* case.

Antelope were known for their racing instincts and their tendency to cross in front of their rivals. The Winchester 257 Roberts was loaded.

His phone rang.

CHAPTER NINETEEN

Lyn wasn't about to give up on Dan. "Hi, I'm sorry about bringing you cookies while you were working so hard. I'm over at the Love Shack, feeling pretty good after a tiara party. You know where I am, the little cabin on Clint's family's ranch. He said I could use it anytime. Why don't you take a break and come over?"

He knew he was going for it again. He could quickly drive home, get his truck and be at the Big Creek Ranch in minutes. Maybe he did need something to relax him.

He ran hot and cold but she knew he loved Clint's ranch. He had hunted elk with Clint on the property and had commented on how great it would be to spend some time in the Love Shack. "Bang, bang, on the door baby, bang, bang."

Clint always left the door unlocked. The Love Shack was on the north side of the property, far from the main ranch house. No one lived on the ranch except the eighty head of horses that Clint kept on his place.

Now all Lyn had to do was "drop the line" so to speak and she knew she'd have no problem reeling Dan in. Not all the dolls fly-fished, but Lyn did. She thought men were very similar to trout. It was just a matter of casting the right fly. If they didn't respond to one presentation you tried another. The question was always which ones were the keepers. It was way easier to catch and release. Lyn could read the waters and knew Dan would be there. This was about as simple as fishing a stocked stream.

Her intuition was correct. He was coming. The ranch was south of the Antelope Club off the highway. Big Creek ran through the property right behind the Love Shack. It was fabulous to hear the flowing water inside. She lit the many candles scattered around the room and plugged her phone into the sound system. She knew Dan preferred the songs he grew up with, so she played classical country selections like Marty Robbins' "Gun Fighter Ballads." After all he was *Sheriff* of this western county.

Lyn checked the stocked bar and poured herself a glass of Pinot Grigio. The bed was in the center of the room. She slipped on a tight fitting white corset with a garter belt and white thigh-highs to match. Looking in the mirror, it seemed as though something was missing. Not exactly country girl, but she was certainly in the country, so she popped on a straw hat that was hanging on the elk antler rack. Perfect. She was ready for her cowboy. She walked outside and sat in the rocking chair on the front porch. That was the beauty of the Love Shack, no one was around.

Dan drove a Dodge Ram 3500 when he wasn't working. The sound of the engine was such a turn on, purring like a huge, sexy cat. Lyn loved cowboy hats, big trucks and big cowboys. He came driving up with a stock trailer hitched behind his truck. The sight of his hat, the truck and the trailer was an ultimate thrill, so manly, so unlike her husband. As he walked through the long green grass she could tell he liked the sight of her. This was what Montana was all about – raw, uninhibited sexuality in the wild.

He was all over her in seconds, pulling down the front of her corset, kissing her exposed breasts. He willingly followed her inside and thrust her onto the bed all the while massaging and kissing each nipple, lightly teasing her with his teeth. She could feel the bulge in his pants. She wanted him inside of her but when she tried to unbutton his jeans he took her hand away, while still massaging and pulling at her chest. This was something new, and she was loving it.

"Oh my god, what are you *doing* to me?"

Lyn could feel waves of heated excitement rolling from her breasts into her core. The sensation was resting between her legs even though he wasn't touching her there.

"Don't talk."

It was as if she was riding the rapids on the Yellowstone River in high waters and she couldn't hold on to the raft tightly enough. As soon as she thought she was cresting the largest wave in the river, another one fell right in front, covering her so that she was so wet she couldn't see or think. She would start to prepare for the next roll of raging waters when a new set, out of nowhere, hit. It was exhilarating, dangerous and terrifying. Dan was the whitewater river guide, steering and maneuvering her, pulling her nipples, squeezing and biting, taking her down through uprising swell after swell that rippled and pleasurably tore through her body. She had to have been inside the "green room" of rivers.

She didn't see the huge final one as there wasn't time to gather any bearings. It was upon her before she was cognizant of anything happening to her body. The river tsunami enveloped the vessel with its powerful force, flipping it upside down. She was suddenly thrown and catapulted deep into the waters of her own pleasure. Gasping for air, she couldn't breathe. Dan grabbed her as she was falling, sinking deeper and deeper. She couldn't breathe and her body was quivering and shuddering. She was struggling to find the surface. She could feel his strong body holding her securely as she thrashed to the top. It was scary, thrilling and euphoric all at once. When she did finally push her way into consciousness Dan was inside her. He was holding her tightly grabbing and squeezing her ass. She held onto his neck while still drowning in her own ecstasy.

Dan was taking her in his own way, gently now, slowly bringing her back to life. She heard noises. Oh my. She was making the sounds, the sighs. He was thrusting harder now, deep inside of her, forcefully and vigorously he came crashing into the depths of her being. Silence. She had no idea how long they'd been inside making love in the big soft, oversized bed. Lyn could hear the rushing waters of Big Creek through the open window. It was suddenly very, very warm. Dan was caressing her again. She tried to divert him by kissing his hands.

"You came while I was kissing your breasts, you

know."

"I'm not sure I know anything. I'm not sure that was even me. I've never felt anything like that before. Dan, oh Dan, you're the best lover I've ever had." She always told her lovers that. Men loved to hear they were the best even when it wasn't true, even when she had to fantasize about another man to make herself come. But this time, she meant it. No one had ever come close to bringing her to the heights Dan had just taken her. Yep, he was a keeper.

"You're not so bad yourself." Dan was extremely confidant when it came to the bedroom. She wasn't the first woman to tell him that. "There's more, you know, where that came from."

There was a part of him that wanted this woman, but wanted her all for himself. He knew he was sharing. He knew soon she'd return to her palatial home and fix dinner for a jerk who thought of her as just another possession. But for now he'd enjoy what lay next to him. True, she was nosey, was always into his stuff, and he ran hot and cold about her, but he loved the attention she gave him, no matter that sometimes she could be so annoying.

"What's the stock trailer for?"

"I'm moving Stacey's horses over to Jean's. Jean is one tough lady. She told me point blank, 'You're our Sheriff. Known you since you were a little tike. And now it's up to you to find who killed my niece and I guarantee it had to do with money.'"

CHAPTER TWENTY

Later Dan met Nick at the Northern Pacific Beanery, a large honey and red-colored brick restaurant that sat next to the railroad tracks. It was at least a century old. For as long as Dan could remember, nothing much had changed except for the ownership. The Beanery was in the center of town, next to the depot. Originally it was the Northern Pacific Lunchroom, a huge diner for locals, railroad workers and tourists traveling to Yellowstone Park. The walls were still covered with railroad posters, the ceiling was twenty feet high and the chairs were black metal. The place could seat a good seventy people although it was only during the summer, high tourist season, when it was filled. Dan sat with his back to the wall.

Stella, the waitress, was as easygoing and friendly as the atmosphere.

"Hi, Sheriff. How ya' doin'? Let me guess, chicken fried steak, biscuits and gravy."

Dan nodded. "You got it, lamb cake." He'd been ordering the same thing for most of his life. Sometimes he liked the buckwheat pancakes but the biscuits and gravy were as routine as the rumble of the frequent trains shaking the building.

"Stella, this is Nick. He's out from New York."

"Welcome, happy to meet ya'. And what would you like, sir?"

"A latte with an extra shot of espresso," said Nick.

The waitress shook her head, sighed and smiled at the Sheriff before speaking to Nick. "Sorry, just plain old coffee, regular or decaf. Which do ya' want?"

"Regular, is fine."

"Sure you don't want pie? We have huckleberry today."

Nick glanced over at the refrigerator cases filled with desserts above the long counter.

"Ok, pie sounds good."

Nick looked at Dan. "Thought a beanery would have an assortment of coffee beans."

"Beanery is the railroad term for 'eating house.'" This guy was going to be about as painful as a root canal. "Ever been out here to fish or hunt?"

"Usually I go to Colorado or Idaho," Nick replied. "Have a client who has a big spread outside Aspen and another one south of Sun Valley. I especially like the bird hunting in Idaho."

So the guy was at least a bird hunter but he hung with fat cats. "Always been a PI?"

"Nope. Used to be a Jersey cop."

Dan wasn't impressed. He wanted to solve this case on his own and the last thing he needed was some big city shit coming around and sticking his nose in his case files.

"What's your relationship like with Scott?" asked Dan.

"I've worked some cases for him," said Nick. "Frankly, he's not my favorite client. We met at a club in New York a couple of years ago. He wanted to know if I ever do 'contract' work. I mean, even if I did, that's not the kind of thing you ask a guy in a club while you're getting a lap dance."

"So you're here to represent Stiles, but you don't even like Stiles," said Dan.

"No, I'm here to find out why Stacey Olsen died. Of course the board would love me to clear Stiles, but I have some of my own theories regarding him. What's your take?"

"Wouldn't piss in his mouth if his teeth were on fire. He'll do anything to promote his agenda. Not much different than a lot of these new assholes up here." He gave him a steely look.

"Got it. Then I think we're on the same page. I just want to get to the truth and I think some of these Ladies Who Lunch may be able to help us. Ok if I work that angle? I'm old friends with Sophia Whitman and she's introduced me to the gals."

Of course this city slicker would want to get in with the Dolls right away. He was probably here to chase some tail and solve the case. Dan could sympathize, just as long as Lyn wasn't part of the discussion. Their relationship ran from very hot to sometimes nothing in his mind, but he still needed to know she wanted only him.

"Sure, get to know the local color. Despite wanting everything all the time, these ladies lead pretty empty lives, so not sure how much they'll have to say." For good measure he added, "I'm already interviewing Lyn, so no need to be in touch with her."

"Fine by me. I've also got computer access and the

accounting books from the Club and I'm going to go over those. I've got a guy in New York who knows more about this stuff. I may call in a favor if I can't get deep enough on my own."

As much as Dan hated to admit it, this guy was being helpful. Nevertheless, he still needed to know this was Dan's town.

Dan knew everyone in the diner. One by one, they came up and greeted their Sheriff. It made him feel proud and in charge and gave him a boost of confidence next to this big city PI. Stella dropped the check with a wink at Dan. He pulled out his wallet, but Nick threw down a fifty-dollar bill before Dan could offer his cash.

"This one's on me." Nick said, with what Dan noticed was a rather smug smile.

"So how about we go check out that crime scene?" Nick asked. "You want to me to follow?"

"Sure."

★★★

Once they arrived, Dan started poking around the rubble and charred wood with his Leatherman knife.

"What're you finding there?" asked Nick.

Dan didn't look up. "Not much. Because of the severe force of the explosion and the fire, everything's scattered throughout this place."

"So still no point of origin known?" Nick asked.

Dan looked up at him, and with badly concealed irritation said only, "Nope."

"Looks like you and your guys have sorted the

timbers, though. It's a good start."

"They've found which pieces of wood are softer than others, where the fire burned first and longest. The less charred wood would have been farther from the point of origin."

Dan and Nick walked the area separately. After about a half an hour, they reconvened.

"Take a look at these," Nick said. He had been sorting through the mounds of blackened debris and came across pieces of terracotta tile from the other side of the scene. "I think they have similar patterns as those pieces of softened wood."

"The wood is from her kitchen ceiling. The scorch patterns match."

"Then do you think the blast could have started in the kitchen?"

Dan squinted at him, "Whoever did this must have known that Stacey would use the side door entrance by her garage," he said. "They would've set something to go off the second she walked in. Probably loosened the propane tanks to cause a leak in her basement. But what sparked it?"

"The scorch mark on the ceiling," Nick said. "Makes me think it was a light bulb."

Dan stared at him. "Light bulb," he said.

"All the arsonist had to do was drill a tiny hole in one of her incandescent bulbs, a regular 75 or 100 watt, fill it partially full of gasoline and then add some dishwashing soap. When she entered her kitchen and flipped the switch...bang. More than just the lights went out."

Shit. This guy was smarter than Dan figured.

"I've seen it a few times before."

"Could be," Dan said. "I'll check with the lab. It's a good theory. But it still doesn't tell us anything about who or why."

They both fell back into silence and went their separate ways through the ruins. After a while of digging around and finding nothing, Nick said he needed to get to his place in Chico. Dan had told him how to drive to the resort, along the road that had once been an airstrip, then said goodbye. He dug some more in the rubble until his frustration was as dark as the soot.

He went over to the pasture to catch Stacey's horses. The neighbors had been feeding them. Some people didn't think horses had many feelings, that they were working animals, just more stock that you bought, sold and bred. Dan didn't agree. They knew quite a lot and had to have experienced all that happened.

CHAPTER TWENTY-ONE

She had kept the flash drive with his photos close, inside her pocket. She popped the little red memory stick into the USB port of her laptop then stopped. She thought she'd heard the garage door open. She quickly tiptoed from her bedroom into the great room. No noise. She must have imagined it.

She opened the photos she hadn't seen. More BDSM. More men? There were women too, showing *everything.*

As she sat staring she took a deep, exhilarating breath. Dark, dark Michael. Well she could dip into the murk, too. Suddenly not the spectator but now the performer, Katherine opened her closet and went into her sachet-scented, satin-lined drawers. She pulled out her black garter belt and snapped on her black nylons, and added tall, black patent leather heels. No panties. She added her new leopard bra and sat with her legs apart in front of her full-length mirror. She brought up her camera on her phone. Snap, snap. She moved in closer to show even more. She took close-ups. Click. Click. She tilted her head back in ecstasy and caught her mouth begging for more. She must have taken dozens of photos. Was it the posing or what she was about to do that was so euphoric? She stopped to review her shots. Nice.

She found her cozy sweats and went to work. Michael

had no idea with whom he was really fucking. Her hobby was coming in handy. She pulled up a photo editor and put a Michael porno shot next to her own. First she enhanced her body and makeup. With the flick of the brush she erased at least a decade. Then she cut herself out of her shots by carefully outlining each image, like tracing in a color book. She pasted her partial photos carefully into Michael's photos. She was screwing with him and it felt so good. *I'm so sorry I don't have a dick for you but you seem to get off both ways. Merging the familiar with the obscure. What is real, what is fantasy? Are they the same, my dear husband?* With the first shots she didn't add her face. Would he recognize the boobs? Let's fuck, Michael. Whose pussy? Cut and paste. She chose about twenty photos and in the last few she added her face. *I'm playing your game, sweetheart.*

Katherine texted Michael her montage.

★★★

She had expected a quick response to her photos, but here it was, three hours later, and she had heard nothing. She wanted him to spin on her mixed message that he could and couldn't fuck with her. His silence was probably a sign that he was disturbed. She loved it.

Katherine heard her phone vibrate on her nightstand.

"Hi, Sophia. You topped all your personal bests with the party today. I think everyone had a great time. Including the unexpected visitor." She hoped Sophia would get the hint and say something about

Nick, but she didn't.

"Are you going to the Zig showing tomorrow?" she asked.

"Oh, that's right," she said. "Which gallery is it? Mountain Images? I have the invitation somewhere. I've been a little distracted, you know, but it does sound like fun." She knew there was no chance of sneaking out with Jean for a WPR day.

"This one is at Zig's home in Suce Creek. Come," said Sophia. "I think you can use the change of pace."

"You're right. Not sure if Michael will be here..."

"Why don't you just assume you're going without him? Have you talked to him about the photos yet?"

"Nope." For now, she'd keep her montage to herself but maybe once he responded she'd share something with Sophia. Taking a deep breath, she smiled. "I'll drive tomorrow. Pick you up at five?"

"Fine." Sophia rang off.

Her phone rang. It was Sophia again. "What do you think you'll wear?"

"Sophia, you just asked me to go with you a couple of minutes ago. But, hmm, for an art showing? Probably black jeans, this new patterned-tweed jacket I got and my Gucci boots with the gold zippers," Katherine said. "I don't really know, but does that sound okay?"

"You always look great. Yes. That's perfect. I want to wear this over-the-top blouse I just bought online, but I'm not sure what pants to wear," said Sophia. Katherine could hear the stress in her voice. With her triumphant tiara party barely in her rearview mirror, she already had to worry about defending her crown as the Doll who dressed perfectly for every occasion. "I think my new dark jeans may work with the top. I think I'd better start sorting it out now. I'm glad you're coming with me."

"Do you think Nick is going to be there?" Katherine asked. It was a blatantly off-topic question, but she was too curious to be subtle.

"He seems to be everywhere," Sophia said.

"He was certainly everywhere at your party. And you're meeting him tomorrow, right?"

"He's calling me tomorrow," said Sophia coolly. "I haven't said when I'll meet him."

Katherine paused. "May I ask you a question?"

"You will anyway."

"How did you end it with Nick? I saw the way he looked at you."

"Katherine. Did you *watch* how he worked the party?" There was a long silence and then she came back in a cheerful voice, declaring the subject closed. "See you tomorrow."

CHAPTER TWENTY-TWO

She sat in front of her dressing table, inside her marble bathroom, naked. Alissa loved to wander around the house without any clothes on. Brad didn't like it but that didn't matter; Brad, as usual, wasn't there. She used to pride herself in being Brad's faithful wife, but she was sick of waiting around for him. He expected her life to fit into his erratic bank consultant schedule—and for her to be oblivious to his blatant cheating. Well, since she wasn't going to be hooking up with her husband tonight, she might as well pursue the newest male in town, Nick Conti.

She'd had a wax yesterday. She giggled. She called it "waxing down her surfboard" and she was ready to ride. Her body was perfectly smooth, her nails and hair looked just right. There was nothing boring about this day: a tiara party followed by an evening with a very attractive private detective. Sitting with him on Sophia's couch, Alissa had smelled his breath— something minty mixed with a hint of a musk she didn't recognize but made her eager for more. The anticipation was always part of the thrill.

She was glad Nick was staying at Chico Hot Springs. Chico made living in Paradise Valley palatable. It was a favorite resort for so many different types of people, from the locals wearing their Carhartt working garb, to movie and rock stars who had second homes in the

Valley. Celebrities liked it because it was a hidden spot where they could get away unnoticed and no one gave a damn about who they were. Chico brought out the individual in everyone. It was western and funky, full of low-key decadence. It was the perfect getaway for anonymity. It could be one o'clock in the morning and like a kid, Alissa would sneak down to the Saloon at Chico and the place would be hopping with life.

She had always been good at sneaking out. During her high school years in Mission Hills she would put her parents' BMW in neutral and silently roll it out of the driveway, down toward San Diego. Armed with a tube top, low-rise jeans, and a fake ID, she'd head to the beach to meet her surfer friends making the beach pub crawl, sometimes ending up in South Mission at the Pennant, other times she'd make it all the way up to Bully's in La Jolla. Too bad Bully's had to close. She'd be back home and tucked in bed before her mom, dad, or the pageant committee had a clue.

Brad would still be snoring loudly as she snuck into the house and slipped into their bed. She loved the feeling of being just a little bit naughty. He was just like a parent, always trying to control her. Her "degree in Brad Fairbanks" was turning out to lead to nowhere.

As she finished rubbing perfume in between her thighs she admired herself in the full-length mirror. She rocked her hips and squeezed her nipples. Brad Fairbanks' wife was headed into the powerful embrace of a new man.

Chico was a short ride from her home and

thankfully her nanny was putting her son to bed so Alissa could sneak away. Meeting Nick at the tiara party was exactly what she needed in her humdrum day. She felt a sexual pull to him and those gorgeous brown eyes had been undressing her as he gave her his card and casually dropped the enticing fact that he'd be staying in the caboose car at Chico—one of Alissa's favorite spots at the resort because it was on the far end, bordering the forest.

Alissa didn't bother knocking; she walked in, opened her full-length fox coat and dropped it to the floor. She watched Nick scoop up her full view, the jeweled G-string, her expensive breasts bursting from a red teddy and her long tanned legs rising from a pair of fancy embellished cowboy boots.

His overly appreciative expression gave her the compliment she sought. Her eyes danced with the atmosphere. The coziness of the interior was the perfect remedy to the windy night. A fireplace was lit in the corner. The red velvet wallpaper, cherry floors, and quilted black-and-white bedspread recalled the decadent days of the railroad era.

"Well isn't this a pleasant surprise," Nick said, getting up from the bed and walking over to the wet bar.

"Hello," she said as Nick offered her a glass of champagne.

"You give new meaning to 'opulence in the wilderness.'" Nick licked his lips.

"Hunting season and you won the tag." Alissa took a long swallow of the champagne. "You know, Chico is known for their spa, and you are getting a very personalized session. I brought my coconut oil."

She undid the buttons on his shirt. She kissed his chest once. He reached to undo his belt but she pulled his hand away.

"Let me do it," she said.

Loosening his belt and dropping his pants and boxer briefs around his ankles she sashayed backward to the bed, welcoming him to follow her. He lay down on his back, watching her slip off her thong and heels.

"You'd better turn over." She noticed Nick was getting ahead of himself. "I'll start with your back."

"Hmmm, okay," he said. She could tell Nick was usually the one to initiate, but he seemed happy to follow her lead.

Alissa smoothed the oil over his shoulders and arms. He tried to turn over to kiss her. She pushed him back down and began to massage his inner thighs.

"Not yet," she said.

She rolled the palm of her hands onto her thumbs with an upward motion, giving just enough pressure with every move as she worked inch-by-inch up his legs and then made her way up his back. He had goose bumps. She thought about Brad for a moment, wondering when the last time was that she had touched him like this. She slid over Nick's body so he could feel her rubbing up against the skin of his back. She used the side of her hands in a chopping motion, running up and down each arm, followed by each leg. Then she lightly used her long, sculptured fingernails in tiny circular motions all over his back and butt. Just as she felt him drifting off, she turned him over.

She found her glass of Cristal and drank the rest. Nick's eyes were glazed. "I think I need a little more champagne," she said. She went over to the credenza and poured another glass.

"Whatever you need, works for me," said Nick.

Alissa looked at herself in the mirror above the bed. Nick bent up to try to kiss her. She shoved him back down.

"I want you to watch," she whispered.

"I have no intention of closing my eyes," he said.

Alissa slowly rubbed the oil everywhere. She was watching herself in the mirror at the same time, knowing exactly what Nick could see.

She took her time with him, teasing him and keeping him rapt with every move. He reached for her, building the sensations between them simultaneously, slowly and steadily until they reached an explosive culmination. They lay there in contentment until the ringing of her phone spun her out of the moment. God, why now? She always kept her phone on—the hassle of being a mom.

"Señora," her nanny, Carmen's voice came through the phone, "the baby is asleep now. Do you want me to get *algo especial por el* señor when he comes tomorrow?"

"No, it's fine, Carmen. If there is anything, you can do it mañana. Thank you. I won't be very late this evening. Gracias y adios."

"Adios y buenos noches a usted."

Nick had pulled himself out of bed and put on a robe. It was so annoying how easily a toddler could ruin the mood.

"So, at Sophia's, you told me your husband was a good friend with Stacey Olsen."

"Oh, Nick, can't we just continue? That was only round one. I want more of you. I hate talking about Brad. Brad, Brad, Brad. It's always about Brad."

"Well, I can tell you some great things about the guy. He has spectacular taste in women. An eye not just for breath-taking beauty, but also extraordinary talent." He brought over the bottle of Cristal and filled her glass.

She sighed. She would be patient. "Brad knew Stacey well enough to talk. A lot."

She crossed her legs and was rocking the top one up and down again while twirling her hair in her fingertips. It was the kind of thing that Brad used to love, and she hoped it had the same effect on Nick.

"One of Brad's specialties is loans. I know Stacey knew something bad was going on with Scott and the Club. They talked on the phone all the time and I listened." She smiled and tilted her head. "Stacey was super impressed that Brad had been a SEC big shot and was always asking him questions. One conversation I heard was about a week before she died. The timing with the explosion and Stacey's death has bothered me a lot. Stacey must have been telling him about a loan or something with the Antelope Club. I don't exactly know what his relationship was with her. But it takes two, you know." Then, as if an afterthought, she said, "Of course, no matter what she did with my husband, she shouldn't have died."

"Do you know what kind of loan it was?" asked Nick.

"I think it was this large loan they got to buy all the additional sections of land for the Club. I heard Brad ask about the appraiser trumping the numbers. That would have really made Brad mad because he's such a prick about anything to do with loans, especially if he knew Scott was doing something underhanded." She leaned toward him and tried to open his robe.

"You're helping me a lot, you know," Nick said. He kissed her playfully on the neck.

"Boy, are you a hard worker," she said with a laugh. Then she changed her tone, "Brad also said something like, 'You don't know where the transfers went?' And then the next night she called again. Brad didn't know I was home and I heard him say, 'Scott heard our conversation?' Apparently Scott was pissed Stacey had talked to Brad. In Scott's mind that was like an act of treason. He demands loyalty."

She had her hand inside his robe, stroking his cock while she spoke. "What do you think *she* had that I don't?" She hiccupped. "Sorry, that was rude. She's dead. But I never understood what was so awesome about her."

She continued. "Stacey told Brad she knew someone had been into the Club's financial records and she confronted Scott about it. Then she told Brad that somebody almost ran her off the highway. Acting all terrified. Well, I guess maybe that could be true, after what's happened. But I thought it was a lie then. Now I don't know. She was such the flirt with him on the

153

phone. On our house line! I brought it up once and he told me it was all in my head, like I was imagining it, that I'm craaaazzy. Brad's such a man-whore. I'm sure he was on her long, long, loooong list."

Nick breathed heavily into her neck, she'd started pulling at him, rather than stroking. "You know who the crazy one is, don't you? Your husband...to neglect a woman like you."

She suddenly lost interest in Nick, both hands searching for her phone. "We need to go down to the bar. It's almost time for the Pacific Time feed. He expects me to watch him on TV tonight and I've already missed the East Coast feed."

"Got it covered," Nick said. He had his flat-screen TV up in seconds. "Here, find him." He handed her the remote. Alissa hit all the wrong buttons, losing the signal and throwing them into black-and-white snow. Nick took it back and punched the signal up again, scrolling through the channels quickly. "There he is," he said. "Tell me you didn't buy him that tie." He winked at her.

"He buys his own. Doesn't like my taste. He says I have no comprehension of 'East Coast Prep.' Like I even want to. Stripes are so boring."

"He really takes center stage, doesn't he? No hesitation cutting off the moderator. Interesting."

"Nothing's interesting about Brad, no matter what he says."

"His past work with the SEC is showing. He's talking about regulations to increase the transparency of dark pools."

"Dark pools? We never had a black bottom pool," said Alissa with a pout. She started to gather up her things. This evening was turning out to be a bust. Sure, he was hot, but like most guys in front of a TV, he was lost to her.

Nick was focused on the screen. Brad was saying, "In the quest for more revenue, there has been evidence that some exchanges have worked with HFT companies to give them an unfair edge over traditional investors."

"Who cares?" pouted Alissa as she started to get dressed. She tried to fasten her bra. It wouldn't snap. After several attempts she turned it around and fastened it on her waist and turned it back and pulled her breasts into the cups.

"Sounds like he's talking about the conditions for a perfect financial storm," Nick said, his eyes still focused on the TV.

Alissa only glared at him as she pulled her teddy, nylons and G-string out from beneath the sheets and put them into her oversized bag. She put on her boots and wrapped herself into her fur coat. At least she'd be able to send Carmen home earlier than usual—perhaps with a little extra cash, just in case she could smell Nick's cologne.

Brad continued, "Think of the 'flash crash' back in May of 2010, when the markets plummeted for no apparent reason, but think a hundred times the size. If computers create a crash that lasts longer than the flash crash and depositors make a run on the banks, we could be facing another 1929. Or worse. This could be a financial Black Plague."

Alissa stomped her heels, hoping to pull Nick from his TV trance. "It's always about Brad. You're no different from everyone else. Oh so enamored with everything my husband has to say. Well, I say, fuck you!"

She flung the caboose door open into the bolting wind. She stomped out, pushed the door closed, and got her fur coat caught in it. She angrily jerked the door back open, gathered up her coat, and this time successfully slammed it shut.

CHAPTER TWENTY-THREE

Dan pulled into his driveway and sat looking at his dark house, wondering why he should hurry to get inside. Everything would be exactly like he'd left it, in little organized piles; piles of papers, piles of feathers waiting to be tied into imitation flies for fishing, piles of washed but wrinkled laundry wishing for a woman's folding touch. There wasn't even an eager dog waiting for him.

He sat thinking of Stacey and the fire blast until he got so agitated he had to move and headed into his house, leaving the day's garbage of paper coffee cups, soda cans, and candy bar wrappers inside his truck. Why did Nick need to forge through his well-plowed fields? Was he there to overturn more earth and solve the crime or cover up someone's carefully planted seeds? As much as he wanted to believe in Nick, he didn't trust anything about the Antelope board's motivations.

It was damn irritating he hadn't thought of the light bulb theory first. It was hard to locate the source of irritation: Nick, or just dealing with a crime that never should have happened in his hometown in the first place. If the theory was right, then whoever did it was probably someone who had access to both the Antelope Club and Stacey's home without causing suspicion. Which meant it was someone who either lived there or was a part of the daily traffic of service folks. That was, unfortunately, a surprising number of people.

It wasn't until he was in the house that he thought of Lyn. He supposed he should give her a call soon. He knew the sequence. Now she was back, sweet as ever. The Love Shack had been great.

It was like the woman read his thoughts. He looked at her number flashing on his phone, and suddenly he didn't feel like talking, although it had been a great time with her in the late afternoon. He thought of letting it go to voice mail but knew she'd just keep calling back until he answered. He picked it up.

"Hi." It was her sultry voice. He went into his liquor cabinet and pulled out the bottle of VO. He poured himself a glass as he listened. "Dan, do you think you could come over? The heat is off at the house. Eric is gone and I'm freezing."

"This happened before. Go down into the furnace room and push that little red button."

"I'm feeling kind of, kind of dizzy. It's so scary down there. Please, Dan. You know how much I appreciate you and you know I'll make it worth your while, like a second round!"

He felt a twinge in his balls but not really enough to make the trip. "Find your flashlight. The one I gave you. It's by your bed, in the nightstand drawer. Take it with you. I'll stay on the line while you go down the stairs."

"Okaaay."

Had she drunk more after he'd left her?

"Found it. I'm going down there, like a good girl. But you know how I can be so bad. Come on Dan, come over, please?"

More twinge. Maybe he would go. He needed the diversion, something more to think about than Nick and Stacey. Of course, he had told Nick he'd interrogate Lyn—maybe he could go over with the pretense of forgetting earlier and remembering now. She usually made him feel a lot better. Except when she made him feel worse.

"I don't see the red button anywhere. It used to be right in plain sight."

"Calm down. Take your time. It hasn't moved." He couldn't listen to his own advice. He was on some sort of verge. Irritated about everything. He finished off the whiskey.

"Nope. It's not here anymore."

"Jeezus. Do you see the fucking little red button, underneath the furnace? Push it and the pilot will go back on." He was probably talking a little too loudly, maybe shouting.

"Found it. I heard it light up. But it's still so cold. Can't you just come over? I remember when you used to always come up for the tiniest little problem. What is it, Danny?"

No one called him Danny. That was a cutesy name for a child, the name he hated being called as a kid.

"Danny? You there?"

He hung up. Why did she have to spoil a perfectly great afternoon? There was no pleasing her for over several hours. Now he'd have to endure her barrage of repetitive calls.

Dan flung the phone onto the table and went to his big freezer. From deep inside he dug out a small parcel wrapped in white butcher paper. Elk steak would be perfect tonight. Yep, a little ES and a little more VO. He popped it into the microwave for a quick thaw. Once thawed, he dipped the whole thing into his flour jar. He put the steak on the butcher block and added salt and pepper. Why did he let her get under his skin? Adding some oil, he slipped the steak into the well-seasoned cast-iron pan that always sat on top of his electric stove. Lyn was as irritating as Stacey's case.

The difference, he supposed, was emotion and control. You took the emotion out of the situation and things began to clear up, necessary when working on a case. Maybe that was why he had always found relationships so difficult, why nothing worked out. He couldn't let go of the emotion. He used to think the problem was the women in his life. Lately he'd begun to wonder if it might be within himself. Maybe the women had seen something he didn't. They were always talking about his need to control. When it came to control, he'd certainly picked a winner in Lyn. He would never be in the power seat with her. Even hanging up on her gave her power to make him miserable.

His phone was ringing, shaking, and ringing. Did she think he'd always do whatever she wanted but only whenever she was free? She acted like he was nothing more than a hired tool belt. Or a hired tool.

He needed to focus on anything else. He thought of how he needed to go riding up the Emigrant trail and retrace steps. Soon. He started to pick up his phone to call Katherine but remembered it was way after business hours. He poured himself another drink as he watched his phone quiver.

CHAPTER TWENTY-FOUR

Wednesday was another day in the office when the coffee wasn't strong enough or hot enough. His phone rang. Forensics in Helena was never quick about anything, but they miraculously had his results back. They were e-mailing him the information.

The lab conclusions from the explosion came in like a hospital x-ray report, with a detailed diagnosis and summary. There were shards of glass in the ceiling and walls. They showed trace elements of a petroleum product, along with a chemical you might find in a detergent. The petroleum accelerants had been present longer on the inside of the bulb than the outside, like a blood-splatter pattern exiting a body.

So Nick was right. He was now officially working an arson case, and a death caused by arson was homicide. He figured he should let the guy know, but he needed to call Katherine to set up their trail ride first.

Dan walked into the outer office and saw one of his deputies ready to leave the building. Everyone called him Beef. He was big, reliable, and kept his ear to the ground.

"Dan. How ya' doin'?" asked Beef. "That big-time city guy giving us any help?"

"He's got some theories," said Dan.

"He's got some action going on, too. Drove by Chico and got a real good look at Alissa Fairbanks's car in front of his cabin."

Dan smiled. Not much ever evaded Beef. He was just glad his deputy hadn't said it was Lyn's car. Trust. That was another issue the former women in his life always mentioned. They said he couldn't trust them.

He forced his mind off Lyn and focused to the task at hand: calling Katherine. She picked up on the first ring.

"Hi, Dan Bentley here."

"Hello, Sheriff."

"Hope I'm not disturbing you, but I was wondering if you could make that trail ride on Monday? The weather should clear out by then and I'm thinking you'll be healed. Are you free?"

She cleared her throat. "I guess my horse needs to get out. My ankle is better. What time?"

"Let's meet at the trail head at ten."

"Great."

She seemed either irritated or was waiting for him to say more. "All right, then, bye," he said.

"Bye. Until Monday."

Why did he feel so jittery about her? It made him angry—the last thing he needed was to think about another Paradise Valley Doll. They were all connected, like a diseased family tree—an aspen with bark beetles.

"Hey there, Sheriff," It was Nick, walking in like he owned the place. Dan was glad he didn't have to make another call. He could tell Nick about the forensics in person.

"Shit. So I was right!" Dan hated Nick's smug look.

"Well, I reached out to my contact in New York. There're some things on the books for the Antelope Club that looked off to me; I think Stiles was up to something and Stacey may have been helping him hide it."

Dan motioned Nick to take a seat in the chair across from his desk. He removed his note pad and packet of chew from his shirt pocket, ready to get down to business. "Ok, what else?"

CHAPTER TWENTY-FIVE

The day was brilliantly beautiful, as if God's lighting director had set the scene. Katherine had taken her camera hoping to catch a few good shots. A light dusting of snow had fallen. The sun was creating quilted shadows on the mountains as Katherine and Sophia drove to Zig's.

"Look at the way the light is hitting the landscape. I can never quite get the photo that captures it all," said Katherine.

Little puffs of cotton-ball clouds were lying low against the mountains. Rays of sun danced over the river, creating thousands and thousands of little sequins that bobbed along with the current. Blues, whites, grays and shades of golden wheat created a visual masterpiece.

"It's nice to hear you sounding good," said Sophia.

"It's as good as I can make it. I've got more to tell you about Michael but I don't want to wreck the moment." Katherine pulled over and took out her camera to capture the landscape.

Sophia always respected her hobby. "Ok, whenever you're ready."

They passed the bison grazing in Pine Creek and Katherine was glad they were behind fences. She had learned how to drive through herds of buffalo down in Yellowstone Park, but it was always unnerving, as one never could be sure when the beasts were going to decide to charge. Their big dark brown eyes, looking so innocent, were deceiving. Typically, there would be fifteen or twenty of the mangy, bulky beasts spread across the road and walking very slowly. At first, Katherine had stayed back and followed them, unsure of their behavior, but she had soon learned that if she slowly drove into the herd they would part to either side of the road single file and she could slide through.

The turkeys were out. They survived Thanksgiving each year even though hunting was a way of life in Big Sky country. Most of them had probably survived through the code of Montana hunters. Only a wimp, like an out-of-towner, would kill a turkey walking near the little country Pine Creek Store.

They came down a curve. The old wooden barn on her left was her cue to turn right onto Suce Creek. She had heard of the many branding parties that took place on that property. But the Dolls weren't invited to those events. They didn't understand the importance of the cattle business and thought the ranchers were unfairly hurting the calves.

Zig had emailed everyone a hand-drawn map— artful, of course, with a bold use of color—even though the directions basically amounted to "keep going until the road ends." They passed over the little bridge and headed east into Forest Service land. Soon, just as the little tan pebbles on the map depicted, they came to the grand log archway, adorned with the white bison skull of Zig Boone's Buffalo Ghost

Ranch.

The property was on eighty acres that had been a homesteader's ranch back in the late eighteen hundreds. The buildings were all dark gray now, sighing with slight swags of contentment.

Her phone rang. It was Brad. She didn't answer.

Katherine felt her adrenaline spike.

***

The room felt cool in contrast to the visuals on the walls. Katherine could hear the click of her heeled boots above the buzz of conversation as she strolled from one painting to the next. Behind her, the room whirled with movement: champagne and wine flowing, hors d'oeuvres being passed, art patrons greeting and schmoozing. Katherine had wandered away from Sophia and the Dolls to form her own opinions of the work.

"Warriors," the exhibition was called, and like most of the work Zig Boone had built his reputation on, the dozen or so new paintings focused on Native Americans. But they revealed a fresh direction for the artist. Known for his expansive use of color, swept onto the canvas with the abandon of abstract expressionism, here he relied on shades of white, brown, and black—until closer examination revealed a quick splash of color. Like the green flash of light before the sun set into the Pacific Ocean, Katherine thought, there for just a nanosecond but transforming the whole.

The invitation-only guests included some of the

affluent from nearby Bozeman, mainly the Bozeman Symphony crowd, along with a few art professors from Montana State University, and, of course, the BM of the BS and their Dolls. Marie broke away from Scott and came running up to Katherine.

"Oh darling, so good to see you," she said as she kissed Katherine on both cheeks. Up close she looked very tired, although she was pushing the bubbly social energy as hard as she could.

"I can't believe you're back so soon from your trip to Paris."

"We only made it Minneapolis. Oh sweetheart, didn't you hear? My Trevor didn't quite turn out to be the guy I'd hoped."

"How so?"

"Let's just say he wanted to watch *Brokeback Mountain* instead of enjoying champagne and lobster."

"Oh, Marie, I'm so sorry." Sometimes Katherine managed to feel sorry for Marie. She knew Marie and Scott had a loveless marriage. He was no prize, but his money allowed Marie the life she led.

"Imagine me with our glasses of Taittinger, walking so sexy to the plush white bedroom in the plane. Mood lighting, of course, cozy atmosphere, perfect for joining the mile-high club. Instead of getting my rocks off, I find out I'm suddenly a fag hag."

Katherine could picture the pathetic scene perfectly and again, she felt oddly sorry for Marie. "Well then, that was a bust. But cheers to bigger and better," Katherine said.

"And straighter," replied Marie.

She wanted to prod. The questions came back to her mind, the ones that accused Marie of Stacey's murder. But surely whoever orchestrated such an explosion would have needed a bit more between the ears than Marie. She certainly had motive, what with the blatant secret that Stacey and Scott were having an affair. But clearly her position as Mrs. Stiles mattered to her enough to suffer an endless string of humiliations, both self—and Scott-inflicted.

She caught Brad out of the corner of her eye. Alissa hadn't come, saying that she had Tyler's cold and a fever. Brad was motioning for her to come over and she felt her breath catch.

Gratefully, Sophia appeared beside her. "Excuse us, but Katherine here has never met Zig and I intend to fix that right now." Sophia escorted Katherine toward the artist. Katherine knew she was one of the few guests in the room who didn't own one of Zig's paintings. The *Big Sky Gazette* had recently called him "the most important local artist in decades" and predicted that his work would someday hang "in the world's finest museums." Owning one of his larger canvases was nearly a requirement for the Dolls. Sophia and John Whitman had the largest work he had ever created hanging in their entrance hall.

As Sophia introduced them, Boone looked straight into Katherine's eyes and kept his hand in hers just a heartbeat too long. She could see very well why the Dolls were so fascinated with his work, or at least with the pretext to spend time with him that buying a painting gave them. He was electric, about as beautiful as the images he created, large in stature but larger in presence, with jet-black, slicked-back hair and deep, dark eyes. Tattoos covered his thick, long arms, making him look edgy and provocative. Zig Boone *was* art. And he was set in the perfect frame: a polished, soft chambray shirt, imported gator boots, and tight denim jeans.

"This painting is incredible," said Sophia. "I can hear the crickets."

Katherine wondered if Sophia had already had a little too much to drink. The canvas showed warriors battling against a winter landscape.

Zig was a pro. "I'm glad you like it."

"You're a wonder, Zig," said Sophia as she gave him a quick kiss on the cheek. It was the perfect gesture, of course. Katherine suddenly saw Sophia with a vivid detachment she'd never had before, as if seeing her on screen. It struck her then how the Dolls always exuded an air of individual performance, as if each were starring in her own twenty-four hour reality show; Group shot, take camera one. Hold that smile please as you speak to the others. Steady as we move in for a close-up. It was if they were responding from direction above, getting their cues off the "God Mic." Sophia drifted away, leaving Katherine alone with Zig.

"Quite the diplomat you are," she said. "I know we're all supposed to see different things in a work of art—but please tell me there are no crickets in there."

He laughed a deep, sexy chuckle. "Who knows? Picasso said the artist paints objects as he thinks them, not as he sees them. Maybe I had crickets on my mind that day."

Katherine laughed in turn. Then she heard herself saying, "And I suppose you'd agree with Picasso that 'Sex is art.' Or 'art is sex.' I forget which way he put it."

"I think he said, 'Sex and art are the same thing.' Funny you should mention that."

"Funny why? Sex and art clearly are the same thing. The man was a fucking genius." Katherine felt at home all of a sudden. She was back at an art opening in New York speaking to someone even more famous about some other work of art and her confidence bolstered again.

"Come over here a bit," he said. "I want to be out of earshot from the rest. If you don't mind my saying it, I get the sense that I can talk to you in a way I can't talk to my usual customers."

"Why? Because they aren't talking about fucking while looking at your paintings?"

"Very funny. But if people here really knew what my other art is like I couldn't sell a single thing in this room."

Her heart quickened, but she kept her cool and smirked. "Meaning it's got to be either violence or pornography."

"I'm not into violence of any kind," Zig said. "And I find porno flat and raw, not artistic." She could tell him that recently, she had found that not to be true, but let it rest.

"Then what do you mean? What are these paintings

that would horrify everyone in this room?"

Zig smiled. It was quite a smile, slow and broad, inti-mating, a great deal more than amusement. "They're not paintings at all. I've been exploring black-and-white photography."

"Okay," Katherine said. "I minored in photography. Loved social realism. I wrote my senior thesis on Dorothea Lang. That was a long time ago, but is it anything similar?"

"She was interested in showing the soul, I'm more interested in images of the body. Some of them erotic. Most of them, actually. You're from New York, which means you must have had exposure to erotic art. I've heard about you, the big, swinging female dick."

"If you're trying to flatter me, it's not working."

He continued as if he hadn't heard her. "Montana is a very conservative place," Zig said. "And despite its apparent vastness, it's also a very small place, at least where the market for fine art is concerned. I'd just as soon not have the gossip wires humming with the news that Zig Boone takes naughty pictures in his spare time. But I would love you to take a look at my other gallery. It's over to the side of the house in the shingled building. Go look and tell me what you think. I'm in need of a new market. Maybe New York would appreciate my work. But maybe I'm over-thinking it," he continued. "That's why your opinion would be so valuable. You could give me a read on whether your social set would be more open to that kind of work."

"Do I get an agent's fee for this market evaluation?"

"Just let me know what you think, Katherine." There was a breathiness when he said her name that she liked.

"I shall," Katherine replied, as Brad slid up and a Bozeman professor and his wife cornered Zig for conversation.

"I'm getting a little jealous," said Brad.

"No need," Katherine replied with a sly smile playing across her lips. It felt so good to have Brad close. It was shockingly glorious that he had ended up in Montana. She never was sure if he'd come because of his friend on the senate finance committee, or because of her, and she'd never ask. She probably should have cut it off years ago, after he'd outlived his usefulness, but he was difficult to resist.

It had all started with *the interview.* When Brad was with the SEC, he had questioned her intensely about the validity of her loans. She had been the one who helped create and approve loans that most people wouldn't be able to pay back. She was responsible, but she wouldn't become a whistle blower about her associates. Brad knew of the deceit, but thankfully, he was bribable and it hadn't cost her a dime.

Maybe she *was* like a guy. She could compartmentalize. She could easily cut out thoughts of Michael or Alissa and just get what she needed from Brad. Years ago she had played with him because she had to save herself and her company from the feds, but now she had Brad because she wanted to, and since they were both solo, she decided to take him to Zig's studio. They slipped away without being noticed.

The first thing they saw was a collection of antique stone dildos. Brad ran his fingers over them and then picked one up and teased her, using it like a massage stone on her body.

She was overwhelmed with the erotic images. "Will you look at these walls?" She thought she'd been quite the selfie artist of lust and art but Zig was superior. Did he use a telephoto lens or did the models really let him get that close?

As she scanned the walls, she found her eyes drawn to a single photo. There was something strangely familiar about it. It was a simple female nude, cropped so that no face was showing. It was all black and white except for a streak between the model's legs, where Zig had added a most unsubtle touch of pink. Katherine tried to understand what was so familiar about it, but nothing made sense.

Then she noticed Zig had added another tiny bit of color, a flicker of green at the periphery. It took Katherine a moment to realize that she was looking at stones, probably emeralds, set into a belt. The flashy, tooled-leather western style belt that snuggly hugged the woman's waist was something she'd seen before.

The room was warm, almost too hot from the wood burning stove set in the center. Tiny laser-like spotlights illuminated image after image, ripening them, burning life into them. It was euphoric, startling, and dream-like all at the same time. Her body felt heavy, almost as if she were sleepy or mesmerized, and yet at the same time she felt intensely awake.

She walked to a large, straight-backed wooden chair

in the center of the room. It was diamond tufted with leather upholstery and brass studs. The arms were thick wooden carved claws that curled inward with a suggestive power. It had to be an antique, maybe from the eighteen hundreds. To Katherine it seemed to contain an old, dark force. She didn't resist as Brad guided her into it.

She felt her body sink into the cushy, leather tufts. Her arms rested on the claws. She had an image of herself as Alice, dropping down, down, down into a long, dark tunnel, but into a Wonderland that felt warm, wet, steamy. Her eyes felt heavy. She wanted to tell Brad that it was too hot in the room. She tried to fight off the sleepy sensation and get up, but Brad pushed her ever so slightly back down into the chair. He walked across the room and picked something up off a shelf.

"Relax, Katherine," he said.

"I am relaxed," she murmured. She thought of telling him that she was overwhelmed, possibly coming down with the flu. She thought of asking if she'd been drugged. But those were like someone else's thoughts, far away and without emotion.

She tried to keep her eyes open as she scanned the walls. It was beautiful work, she could see that now, far more stunning than she'd realized at first. Every photo was playing to her like an instrument, coming together in a symphony of light and dark and sensuality, beckoning her to come closer, to join in their movement, to dance in their rhythm.

She felt his presence before she saw him, warm,

powerful, and strong. Brad was naked. His perfectly tanned, brown body was oiled, making every beautifully delineated muscle gleam. His hair flowed back from his face, recasting Brad somehow in the image of the warriors in the paintings in Zig's home gallery. As he saw her staring at his nakedness he leaned into the chair and began kissing her. His lips seemed to probe her, pull her, take her down even deeper. He kissed her neck and squeezed her breast as if he was an artist, massaging paint out of an oil tube. He knew just how much he needed to do to create the sensation she craved. Katherine hadn't remembered getting undressed but she was naked also. It seemed so easy now, so right, so inevitable.

"Do you know what I want to do with you?" He had pulled her out of the chair and alternating between the thrust of his own body and what felt like stone, what must have been the long, thick black marble dildo they had seen when she first came in the studio. She laughed to herself; this was a whole new meaning to "hot rock massage."

Brad was again creating a masterpiece within her. It was like being inside one of Zig's photographs, forced to feel sensations that dissolved her, rocked her, tempting her, baiting her on to a new awareness of passion. And how he taunted her. When he felt her begin to slide into a shattering release, he'd stop and pause until the wave had passed, then tease her with light, fluttering circular motions, like the strokes of a paintbrush. She had never seen Brad this way, he became smooth but savage, pulling her hair, biting and gnawing her back, devouring her with primal intensity. The black dildo had been cold and thrilling but his firm and wide cock was warm which made her even hotter. He was the master and she was his new creation. She became the shadow moving into the light, following his artful strokes, letting him lift her to the next level of explosive surprise. Then, her body was quivering, her whole being was trembling into the release of unnamed sensations. Soon she was floating, carried by a slow, gentle current, with no sense of time or space.

Slowly Katherine came back to her body. Her hair felt matted with the same salty sweat that ran down her face. She tried to sit up in the chair and get her bearings but her head was still groggy. She felt clumsy finding her clothes. Brad had a smile on his face.

"We need to get back to the party, you savage. Not that anyone will have missed us."

"Well that was truly something. You always surprise me."

"Now get your shoes, Brad, and fix your hair."

★★★

Back at the party she shouldn't have been surprised that Sophia's shrewd eyes never missed a beat. "You disappeared with Brad, and Zig seemed quite interested in you."

"Zig just wanted my opinion about his work." Katherine said. "So I brought Brad to see his other artwork."

"Your opinion. And did you have a past career as an

177

art critic you've never told me about?"

"Well. I briefly declared myself an art history major in college," Katherine said. Not that Zig had the faintest idea about that.

"Ooh la, la! Well, good that you stuck to business. In any case, I just think you should be careful," Sophia said, lowering her voice.

"Sophia, stop it. You really think you know everything, don't you?" Katherine said it as light-heartedly as she could, but she knew the irritation came through. The irritation was something she didn't like about herself. It had been great with Brad but she knew this was the Katherine she didn't want to be anymore and a lot of that had come from getting to know Jean and the WPR.

"I just think you could be setting yourself up for trouble, that's all. After all you've been through with Stacey and with all the Michael stuff," said Sophia, more softly this time.

"I think what I am," she said to Sophia, "is hungry. Point me toward the hors d'oeuvres."

Sophia dropped the subject but didn't stop watching her.

The next time Zig came around to them, Sophia said she was interested in purchasing one of his smaller framed pieces.

He brought Sophia over to speak to her alone, but came back to Katherine. "So what did you think about my photos?"

"I think you're talented. The best. New York would think you're a star. But Zig," she said. Her voice quavered a bit and she started again. "Zig, may I ask you a question?"

He paused and looked at her with his big sly smile again. "Sure, shoot."

"Remember your photo of the model with the green belt?"

"Yes?"

"Is that Stacey Olsen?"

"I never reveal the names of my models. Nor do I kiss and tell. "

For the moment, fair was fair. Neither did she.

CHAPTER TWENTY-SIX

Michael wanted to focus on work, but Katherine was gaming him, sending whorish pictures of herself. Did she really think she could compete? So much for his security. He'd been lazy, never locked his private stuff, thinking she was oblivious. It annoyed him that he even had to worry about her.

He turned to his central screen and stared at the pulsating glow. He'd gotten the texts yesterday but had no clue how to respond. Had these pictures come from one of his slaves, he'd have been able to get off right then and there, but his wife wasn't illicit or forbidden, she held no mystery or challenge.

The key to Michael's success had always been vigilance. So he had slipped with her, but never in his business. He checked every detail, considered every variable. He had rarely used his own money to build his empire, shifting the entire risk to his clients. They had been so eager to believe their investments would succeed that they accepted his twelve percent return with no questions and no audits. He thought they might have been more skeptical after the Bernie Madoff meltdown, but he was reassured to see that greed still smothered caution.

Michael had steadily built his relationships with big brokerages and clearing houses across the globe. His stellar reputation gave him Direct Market Access to all the international exchanges. It was like amassing unlimited credit. BotDom owned racks of computers near all the major exchanges, New York, London, and Singapore. He used an electronic communications network that cut out intermediaries. HFT was nothing more than a system of trading stock that used superfast computers to place huge numbers of orders at very fast speeds. His complex algorithms analyzed the markets and placed orders based on the immediate conditions, before a human could blink an eye.

He'd had a fiber-optic cable laid from Lolo to the prairie and then, piggybacking on other cables, all the way to New York, with lasers to fire data impulses along it. His racks talked back and forth to each other with missile speed, slipping in orders with almost zero latency as his systems shared information simultaneously.

But even now, even at the top of his game, he had to be constantly vigilant. His algos for lightning-speed trading typically worked for a while, but then, for reasons no one knew, they stopped being effective. Michael thought it could have been a sort of Heisenberg Principle of cyberspace, that his bots were actually changing the market as they mined data, constantly requiring him to build new models to adapt to their own creations.

No one in the world had as full a grasp of the field or as vast of an array of research formulas and models as he had. But the data gathering that had enabled him to amass his great fortune had now brought him an awareness of the new reality. His research showed that soon he was not going to be able to move through markets at his usual speed, because the inefficiencies of the markets he had so successfully exploited were dissipating. His algos were creating an irreversible immunity to their own inefficiencies. He was turning science fiction into science fact. He had, in effect, created his own Frankenstein. An electronic Frankenstein on speed.

Plus, the taxation debacle was growing. Europe was taxing orders. In the short run, all that did was drive new customers straight into his domain, but it wouldn't be long now before the same thing happened in the US, before the new federal regulations being written by people like Brad Fairbanks and his former SEC henchmen would start taxing cancellations of high-volume trades or requiring transaction fees on multitudes of trading orders. Maybe they were drumming up legislation to require all orders to go to the NYSE first. It made no difference to them that BotDom Technologies provided liquidity to the marketplace. He would no longer be able to accrue instant fortunes by zipping in and out of the dark pools of what he called "BotDom Land." Legal changes took time, though, and the required software changes still more time.

They thought they were closing his window, that he wouldn't be able to keep playing his game much longer. But that was fine with him. Because everything that made this game harder to play also set the stage for the endgame.

CHAPTER TWENTY-SEVEN

Dan was in the office early again that morning, hoping for some good news. He was working a case, yet he couldn't shake the feeling that he should have taken Lyn up on her offer the other night. Sure, she was crazy, but she was a fine piece of ass and he could have used the second release of another whirl that came with an evening between her sheets.

Although email had spread across the rest of America swiftly, internet connections could be spotty in Montana, so Dan did most of his work the good old fashioned way: hitting the streets and talking to people. Despite that, his deputy would boot up the old HP every morning and open Dan's email for him, just in case there was anything other than spam.

The message at the top of his inbox was from Nick Conti. Just like a New Yorker to email rather than phone or come by. The subject read; "Read this and call me."

Dan hated the implication that he was at Nick's beck and call, but he did as instructed.

To: Dan Bentley
From: Nick Conti
Re: Read this and call me

Dan: Lots to talk about in person, but I wanted you to have this email my contact was able to dig up. Seems we've got someone else to interview.

Talk soon,
Nick

To: Mstiles@antelopeclub.com
From: Solsen@antelopeclub.com

Marie,

One of our members recently brought a guest to the clubhouse. The woman claimed to be an antique expert, specializing in Italian Renaissance furnishings. She asked where we had purchased the oversized credenza on the wall facing Emigrant Peak. I told her you had done most of the decorating and acquiring of art. She said she was most certain the piece was not an original and suggested I let you know. She could have been mistaken but I'd appreciate you getting back to me on the matter.

Thanks,
Stacey

If Marie was making fraudulent dealings in the art world and pocketing the money she wouldn't have liked Stacey catching onto her scheme. Now that sounded like a real motive to Dan, way better than crazy jealousy over a husband she obviously couldn't stand.

CHAPTER TWENTY-EIGHT

Lyn had finished trying on several new items in the box from Saks in San Francisco. Amazing how five thousand dollars' worth of clothing could be wrapped in tissue paper and fit into such a small parcel.

She loved her stylist. He worked in the Fifth Avenue Club, where clients were coddled and pampered. He had been outfitting her for years. When she'd lived in San Francisco she only wore St. John. The knits were perfect for any Bay Area society function, plus they traveled well. But in Montana they looked so matronly, so he had transformed her into someone trendy and adventurous. He had no problem finding things even from the fifth floor, junior-looking things, that thrilled her to the core. When she met with him on her frequent trips back to the city he was brutally honest. She would see the scowl on his face or the tapping of his foot when she was pushing it.

But the scales had tipped as Lyn had gotten older. Now she liked to press "vavoom" to the max. When she was back in the city, it was Stephan's boss, Carolina, who did her best to convince her to stick with age-appropriate dignity. Most of the Dolls had the "Mountain Lauren" or "western glitz" looks in their wardrobes. Lyn knew a native Montanan woman would never dress in overly flashy western attire, but she didn't care, just like the rest of the

Dolls. She wanted to look young and hot. Carolina would die if she saw how she rigged some of her Double D designer western outfits, shortening skirts and tightening tops.

This outfit was perfect. Stephan had sent everything she wanted: a ragingly awesome pair of leather pants and a woolen, tight-fitting blazer with a see-through black mesh top to wear underneath. He knew her figure well, and it hugged all her curves just the way she wanted. And the boots were the finishing touch, sculptural yet understated, but sturdy enough to prance stylishly through the valley's mud and grime.

She looked good, way too good to stay home. It wasn't even noon yet but she already had a little buzz going. She couldn't remember if she'd taken one or two Ativan. Her doctor had been understanding when she said she'd accidentally dropped the week's dosage down the drain. She always felt nervous, as if something that she couldn't control was going to happen, but the Ativan calmed her down and let her sail through her anxieties.

Today she wanted to be seen and appreciated, but she knew Dan was probably at the office trying to figure out all that Stacey nonsense and wouldn't want to be bothered. And, truthfully, she was in the mood for a new conquest.

Nick Conti was a private dick she wanted to see more of. What little she got at Sophia's party had been enough for one round with her vibrator, but she was ready for the real thing. He would be the perfect distraction—especially since his time here would be brief. He was so handsome, so manly in his Italian-style, big city way. Said he'd lived in Jersey most of his life. His parents were teachers but he had always been the rebellion, walking the wild side until he switched it up and became a cop in New Jersey. He had a toughness about him, like a muscled up modern day superhero ready for the ring. It did make sense that she got the feeling that he worked for the mob in New York, or maybe she was fantasizing too much, but he had looked good in his Italian suit and shoes.

She wondered if he'd recognize these Italian boots? Probably not, but he certainly seemed the type who would love a see-through top. "Oh, Nick," she said aloud, "If you're around, this could be your lucky day."

She headed down to Chico Hot Springs, but she wasn't sure where he was staying. She was taking a chance that he'd even be on the premises, but she didn't want to spoil the surprise by calling him, so down the hill she drove.

The desk clerk had been her former housekeeper. It was such a small town she usually had some sort of connection wherever she went.

"Hey, Lyn. What're you up to?"

"I'm looking for a guest. Nick Conti. Do you know what room he's in?"

"I believe he was down at the pool earlier, but I thought I saw him head up to the Caboose. You know where that one is?"

Lyn was already on her way up the hill before the clerk could finish. She was hoping to catch him in his room, but on the way she saw Nick over at the stables. She threw her car in park and waved, motioning him over. He was at her window in a flash.

She followed his eyes. They swept over her face and stopped on her generously exposed cleavage, just as she had hoped.

"Are you thinking of taking a ride?" she asked.

"I might. It's been awhile." He smiled slyly. He leaned in a little closer. She could smell his cologne. It was sophisticated, with a hint of lemon. His eyes were softening.

"Where are you headed?" Lyn asked.

"Down to the Grill."

"Get in. I'll give you a lift."

"It's not that far," he said, "but I'll take you up on it."

He hopped into her Range Rover. She drove past the front of the main lodge and pulled around to the Poolside Grill entrance. There weren't many cars in the lot.

She turned to face Nick. Her head felt light, as if she'd been drinking, but no, that was just the pills. This was still her favorite drug, a new lover. She knew she could have him. He put his left arm on the console and leaned toward her, ready to get closer but stopped abruptly.

She hadn't heard the engine of the car that pulled up next to them. Lyn had shut off the outside world as if nothing but Nick existed.

"We've got company," said Nick. "He wasn't supposed to be here for another twenty minutes."

Lyn looked out the passenger's side window to see the vehicle she knew so very well, Dan's Dodge Durango. Her heart stopped. She knew how jealous he could be. Thank goodness they weren't doing anything. But what was her excuse for being at Chico with Nick in the car? Any hint of disloyalty was good enough for Dan to ignore her for days—this was not good, not good at all.

"You didn't tell me you were meeting the Sheriff," she said. Her voice was barely above a whisper.

Nick was surprisingly cool about the disruption. "I'm briefing him about my end of this case. I'll give you a call." He opened his door.

She heard herself say, "I'd like that."

Dan was out of his car, peering through the window at Lyn. He didn't need to speak. She knew the look, that look of betrayal. He was always either on or off, and it wasn't too hard to figure out this was an extreme version of "off." His face tightened up and his eyes darkened, turning to gun-metal gray.

Dan turned away and walked up to Nick. The two headed into the Poolside Grill. Lyn's anxiety was escalating, starting to turn into panic, so she began digging through her new bag looking for a stray Ativan. It was a perfect bag, stuffed full of every emergency provision known to woman: makeup for eyes and face, nail polish and files, hair spray, toothbrush, personal deodorant, dental floss, ibuprofen, protein bars, lotion and creams, an assortment of perfumes, and a tiny notepad. Where the fuck were the Ativan?

Why hadn't she made sure Dan wouldn't be going

to Chico? Why hadn't she asked Nick why he was going to the Grill? What was she supposed to do now? She rummaged through her purse, praying that at least one of the tiny pills had fallen out of the bottle. She could picture the full bottle sitting next to her bathroom sink; why hadn't she put a few emergency pills in the ibuprofen container? At last she found one in a little pocket. She swallowed it dry. She knew it might be too much, on top of the other two, but what other choice did Dan give her?

If her husband had driven up and found her in the car with Nick, he barely would have given it a thought. Losing Eric scared her so much less than losing Dan. She knew he could smell her disloyalty. It wasn't fair. She dug deeper in her bag.

★★★

Tap tap tap. Tap tap tap. His head was pounding and his heart sounded like it was on speakerphone inside his body. It was quiet inside the Chico Poolside Grill. They took a table looking outside into the thermal pool that stayed heated at a warm ninety- degrees year-round. A few guests were swimming and a couple of kids were floating around on Styrofoam noodles. Dan sat facing the door. The waitress brought them plastic-covered menus and said she'd be back with Dan's Diet Pepsi. Nick ordered a PBR.

"I think I'll have the 'Talkin' Turkey' sandwich," said Nick. "Looks good, turkey, bacon, and sun-dried tomato mayonnaise. Ever had that?"

Dan didn't answer. He didn't look at the menu, just

ordered a burger and fries when the waitress came back.

He wanted to say, *So you're fucking her, too? First you come in here and push through my investigation and now you're pushing in on my woman?* He wanted to take Nick outside and beat the crap out of him. But he didn't. Dan didn't say a thing.

"Spoke to my IT guy," Nick said, pushing the conversation forward. "He's found some interesting trails. The Olsen woman had Stiles' books set up for his board and Club members to show a simple, straight-forward, steadily profitable enterprise. Then she had another set of records, probably only known to the two of them, showing an insanely clever path of money transfers. The asset allocations were muddled, sometimes leading nowhere, which most likely meant they somehow lead to Stiles. The regular books revealed large sums deposited into Marie Stiles' accounts for decorating the lodge."

"Yeah," added Dan, "And there was that email."

Dan was softening as the Diet Pepsi hit his stomach. He was ready for those fries and burger now. Maybe if he wasn't so goddamn hungry, he could stop being upset about Lyn and whatever the hell she was doing with Nick in her car.

"Right. So Marie had motive beyond the fact that Stacey was doing her husband, which everyone knew. Stacey was questioning if her purchases for the clubhouse were forgeries. Marie could have been purchasing forgeries and pocketing the money. With that email, she knew Stacey was on to her scheme."

"Have you interviewed Marie?"

"Not in detail," said Dan. "Spoke to her the day of the accident. Told her I'd get back to her. She seemed concerned about Stacey, sort of cordial, but her behavior wasn't very different than any of the other Dolls."

"All right, so back to Stacey. I assume you're checking her cell phone, email, telephone bills?"

"Yep. Got a postal search going on too. We'll get it down to a profile and summary. Should be soon. Been trying to trace the source that sent her the last email she opened. Looks like it could have been from offshore. Ask your friend what he knows about that. I've got people still shifting through the ashes to see if they can find the iPad. Not that we'd be able to recover anything if it's in the condition of the rest of the rubble. Anything else on Stacey's office computer?"

"So far, nothing out of the ordinary. Just the usual, read most of her news online, frequented the financial wires, some porno activity. Just about the same you'd find on anyone's computer in her capacity. I took the liberty of taking snap shots of the accounting anomalies to show you how they lead to nowhere. Plus, I added some of Stacey's porno pages from her computer. Might as well make this case just a little more entertaining than it already is." Nick rolled his sarcastic eyes. "Here, take a look."

Dan was momentarily surprised. He scrolled through Nick's screen shots slowly. It showed deception alright. Nick's guy in New York had done well but

Dan wasn't about to mention it. And the porn shots looked like the norm. Just sort of surprising it was Stacey's norm.

A waitress came up to ask if they'd like refills on their drinks while the Sheriff was immersed in digital discoveries. "What's a pretty girl like you doing out here in the middle of nowhere?" asked Nick.

Her mouth wasn't as pristine. "I could ask the same of you. Ever heard of paying the rent by yourself with three kids at home to feed? Ever hear of working two jobs just so the electricity doesn't get turned off or that you have enough propane to last through the winter?" She looked down at her apron pocket and then looked back up at Nick. "Sorry sir, didn't mean to be rude."

Nick replied, "Not a problem. Was just trying to make conversation. Life can be a bitch." In true Nick Conti style he handed her his card, smiled and said, "I'll be staying here for awhile."

She looked at him with a smile layered over disgust and walked away.

"What the fuck? Nick. You think she's some kind of gin soaked honkytonk? People out here have something called *pride*."

His head started to pound again. He kept looking at Nick's screens but he felt the urge to punch him. In his mind he was a wannabe john in a crowded smoke filled bar. He had to slow down. Probably wasn't the first time that pretty girl had been hit on but he didn't like it one bit that it had been from someone with him.

Nick was city-slick, brash and too impolite for the country, although he did have a bit of modern Sherlock in him. Things he wouldn't have thought to do like the New Yorker's phone copies, or maybe it was just that he'd never thought about women looking at porno. But Marie, nothing would alarm him about her. Stacey, yes.

"Ok. Can't resist a pretty girl. I walked right into that one. Most women I've met tend to be flattered. Hey, aren't we all mining for something? So first off I suppose we'd better talk to Marie, right?" said Nick.

"Yup. I'll call right now.

"Marie, this is Sheriff Dan Bentley. Nick Conti, who's working this case with me, and I would like to meet with you as soon as you have time." Dan wasn't sure if Nick could hear her overly sweet invitation for later this evening.

"Why thank you, ma'am, we will see you tonight."

"Ok, we meet at Marie and Scott's home. You know, it's the largest home in 'Diamond Peak'. Looks like it could be the Antelope Clubhouse. Right off the first hole. Tee off time, eight tonight. You can't miss it." Dan chuckled.

CHAPTER TWENTY-NINE

Katherine had given up wondering when or if Michael would ever comment on the pictures she sent him. The only question for her now was how they would behave when they saw each other again, with that unacknowledged act of one-way intimacy.

And Alissa. She kept calling to chat. Tyler this, Brad that. Katherine was purposely aloof, actually embarrassed, but that didn't stop Alissa from reaching out. She had to admit she was beginning to feel badly for Alissa. How could she continually blow off someone so unassuming? It was digging into her core, making her feel terribly.

Brad was travelling; thank god he wasn't calling her also. When he was around, they rarely spoke on the phone—it was usually just a text or two about where to meet. She supposed Brad had become her chosen drug to continue taking when she first moved to Montana but she felt so dishonest, a little morally sick that made her stomach quiver.

Katherine went down to the stables and rode Triumph in the arena. Although she rode English she preferred riding western, quite the anomaly for the East Coast. Triumph had won first place in a national western pleasure category years ago but that was with a trainer showing him. Katherine thought the ring was never as good as the trail but it was better than not riding at all. Cluck once, and he was in a walk, cluck twice a trot, three clucks and they rolled into a canter. She and Triumph melted into one fluid motion. She glanced down on the inside leg to make sure Triumph was on the right lead. "Whoop," and back to the trot.

Round and round she went. Going through the commands, going through the motions. Forcing down emotions. Triumph tripped and slipped down into the sand. She pulled him up almost losing her balance. She thought of what Jean had always said, "The only safe horse is a dead horse." She wondered who felt that way about Stacey.

When she arrived home there were two jars of canned pickles and a huge heirloom tomato. Katherine put them inside and walked over to Jean's house to thank her. The log cabin always had memorabilia that had amazed her, like the one with her father standing between President Truman and Oscar Chapman who was the Head of the Department of the Interior. She had said her father had worked for the federal government. And stopped there. She eventually found out it was for Yellowstone Park. Her family had been well respected for generations. Gradually Katherine had put the pieces together about her life. She was born in January of 1947 when it was twenty below zero. Her family had grown alfalfa as long as she could remember. Jean had a degree from University of Montana. The horse that she had grown up with was named Bill, a mustang her father got for her off the Nevada desert. "Now I ride Rocky, the Appaloosa," Jean had said.

When Katherine got to Jean's she noticed someone working in the fields.

"Don't you have a son?" She'd wanted to ask Jean before, but wasn't sure how to bring it up.

"Yes, Will. He's not interested in farming. He was a little ornery growing up. He was quite the challenge to his father and me. Did his chores with an attitude. But at the same time he could be so loveable. As he grew to be a teenager he was more interested in drugs and alcohol, even though he knew we were shorthanded, but I have always loved him so deeply. His father did too, but finally he took him downtown to an old broken down hotel where the drug addicts lived. He asked him if this was the life he wanted. And that cured the drug problem, but the alcohol, that will probably always be a part of his life, like his grandfather on his dad's side."

"All families have their problems."

"Will is a good boy. I couldn't force him to take over the family business even after his father died. Maybe that was what frightened him. Seeing the farm machinery crush his father like that. So when he became a fishing and hunting guide I was relieved he'd found something he enjoyed. Some term him a 'Legendary Outdoorsman.' I'm glad he's living his dream, always outdoors and making a living, sharing his knowledge about wildlife."

"So it is *your* Will that's the 'go-to-guy' when the famous around here want to hunt and fish."

"He doesn't just take anyone on the river or into the mountains, which makes him a favorite of celebrities and well-known authors. He is not fazed by status, always just as happy on the river with the stars or in the mountains with his local friends."

Stacey was the closest female family member to Jean. Katherine knew she wasn't going to say much, but Jean surprised her.

"I suppose part of his clients are those monsters of the Antelope Club. These Antelope people running the place don't care a bit about other people, all they want is money, money and more money. I'll bet Stacey wouldn't put up with any kind of fraud. These last two months she told me she was afraid, scared of what was going to happen to her. And now she's gone." In a rare show of emotion, Jean sobbed.

Katherine hugged Jean and was a little surprised Jean let her. "I've seen a lot of people die from accidents around here during my life," Jean said. "But it was always either a natural cause, a car collision, death from the environment like drowning in the river, perhaps a misstep and falling off a cliff or even lost in the freezing snow. Bear attacks or snow mobile accidents cause death but I've never seen anything premeditated like this was. You know Montana has a personality of its own. Before the Antelope Club came here, being honest and forthright were our standards. But now these big money men come in here and kill my niece who was probably telling them to reveal the truth. I was all the family Stacey had, and now she's gone forever and the big talk, big money and big violence have destroyed the peace around here." She said in a lower voice, "I know she liked a variety of men, but killing her? That's a little farfetched to imagine. She always stayed friends with everyone in the community, inside and out of the Antelope Club."

There was a knock on the door. Jean went to open it and there stood a young cowboy, must have been her working hand, standing with his faded jeans, a tight dirty t-shirt and a straw Stetson hat. He was tall but looked older than he probably was.

He took off his hat and said, "Excuse me, ladies, but I've been having problems with the baler all day. I think I'm going to order a couple of new parts."

Katherine noticed a softness in Jean's eyes that she'd never seen before.

"Why don't you come down around suppertime and we'll discuss it," Then turning to Katherine she said, "Oh, excuse me, Katherine this is Everett."

"Nice meeting ya' ma'am." He turned toward the door and made a rapid exit, as if he had interrupted something important.

"Well he sure is a cutie," said Katherine.

This time there was no softness in her eyes. Jean looked out the window as she spoke. "He's a hard worker. Came here looking for work just at the right time. Ranch hands come and go. This one has stayed longer than most and is a friend of some acquaintances I have down in Wyoming."

Turning back to Katherine she said, "Something is always breaking down here. Will comes and helps when he can, but he's so busy with clients. Hard for a decent woman to make a living from alfalfa. I don't mind the work one heck of a bit, but sometimes, like this, I get mighty tired of fixing things. It's not as though I can't remember the good things. When I was only five, I was fairly tall for my age, and my dad put telephone books on the driver's seat of his truck so I could drive and he could throw hay to the cattle. Boy, did I think that was fun!"

Katherine knew she was pushing it by asking her question but she did anyway. "So, Everett comes up here from the bunk house for supper?'

Jean gave her a sub-zero look that would freeze nostrils. She continued to look out the window into her fields, now turning gold. "Sometimes. Mostly he cooks for himself in the bunkhouse. When I had more people working for me, like my mom and dad did, we always made meals for the working hands. Now that things have slowed down and I'm not farming all the land, Everett can do the job, and with a little help from me, things work out just fine."

Katherine wondered exactly what "fine" entailed but it was none of her business.

CHAPTER THIRTY

Dan was headed into town. After lunch with nit-picking Nick and a brief nap at home he hoped his office would give him some clarity. It felt like he was making little progress. The sun was bursting in and out of the clouds, putting a spotlight on Dexter Peak. Dexter was his personal landmark. He could always tell how far up or down the valley he was by his proximity to the eleven thousand- foot peak, and the angle at which he saw the mountain. It was facing him head on as he looked east, like a woman's breast with an erect nipple, so he was about fifteen miles from town. The mountain was gray and pink. A sharp slice of light cut through the clouds, turning the alfalfa fields into bright golden strips rolling up the slope to the Absaroka mountain range.

He was driving at the comfortable speed of seventy miles per hour. The vehicle ahead of him was gaining distance so he accelerated. They were over the limit now, but nothing out of the norm for a two-lane country highway. He recognized the vehicle only too well, a silver Land Rover with plates starting with 49, meaning Park County. He flashed his lights. What the hell, he put the strobe on also.

Dan was out of his car and up to her side window before Lyn could climb out.

"Stay in your vehicle, please. You were speeding.

I need to see your license, registration, and proof of insurance."

"Dan, I'm sorry. I wasn't doing anything with Nick. Can't we just go somewhere and talk about this?"

"I'll tell you one more time. License, registration, and proof of insurance."

"Dan, come on."

She reached into the console and gave him the registration and insurance card, then pulled her license out of her wallet.

Dan looked at the photo and then looked at Lyn. He'd never seen her license before. Never had a reason. The woman in the picture was quite different from the woman who sat in her car. He said what he'd wanted to say so many times before to motorists.

"Hair, brown. That's changed, at least a couple times since I've known you. Weight?" Lyn had to weigh about 140 pounds, but her license lied just like she'd probably been doing throughout their relationship. "So you weigh 118, huh?" This, he knew, was probably harassment, but she deserved it.

"Jump in the backseat and find out. I'm pretty light when I'm on top." She was smiling. Damn her.

"I'll have to run this. Stay in your car. I'll be right back." The backseat of her vehicle had seen plenty of action, and it was tempting to play out her cop fantasy, but he was angry and in no mood.

He knew he wouldn't be right back. He got into his Durango. Didn't run her license, just waited. He'd make her sit there a good seven to ten minutes to get that smile off her face and think of what she had done

202

to him. Think of who really had the upper hand. Cars were slowing down to see who he had been pulled over. Let them gawk. The light bar had red and blue lights circling in a wide radius while the strobe light looked like a flash camera going off, taking hundreds of pictures. No one messed with Dan Bentley.

★★★

His cell phone kept ringing and he kept pressing ignore. They could all go fuck themselves. Originally he was heading into town and into his office but as he came up to the interstate he found himself veering to the right and going toward Big Timber. He was heading for his aunt's place, where he could take a ride on his favorite horse, Newman. The weather wasn't perfect but that never stopped Dan Bentley from riding. What did he always say? "There is no bad weather, just poor choices of clothing."

Dan always traveled with necessities in the back of his car, his long, yellow rain slicker, an Australian oiled canvas coat, vest and gloves. Even his saddlebags. When he wasn't riding, the brown canvas bags kept the basics all in one place, a few candy bars, a compass and a spare set of binoculars. The only thing he didn't have was a pair of chaps, but he figured there had to be at least one of his old pairs still hanging in his aunt's barn. A ride out in the open was what he needed. He had to clear his mind. Think. Get a grasp. He wasn't stupid. He knew he was messed up over all the wrong things.

Aunt Ellen wasn't home. The small white farmhouse

was silent. She must have gone to town. The doors had never been locked as long as she'd lived there. She thought there was no reason. Dan had seen enough as Sheriff to think differently, but nothing would change this woman. She was as strong and sturdy as the barn his father had built for his sister and her husband over fifty years ago. Newman was grazing with the other horses. Hard to miss, a big chestnut standing about seventeen hands, and never difficult to catch. Dan walked right up to him and slipped on his halter.

Newman was as seasoned and weathered as the old saddle Dan preferred. Riding in his own saddle on his favorite horse was like wearing a pair of old shoes that fit just right. The bumps and little ridges in the saddle had been molded by hundreds of hours of his body against the leather. Dan had him saddled and out in the open fields in minutes. Newman was great on the trail. Nothing bothered him, not deer or even moose. The scent of a coyote or wolf didn't faze him. The air was cold and invigorating, just what he needed to clear his head.

Thoughts of Lyn were blowing around like tumbleweed with no direction. Had he believed he was in love with her? Maybe he didn't even know what love was. Whatever it meant to him was different from what it meant to Lyn, that was for sure. Wasn't that true with everyone? Did anyone know what it meant? Probably not. Was it even necessary that both people love with the same intensity? Maybe love was better when it was complementary, not identical. When it was sane and sensible.

When he thought of it that way, the whole thing with Lyn looked like a joke. How did she make the slightest bit of sense as his woman? Why should he even care about her? It was a waste of energy even being angry at her. He should have waited and watched before pulling into the lot at Chico, that's what. Then he could have seen with his own eyes just how much he really meant to her. The bitch.

He pushed his butt further into the saddle, dropped his heels a little more. It was going to be a long ride.

He was making the big loop, which would take him into the evening. He rode along at a fairly good pace. The temperature was dropping quickly but he was still comfortable on Newman. Why couldn't he find a relationship with a woman as good and easy as he had with his horse? They moved as one. He was sure some people were lucky enough to find that kind of companionship. He knew what Newman would do next, time and again. Like the way he acted when Dan cinched him up, blowing and pushing out his belly so the saddle wouldn't fit tightly.

Dan stopped, dismounted and pulled the strap out and tightened the cinch around his girth. The back one was loose, too. He normally checked his cinches before he went out, but he had been too preoccupied. That wasn't like him.

Dan was back up in one fluid motion. The wind kicked up, and Newman threw his head. It was gusting, bringing something in. A storm could come out of nowhere in the mountains. He thought about calling into the office but usually his phone didn't work out there anyway. They'd just have to get along without him for a few hours. He put on a little pressure, squeezing his legs. He'd need to get a move on if he planned to get back at a decent time. The horse pushed into a trot and then a gallop, like a well-tuned car moving through the gears.

The wind gusts were accelerating, roaring through the valley, trying to rip open his long yellow slicker. He was having difficulty keeping his cowboy hat on and finally let it fall behind his neck. Held by the small neck rope, it bounced and flapped on his back. Newman was beginning to act up, throwing his head again and again. Horses had a keen sixth sense. It was as if they felt what was about to come. Horses were known to feel an earthquake before it hit. When Dan pulled back on the reins, Newman bounced his head up and down the way he did when he wanted to gallop.

Dan let Newman set the pace. Maybe the speed and the wind would help clear his head. He kept hearing all the sweet things Lyn had ever said to him and wondering if she meant even one of them. Was that all he was from the beginning, just a diversion, something to toss away as soon as a new toy comes to town? He'd always heard that women wanted love and security. But that was it, wasn't it? He could almost hear the pieces clicking in his head. She had security with her husband. And she probably had some kind of love with him too, after all the time they'd been together. Not passion, but maybe that wasn't real love anyway. He needed a woman who would let him love her, who would appreciate the kind of security he could bring, not a billionaire's version of security.

The clouds were coming in behind him, from the west. When he'd left Aunt Ellen's they were just normal grey, looking like gigantic rolls of coal-colored cotton in the sky. Now, as he moved through the valley, a thunder squall behind him was growing darker by the minute. The sky had turned a blackened navy blue. The Crazy Mountains to the north were darker still, silhouetted like shadows on shadows. The wind was blowing right through him now. Even though he was wearing layers of clothing, a padded, quilted vest, jacket, slicker and his chaps, it felt like he was riding with nothing to protect him. His hands were brittle and cold underneath his deerskin gloves.

Nick Conti. That asshole. He thought he had the right to come into his town and turn everything upside down with his fancy, sophisticated city ways. He'd get what was coming to him. Dan controlled the county. The investigation was his. So was Lyn. Not that he wanted her anymore.

Hell, it was crazy, he knew that. He knew Lyn was the worst possible woman for him, and the fact she'd gone after Nick proved it, but he still wanted her to regret choosing Nick over him. He knew the worst fate he could wish on Nick was getting mixed up with Lyn. The wind wasn't clearing his head. It was scrambling it up.

The landscape over in Big Timber was different than up in Paradise Valley. It was prairie land with lots of cheat grass and sage brush, small little bushes that

Newman rode right through, even in tough weather. The valley was wide, open and void of trees. He was out several miles now, following a narrow game trail, where the deer and elk had cut through the valley.

Yeah, it was crazy, he thought. But so what? He knew what he wanted. He wanted to make them both wish they'd never crossed Dan Bentley.

The lightning opened up the sky in a gigantic flash. The thunder took him by surprise, surrounding him, crackling as if the sky had broken and shattered around him. The explosive bang was tremendous, reverberating and splitting on top of him. There was no cover. Newman reared. Dan hunkered down on the saddle and pulled back the reins, but the horse was in a fury and tried to throw him off. Dan pulled the reins to the far right to get him to go in a circle and refocus, but just as he did the lightning struck again, this time louder. Newman straightened out and tried to bolt. Dan slipped on the saddle but regained his balance. They traveled on, the big man on his big horse, sorting though treacherous terrain and unfamiliar, uncomfortable emotions.

First came the rain, blowing in gusts from the heavy winds. The area was commonly termed by locals as the third windiest place in the country. Dan was used to the wind, even these stiff, raw blasts blowing at least eighty miles an hour. Newman was fighting it all the way, rearing, sidestepping and refusing to go forward. Then came the hail. At first they were the normal pea sized balls but they were coming down in sheets like a continuum of BB gun pellets. There was nowhere to move to shelter, not a tree or large group of boulders. Newman was fighting him to let go. With the next bolt of lightning came thunder, and then hail like Dan had never seen before. Icy stones the size of lemons that hit like fastballs, pitched from an arm that had no mercy for man or horse.

Newman let out a cry and twisted while rearing. A huge chunk of ice slammed into Dan's cheek, tearing the skin. It stung. He knew his horse must be taking painful pelts too. He had to let Newman go. Neither one could protect the other. He threw himself off the saddle and rolled to the ground as Newman galloped into the storm.

The hail was coming down heavier now and larger. Dan had no cover. His hat had blown off. When he tried to get up, the wind pushed him to the ground. He was forced to huddle in a fetal position as the fierce balls of ice pounded his body. He held his face in his hands as the wind thrust onslaught upon onslaught of the frozen bullets, some elongated with small spikes, most of them rounded, but all of them bigger than he had ever seen. They hammered his body in savage attacks, then ricocheted off to the ground. His adrenaline had kicked in but he had nowhere to go, nothing to do. He'd never felt so powerless.

Then he got it. This was a higher power pulling down the wrath of awareness. It was a deal-making moment. He heard himself say, "All right, you made your point. I'll stop if you stop."

The chunks of ice grew smaller. The winds were beginning to carry the hail further down the valley.

Finally, he could stand. His face was bleeding. The pain pelted him where the hail had hit his shoulders and legs. There was no sign of his horse. He could only hope he had headed back to the barn.

Powerless. He remembered that feeling. He had been unable to stop the lashing wind and the bombarding hail. But the storm was moving on, as it always did in Montana. He had to move on, too. Get past his emotions. They were what always tripped him up, time and time again, especially with women. He was soaking wet, he was bleeding, and he was miles out on the range without a horse. He had no choice but to put one foot in front of the other.

He had only two things he could count on. One was his mind. The other was inside his vest. It hurt to use his arms to tear open the layers of coats, but at last he found the little can. He tore off a wad of chewing tobacco and pushed it into his cheek. Alright, then. He was the Sheriff of Park County, goddamn it. He knew right from wrong.

CHAPTER THIRTY-ONE

The Stiles home was furnished in big money, Big Sky, western décor. The ceiling was high, with massive glass windows looking up to Emigrant Peak. A grand piano sat in one corner. The room felt like a hotel lobby, with several sitting areas. Over each hung a chandelier made of huge upside-down glass bowls trimmed with copper and elk antlers. Dan hadn't been there before. He was taking everything in, wondering if their home was adorned with fakes, too. The butler escorted him to an overstuffed suede chair with a fringe-trimmed bottom.

The details were pure cowboy-and-Indian. A cattle brand was centered on the back of the chair, and a Native American throw blanket hung on one side. On the floor was a fine rug in orange and blue tones, a Navajo blanket. A bronze Remington statue of a horse trying to throw his rider stood in the center of the coffee table. The room tried to exude wealth but it gave Dan the chills. It wasn't just pseudo-Western, it was a pseudo-home, too.

Nick was a few minutes behind Dan and the butler now let him in and ushered him to a cowhide chair. Dan was feeling better after his painful trail ride—and five hour walk. He didn't give a fuck about Lyn, even though he could tell she felt badly and embarrassed about whatever she'd been doing with Nick, and he was sure she'd be enticing him with a sexy text or two tonight to make up for it. After the butler was out of earshot Dan said, "I got that forensics report back."

"What happened to your face, buddy? Looks like you took a beating," said Nick.

"Got caught in a big hail storm. It's nothin.' It looks like you may have been right about the light bulb."

Before Nick could comment, Marie appeared at the top of the wide, curving staircase.

Dan attempted not to, but couldn't help staring. She stepped down slowly and dramatically, like Scarlett O'Hara greeting Rhett Butler, except dressed like Pocahontas. She wore a beaded, full-length gown made of deerskin. She looked gaunt, as if she hadn't eaten a meal in a long time, which only made her breasts look unnaturally large. The effect, when combined with her nipped and tucked face, was of something not quite human.

"My, my," she said. "Aren't the two of you quite the sight?"

At long last she reached the bottom of the stairs, looking straight into Dan's eyes with a flirtatious smile. "It's been a while, Dan."

He'd seen her nearly a week ago; that was often enough. Dan nodded the way cowboys do to females, tipping his hat and acknowledging her politely but unenthusiastically. Then he removed the hat and set it on an end table next to the oversized leather couch.

"And Nick, so nice to meet you." She held out her left hand, adorned with its ten-carat diamond ring, and waited for him to kiss it. He didn't.

"Nice to meet you, too."

The butler came in and asked what they all wanted to drink.

"I'll get the drinks." She dismissed him rudely, moving to the bar and first pouring herself a tall vodka on the rocks. She added a splash of water and took a long drink before addressing them. "And what will you two have?"

"Diet Pepsi for me, if you have it," said Dan.

"A scotch and water would be fine," said Nick. "So, I understand you had to come back from Paris earlier than you hoped."

"I never got to Paris. I had a problem with my horse trainer. I found out inflight that he had totally misrepresented himself in terms of his expertise."

Dan couldn't help but stifle his smile. How could Marie not know that Trevor would be going to enjoy the swish in Gay Paris?

"I had to dismiss him and turn the plane around to find another trainer as quickly as possible. I have six horses showing in two months at Nationals without a trainer. It's a disaster."

"I thought you usually went to Paris to purchase antiques," said Nick.

"I do." She replied with a certain snippiness. "And I'll need to go back soon. But first I have to settle the horse situation." She gracefully sat on a couch and smiled, suddenly all sweetness and light. "Paris is full of such wonderful art. You've probably heard that I'm in charge of decorating the lodge at the Club. It's almost finished but I'm still looking for just the right final pieces."

Dan asked, "How many times have you been to Paris in the last year?"

"Oh, I'm sure it's been about a dozen," she said.

"You buy new furniture about once a month?" Nick asked.

"Perhaps." She replied, taking a swig of her vodka. "I guess it just depends on the month!"

"Do you work with an antique dealer in Paris?"

"The best, of course."

"What's his name?"

"Henri LaClaire," said Marie.

"Was that *La*Claire or *Le*Claire?" Nick asked, typing notes quickly onto his phone.

"Are you buying originals or fakes?" asked Dan. Might as well cut to the chase.

"I beg your pardon?" asked Marie, in grand arrogance mode.

"Reproductions," Nick said sharply, with a glance at Dan. "Many institutions use high-quality reproductions rather than take on the complications of investing in genuine antiques."

"Of course I'm buying originals." Her tone dripped with condescension.

"And you have receipts for those," the Sheriff said.

"Naturally. Is there some issue with my purchases that I haven't heard about?"

"That you haven't heard about?" Nick questioned.

The sharp edge in his tone caught Marie's attention. She eyed him carefully, then walked slowly to the entertainment center and turned on the music. With her back to the men she said, "What are you asking?"

"Didn't Stacey Olsen talk to you about a Renaissance credenza that a visitor insisted was a counterfeit?"

She turned back to them. Walking toward the men, she rolled her hips slowly underneath the soft leather dress, scanning Dan's body with her eyes, visually fondling him, then bringing her eyes back up to his and licking her lips. She did it well, he had to give her credit, but he wasn't one to be fooled. Of course, she could have been looking at Nick just as easily—it was hard to see if he was taking the bait.

"I believe what you're referring to," she said, "was a lady who apparently didn't know antiques as well as she thought she did. Or wanted others to think she did. Of course, I had no trouble proving its authenticity."

She wasn't abandoning her routine, letting her eyes drift down.

"And you have documentation on that?" Dan snapped.

Marie turned to speak, but she was interrupted by the sounds of a door swinging open and heeled boots hitting the highly polished wooden floor. Scott looked surprised to see Nick and Dan.

"What is this?" he said.

Dan started, "We were just asking your wife..."

But Scott wasn't talking to Dan. "What the hell are you wearing?" he yelled at Marie with no attempt to hide his disgust. "You know we have to be up at the Club to meet the Spanish Contessa and her husband. They just landed. Go put on some real clothes!"

"Oh, my, I forgot they were coming this late," said Marie, affecting a grander than grand attitude. "The Contessa from Spain and her Norwegian husband. I'm sorry, gentlemen. Can we continue another time?"

Dan nodded and stood. Nick followed his example. Scott was heading out of the room, but Nick called after him, "Scott, I left you a message this morning. We'd like to speak with you early next week."

Scott didn't acknowledge him.

CHAPTER THIRTY-TWO

Katherine wasn't the type to visit, but she wanted company. She swung by Sophia's house on the way down the hill to her own. The two sat in Sophia's kitchen while Sophia bound a book she was making. She served tea and macarons, using her fine china, as always.

Sophia's latest remodel of her kitchen had bucked the "trophy kitchen" in favor of functionality and friendliness but she hadn't omitted elegance. Her white marble island had tabletop lamp shades that were covered in the same light blue fabric as the stools. Sophia had an arrangement of green, white and blue hydrangeas centered on the island in a white Tiffany weave vase that matched one of her many sets of china. Versace's Medusas on his tall white-wine stemware peered out from the French glass cupboards on the wall.

"I'm still wondering why you left Boone's reception with Brad," said Sophia abruptly. "Alissa's husband. *Married* men. Maybe you and Stacey shared more in common than I imagined."

"Wow. There's a stretch."

"Alissa looks up to you. She is constantly hurt by her husband's unfaithfulness."

"I've known Brad for a lot longer than I've known you," but she couldn't say it like she meant it.

"What's that supposed to mean? Please tell me you're not fucking Brad Fairbanks. You're worried that Michael is cheating on *you*. What are you *doing?* Is this just something *I'm* fabricating?"

Katherine was used to denying the reality about her behavior with Brad. She had always believed she was protecting a higher principle, protecting her associates back at Stanford and Jones, protecting herself.

"Brad is a long story from the past. There was a different code." And now that code didn't seem to work like before, but she wasn't going to further anything Sophia suspected.

"I've always admired you for your balls, but sometimes I believe you think with them."

"You're not just questioning all this to keep me from asking about you and Nick, are you?"

Sophia was carefully pasting each parchment page into the binding of her book as she spoke. "I told him I had a perfect husband and that I wasn't like a quilt— he couldn't just pick me up where he left off. I don't even think he was listening. Once he got the message that the candy store was closed, all he talked about was Stacey's death. Mostly questions about Scott. I could tell he wanted me to help him, just like the old days...which I'd be happy to do, if it meant he'd get out of here and go home sooner. But right now there's really nothing I *can* do."

"I'm supposed to go back up to Emigrant Peak with Dan on Monday. He wants to see if I can remember anything new about what Stacey mentioned or did," said Katherine.

"Dan, there's another one. He's attractive, with the Stetson, the badge and all. Michael, Brad, and Dan. No wonder you seem preoccupied."

"Oh yeah, that's just what I'm after. Lyn's sloppy seconds. A guy that doesn't wash the blood off his hands."

"What do you mean? He seems like a straight shooter to me."

"I mean that he came to the Murray with elk blood on him."

"Disgusting. But maybe he wants to go on that ride because he's interested in you."

"Right. If he's at all nice, it's because he's delusional and thinks he can get more information from me about Stacey."

"Ok. And what's going on with your husband? What's the latest with Michael?"

"Michael's the tricky one. Okay," She paused to exhale. "Confession time." Katherine explained her nude selfies. "I sent them three days ago and I haven't seen him or heard a word."

"Hmmm." Sophia had an approvingly wicked smile on her face.

"I thought I could wake him up. But he's just... he's about as stable as a low-pressure system over the Rockies. I never know when he's about to storm and for how long, or when he's just suddenly going to turn icy cold."

"I bet he loved them. Maybe he's going to surprise you when he gets back from Lolo."

"I don't want any more Michael surprises.

Sometimes I think it's all my fault, and sometimes I think, oh, there's nothing really wrong, it's all in my mind."

"Listen to your gut, Katherine."

"I *am* listening and I think there is something really wrong."

"Then keep looking. It takes patience."

Katherine pulled her mouthpiece out of its case in her handbag and shoved the clear plastic guard into place. This Michael conversation was sure to make her driving even more stressful, despite the short trip home.

★★★

Instead of driving down to her house after leaving Sophia's, Katherine drove back to the highway and headed for Yellowstone Park. She didn't feel like going home. Michael was supposed to fly in from Lolo, and she had no desire to see him. No, Sophia didn't get it. The old Michael would have already jumped with a sexy response of his own after those photos. He wasn't playing nice. He wasn't hostile. He was just distant.

As the sun began to set she headed for her favorite spot, Point of Rocks. She pulled off onto the Old Yellowstone Trail and drove up over the side of a cliff and down past the Yellowstone River to see the antelope grazing in the fields. They always seemed so peaceful. They stuck together and followed each other, one by one, down their game trail. She loved their fluffy white rears and black horns. Sometimes something spooked them and she got to see how fast they were. They were the fastest animal on the continent, they could outrun anything, even wolves and coyotes. Katherine made a high-pitched "eek-eek" sound that Jean had taught her to draw their attention. She'd made the ridiculous sound many, many times before and laughed for a moment remembering Jean's comment that she couldn't fail, just about anything could draw their curiosity. The antelope all turned their heads, froze for a second, and then went back to grazing.

With a sharp pang of sorrow, she realized that she felt a deeper connection with the pronghorn than she did with her husband. They were predictable, at least. And although their lack of interest in her was as great as his, theirs at least seemed benign. She watched them graze and wander until the sun slipped behind the mountains and darkness eclipsed their slender silhouettes. She sat and thought for a while, enjoying being alone, delaying the inevitable unpleasantness that waited for her at home.

The house was dark when she returned. She assumed Michael had gone to sleep early as he often did, so he could wake up in a couple of hours and work. But when she opened the bedroom door, she found him reading in bed.

"You're still up?" she asked.

"I was waiting for you to come home," he said.

She braced herself.

"I've been thinking about going out alone for an evening."

"Okay," Katherine replied, raising an eyebrow. "Just the two of us?"

"Exactly. I've got a special place in mind that I've wanted to bring you to for a while."

"You and I. Alone."

"Yes, that's what I said."

Her heart jumped in her chest. This was a small step, but it was something. "Where do you want to go?"

"It's a surprise."

Katherine could only look at him for a few moments. Then, very tentatively, she began to smile. He matched her smile, and hers grew wider and wider.

"Sounds great," she said. "When?"

"Well, what about tomorrow night?"

"Saturday night is the Library Fund Raiser. We always go." She saw the smile drain from his face. "But I can give the tickets to someone else." Alissa, she thought to herself. That would be a bit of kindness to help her conscience.

"Good," he said.

She dropped onto the bed beside him. She didn't quite have the nerve to touch him yet, but he laid his hand gently over hers. "Michael, I've been thinking about us lately. I've been wondering what has been going on with you, and..."

There was so much she wanted to ask him, but right now she just wanted to enjoy the sight of her husband coming back to her.

"...tomorrow night sounds great," she finished her

sentence.

"Wear something black."

Michael turned off the light right along with his temporary charm.

CHAPTER THIRTY-THREE

Dan spent most of his day chopping wood. In two days he'd be going up Emigrant peak with Katherine. A city hot shot that thought she was above it all. She may have been smart about money but she was wrong when it came to the way things worked in Montana. He was dreading the encounter when he should have simply been looking forward to the chance to learn more about the moments before Stacey's house went up in flames. He swung his axe hard into the next chunk of wood.

Even though it was a Saturday, the Sheriff rarely had a real day off, and he needed to go into work. The first heavy snow had been forecast and he had to sort through mounds of paperwork. He used his twenty-minute drive from his house to the office as his contemplation period.

When he arrived at his office, he grabbed a cup of stale coffee and sat down at his desk. The next time he looked up, he could see the snow coming down and the wind whipping it up like a fine ice swirl inside a blender. He had been in his office for hours. A winter-weather advisory had been posted. It was a matter of time before power outages and accidents would tax emergency crews countywide.

Duane walked in. "I followed up with the hooker, the one who had the john who complained she wouldn't let him finish."

"And?"

"She's not a prostitute like we normally see. Maybe this was her first time. I don't know. She's twenty-four. Born in Butte. Sort of a sweet girl, although kinda goth, one too many piercings."

Duane could be irritating. He had a problem with too many details and Dan wasn't in the mood for it. "Get to the point," he said.

"Well, she wondered if we knew anything about a character named Pussywhip."

"Duane." The sheriff paused. It was all he could do to keep his composure. "Pussywhip, really? Why does she want to know?"

"She said she just disappeared. And a lot of her friends knew her and she wondered if we knew anything."

"Duane, a lot of people disappear or stop going out. Maybe's she's sick. 'Pussywhip,' for Pete's sake. What kind of name is that?"

"I think it's kind of funny," said Duane. "But this girl was serious."

"A serious hooker." For the moment he wanted Duane out of his office. Dan paused but didn't look at his deputy. "Okay, what the hell. Check into it."

He wasn't surprised when the emergency calls started. He sent a deputy for a two-car collision in downtown Livingston. An ambulance was on its way. Dan wondered why he hadn't heard from Park County Fire Chief Mark on a night like this, but just as he was thinking of him, in came his call.

"I'm down in Gardiner almost to Yellowstone Park. Send a deputy to the Sinclair Station and an ambulance ASAP. My radio isn't working. I've got an injured woman whose car slid on ice and spun right into a gas pump. Can't believe I was down here at the exact time. It took me a hundred and seventy-six damn seconds to pry her out of her totaled vehicle. Should have taken me no more than twenty, but the lock on the inside of the driver's door was jammed. Then I finally pulled her out of the van and the entire vehicle burst into flames. Got the fire under control but the woman's in shock, not sure how badly she's injured. She's conscious but probably has a few broken bones. Wish we weren't so damn far from Livingston. My volunteer firemen were here in minutes."

"There's a deputy not that far away down at Tom Miner Basin. He'll be there soon. It's going to be a long, ugly night."

"I'd say so, Dan. Got her wrapped in blankets on a gurney inside a truck. It's ugly but it could have been gruesome. If we can get her stabilized tell the EMTs we'll meet them on 89. We'll start coming back to town as soon as I think it's safe."

"Stay in touch, buddy. She's damn lucky to be alive."

CHAPTER THIRTY-FOUR

Katherine wore her new, tight, black satin jeans with a black leather jacket and high-heeled black boots; online purchases since the stores in downtown Livingston certainly weren't high-fashion boutiques. She applied her makeup with special care, adding a little shimmer to her face powder and piling on Ruby-Lite, her favorite dark-red lipstick by Chanel. No one carried Chanel in Montana, but David, from the cosmetics counter at Bergdorf Goodman in New York, was more than happy to ship her three or four tubes at a time. She was going to do whatever she could to make sure this night was special.

Michael wasn't telling where they'd be going but for once in a very long time, he opened the door of their Tahoe to let her slide into her seat as a gentleman would. She was ready for the attention that Michael so rarely gave her. He had said it would be a bit of a drive and the evening wouldn't center around food, so Katherine had grabbed a quick yogurt and protein bar before leaving. Just the idea of being out late excited her. She missed their long-ago nights in Manhattan, Michael's chauffeured sedan whirling them from restaurants, showings, the theater, and parties until nearly dawn. No Antelope Club members ever went anywhere late in the evening because everything closed down by ten.

Michael seemed to be in a good mood as he drove, pleasant and upbeat, even complimentary. "You look great, Katherine."

He never commented on the way she looked anymore. Then again, he seemed so happy she thought she could have been wearing just about anything and he would've said something nice. It was strange behavior but she certainly wasn't going to complain.

"Katherine, there are so many things I want to share with you. Most of the time I guess I don't know how to go about it. You're always so aloof."

She could never recall him saying anything about sharing or communicating, not even in their earliest days.

"You know you can share anything with me," she said as she reached over the console to hold his hand.

"We'll see," said Michael. Maybe he was going to tell her about his computer photos.

They said nothing else for a while, just listened to music as they rode in silence over the pass and down into Bozeman. Michael concentrated on his driving as gusts of wind buffeted the Tahoe. A big cold front was moving in quickly.

As they bypassed Bozeman and continued west toward Belgrade, he said, "You've always told me you have an open mind."

She turned up the radio, thought for a second, then turned it down. "I do. Sometimes I think you don't even know who I am." Since he didn't seem to want to bring them up, she braced herself and finally asked, "Did you like the photos I sent you?"

"You'll see," he said. He sounded almost angry.

"You're starting to sound like a parent," Katherine said. "'You'll see, we'll see.' So where are we going? Tell me."

"I can guarantee you, it's a place you've never been before," he said.

Michael exited off the freeway and headed for the industrial part of town. It wasn't a restaurant and it couldn't be a hotel. A bar, maybe, but why would he drive her nearly all the way to Three Forks to go to a bar? He was so vibrantly "on," but somehow not as happy as when they'd started. Edgier.

He slowed down and turned into a gravel parking lot in front of a gray, corrugated metal building. The lot was jammed full of cars.

"We're here."

"This is where we're going? Into a warehouse?" Katherine asked.

He got out and crossed to her side to open her door, another first in a long while.

A cold wind whipped her as she stepped out. He held her hand tightly, intimately.

★★★

A man dressed in a black spandex bodysuit nodded to Michael as they walked in the door. Katherine saw a couple of masked figures in the far end of the room. It was so dark, she couldn't make out her surroundings. But the smell told her something was off. It was sweet, sickening.

Katherine had never seen her husband so turned-on,

he was like an eighteen-year-old boy. As her pupils began to dilate she was able to make out more figures. At first she wasn't sure what she was seeing. A woman brushed by her in a cat woman outfit. She thought she saw a man with his balls hanging out and nothing on but ass-less chaps. She turned the other direction and saw a bar with women kissing and fondling other women.

She heard the crack of a whip. Then screaming. She looked into another room. A woman's hands were tied above her as she lay on an X-frame, naked. Her legs were spread apart. Each ankle was tied to the frame with thick brown rope. She was blindfolded. A man dressed in only black leather pants was whipping, then stopping, and whipping her again.

Katherine grabbed Michael. "Where *are* we?" She felt a light sweat cover her body. "Michael, I need some air."

"Shut up." His tone was frightening. As bad as Michael could be in private, he never told her to shut up in public. But maybe this wasn't public. She was far away from any reality she had ever shared with her husband.

"Michael, what is going on?"

"Katherine, calm down." There was something fierce in the way he said it. "It'll be fine."

"I need to go outside," Katherine said.

"Be quiet." He led her to a small bar where they took seats on high stools. Michael ordered them each a double scotch. She jumped. A woman was sitting underneath them, on the floor. A chain was attached to a nipple ring in her breast. The guy holding the chain addressed Michael.

"Polaris. Nice to see you. Who's your new friend?" The woman on the floor began to rise to take a look at Katherine. The man kicked her. "Get down, you bitch."

"Polaris? Michael, who the fuck is Polaris?"

Michael put a hand firmly on the back of her head and whispered into her ear. "This is important to me. I want you here." She kept waiting for him to tell her he was playing some sort of joke, but her intuition screamed that it wasn't going to happen.

She closed her eyes and tried to sort through it all. This was the "special" place he wanted her to see. A dream date filled with the smell of blood, screams, and the sound of whips. And he had been here before. Many times. They knew him. This was the side of himself he had wanted to share but didn't know how. The computer images were nothing compared to this.

"Michael," she said firmly. "Let's go. Now." She looked over to the other side of the room for the exit. She saw a man with nothing on but a black-felt cowboy hat. He was on all fours, bound by black-leather straps to the top of a wooden table. A huge, red-plastic cock was attached to a metal rod. It was some sort of machine. Two naked men were watching and jerking off while the man in the black hat moaned.

"We're not leaving yet," Michael said. "I'll be right back."

And suddenly he was gone.

Katherine had to flee. She was turning on her seat,

when a woman with clamps attached to her exposed nipples came up and sat down at the bar beside her.

"So, you're new around here. Kind of brave to be coming to Kinkster with Polaris." She looked Katherine up and down, shaking her head with a smile that ranged somewhere between pity and sympathy. No one ever looked at Katherine in sympathy.

"What do you mean?"

"I suppose Polaris didn't tell you about one of the last times he was here, did he? About the so-called accident?"

Katherine froze. "What accident?"

"He tied up a member in a dog collar, way too tight, in one of the dungeon closets. Didn't tell anyone. Left the club with someone else. They found the guy hanging from the collar about 3 a.m. He was blue-gray, almost dead. Polaris was so cavalier, saying he'd forgotten, and he meant no harm. He's one dangerous player."

A creature covered in a black-leather mask with a metal zipper over the mouth came up beside them. The woman quickly moved on, leaving Katherine face to face with him.

"You are my most lovely dream," he said, running his fingers down her chest.

She could see the familiar blue eyes through the mask. It was Michael.

"Take off the mask, Michael." She reached for the zipper.

He brutally shoved her hand away, saying, "What happened to that open mind of yours, Katherine?

Hmm?"

Michael put his hand behind her back, guiding, almost pushing her off the bar stool to the other side of the room. "People are here because they want to be, doing what they want to do. It's very liberating."

Her husband looked like something from a torture chamber. She saw a grown man in diapers. The smell told her he had been that way for a long while.

She kicked herself into survival mode. She had done it before, but not for a long time. She used to do it on the Street and in her previous marriage, to keep herself calm and objective. She capped her senses, stopped, and took herself out of the situation. She ceased feeling, especially anything for Michael. A therapist had once told her it was fine for work but not a healthy practice to do in her marriage. Healthy marriage practices no longer seemed relevant.

A woman in black leather shorts was talking to Michael. She beckoned him to follow her into another room. Michael winked through his mask at Katherine, an odd expression from someone who never winked. He grabbed her hand and pulled her through two doors.

She hadn't heard the new screams from the first room. It must have been sound proof, padded in black vinyl. A man was hanging from the ceiling in chains attached to his wrists. He was being pushed back and forth and then whipped. Every time he screamed he was flogged, whipped again and again by a man in a leather G-string with the physique of a sumo wrestler.

"That's Tay," explained Michael. "Abraxas is his

slave."

"And Tay wants him to do that?"

"He does."

The more Michael watched, the more drugged he became. He was in another realm of existence.

He ran his hands down the sides of her arms. "He does what he wants," he said as he put his hands over her breasts.

Katherine slapped him.

"There," Michael said. "I knew you'd catch on."

"Michael, stop. Just fucking stop."

He pushed her through a doorway. This one didn't lead to a room. She felt the walls hard against her back. It was a closet. Or a dungeon. Dark except for a deep blue light shining on a hook that hung from the ceiling. As he came closer, raising his hands to her neck, she shrieked. But he had closed the thick door behind him. No one would hear her now. He lunged at her, grabbing her neck with one hand while the other snapped a studded collar on with frightening dexterity.

He was going to hang her, like the man who almost died. He was going to kill her and no one would know.

He tried to tie her hands but she scratched him and kicked him.

"Come now," he said. "My little Hellbitch."

He was lifting her, trying to pull her collar up onto the hook. She clawed at his hands and screamed, but he kept lifting. He was strong, much stronger than she knew. She felt her feet leave the ground. The collar caught on the hook. He let go and she hung there, kicking into the air. Her breath was almost completely cut off, and she tried to scream again.

Michael leaned against the door and watched with pleasure. "Stop your screaming. Even if they hear you they'll think it's all part of your fantasy."

She stopped struggling and stared at him, rasping. "Michael. In the name of God..."

"I thought you would like this little party after the nasty pictures you sent me. Yes, you are my party *Doll*. I like to take Dolls apart, limb by limb. "

There was a knock on the door. Michael's eyes looked enraged at the interruption. He didn't move. Katherine pleaded with her eyes, but he only stared at her. Then the door swung open.

A caped, semi-naked man dressed something like Darth Vader peeked inside. "Everything okay here, Polaris?"

Michael nodded. "Just showing our new friend a good time."

"Sure thing," said Darth Vader. But he didn't leave the doorway.

"Get me down," Katherine said. Her voice was hoarse.

Michael unzipped the mask and slid it off his head. Maybe he was trying to look sane or unthreatening, but the huge, Joker-like grin on his face belied him. "Ah, come on Katherine," he said as he unsnapped her collar. "I was just playing with you. Lighten up, have some fun."

Katherine pushed herself away from him and

stumbled back to the padded room. She ran from room to room, looking for a way out. She stopped to catch her breath.

"You can't run out now." It was Michael's voice.

She wheeled to find him right behind her. "What are you doing?" She looked into his eyes, hoping to see the sane Michael, if only a glimmer, but only this new creature was there. "What do you want from me?"

"Katherine, relax." He brought his body against hers. Something sharp poked her belly, like a knife. He held it so no one could see. "Just let me lead. I'll teach you to like this. Teach you to be my good little whore, like in your texts."

"Sorry. I don't want any part of this."

"You'd better learn, Katherine. You'd better learn to do things my way. Very soon, nothing's going to be the same."

"Well, you're right about that. After tonight, nothing is going to be the same. Ever again."

His eyes crinkled. He found that amusing. "You think I'm talking about us, don't you? You think I'm talking about our tiny, empty little marriage. Well, this'll be a bit bigger than that."

His face twisted. Katherine felt the sharpness jab deeper into her skin. Michael's voice took on a strange intensity.

"Economies will collapse. The world will be divided into the vast masses of the have-nots and the few haves, the very few wealthy and powerful who will look down on them from heights of luxury, and laugh."

She could only stare at him.

"You could have been one of the chosen few. You could have been the good little Hellbitch whore for the few. But now..."

"Yo, Polaris."

A muscle-ripped younger guy was walking up to them, wearing nothing but a cock ring and black socks.

"Tyrone," Michael said.

They held each other's gaze. There was an energy between them, and suddenly Katherine didn't exist. Michael let his hand and the knife it held drop away from her belly.

"What's up?" asked Tyrone.

Michael didn't answer. He nodded toward Katherine and gave Tyrone a face that said, *I'm stuck with her.*

Katherine slipped her hand into Michael's pocket, searching for the keys.

"So where's Pussywhip? Haven't seen her for a while."

Michael jerked away from Katherine's hand without looking at her. "How should I know where Pussywhip is?"

"Hey, you know, I just thought..."

"Where do you think you're going?" Michael snapped alert as Katherine pulled away from him and started walking.

She kept moving across the room, quickly. Michael seemed unable to follow, either because he didn't want to go chasing her in front of witnesses or because

Tyrone's magnetism held him where he was.

Katherine told herself to stay above the scene, outside her body. Keep going, find the door.

She saw it: a glowing red Exit sign. Even in her current frame of mind, it struck her as perversely funny that a slice of hell like this would still observe the state fire-code on clearly marked exits.

She surged toward it. Her hand hit the panic bar. The door flew open and she was out into the cold, clear Montana night. Her fist tightened on the car key she had fished from Michael's pocket, and at last she let herself break into a run.

★★★

The weather outside was deteriorating quickly. A blanket of snow had started to fall, making it almost impossible to reach the car in her heeled boots. Katherine slipped on the side runner but pulled herself up and into the Tahoe. It was freezing inside. She thanked god for heated seats.

Her experience riding her horse in the mountains had taught her how to notice her surroundings and remember landmarks, a skill she applied almost unconsciously even on city streets. She pulled her mouth guard out of her handbag, thankful to herself for packing it earlier—her teeth would be grinding this entire drive.

Even with the limited visibility she found her way quickly back to the interstate. A voice in her head warned her not to drive late at night in a snowstorm, but nothing mattered now more than putting mileage between herself and that nightmarish place. A few miles on she saw the taillights of a semi-truck with a trailer and pushed herself to catch up to it. The truck was throwing snow, so she kept her distance, but its tracks provided a relatively clear avenue for her wheels. As the snow fell harder, though, she could barely see the tracks in front of her and had to depend on the grinding noise of her tires on the rumble strip to keep her from driving off the highway.

Interstate 90 had only two lanes in either direction, cutting through the steep mountainous pass that separated Livingston from Bozeman. On a night like this, that meant little room for error. Soon the truck ahead of her was vanishing into the whiteness. Now the whiteout was complete. In her disorientation she couldn't be sure where she was traveling or how fast she was going. Her white knuckled hands clutched the wheel as she struggled to keep her car moving forward, praying that she'd stay on the road.

Total disorientation. That's what she'd been experiencing since Michael had first led her into that club. Everything she had known was a lie. Her marriage was a farce. And Michael. God knew what Michael really was.

Suddenly the semi was just ahead of her. In her anger she'd been pressing down on the accelerator. The highway curved and the truck slowed further. She knew the smart thing was to brake and slow to a crawl, stay well behind the diesel monster, but her adrenaline was pumping. She wanted this drive to be over. She decided to pass. She turned the wheel to the left and stepped on the gas.

In a split second she lost control. Her car was going to the right, not left, and heading straight into the truck. She cut the wheel back and missed the back of the trailer by a foot, but she couldn't correct the steering wheel as she slid, skidded, and spun to the right, like a snowbound version of a Disney teacup ride. Suddenly the vehicle whirled around and shot in the opposite direction. She saw it coming and there was no stopping it.

As she hit the concrete center divider she screamed, thinking her life was over. But she bounced off and spun once more. The car slid over the rough sleeper lines on the shoulder facing the precipice below. She stepped on the brakes but she was moving sideways, skidding into the grim reality of northern winter. The Tahoe came to a halt when it slammed into a pile of snow that had been pushed to the side of the road.

Everything stopped. There was nothing but silence and white falling snow.

CHAPTER THIRTY-FIVE

By the time Dan arrived, the highway patrolman had dug out the snow to open the driver's door.

"She's lucky to be alive," he said to Dan.

Dan heard sirens coming in their direction.

"Are you all right?" he asked Katherine.

"I just want to go home," she said. "I'm fine. Nothing hurts that terribly."

Dan watched the patrolman ask questions while Katherine did her best to answer.

The tow truck and ambulance descended upon them about the same time. Her vitals were normal and only her lower back was a bit sore. The tow truck driver from Livingston didn't think there was substantial damage to her car. If you were going to crash sideways into something, he mused, it was probably smart to choose snow.

Dan noticed that Katherine didn't seem to care one way or another. "She'll need a ride," he said. "I'll get her home."

Dan helped Katherine into the Durango and wrapped another blanket around her. He could sense that there was more to this story, and more troubling her than this crash but he'd find out in time. For now, he just needed to get her home.

It was early morning now. The snow fell softly as Dan stayed in the right lane, taking it slow and steady.

"You're going to be fine," he said. "As far as any bodily harm."

"What's that supposed to mean?"

It wasn't the time to be harsh. "You're not the only one who's miscalculated on that pass. Every summer the winds blow huge semis off the interstate and every winter there are a lot of accidents like yours. Except most don't end as happily."

Katherine was clearly still in shock when they arrived at her house. "Where's your husband? Is he home?" asked Dan.

"No, he's not here. No."

Dan saw her shiver. "Let me get you into the house then."

Katherine was quiet for what seemed like a long time.

Finally, she smiled. "Thank you. I'm just not quite feeling like myself."

"You'll get there," said Dan.

"Thanks for bringing me home." She paused again. "I'm still planning on going on that trail ride with you."

"Sure thing. You're welcome and glad you want to go, but now Monday will be too soon for you to ride with any kind of back pain. When you're feeling better we'll reschedule."

"Ok, thank you. Sounds good."

It was good enough for now.

★★★

"I can't believe you made me come to this," said Katherine. "I can't believe I can walk after last night."

Katherine and Sophia were sipping wine and standing in front of the grammar school's front lawn where a large brown and white cow was grazing between melting patches of snow. It was a breezy Sunday afternoon. The sun was out and most of the snow had melted from the day before. Low temperatures never stopped Montanans from being outdoors. When it dropped into the teens they might finally go inside, but today was warm, and the community seemed to be enjoying the fresh air. Besides, this was a big day for Livingston: the Cow Pie Fundraiser followed by a local rodeo where everyone from miles around came to watch their friends and family.

"It's what you needed and you know it," Sophia said.

"I knew I needed the Cow Pie Fundraiser?" But she did. She needed anything that would get her out of the house and among other people. Her back pain was hardly a bother. To say she was pissed at Michael was an understatement. Michael hadn't come home after the club. Of course, she had taken their car and cabs were scarce in Montana, but that wouldn't stop Michael from summoning a ride.

She looked at the map of the lawn she'd been handed. It was divided up into little uneven squares, like states. "So, I place my money on where the cow's going to drop her first patty and if I win, I get the cow. A real cow."

"The cow or three hundred dollars. The school gets the rest. Weren't you listening when they explained all this?"

Katherine shook her head. "I was trying." She kept hearing other things. Michael's voice. His laugh when she was hanging from that hook.

Even if the past is left behind, there's no guarantee it won't appear in the present. And Michael was violence backed by money and power. Worse, his abuse was for fun. Then there were the other things he was predicting, near the end, that she could barely follow. Armageddon.

"Katherine, are you there? Are you listening to me?"

"I'm here."

"I think you should call some of your friends back in New York," Sophia said. "Tell them what you do for fun now that you've moved to the real America. If an angel had come to me when I was sitting in the waiting room at *Marie Claire* and told me that in ten years I'd be betting on the landing spot of a pile of cow dung," Sophia sighed, "I'd have thrown him out the window. But now, honestly..."

"Now what?"

"You know I came *that* close to winning last year?" She made a gesture that brought her perfectly manicured fingers just inches apart. "Seriously, it splattered an inch from the edge of my square. Well, this year, I *want* it."

They both laughed at that. But Katherine couldn't keep the laughter going long. "How long will this eff'n thing take?"

"Just pick a square." She paused. "And stop thinking about last night."

"It's about what he's going to do next. He's not just kinky. It's more than S&M, Sophia. He's dangerous in a very sick way."

"Is it possible that he was just experimenting, looking for your reaction, hoping you liked it?"

"I think a good part of him, somewhere in the dungeon of his algorithmic mind, wanted me to join, but he was way too lethal."

Katherine saw Marie, Alissa, and Lyn, coming toward them. The last thing she wanted to do now was listen to their circuitous chitchat, but there was no way to avoid them.

"Did you pick your square yet?" called Lyn. "Is it true the winner gets to keep the patty, too?"

"I'm betting she goes under the tree because she'll want shade," said Alissa. "I bought the closest square I could find to the tree."

"That's actually kind of smart," Lyn said. "I know nothing about cows or cattle. I don't even know what kind she is. Is she a heifer or a Hereford?"

"Oh my god," said Alissa. "A heifer is a young female cow who hasn't had a calf and a Hereford is a breed. That could definitely be a Hereford out there, but beyond that, I don't know. Maybe it's a heifer Hereford."

They all laughed.

A deep voice came from behind. "That's not the way you say it. She's a Hereford heifer."

Katherine and Sophia turned around to see Dan

and Nick join the group.

"A Hereford heifer," said Alissa. "Well, now I know. I can't wait to impress my next houseguests and teach my little Tyler."

"You ladies are a breed unto yourselves," said Dan. "Bet you don't know the difference between a dairy or beef cow."

Lyn gave him one of her pouts. "Does it really matter?"

Katherine didn't like being lumped into the group of "ladies." Especially at times like this.

Dan looked at Lyn, lifting his eyebrows. "Probably not. At least not for you."

Dan glanced her way. She nodded, giving him one of her confident smiles. She could see Lyn, noticing Dan's gaze and visibly stiffening. Katherine was about to thank him again for last night when Lyn took two steps toward Dan. Unfortunately, she'd worn high heels. One heel sunk into the moist lawn, forcing her to kick her foot out of the shoe. Everyone stood there and watched her pull out the muddied spike.

"Well that's a whole new definition for 'fuck me heels,'" said Marie.

"Very funny," snapped Lyn as she tried to wipe the heel off with a used tissue from her hand bag.

"At least now they go with that dress," sneered Marie, pulling back her head with a snobbish disgust.

A bitchy line, Katherine thought, but Lyn did look a bit like an over-aged lady of the night. The dingy fur wrap in the middle of the day didn't help any. Her clothing choices had been growing more extreme and more erratic. Katherine wondered if she were getting dressed under the influence.

Lyn leaned on Dan as she put her shoe back on. Dan was trying to act as though he was looking out over the lawn, but he was clearly keeping Katherine in his peripheral vision.

"When is that damned heifer going to shit?" Sophia asked.

Katherine snorted a laugh. Sophia didn't usually swear unless she'd had a few, but John wasn't there to notice. Then Alissa came up to her, looking oddly nervous. "Where's Michael?" she asked in a whisper.

Perfect. Was he sleeping with her? Maybe she deserved it. Nothing would surprise her now. "Work."

"I've called you and left messages but never heard back." She dropped her voice further as she continued, "I've been eavesdropping on Brad. I think it may have something to do with Michael and his trades. It's different from what I told you at the tiara party."

Oh, more innocent than Katherine thought, "What is it?"

"I'm not totally sure. But I'd like to talk. Maybe I can come over."

"Of course, anytime," said Katherine. Then she added, "But call first." She still didn't know how long she was going to be able to stay in her own house.

Sophia waited until Alissa had walked away, then positioned herself so no one could hear her.

"So, what more were you going to tell me? About Michael?"

"Okay," Katherine said. "He has a code name at

this club. Polaris. And..." She stopped because she had to wrap her mind around the idea. "I think he has 'things' with the people there. Both women and men. And people asked him where 'Pussywhip' was. Like she was his regular partner." Her speech sped up. "And I think Pussywhip might have been Stacey."

"Stacey? What makes you think that?"

Katherine looked at her and hesitated. "Because when I was in Zig's studio I'm sure I saw a photo he took of Stacey naked."

Sophia shook her head and bit her lip. "No wonder you're not yourself. But okay, okay. So Stacey was into kinky sex, and Michael's into kinky sex."

"And Michael is violent and Stacey is dead."

"Her house was blown up. That doesn't sound like S&M."

"Sophia, for god's sake..."

"I think it would be a good idea for you to talk to Dan about what happened with Michael. Honestly, I can't believe you didn't tell him last night."

"Tell him my husband is a freak? That he took me to a BDSM club and tried to hang me? I can tell one thing about the Sheriff. He doesn't trust me. Thinks I'm an outsider. Plus, how long before that's all over the Paradise Valley grapevine?"

"Katherine, if you really think Michael is a physical threat to you, you owe it to yourself to tell Dan. He may be able to protect you."

"Just go up and tell him, huh?"

"Well, not *now*. But call him as soon as this is over. He's the Sheriff. I'm sure he's heard worse."

Dan was talking and laughing with some older ranchers, Jean and a few of the Wednesday Pine Riders. They were all wearing their cowboy hats, with padded vests and faded jeans. Some wore their shiny belt buckles sporting rodeo prizes of days gone by. They made a fine-looking scene, huddled together like the retired Marlboro set.

"No," Katherine said. "If I'm going to tell him, I've got to do it before I talk myself into thinking it's all in my head."

"Katherine..."

Katherine shook her head and walked toward Dan. She caught his eye, and he peeled away from the ranchers.

"How are you feeling? How's your back? I'm surprised to see you here."

"I'm doing alright. I want to thank you again for last night. The body shop thinks the car won't take too long to get fixed."

"Glad to be of help and that you're feeling ok. We really need to get back up on that trail. Would the day after tomorrow work? Let's say ten?"

He hadn't picked up on her distress. "Okay."

He changed the subject. "Did you pick your square?"

"I did. How long do you think it's going to take? The cow, I mean."

"If you get impatient, you can always sneak out there and slip her some Maglax." He paused to look at her more seriously. "I think she's not the only one around here who's a bit nervous. How are you doing,

Katherine? Truthfully."

So he did notice. She saw the fray on his Croakies and his plaid shirt was woolen but probably twenty years old. She supposed it fit his style.

"I've been better. I'm fine physically but I'm worried about my husband." Katherine told Dan about Kinkster and how Michael was a regular, calling himself Polaris.

"Everyone kept asking him about a woman named Pussywhip."

"Pussywhip. That name has come up before," said Dan, writing in his notebook.

Katherine felt uneasy as he started scribbling notes. She didn't want to open an investigation, but she was also impressed that he seemed unflappable as she described the club.

"Did you see any activity there that you thought might be illegal?"

Like hanging your wife? She had to cut to the heart of this now, tell him what was at the core. "Dan, it wasn't just the club. It was Michael. He..."

"She's pooping!"

Screams and laughter carried over the lawn. Katherine looked. The cow was pooping all right, but not just one little mound of cow pie. Dan looked out into the grass where the officials were running.

"It's going to take skill to sort out this crap," he said. He grinned at his own joke. "Looks like we could have more than one winner, the way that stuff is flying." He stared out in the direction of the cow. Then he paused and looked back at Katherine. "We'll talk more. Are you worried about your safety?"

"I'll be fine." She wanted to admit she was scared, maybe for the first time in her life, but couldn't find the words to ask for help. Not without filing charges against Michael, and that sounded too awful to contemplate. And for a woman used to taking charge, she had no idea what to do.

Manure was squirting everywhere.

CHAPTER THIRTY-SIX

Everyone was so incredibly stupid. Stupid or cowardly. Short-sighted. Walking merrily to the slaughter. The Hellbitch had been no exception. Not that he had ever for an instant expected her to take the chance he was offering her. He knew all along he would be leaving her behind. He just liked knowing that he'd given her a last chance and she'd thrown it away. He liked picturing her trembling under the point of his knife, squirming in fear, desperate to get away from him, not even dreaming that she was dooming herself. This way he got to sleep peacefully, knowing he'd given her a chance, and yet he still got to picture her falling into economic hell with the rest of them. She'd be so sorry then that she didn't let him have what he wanted, but it would be too late and he'd have nothing to apologize for. It was ingenious. Cruelly, sadistically, ingenious.

Although maybe he'd rushed things just a tiny bit. He had to admit that. Maybe the terror in her eyes when she was kicking and writhing on the end of that hook had turned him on a little too much. He hadn't planned on revealing what was coming just yet. Now he had to consider moving quickly, just in case she was starting to put it all together. But that was okay. That was part of the fun, speeding it up when you got to the edge. Fighting to hold your pace but feeling it heating up in your balls, having to pump faster, faster, faster until it exploded.

It was time anyway. Yes. There'd been a bit of unrest with a couple of his investors. He could make it happen in two weeks, even less. He'd have the crew run tests on the hardware in the morning. He'd stall the investors, that was never difficult. He could promise them anything, because he wasn't returning any principal to anyone. Why should he? It wasn't theirs anymore. Soon they wouldn't have anything anyway. It was time to fuck them all. He had already converted nearly all his positions into hard assets. Gold, diamonds, emeralds. Moving them to an island off the coast of a banana republic where he'd already bought the silence of the government. His hard, hard assets swelling every minute, getting ready for the explosion. Everything would be about hard assets, and he'd be the hardest and the biggest of all.

He shoved forcefully on the back of Tyrone's head and started to pound. It was time.

★★★

Stacey under five or six feet of ashes. Buried Silence. Katherine knew the pieces of the puzzle weren't all there but some of them were starting to fit. Now she was afraid.

The house seemed exceptionally quiet and she was on edge, not knowing if Michael would return or where he had gone. Her body felt a bit sore, but at least nothing was broken.

Kinkster. She had a name for what she had only

been able to think of as "that place." That made it less frightening, somehow, such an ordinary name. She started seeing it again. In the middle of the bright afternoon, all she could see was the darkness, the red and blue lights, the shadow figures of the bizarre participants. She could smell the place again. Hear the whips and cries.

She hoped "Pussywhip" had not been Stacey. It sickened her to think that all the time that Stacey had pretended to be her friend, she'd been sleeping with Michael.

Maybe Dan and Nick would go to the club to get more information. She could imagine Nick wanting to slip into that scene, but Dan? She had a sudden image of him in black leather chaps, a studded vest, and pointy-toed cowboy boots. And his hat. No, not Dan.

There had to be some kind of membership protocol anyway. It was a private club. The only way Dan would be going in would be if he pushed through with a warrant, and he wouldn't learn anything that way. Probably no one could get into that place except Polaris's new playmate, Katherine herself.

The thought jolted her. Katherine had to get out of the house. She went for a walk down by the Yellowstone. As she sat on a big boulder watching the river she tried to let it go. But it wasn't like throwing a stick into the current and watching it disappear. The thoughts kept circling back. In the roar of the river she heard Michael's voice, his insistent murmuring, his absurd babbling. What was he telling her about a financial collapse? Maybe she needed to talk to Brad. With her clothes on this time.

She wished now that she had learned more about Michael's mystery. She remembered what Jack had always said back at Stanford and Jones. He had warned her there was something not right about Michael, something almost spooky. At the time, she'd attributed it to Jack hating Michael. He'd been Michael's old partner when he had started his first high frequency trading company. Jack left before Michael had come into the big money, citing that Michael worked only for Michael and never worked as a team player. He claimed Michael was growing as crazy as an algo gone wild and worst of all, he knew for sure Michael was skimming on their skim. Jack never pressed the accusation. Katherine had always known Jack was the cool headed one. For a while, he was out of a job. Even though Michael wasn't happy about it, Katherine had helped Jack get a position at Stanford and Jones back when she was a trader, before she got into sub-prime loans. Later on it had been Jack who had helped her start her mortgage foundation fund, which he ran faithfully to this day.

Now she wished she'd listened more carefully to him. She thought of calling him, but had no idea what to ask.

She called Sophia.

Without even saying hello, Sophia asked, "So, did you tell Dan?"

"I need to ask you a favor," Katherine said.

"Okay. Sure. What is it?"

"I need you to help me. I have to go back there. It's the last place I want to see again in the world, but I have to if I'm going to find out the truth about Michael and Stacey."

"I can't believe I'm hearing this."

"Sophia, do you still own that leather cat suit you wore for Halloween last year?"

"Katherine, it will take more than a borrowed cat suit to make you look like a sexual adventurer."

"Spare me the sarcasm. I'm not talking about borrowing it."

There was a long silence from the other end of the phone.

"Wait. What?"

"I can't go alone. I know I've got to go back there but I don't want to walk up to that door by myself."

"And you think they'll let us in."

"Single women dressed to 'play'? Probably. Especially if they recognize me from the other night."

"Don't you think this could be dangerous?"

"The way everyone was talking, everything that happens there is consensual. They even have Darth Vader to check on situations that look dodgy."

Sophia's nervous laughter was unusual. "The place sounds so horrible. And how are we going to get out when we want to leave?"

"We're going to walk out the door," Katherine said. "That's how we're going to leave. You're surprising me, Sophia. You're usually so fearless."

"Won't they want us to participate?" asked Sophia with another nervous laugh.

"I don't doubt that they will. Which is when we say, 'Maybe next time, thanks.' Michael was the only one I felt afraid of. That's part of what's so disturbing about this. He wasn't like the rest of them."

"You're sure we don't have to get whipped and tied up?"

"I'm positive. If we're uncomfortable we'll go to the ladies-only section." Sophia needn't know what that meant.

"What are you wearing?" asked Sophia.

That was more like her friend. Once the Dolls got to thoughts of wardrobe selection, they were committed. "I think I'll wear a very short skirt, fishnet stockings and a black lace top," said Katherine. "Your leather cat suit is perfect."

"Okay," said Sophia. "I think this is a bad idea, but I'm going with you because I think it would be far worse if you went by yourself."

"I don't like it either. But my husband and my friend could have been having an affair behind my back and my husband may have had something to do with her death. Stacey said she needed my help when we were on the trail. Maybe it was because she knew about Michael."

"That's kind of a stretch, Katherine."

"Maybe. But what if I'm right?"

"So when do we have to do this?"

"Start getting ready. We have to do it tonight. Late. After I get back from the rodeo."

CHAPTER THIRTY-SEVEN

The rodeo on the Livingston fairgrounds was a huge local celebration to fund junior rodeos across several counties. Sophia went once, saw a horse hit the side rail and die in front of the audience. She never attended again. Stock animals in Montana were seen differently. Katherine remembered a trail boss on a WPR day tell her that her horse wasn't a pet, like a dog, and she should never try to bribe her horse across a creek with a carrot. Someone else had yelled, "That is what spurs are for, girl." Again, she had felt like a fool, but Jean had been watching and quickly wrapped a rope around her saddle horn and yanked Triumph over the water. He jumped over the wide stream, almost into the bushes, but Katherine had held on and squeezed her legs tightly. She had at least figured out that chaps weren't just for show horses. You wore them to protect your legs.

Katherine was going with Jean to the rodeo and had asked if Alissa could come with them, as she found a babysitter for a Sunday night. Jean didn't sound too excited about Alissa tagging along, but agreed. Jean rolled with life, which was another characteristic Katherine envied.

This rodeo was different from the Fourth of July Rodeo in Livingston that attracted so many tourists; this was for locals. There was the usual bronc riding, calf roping, barrel racing and of course, bull riding. Katherine was so excited to go. Jean chose to sit next to her WPR friends, and Katherine and Alissa were off to themselves at the end of the row. There were lots of locals watching while sitting on their trucks' tailgates.

Barrel racing was Katherine's favorite. Especially watching the women riding so fast from barrel to barrel, cutting around each one so swiftly and then racing back to the finish. Once in a while, when someone hit a barrel on the turn, you could hear the crowd sympathize all at once because that lost her coveted points. Speed and skill was what made it so enthralling for Katherine.

Calf roping was the event that Alissa couldn't take, a timed event between a calf and a mounted rider. The cowboy gets the calf by throwing a loop of rope from a lariat around its neck and then jumps off his horse to run to the calf and tie up three of the calf's legs together. It goes quickly, and they of course free the calf in seconds as soon as it's completed, but Alissa wasn't quiet about her thoughts that they were "hurting the baby cow."

Close to the end of the rodeo, Katherine suggested they go to the corrals by the chutes. She wanted to see the livestock after noticing a stern scoff from a WPR rider who Katherine didn't recognize. She was staring at Alissa's very, very short and fringed skirt, which didn't help.

A full bar with hard liquor was always at a Livingston rodeo. Katherine had distracted Alissa on the way in, but now she saw the bar and Alissa had to stop. There wasn't any champagne and only cheap white wine, so she settled for a double vodka on the rocks. Katherine had a scotch. Alissa downed hers like a glass of lemonade while Katherine sipped. Alissa ordered another and they headed to the corrals. After Alissa tripped over into the dirt they saw the bulls first. They looked so docile compared to when they were in the ring.

As they rounded the corner Alissa, probably feeling the immediate rush of all that vodka, squealed, "There's Gram and Cody! You know, Katherine, my fix-it dryer guys! They look even cuter in their cowboy hats and chaps cupping their cute butts."

Katherine knew they'd already been in the ring, although Alissa hadn't been paying attention.

"Hey Mrs. Fairbanks, how are you?"

"Alissa, remember? Just great, this is my friend Katherine. Have you already ridden?"

"You didn't see me?" asked Cody. "I got a perfect eight, riding that bull right over there." He pointed to a very mean looking one. "The most dangerous eight seconds in any sport."

"I did see that, but I didn't know it was you. I would have given you a ten."

Both cowboys looked at each other and Katherine jabbed Alissa.

"There is no ten, it's extremely hard to stay on a bull, especially for eight seconds," said Katherine. She could tell the boys were snickering about Alissa's comment, even though they were staring at her skirt revealing most of her legs, but they were polite.

"Well, we'll never forget fixing your dryer, um, ma'am. That was one hell of a day, besides helping the stupid FedEx guys."

They heard an older man calling to Gram and Cody. "Well, we'd better be going ladies." Gram winked, "Maybe next time? Call us if you need *anything*."

Something was bothering Katherine about FedEx guys but she couldn't place it. Maybe it was just Alissa, her double vodka, her skirt, her not getting the rodeo scoring, she wasn't sure. On the way back they saw Eric and Lyn. Then they noticed Sheriff Dan watching them, although Lyn didn't seem to notice. Uncomfortable.

It was a rare sight to see Eric and Lyn walking warm in arm, rare to see them out as a couple, and Katherine and Alissa were happy to see them. Katherine asked if they could have a ride home. She didn't want to damage her reputation with the WPR with Alissa along. She told Jean they had found a ride and Jean smiled as if she'd garnered the eight.

CHAPTER THIRTY-EIGHT

He couldn't put it off any longer. Lyn had greeted him with a warm kiss and offered him a Diet Pepsi. Then she sat down next to him on the couch and began to rub her chest close to him, her usual romantic precursor to more. For a moment he thought he might hold off a little longer before saying it. She could make him feel so good.

She must have sensed his tension, because she suddenly tried to change his focus.

"Are you getting anywhere on Stacey's case?" she asked. "You know she hid Scott's shit, right? And he was into *big* shit."

Maybe she had more information than Dan thought. Perhaps he should interview her after all. "What do you mean?"

"Doesn't take much to get that she had to cook his books."

"Do you know this for a fact?" Nick had already found this info, thanks to his New York connection, but if Lyn had first-hand knowledge, maybe she could be more useful.

"I know lots of things. I imagine you're aware Scott wasn't her only lover."

"Like whom?"

"There's a so-called 'list.' You need to check it out, Dan. For all I know, you may be on it. Maybe she was just like you. Although I get the feeling you're moving on to Katherine now. I saw you talking at the cow pie. What is it Dan? Are you playing another one of your games of hide and seek or seeing how many of us you can reel, rope, and ride, hmm?"

"Lyn."

"And which one of us bucks the hardest, hmm?"

"Lyn, listen to me." He'd started downriver now. There was no paddling back. "You're a beautiful woman, but we both know it can't work. You know you're never going to leave Eric, and I can't spend my life waiting for the final round that I'll never qualify for."

She was leaning in on him again. He could feel her breath on his neck. "If this is about Nick, he means nothing to me."

"It's not about Nick."

He could tell she wanted him even more now. She always did when he pulled away. She tried to move in closer and kiss him but he gently and firmly pushed her back. He wanted to know about what she knew about Scott, but he wanted her out of his life even more.

She wasn't trying to kiss him now. Her face had turned to pure hatred in a couple of seconds. "So this is when you ride off into the sunset, is it? Just throw me away, like a piece of trash."

Dan ran his hands through his thick hair and grabbed his hat. He centered his Stetson and then straightened his huge silver belt buckle. Tipping his hat he said, "Good day."

She tried to embrace him as he attempted to walk past, but he kept walking. "Dan, you can't do this to me." Now she was starting to cry. "I can't make it without you, Dan. My life is too horrible."

He stopped at the door. *There were many theories about arguin' with a woman and none of them worked.* "You'll be fine. In your life there's always a new rider up before you know it." He wished he had a card for one of his former rodeo buddies down in Cheyenne so he could hand it to her like a businessman leaving an old job. *Here, call Tucker, he'll service you in a flash. He loves head throwers.*

"You'll regret this, Dan. No one will ever treat you as well as I do. Ever. And I've got so much more to give."

He looked her straight in the eyes. He opened the door and kissed her on the forehead. He paused and tipped his hat. "I wish you the best."

CHAPTER THIRTY NINE

She couldn't remember how many Ativans nor how many Oxies she'd taken. Her head was filled with rage and the pills weren't calming her down. She had to punish him. And not just by bad mouthing him all over the county. Not just keying his car or sending him a box of manure. No. Not for something like this. For this he had to pay. Dan Bentley had messed with the wrong woman. It would seem like a tiny accident. Yes, just a little accident that would take away what he valued so greatly.

The next thing she knew she was driving toward town. Horns honked. She waved back as she navigated from rumble strip to rumble strip, swerving down 89 South. She was humming to herself. She turned up the music. The best part was that it wouldn't be over quickly. It would be slow. He'd realize gradually, horribly, what was happening, but he couldn't do anything about it.

Lyn entered Western Drug. She had to do it before Dan remembered she still had his key. She purchased the little gray bottle quickly and headed back to the valley. Things were looking a little blurry so she slowed down. She held the little white bag in one hand and the steering wheel in the other.

Checking to make sure the Durango wasn't in his garage, she hurried inside and headed straight to the bathroom. She knew when Dan got around to taking a shower he scrubbed his scalp thoroughly. He played the man's man, but he was more vain than anyone knew. That's why this was going to hurt. That beautiful, thick head of hair that he loved so much.

Lyn dumped out most of his shampoo and filled the rest with Nair for Men hair remover.

She left, taking the key with her. Not that it would matter. For certain he'd be changing his locks.

★★★

Dan and Nick were back at Marie's house, hoping to finish the conversation they'd started the other day. Nick's guy in New York, Allen, had found more layers of money transfers. It was like a system of caves. One dark channel led to another and another, deeper and deeper to the point that Dan wondered how they pulled it off as long as they had.

Marie's part of buying antique replicas and pocketing the difference between the originals was becoming clear, but Scott's part was still obscured. It was obvious he'd moved a lot of liquid capital but less obvious where it went. The trails were surprisingly sophisticated for a standard-issue CEO swindler like Scott Stiles. Stacey had to have known what they were both up to, because Allen found the hidden trails in ghost files on her computer, but she probably didn't have the chops to pull off anything like it. Stiles must have had someone to help him.

Marie welcomed Nick and Dan this time by herself, no butler at the door. The house seemed dark and cooler than before, but perhaps it was the wind outside that brought in the chill.

Dan didn't take off his hat. He wasn't in the mood to answer questions about his new look.

"So, how have you two been?" Marie asked, sounding falsely bubbly.

Dan ignored her, looking at an antique cabinet. "Didn't see this before."

"It's from Florence, seventeenth century. It was quite a steal."

"I'll bet," said Dan. "You've got a lot of steals in here, don't you?"

"I beg your pardon, Sheriff," said Marie.

"Marie, mind if we have a seat?" Nick said, obviously trying to soften the tone. "There are some questions we need answered."

"Please, go ahead."

Marie wasn't smiling. She sat straight up in a large chair near the sofa where both men settled. She pressed her lips together tightly. No, the chill in the room wasn't just about the outside wind.

"Marie, we can do this the easy way or the hard way," said Dan. "Try your very best to be honest and then you can get back to your shopping or gossiping or whatever else it is you and your friends enjoy."

"What is this about, Sheriff?" She waved her hand beside her face and attempted a mock smile to show she wasn't scared.

Dan cleared his throat. "We've gathered a lot of evidence regarding your purchases for the clubhouse. I've been working with Interpol and have been reviewing the Antelope Club's books and Stacey's account records."

Marie glared at him hatefully.

"It's very simple," Nick added. "We have documents from Interpol showing shipments of furniture and art pieces insured at a fraction of what you reported to Ms. Olsen to have paid for them in Paris. Why would anyone underinsure such priceless pieces? Unless, of course, they weren't the real thing."

Marie remained quiet and Nick continued, "We also have bank records showing large sums of money transferred into your account prior to your trips to Europe. We've located an offshore account that had sums deposited about the same time as your corresponding buying trips."

Marie's tense, icy act was melting quickly. She was fidgeting, pulling non-existent lint off the chair, looking down.

"Mrs. Stiles," Nick said with calculated warmth. "Marie. It will be so much easier for everyone if you could just explain."

Marie looked up at him. For an instant she looked as though she was about to rage at him. Then she began to cry. Not what Dan had expected. She wasn't just getting misty eyed, either, or sniffling. She wailed. It was streaming out of her like water from a pipe broken by the cold. Or a septic tank explosion.

"It's not my fault. You have to listen to me. Scott has been up to a lot of sneaky business with the Club's money. He was lying to them and he was lying to me. Our marriage is dead, dead. It's been dead for a long, long time." Mascara was running down her cheeks, making her look like a weary raccoon. "This is all about Stacey." She was slipping into some kind of Southern accent. It was like Tammy Faye Bakker had come back to life. "She was his lover, you know. Everyone knows. He had plans to leave me for her. I was just building a nest egg for when he finally left me. When my settlement came, I was going to put all of the money back." Then some venom mixed with the tears. "And you *know* my settlement's going to be big enough to pay it back with interest."

Dan's voice was fierce. "How much did you steal?"

"No! I wasn't stealing! It was just a sort of loan. I swear to the Good Lord I was planning to pay back every cent."

"Except you didn't tell anyone about this loan."

"My lawyer told me to transfer the funds."

"Your attorney advised you to purchase counterfeit antiques and pocket the difference?" asked Nick.

"Well, it wasn't that simple," Marie began.

Dan interrupted her. "When did Stacey discover what you'd been doing?"

Marie's eyes grew wild. "I was going to straighten things out with her. I swear I didn't kill her. I didn't. Dan, you have to believe me. Please believe me. Nick," she said, entreating him with her Tammy Faye eyes. "You believe me, don't you?"

"Marie, I'm sorry to hear that you and Scott were having so many problems." Nick used his soft voice. "That must have put you under a terrible strain."

"Terrible," wept Marie.

"And it must have been hard watching your husband play fast and loose with the Club's investments," said Nick.

"It was awful," Marie said. Then she caught herself. "Of course it's not that I know, really, what Scott might have been doing."

"You said he was up to a lot of 'sneaky business' with the Club's money,'" Nick said, glancing at his phone as if checking his notes.

"I don't actually know anything about Scott's business," she said hastily. "I was angry. That's all."

"Marie, if you'll help us understand what Scott was up to," coaxed Dan, "I don't think anyone will be as concerned about your antique purchases."

"I don't know anything," Marie said. She stood up. She was shaking. "I'm not going to say another word. You'll have to talk to my attorney."

Dan looked at Nick and laughed. "Amazing how long it took her to think of that one!"

"I want you out of here," Marie said, her voice getting louder, but quavering. "I want you out of here now. If you want anything more from me, you'll have to talk to Charles first. Scott's and my attorney."

Dan stood. He touched his hand to the brow of his hat, but instead of tipping it, he shoved it further down on his head. "You can be sure we will."

When they got outside, Nick said, "Well, we got an admission, at least. And plenty of evidence that she and her husband weren't working together in this. I would've liked some more time with her, though."

"Look," Dan said sharply, "I know what you're

thinking. We could have gotten her to help us inves-
tigate Scott. But take it from one who knows—you're
never going to get anything out of these Dolls but
lies. Lies and games. That's all they know."

"Okay, then," Nick said. "Let's get back to work on
the husband."

"Should be less sickening."

"By the way," Nick said, indicating Dan's head. "I
like your new look."

"Fuck you," Dan said, and stalked away.

★★★

When he finally got home and looked in the mirror
he felt like he needed a piercing to match. There was
his tanned face, neck, and ears, and looming above
them was a butt-white dome. He wasn't the first bald
Sheriff of Park County, but he knew he was the first
to go bald in one day.

Not like he'd had any choice about shaving, not after
his hair started coming out in chunks in the shower.
He had smelled something foul as he was scrubbing
what he thought was shampoo into his head, but it
had been too late. Now each day he just had to get
it right, so he didn't look like an even bigger freak.
He never knew it would be this hard, shaving a head.
He wondered if there were special razors or clippers
for this, but he wasn't about to go to the store and
ask. He ran his hand over his shiny orb and studied
himself.

His final gift from Lyn. Maybe he should be grateful.
He could use a reminder that you couldn't just get

involved with a Doll and walk away unscathed; they made you suffer. They were all cut from the same cloth—vain, spoiled, shallow, two-faced, blood-sucking, greedy, and horny. They could all go spin themselves into a masturbating frenzy. They weren't going to fuck with him anymore.

He had more important things to concentrate on. Nothing was going to distract him. Scott Stiles and Marie were going down. They had motive to get rid of the one person who knew of their deceits. Stacey knew Marie was buying fakes and she had to know Scott had stolen Club money. Although she may have been loose with her personal life, Dan knew Stacey well enough to know she was a purist when it came to finance. She wouldn't have condoned thievery and Scott, acting like a feudal lord, had gotten rid of anything that stood in his way.

Today was the trail ride with Katherine. Hopefully she'd remember something. He'd be back looking down on his troubled valley, the valley so low...

"Hang your head over, dear, hear the wind blow."

CHAPTER FORTY

Of course she never heard a word from Dan. She didn't expect to, but Lyn was beginning to believe the joke might have been on herself. It was immature. She had been lost in fury.

Just to put her mind at ease she called Dan. She knew he would never, ever pick up, probably even if it were a 911 call. But, she left a message saying she was sorry for her spiteful behavior.

For once in a very long time, she knew the right thing to do was reconnect with Eric, to bring back even some of the thrill they had when they first married.

When he had finally come home last night after a long business trip, she had greeted him in her sexiest little nightgown that he had always liked. It was a squeeze to get it to look just right, but she wanted to try and stop the nonsense of always seeking a new lover.

When he came home he entered their bedroom. Eric had looked at her with disgust. "Did your lover just leave or what, Lyn? Why are you in that skimpy thing that barely fits you anymore?"

That line was a hard one to swallow but Lyn had come up to him anyway, to give him a warm kiss like the old days, to show her intentions were for him.

"Lyn, stop this crap. What's gotten into you?"

"I just thought we haven't been together, really together, in such a long time."

"And that time is long over, Lyn. Put something decent on. I'm tired and don't want to look at you in that, that thing. I'm going to sleep."

Lyn was now more than offended. She had put on her robe, rushed into the bathroom and sobbed. What a disgrace her marriage was—she knew Eric could hear her. He didn't come in to apologize and by the time she came to bed he was sleeping on his back grinding out loud snores.

★★★

A large network was coming to town to do a feature on Livingston. The host traveled the world on his shows. He was an Emmy-winning television personality, best-selling author and internationally renowned chef. The show's producer had asked Will to be the host's guide of the town and area for the program.

Will had called Lyn. "Hi Lyn, I'm Will Larson, I don't believe we've met, but I'm helping a TV crew who's doing a show on Livingston. I know you have one of the most well preserved sheep wagons in the area. Would it be possible to use it for the program? We'd just need an outside shot, as the host explains the way of life mostly gone by."

This must be the Will she was sure she'd seen ages ago at the white trash party with the singer. She was pretty sure he was Jean's son. "I'd be happy for you to use it."

"Mind if I come by, maybe this afternoon, to take

a look? Otherwise, just give me a time that's good for you."

"Would tomorrow morning work?" asked Lyn. Somehow she was feeling down, mostly about Eric, and for the first time she could remember, she wasn't eager to get another man into her wagon, no matter how cute he was.

"Ok, sure. Would tenish work?" asked Will.

"That'll be fine," said Lyn.

"Thanks ma'am."

"You can call me, Lyn. Do you need directions?"

"Happen to have seen that wagon before, your home is near the ninth hole on the golf course."

"Exactly. See you tomorrow."

"Sure thing."

Normally Lyn would have popped an Ativan to calm herself down about the possibility of a new lover. But where was that going to lead? She felt stuck with her marriage to Eric and felt tired of trying to find attention from other men.

Something was either really wrong with her or really right. Who had she become? She certainly didn't feel like part of the "It Couple" from Pacific Heights in San Francisco anymore. She was tired of Eric not caring, turning his head or pretending he didn't know about her affairs. She knew she loved Eric when they'd first married but that feeling of being loved had never resurfaced with them, nor had she truly received it from anyone else.

★★★

The following morning, when Will came over, Lyn was dressed simply, hardly any makeup and she was wearing a loose turtleneck with a pair of simple jeans. She hadn't seen herself look this way in a long while.

She met him outside and let him walk around her sheepherder's wagon. She didn't offer to show him the inside, her proven seduction site.

But, she did offer him to come into her home. "Would you like a cup of coffee?"

Will looked at his phone to check the time and said, "Sure."

As they walked to her house the UPS guy drove up and hopped out to hand Will a package. Will blushed. As the brown truck drove away Will said, "I think he thought I was your husband, a new driver for sure."

He handed the package to Lyn. It was addressed to Eric. Did someone really think she'd be married to a fishing guide? Secretly she was pleased.

Lyn got out a couple of mugs and quickly made them each of cup of coffee in her Keurig. They sat at the kitchen table and Will was full of stories. Most were interesting but she was especially annoyed hearing that the Antelope Club had been built on a former garbage dumping site.

"I think everyone in town knows except the members."

As if he could read the horror in her mind and what the Dolls would think, he said, "That was a long, long time ago. I'm sure they had to clean everything out before they began to develop this place."

Lyn wasn't flirting with him as she normally would

have. The days of hunting down men had ended with the Sheriff. She wasn't batting her eyes or scooting a bit closer. He was handsome though, his eyes were green and his almost gray hair was thick, combed back, creating just the right wilderness-but-cool look. He was wearing an old Pendleton blue and gray plaid button up shirt with a gray t-shirt underneath. His boots were for hunting, she supposed, surprised that he hadn't tracked in any dirt.

Will was polite and funny, too. He mentioned he had a son. "Yep, I keep reminding him to get that nut sack out of his gray matter."

Lyn knew some of the Dolls would find that statement horrifying but she could see Will was smart and witty. She felt as though she was in a new arena with him. She told him she loved to fish, shocking him, as though no known Doll was ever in the water with rod and reel. "I usually just go down to the shore. I even like to ice fish, but I can never get anyone interested in that."

"Well, you'd be surprised how much water you can cover in a boat. I'd like to take you sometime, your husband too, if he wants to come. Sort of a thank you for letting the crew film your wagon."

"No, Eric would never, ever, fish with me. But I'd like to go."

"Love to show you some new waters. Been a fishing and hunting guide most my life. I like it when I can introduce someone to land and water they've never seen before and love it when they catch a nice size fish to remember. "

His smile combined with those green eyes were sincere and she, for once, in many, many years wasn't trying to seduce him. She simply felt comfortable with him. She also felt safe, like he wasn't going to say something rude, although word had it that he was a Murray's Bar regular, and that meant he hung with the rest of the town's hunting and fishing guides, who weren't known for polite or subtle language.

"The shoot using the sheep wagon will be sometime next month," said Will, "But I'll give you plenty of notice, and meanwhile keep in touch."

Lyn smiled. He had lifted her spirits and it wasn't from a pill. She felt an old bounce in her walk when she accompanied him to the door, and it wasn't about one of her triumphant seductions.

CHAPTER FORTY-ONE

"Thank goodness John is out of town again. I would have had a hard time explaining *this*," Sophia said, motioning to her cat suit.

"Just think of it as a job. Isn't this the kind of thing you did with Nick, ingratiating yourself with people and teasing information out of them?"

"Not people with whips," said Sophia.

"People with guns are less scary than people with whips?"

"Well, since you ask...yes."

"Our purpose is to find out who Pussywhip is or was. The nature of her relationship with Polaris. Whether Polaris has been talking about anything strange or apocalyptic."

"I'd like to know how we're going to find out," said Sophia.

"It's a Monday evening, so things should be slow. Maybe they'll want to talk because there won't be as many there into the pleasure of pain."

Katherine turned up the music. She didn't like driving their huge Suburban as much as her Tahoe but the Bose sound system was just as good. It was too coincidental that Springsteen was belting *The Ties That Bind*. "Start with small talk. How long have they been going to Kinkster? We ask them if they know someone called Pussywhip, who we met at a party once. Then we fake it from there."

"And what if Michael's there?" asked Sophia.

Katherine looked out the window, not wanting Sophia to see her face. "I don't think he will be."

"Why not?"

"Because it's Monday. Big market day. He'll be in the Cave."

"What if he's stayed to hang people from hooks at Kinkster?"

Katherine had to change the subject. "Sophia, just try to block what you see and pretend it's a masquerade party. At a party, you're invincible."

"Do not let me out of your sight," warned Sophia.

Getting through the front door was not a problem. The greeter was Tay, who was hanging from the ceiling last Katherine had seen him, and she remembered his name. Sophia and she looked like they belonged. And they looked good, Katherine had to admit.

Sophia grabbed her arm with a chrome-studded leather glove. "The guy over there has an oxygen mask on, an old one, like in World War II. And the smell. What's that smell?"

"Keep moving. We're going into the room back there. Just pretend like you've seen it all before."

Men kept coming up to them and trying to start conversations, just like guys in any bar except for the collars and chains. And the masks.

A masked Zorro, complete with cape and hat, greeted Sophia. Did she hear him say, "Would you like me to embarrass you?"

Was Sophia smiling at him?

"But I am not your foe."

"Are you into the thrill?"

Sophia ran her gloved finger over the blade of Zorro's sword.

That was enough. Katherine grabbed Sophia. She looked the guy straight in the eyes and said in her best dominatrix voice, "Sorry, Zorro, she's mine." Then she kissed Sophia on the lips.

"What the hell?" asked Sophia.

"Roll with it," hissed Katherine as she pulled her toward another room.

"I'll have a double vodka on the rocks," said Sophia. She looked at Katherine with something between amusement and disgust.

"Scotch," said Katherine. "And I'm sorry about what happened in there. Everything's a game here anyway, right?"

Sophia took a long swallow of her cocktail. "But quite the interesting game. Very slashy. Have you checked out some of the outfits? They give me ideas."

"I'm not sure about you tonight."

"We're supposed to be ingratiating ourselves, aren't we? I could have asked Zorro about Pussywhip."

"Okay," said Katherine. "But I'd like to start by talking to women. They feel a bit safer."

A tall and very thin brunette with long, straight hair approached them. She had on red satin gloves, black satin shorts and a black and red bustier. "Drinking scotch, I see," she said. Then she glanced slyly at Sophia. "Alcohol makes girls so much more receptive."

"But not more teachable," said Katherine.

"Haven't seen either of you here before."

"We must have been wearing different outfits."

Sophia was certainly comfortable. "Your gloves give a new meaning to the Devil wearing Prada."

"Prouda what?"

Sophia spoke with a laugh. "Never mind. If you're a regular, then maybe you know Pussywhip?"

"Yeah, sure do. I used to see her all the time, but she hasn't been here recently. Everyone's been asking about her."

"Didn't she used to come here with Polaris?" Katherine asked.

"Yeah. He's creepy but they used to put on a good show. Really big into suspension bondage."

Katherine looked at Sophia. Here it was. Polaris and Pussywhip. "What do you remember about her?"

"She's small. Don't know about her hair color because she always wore a long black wig, same color as your hair. She was nice. Everybody liked her. Always wore theater-type outfits, not just the usual black. My favorite was her butterfly, sparkly green and blue and black, lots of jewels. She'd flutter these huge wings when Polaris put her in the harness. She made suspension look lovely. Real lovely."

"Sparkly green," said Katherine. "Did she wear a green belt, a Western-style belt, with emeralds?"

"Oh yeah," the woman said excitedly. "That was an awesome belt."

Katherine felt a jolt to her solar plexus. So she'd been right about the model at Zig's.

Sophia saw her distress and jumped in. "You made

it sound as though you don't like Polaris as much as her."

"He's been getting ugly lately. Telling people something big is about to happen and asking if they want to stay with him or be left behind."

"Big, how?"

"Oh, I don't know. His end-of-the-world doomsday—whatever. I'm always hearing somebody predicting the end of everything. I say, if it's all going to end, I might as well have fun tonight."

Katherine's head felt light. She used to think of herself as powerful, but the reality of what she was hearing made her feel small.

The woman in red kept talking. "When anyone asks him about Pussywhip he just shrugs his shoulders and acts like he doesn't care. A lot of us are starting to avoid him. He almost killed a guy once. Not cool. Not cool at all. But they say he basically supports this place. Some kind of millionaire. Heard a few days ago he called Kinkster his 'recruiting center.'"

"Recruiting?" asked Sophia.

"Says he's about to go off to some tropical paradise and take only his 'loyal playthings.' Leave the rest of us to starve or whatever. Honestly, I wouldn't touch the guy with a ten-foot bullwhip."

A fully tattooed woman with nothing on but a face-mask and ankle chains came up to the brunette and they started a conversation, leaving Katherine and Sophia alone.

"You okay?" asked Sophia quietly.

"I don't know," said Katherine. "I think I got my

answer. She said Pussywhip wore a green western belt. That makes me wonder if Pussywhip was Stacey."

"Maybe we should go."

"No. There's more we have to learn. But I could use some air."

She stood up and led Sophia out of the room. They found themselves in an empty passageway with a door at the other end. As they started toward it, the door opened and Michael stepped through, unmasked.

Katherine's and Michael's eyes met. He was dressed differently from before, no mask but skin-tight leather pants adorned with chains and an open vest over a torso sporting quite a few new bruises and abrasions, a noose in his hand. He started walking slowly toward her.

After him came two others, Tay and his sumo-shaped friend Abraxas.

"Well, Michael Hawthorne," Sophia said with mock cheer. "Fancy meeting you..."

In a snake-swift movement, Michael whipped the noose over her head and pulled it tightly.

Sophia froze. Katherine saw rage in his eyes, as though he could kill her for using her real name. But with the rope around her throat and three men in front of her, there wasn't much she could do.

"Let her go," said Katherine, as steadily as she could.

He looked them over like they were a fresh meal and played with the rope in his hand. Katherine saw that it had a second noose on the other end. "You weren't leaving, were you? I've been watching you since you first came in. That was such a kiss you gave our beautiful Sophia. I'd like to see that again."

Katherine stepped back, but she bumped into the mass of Abraxas. He held her as Michael slipped the other noose over Katherine's head, clearly a coordinated move.

"My friends," he said with a grin. "I'd like you to meet my wife, Hellbitch. And her friend, Queen Diva. I think you're going to enjoy getting to know them."

Katherine pulled out of Abraxas' grasp, but as she did, the noose tightened. She saw Sophia's eyes widen as the rope bit deeper into her.

"This is a double noose," Michael purred. "If one of you moves, the slip knot tightens on the other. It's good for togetherness." He took hold of the knot in the middle and pulled them toward the door he'd come through.

Katherine thought of yelling for help but didn't know what that would bring, especially with Tay and Abraxas watching her impassively but steadily.

"Now, be quiet and come with us. You've lived such limited lives until tonight. We're about to stretch your horizons."

"Michael, cut it out," Katherine said. "You owe me an explanation. What was going on with you and Stacey?"

Michael flushed red at that. "I don't owe you anything!"

"Michael, take this noose off us right now," Katherine said levelly, "or I am going to call the Sheriff."

That shook Tay and Abraxas out of their robotic

silences.

"Sheriff?" Abraxas said uneasily.

"Polaris, what does she mean?"

"To hell with the Sheriff!" Michael snarled. "He's not the Sheriff over here in Belgrade anyway. Idiots, primitives, forget them all. No one can touch me, haven't you learned that yet?"

Which is when Sophia kicked him in the balls. He dropped the noose and doubled over. Sophia backhanded his face with her studded glove, tearing his skin. Tay moved as if to grab her, but a nervous Abraxas restrained him. Katherine quickly brought her head close to Sophia's, loosened the knot, and jerked the noose over her head.

Michael looked up at them, murderous hatred in his eyes.

"Get those bitches," he snarled to the two men.

Sophia started banging on the wall. "Get us out of here! Get us out of here!" Katherine had never heard her voice that loud, but somehow she wasn't surprised.

Both doors of the passageway were blocked by other minions of Michael's, meaning she needed a distraction. Katherine shot her phone overhead. The screen showed a call in progress. "I'm glad I thought to put Sheriff Dan Bentley's number in my favorites," she said.

One of the men ripped off his mask. "Polaris, what in god's name is going on?"

"Polaris is stepping aside to let us leave," Katherine said.

He did not step aside, but Katherine and Sophia pushed past him, one on either side, and strode to the door.

Sophia tossed a grin to the shocked, pudgy guy holding his gas mask. "In god's name," she said as she pointed her finger, "I like that."

As they stepped into the parking lot, Katherine had to put a black-gloved hand on the roof of a car to steady herself.

"I think it's time we got out of here," Sophia said.

"You drive," Katherine breathed.

Sophia gestured at the phone still in Katherine's hand as they threw themselves into the car. "Dan didn't answer?"

"Oh, right," said Katherine, "That was my horse vet's number."

"I like your style," Sophia laughed. She pulled out of the parking lot with a spray of gravel. Katherine thought she looked strangely invigorated.

Their breaths began to calm down as Sophia pulled them onto the interstate. "So," she said. "Holy shit."

"Yeah, holy shit," said Katherine. "Michael and Stacey."

"Still a lot to be answered, though."

"Yeah. But now I'm determined to find out."

Sophia smiled. "After tonight, I guess you could say we're bound and determined."

CHAPTER FORTY-TWO

Michael had come home to an empty house, as he expected. He knew the bitch wouldn't confront him. She would be hiding out with her cunt-friend Sophia. He had plenty of time to pack everything he needed for his final trip to Lolo.

His final trip. He had been looking forward to it for so long, never expecting it to come so soon. It was time, though. It was too big of a gamble to stay with the original timeline. Katherine knew the truth about Pussywhip, something he hadn't counted on.

He copied the latest version of his plan of operation on to a flash drive so he could update it on his MacBook on the flight to Lolo. Then he started a hard-drive wipe. Even if anyone decided to look at his home computers, they'd find nothing on them. Or, at least, it would take them so long that he'd be out of the country before they did.

He bounced the flash drive in his palm and smiled. There was something perversely fitting about using such a primitive instrument to convey data that was going to throw the entire world into chaos. A little gadget you could pick up at a local hardware store contained the script for the future of global finance.

He heard the garage door open. Then the familiar click of her boots stepping on the hardwood of the first floor. Her steps were coming up the stairs, straight toward him. She was alone. He looked forward to watching terror fill her eyes when she saw him.

She was at the doorway to his office a moment later. She came in and smiled.

That threw him off, which made him angry. "What are *you* doing here?" he yelled. His voice betrayed a strain, and that made him angrier still.

"Is that any way to greet your wife?" she asked. "By the way, I'm not here to talk about the 'rupture' in our relationship."

She shot him her country club glare while flipping back her hair. Her smile didn't waver. It was her professional smile, her social smile, confident and warm. He was impressed at how well she could pretend.

"I need answers to some questions, Michael," she said. "Or should I call you Polaris? Whatever makes you more comfortable."

"You can call me whatever you like," he said, smiling back at her. He was conscious of his own smile feeling tight, more like a grimace. "May I call you Hellbitch? It suits you so well."

He couldn't believe he was wasting his time talking to Katherine. He had more important things to deal with right now. He had to get to Lolo.

Katherine dropped the smile. "Why'd you do it?"

"Do what?"

"*Why* did you kill Stacey?"

"You're delusional."

"I can see why you would have strangled her." Her voice was unsettlingly calm. "But why would you

289

have her house blown up? That doesn't sound very erotic."

She stood just a few feet in front of him. Three quick steps and he could have his hands around her throat. "What are you playing at, Katherine?"

"Stacey knew something, didn't she? Something about your investments that you absolutely can't allow the world to discover."

Three quick steps.

"Oh, by the way," said Katherine with a phony nonchalance, "I hope you don't mind that I invited Dan over. He could be here any minute."

Word was that the big, brainless bull would do anything he was told to do by whatever rich bitch he was fucking that week. It was probably Katherine at the moment. After years with a man so superior to her, she probably enjoyed having a virile imbecile to manipulate. He stared at her.

"Sweetheart, you look awfully pale," she said. "I'm worried that you haven't gotten enough sleep lately."

He had to get out. He knew she had nothing but postulations, but she and the Sheriff could delay him. He couldn't afford delays now. He shoved her violently aside and headed for their bedroom.

"You...stay out of my way," Michael said.

★★★

After her run-in with Michael, Katherine had gone straight to the equestrian center to meet Dan for their trail ride up to the peak. Her horse, Triumph, was always calming.

Dan had trailered his horse, Newman, to the Club's center. He could have ridden one of the horses Clint had right there. When he'd called yesterday to confirm their ride, he'd told her that riding a different horse was like eating dinner out. It could be convenient, but sometimes it just felt better to stay home. And home for him was in his own saddle on his own horse.

"Dan," she said, looking at what should have been his hairline under the brim of his hat. "Did you shave your head?"

He shot her a look that could have felled a medium-sized deer. "Let's not talk about my head," he said curtly.

She felt slapped. On another day, she knew she would have asked Dan what was going on, but she was in no state for another confrontation.

Dan said nothing as he urged Newman up the trail, not even looking back to make sure she was following. That was fine; she had to give most of her attention to Triumph, anyway. He wasn't as composed as usual and was fretting like a two-year-old gelding, bobbing his head up and down and trying to take the lead on the trail. Most likely he was picking up on her nervousness.

After a while Dan turned on her with a scowl. "Use a firmer hand," he said. "A horse needs to know who's boss."

"I know how to ride, Sheriff."

"Do you? You're riding like a summer tourist right now."

"Is that why you asked me up here? To give me a

hard time?"

He shook his head in annoyance. "Set your reins lower and hold your hands down. Pull back a little so he can feel the tension in the bit."

"He can probably feel what's going on with me," said Katherine. "I'm not in the calmest mood."

"Oh, I know," Dan said. "You've had a lot of extremely serious issues to deal with lately."

"Trust me," she said. "I have." She wondered why the foul mood. This was hard on her to go up the trail where she'd last seen Stacey.

"Uh-huh."

They'd only been riding thirty minutes or so, but to Katherine it felt like a long couple of hours.

"This is where Stacey and I stopped for lunch."

They pulled off into a little clearing under some trees. Dan was off Newman in a split second. Katherine followed. Triumph exhaled as if to say, "About time." Dan's horse hadn't even broken a sweat.

Dan had brought along his saddlebags and removed a little brown sack. He pulled out his paper notebook from his front shirt pocket and read it in silence. He bit off some jerky and took a long swig of his Diet Pepsi. He didn't offer to share.

Katherine drank water.

Not looking up from his notes he said, "You reported you could see the valley from where you and she were sitting. Must have been over here."

He walked over to the edge. She had purposely stopped short of it because she didn't want to see Stacey's house.

"And you say she acted as though she were troubled."

Katherine thought his tone was softer, but only because it was extremely professional. Well, better than him acting like a dick.

"More than troubled. Frightened. As if she knew something very big was going down." She paused, then decided she couldn't wait any longer. "Dan, I think she was right. I think something is happening, something truly huge. Not fraud-in-the-Antelope-Club huge. Like globally huge."

But she could tell Dan was drifting alone inside his head. "Someone set her up," he said.

Dan sat deep in the dirt as if it was most natural thing to do. He pulled his chewing tobacco out of his shirt pocket. He dug a pile of the gooey looking brown stuff out with his fingers and pushed the whole mess into the side of his cheek, making himself look like a lopsided chipmunk.

"Hey," she said, "I need you to listen to me."

"You know," he said, with words muffled by the wad, "from up here everything looks pretty much the same as before your Antelope Club showed up. But everything is different now. Completely different."

"Dan."

"We never had the kind of crime we do now. We had drunks, fights and a few car break-ins. But you people are bringing a kind of theft and exploitation like nothin' we ever thought of, a new kind of violence. Not much different than what the original settlers did to the Natives."

She hated being grouped with "you people."

"Dan, you don't know what *kind* of brutality is out there. Michael's into something terrible."

"Is this about your husband's sexual preferences?"

He looked at her with a scorn that made her blood boil. "For god's sake, I'm not *talking* about his sexual predilections! I believe he's involved in something that could be horrific—economically devastating—and I think he may have killed Stacey because of it." *There, she finally said it out loud.*

He looked as though he wanted to laugh at her but forced his voice to stay even. "Has he said anything specifically to the effect that he was involved with Stacey's death?"

"No, but..."

"Did he ever threaten to kill her?"

"I wouldn't know," Katherine snapped. "But he tried to kill me!"

"When?"

"At that club."

Dan paused, then continued in a sarcastic tone, "He did something violent to you at the S&M club you accompanied him to?"

"Dan, this isn't a game! Michael's dangerous!"

"If you feel unsafe, you should get out of your house." He finally seemed to be taking her seriously, but he was still keeping his tone infuriatingly businesslike. "Stay with one of your friends. You can file a report on any threatening behavior he's engaged in, and if..."

"This isn't about my safety! He was involved with Stacey on a lot of levels."

He snapped at her. "Just because he was having an

affair with her doesn't mean he killed her. By that logic, most of the valley could have killed her."

"You wanted me to help you with the investigation of Stacey's death. Well, I'm giving you a lead you'd be a fool to ignore."

"I have plenty of leads," he said. "They all point in one direction."

"You mean Scott and Marie. You're going to follow that trail until it dead ends?"

"I don't follow dead-end trails."

"In the meantime, Michael could be..." She fumbled for words.

"He could be what? Katherine, if you can't answer that..."

She turned on her heel and stalked back to Triumph.

"Where are you going?" Dan called. "This ride isn't over."

Katherine tightened Triumph's cinches with two quick tugs. "Sorry, Sheriff. I'm afraid it is."

She never looked back as she rode down the trail.

★★★

No one took off on him like that. He flew down the mountain and pulled his horse up next to hers, cutting her off in a whirl of dust. She pulled back the reins and wiped her eyes.

"What?"

"Look, I'm sorry. I *was* listening to you." Dan did feel genuinely bad.

"Thanks, but I don't think you *heard* me."

He dismounted and pulled Newman to the side.

"Get off your horse, please." Working against her wasn't going to help. Despite her haughty attitude, she dismounted. They stood face to face.

"You think you know it all because you're from New York. You think the city way is the only way. That your approach is the only approach. It's your assumed superiority that clashes with life out here."

Katherine look bewildered, as if no one had ever described her like that before, and it certainly wasn't who she wanted to be. He was grouping her with the rest of the Club.

He broke into a whisper, "Move slowly toward me." A huge rattler came out from the boulder right behind Katherine.

She took two steps and with one slick move he pulled the gun out of his holster and shot it in the head. Katherine jumped at the sound.

"It's over. Don't worry."

Dan took his jack knife out and cut the remnants of the head off, then went into his saddlebag and grabbed an old cotton flour sack.

As he picked up the pit viper, Katherine watched. "I remember seeing timber rattlesnakes in summer camp when I was young, but I never saw one this closely."

He put the snake inside and tied it tightly. It was still moving. "Ever eaten a snake? This rattler will make a fine appetizer before buffalo or elk stew. Tastes just like chicken without the bones."

"I'll have to request it at Sophia's next get together." She smiled. Something had opened in her, he could tell. Her mood seemed to soften, so he motioned to a fallen log and Katherine followed.

"Let's make a truce. I'm going to look into what you're saying about your husband. Just please try to respect the Montana way."

"Which is what?"

He knew he was sporting his John Wayne, big cowboy grin as he pointed to the landscape below. "It's about people counting for who they are, not for what they have. And it's about the pureness and the essence of all the nature that surrounds us."

She looked out down into the valley.

"Do me a favor, Katherine. Hold on to this picture. It can live inside of you if you give it a chance."

"You may not know it, but I've been trying. It's ominous beauty is like nothing else, anywhere."

"Give yourself time." When she looked at him he thought he saw a glint of admiration, but just for a second.

CHAPTER FORTY-THREE

The markets would go down, but not Michael, and he was thrilled. His plan was simple. It was a coordinated algorithm that would stampede all the exchanges. His algos would give commands for his computers to start the huge dump, selling off major chunks of stable stocks, like 3M, PepsiCo and Microsoft. If 3M were selling at ninety-eight dollars a share he would sell huge positions in minutes, pushing it to sixty, then fifty, forty and down to twenty. This would trample the markets creating a domino effect that would reduce value and create the immediate sale of massive international stocks, the biggest short in the history of finance.

He had made sure he could bypass all the exchange clearances and safeguards with ease due to his powerful position and credit worthiness in the markets. As he sold off gigantic bundles of reliable global stocks, worldwide panic would start. Traders would see the markets fall and, like always, think they were plummeting because of some event outside their knowledge. It was so damn simple. So that investors wouldn't think it was a tech anomaly, he would explain the panic with his simultaneously prescheduled phony news blurbs and tweets that would bombard the planet over and over again. Glorious retweets of North Korea dropping a little nuke.

The emergency phone rang.

"I don't care if it takes a hundred land crews to clear it up! Get them out there and get it done now!"

He pounded the off button on his satellite phone and threw it next to his seat in the copter. *Fuck.* Everything was conspiring to make this difficult. He'd only had time to pack one bag of essentials from the house, meaning he would have to come back to the valley one more time after nailing everything down in Lolo.

All her fault, of course. He had everything laid out neatly in front of him but now his wife, the Hellbitch, was sniffing too closely, forcing him to speed up his timeline.

When he first called Rick and said he needed the chopper, the fool had insisted he couldn't because he was under stand-by orders from Mr. Stiles that day. Michael had told him that Scott Stiles was in no position to refuse him anything, but the simple-minded could not be reasoned with, and ultimately Michael had to waste time calling Stiles himself. He had lit into the smug bastard, made it clear that he was to instruct his employees that Mr. Hawthorne's needs always had priority, but it hadn't brought him much release.

Forty-eight hours. The new H-hour, the soonest he could see it all coming together. Nearly one hundred and eighty-nine hours ahead of the original target.

He had work to do. A timeline to re-plot. He pulled out his MacBook and dug in his pocket for his flash drive. It wasn't there, which meant he must have dropped it into the pocket of his jacket, which he'd folded up and stashed in the back when he'd switched to heavy down for the flight. He unbuckled and started to climb from his seat when the phone rang.

It was his chief engineer again. He sounded scared. "Sir, there's a problem. While the crews were digging into the pipeline a fire erupted in the manhole, causing a secondary failure. We'll have to fly people in. They say they need your personal authorization to do that."

"*Fuck!*" Michael slammed the phone hard against his thigh. "*FUCK!*" He pounded himself with the phone again and again. The pain helped him think.

Rick glanced at him worriedly.

"Pay attention to your job," Michael barked, and began stabbing numbers into the phone. He was surrounded by worthless morons. He was clearly going to have to supervise every detail himself.

CHAPTER FORTY-FOUR

Lyn didn't expect to hear from Will so quickly, but he had called and asked her if she'd like to go on a float to fly fish down the Yellowstone River.

"Of course! I'd love to go. When?"

"Well, the wind should be dying down, so how about we go today at eleven-thirty? Meet me at Carter's Bridge and we can ferry a car."

Lyn wasn't exactly sure what ferrying a car meant; maybe the services that had your car ready to drive home after a day on the river? But she knew where the Carter's Bridge fishing access sight was. "Sure, I'll be there. Do I bring my rod?"

"No need. I've got it covered along with a little lunch in case we get hungry. You have a license right?"

"Of course." He had no idea how much she loved to fish, just like the other Dolls couldn't understand her love of an arched rod.

"Wear your wading boots. The water's chilly."

At least he had given her credit for having gear, even though sometimes it was tough to know which fly to use, what knot, and which rod, as conditions could change so quickly along the river. Lyn knew Stacey used to hire guides to fish the Yellowstone but this was her first time in a boat. It had taken her forever to perfect her skills, as fly fishing was difficult compared to bait fishing in California's Toulumne River, where she had gone as a child with her father.

She soon understood "ferrying," as they'd left her car at Mayors Landing and drove back to Carter's bridge to launch his boat.

"We're fishing this stretch because with the conditions, there are more fish toward town," said Will.

Lyn was impressed with the way he handled the boat. He was super strong for his medium-build body size. She wasn't going to flatter him with compliments as she did the other men who she wanted to be her lovers. But she did say, "Looks like it takes a lot of strength to maneuver your boat in this current."

"I've been a guide for decades and was a lumberjack up in Washington. When you're constantly working, the strength stays with you."

"But you grew up in Livingston?"

"Sure did. Bet you know my mom, Jean Larson. She's as stubborn as me, I suppose. Would not let those rich fuckers take away her property, no matter the exorbitant fee they offered. Strong genes run in the family. I always thought I'd be a rancher and keep the family business going. Know my mom wanted me to, but after seeing my father killed by a piece of machinery, I didn't want to have a thing to do with farming."

Will handed her a rod. "See that water over there to your right, about two feet from the shore? That's where I want you to put the fly."

She steadied herself in the bow to cast, but the fly landed away from her intended spot.

"Not bad, but let me show you. You're breaking your wrist. You're raising your rod too far back before you throw it forward."

Will threw the anchor down and came up behind her to show her where to stop the line, right above her head before casting it into the water. Lyn could feel the heat coming off his body, warm and strong when they practiced. Next cast she threw herself.

"Now that's more like it."

She could see there was some admiration there and soon as the line hit the water she felt a bite and then the thrill of the pull on the rod. *Yes!*

"Let him run. Give him line. You've got a good size brown on there. Keep your rod tip up but give him slack. That's it. Now let him run a bit more."

Lyn was excited but she knew if she didn't bring the fish to the boat it wouldn't be counted as a true catch and release.

"Ok, now you can start reeling in, but slowly and don't drop your rod tip."

This was thrilling. All she had to do was listen to what Will was saying and it was working. The fish hadn't broken the line. She could feel he was bigger than her normal catches from shore. "What do I do next?" She knew her voice sounded shrill, but she was so excited.

"Just pull the leader in slowly with your left hand. That's it, keep pulling. There he is. He's on the side of the boat now."

Will lifted the fish up in his net. "Look at that! A two-pound brown trout, king of the river." He quickly removed the barbless hook and released him back into the water.

Lyn was elated. "That was the biggest fish I've ever caught out here. Thank you!"

He lifted his sunglasses so she could see those green eyes. "No, you caught it. But it's not always like this. You were very lucky early on."

Lyn had never felt this way about a man. She felt a tenderness for him, and it wasn't about seduction.

"Are you cold?" he asked. "How bout we stop for lunch?"

Lunch was in the boat. Will had brought an assortment of cheeses, salamis, crackers and fruit along with a bottle of wine. He used his pocket knife and served lunch on a paper towel.

"I just have to tell you how very pretty you are. You should see what you look like out here in the boat."

Lyn could just imagine, her hair must be a flying mess and she had put on more sunscreen than makeup. It was minimal. "Thought there was no point in layering on the makeup." She felt she could be herself around Will.

"I like that natural look." He began unscrewing what looked to be a very old bottle of wine. "I've been saving this bottle that my writer friend gave to me. Wanted to wait to drink it with someone special."

So maybe he did like her, but in a natural friendly way. He wasn't coming on to her, he was just pleasant, funny and considerate. When she asked if they'd be floating by a restroom, he laughed.

"They're all around you. Just go up and pick a place

away from the river to pee."

"I've never done this before. Those boulders over there look difficult to navigate."

He was out of the boat in seconds. "Here, give me your hand. I'll walk you up to a good spot and look away."

True to his word, he took her up to a safe looking area behind some bushes. He took something out of his pocket. "You might need this."

"Toilet paper." She laughed. "Why didn't I remember that? I had tissues in my purse," Will seemed to think of everything, so unlike all the men who thought of themselves first. It was so comforting.

After they got back in the boat and finished lunch, they floated through town. It was quiet and peaceful. She didn't catch a thing but some fish had come up and rolled over to take a look at the fly. One got on but broke off.

"What did I do wrong?"

"Nothing. It was a medium sized rainbow trout. Sometimes it just happens. Hey, would you like to come over to my house sometime for a wild game meal? The place is very small and plain. I live in town."

"I'd love to come over." She could see his grin, like she had just told him the very best thing he could ever hear.

"Better yet, how about tonight, fireside. I'll cook most of the meal and bring it up to my buddy's ranch and we can have dinner by the fire pit."

It was just a little soon, but truthfully the way she felt with him made her feel safe. "Sure, I'd love to come. What can I bring?"

"Do you have an old sleeping bag?"

Lyn looked at him with a smile and said, "No. I haven't been around a campfire since college days when a group of us would go to Lake Tahoe. Even then, we slept in a cabin on the lake."

"Then just bring yourself."

This was certainly new for Lyn; she was not the huntress, she wasn't even trying to lock him up into her cage of lust. For the first time, in a very long time, she felt valued, a gift she hadn't unwrapped in many, many years.

★★★

After a change into warmer clothing, Lyn met Will at his house. She'd never known anyone with such a small and simple home, but being with Will as a friend was all she wanted. They drove for what seemed like a long while on dirt roads until they reached the campsite on the ranch. In minutes Will had the campfire going strong. The dinner was fabulous, lamb and a simple salad. It was so comforting to just sit and talk. Will was full of stories about his writer clients who used fishing on the river to clear their minds.

★★★

She too felt clear and vibrant and could never remember having a male friend without the pressure of needing to seduce him. She sensed she was appreciated for whom she was with no strings attached.

She invited Will over the following evening. She'd

never had a man in her home when Eric was gone
—except for her rendezvouses outside in the sheep
herder's wagon. She felt no need to push her vavoom
look and wore a simple t-shirt and jeans.

She offered him a drink but he quickly grabbed
Eric's Grey Goose magnum of vodka and hit it pretty
hard. It was a limited edition and the wings of birds
closed the top of the collector's bottle. This one would
be a hard one to replace. She wondered if Eric would
notice if she refilled it with something inferior. You
couldn't even buy this type around Livingston.

The more Will drank, the more he began to transform into someone else, someone she didn't like
as much. "You know all these rich fuckers around
Diamond Peak here are full of shit. Look at that
diamond on your finger. It's worth more than all I
own or could ever hope to own."

Lyn looked at him like he was another person.
"The Dolls, as you call yourselves, are just expensive
jeweled cunts. I hate being cunted, lied to and manipulated. I suppose you're one of them."

That was enough for Lyn. "Will, it's time to go,"
she said.

"Oh I'll be going alright." He grabbed his baseball
hat and hustled out the door.

★★★

Lyn sat there stunned and confused. No one had
ever talked to her like that; she couldn't help it as
she began to cry. He was downright disrespectful and
rude; is this what he thought about her all along? Lyn

was back to her Ativan. She had to sleep this one off.

★★★

The following morning, she slept in later than usual until she heard the doorbell ring. She sleepily opened the door to find the Will with a huge bunch of wild baby's breath flowers.

"I'm sorry about last evening. I picked these awhile back, saving them for someone special."

An apology was something she hadn't heard from a man in a long while.

"Thank you, Will."

With a sheepish smile he said, " I've got a client coming soon. But I wanted you to have these."

"They're beautiful. I had no idea they grow in the wild."

"Sure do." With a genuine smile and quick wave the outdoorsman hopped into his vehicle and was gone as quickly as a fish grabbed a fly.

Lyn had heard that he was always slightly drunk but he wasn't that way on the river, or at the campfire. She knew he drank hard with the guys, but Will was natural. He said things and did things as the ideas flew into his mind. Although Will probably had no idea, Lyn knew baby's breath signified lasting love or in his case, innocence in the wild. Faults and all, it was great to know not every man had to be a sexual conquest. Refreshingly, she knew Will was still her friend.

CHAPTER FORTY-FIVE

"So, you talked to your guy in New York?" asked Dan.

"Yep," replied Nick, as he leaned back in one of Dan's office chairs.

"Okay, so Allen's been digging more and he found all this crazy financial shit in Scott's background. There were loans taken out and money squirreled away, which he starts defaulting on. Then the usual stunts, new loans to keep paying the interest on the old loans, until he's built himself a regular house of cards."

"He was developing a chain of Antelope Clubs all over the world."

"So, how does he not go bankrupt last year?"

"That's where it gets interesting. The Club got a huge loan from Credit Luxembourg, September 15th, paying off—get this—every single loan he was carrying in full, plus a nice chunk for more operating capital."

"That's a lot of cash."

"Three hundred million. But a couple of months later he's out of operating cash. He gets another loan. Smaller, but the paying entity is listed as the 'Antelope Preservation Fund,' which I assume is someone's lame idea of a joke. But this was no gift. He's paying money back to this fund at numbers that make me think he's paying over thirty percent interest."

"Who charges that kind of rate?"

"Here's the next part. Around the same time, he starts moving the Antelope Club assets away from Morgan Stanley and Goldman Sachs and the rest of them and over to an investor I've never heard of, The Munch Group. Absolutely no idea what they're about, no information on them out there. Soon enough this Munch has every cent of Antelope investments. Not to mention Stiles's personal fortune."

"But the name Munch doesn't appear in the official books at all, at least not to my memory," Dan said, leafing through the case file in front of him.

"This Munch pays some heavy dividends, way higher returns than most investment groups."

"I met a guy down at Chico the other afternoon, John Whitefield," said Nick, "I'm sure you know, he's Sophia's husband." Dan thought he saw a sudden look of sadness or longing on Nick's face, but it passed in a moment. "Anyhow, we got to talking and it turns out he's been trying to get his investment back from Stiles, but Stiles says he doesn't have access to it. I'm wondering if Stiles doesn't have access to his own money. You think Stiles would be dumb enough to fall into a scam just because he's getting high returns?"

"He's stupid, but I didn't think he was that stupid." Dan was excited now. This was far different than any case he'd ever worked and his mind was racing.

"They have his money so they'd hold all the power, that's for sure. Maybe they're moving money in some weird way," said Nick. "Or maybe they want control over this place, or over Stiles, for some other reason."

Things were looking worse and worse for Scott, but that didn't surprise Dan. This looked like prison-term stuff, if they could pin down the details, more than enough motive for him to have killed Stacey if he thought she was going to expose him. But now there was something else, somebody else, lurking in the background.

"Tell your guy to keep digging," Dan replied. "See if you can link this Antelope Fund and the Munch Group at any point. I'll see if I can find out anything about either of them. There's an empty desk outside my office. You should set up shop there for a while. I've got some more details I'm going to run by you."

Sure, Nick was the one cracking open this information, but Dan was still in charge of the investigation and felt good giving orders. "Hey, Beef, bring me in last night's reports." He knew, with the PI there or not, he was running this operation.

CHAPTER FORTY-SIX

Katherine was sitting in the driveway in her recently repaired Tahoe, watching her house. She had seen a helicopter heading northwest when she was on the trail. Still, she wanted to feel sure he was gone before she walked through the door. She knew she had the strength to play it cool again, but she questioned whether that would work on Michael a second time. At last she took a deep breath and opened the front door.

She was barely inside when she heard a knock. It startled Katherine, but when she looked, it was Jean. She had stopped by to tell her about one of the Wednesday Pine Rider's husband's dying and Jean wanted to see if she could attend the service with her. Jean could read Katherine's face.

"Katherine, I know something is going on with you. Is it more than Michael?"

Jean wasn't one to pry, so she must have looked pretty frazzled.

"It's that easy to see, huh? There is. It's way more than marital things. I'm getting worried, wondering if everything is connected. I know that sounds cryptic. Anyway, I'm going to stay with Sophia tonight after one of her parties."

"Now, you listen to me," said Jean. "If there is anything, anything, where I can help, I'll be there for you. You know I know the Sheriff. You know I know this country. Don't do something foolish. Got it?"

"Got it."

"I want you to promise. This whole Stacey murder has me worried too, so count me in."

"Ok. If I need help, I promise."

"And you better let me know what's going on."

Katherine hugged Jean but could feel her stiffen; her hard Montana pride wasn't exactly warm and fuzzy. "I will. I promise. "

Jean looked her straight in the eyes. "Ok, then." She turned and walked out the door.

After she left in her usual abrupt-Jean style, Katherine quickly took a shower, did her face and threw together a few days' worth of outfits and toiletries for Sophia's.

She was at the door, about to leave, when she decided she should make at least a token effort to dress for the "sipping" party Sophia was throwing that afternoon. Even drunk and lost in self-obsession, the Dolls had state-of-the-art radar for the nuances of wardrobe choices. If Katherine looked as though she hadn't dressed for the event, they would suspect something was wrong and start quietly or not so quietly, grilling her. What had Sophia told her about this party? Boas, that was it. Everyone would be wearing a feather boa, because, of course, everyone owned a boa. Katherine had one in the back of her closet from some forgotten Halloween costume.

She stood before the mirror, trying to get her untamed feathers to look presentable on top of her black skirt and crisp, structured top. She draped it into a loop around her neck and tried tossing it would-be casually over one shoulder, but it looked ridiculous any way she positioned it. She knew the others would be wearing theirs in perfect style. She tried wrapping it tightly around her neck.

She thought of Michael and jerked it loose, walking toward the bathroom to put the finishing touches on her lipstick.

From her vantage point, she could see the doorway to Michael's office. Still open. She went in, not looking for anything, not snooping. Somehow she just wanted one last look at that room, maybe to reassure herself that all this insanity was real.

She stood there a moment. She hadn't noticed before how cold and impersonal Michael's idea of a workspace was. She couldn't even sense his presence in it anymore, for good or ill. She turned to go. As she did so, she glanced down. Something on the floor, small, black, and rectangular, nearly hidden behind one of the legs of the desk.

She reached down.

It was a flash drive.

She remembered him holding the drive when she'd entered the room the last time. Something he'd just copied so he could take it with him. He must have dropped it sometime during their fight.

She held it and took a deep breath. It was probably nothing, probably just more porn. But she wouldn't know for sure unless she opened it.

She went back into their bedroom and turned on

her computer. It seemed as though nothing had ever turned on more slowly. By the time her laptop came up she felt almost dizzy. She popped in the flash drive. She shook her head as she braced herself for a graphic onslaught. Then she opened it.

It was locked. An encryption application kept her from even seeing the files. Why would Michael suddenly lock a drive full of porn? But copying it right before he left, when he'd seemed so full of urgency...

She dug through her handbag for her phone.

★★★

Katherine knew that few people, if any, would be able to crack one of Michael's codes. Definitely no one in Paradise Valley, probably even the whole state of Montana. The only one she could imagine being able to do it was Jack Weber.

Jack was a master of HFT code, and as a security analyst he had formerly written software encryptions. Outside of Michael, he was the one certifiable software geniuses she knew. She knew he had appreciated all of her help. Plus, she had saved him in a big way by getting him to pull out of the markets before the crash happened.

"For you," he said, "anything. How soon can you send it to me?"

Of course he wasn't even going to ask about the legality of opening Michael's flash drive. "I should be able to get it out by FedEx today. You'll have it tomorrow."

"Great," said Jack. "I've got a couple other hot items

going right now but I'll get to it ASAP."

"Jack. No. Take a look at it the second you get it. Please. I know I'm asking a lot, but this could be urgent. I can't explain yet, but I'm terrified that something very bad is going to happen."

There was a silence on the line.

"Jack?"

"Katherine. Are you in some kind of danger?"

"I may be. I don't know. Jack, please just see what's on that drive."

"Katherine Hawthorne is finally afraid of her husband. Shit. I always told you there was something seriously not right about him. If you tell me what it is..."

"I'll tell you everything once I know a little more. I'll probably even admit you were right about Michael all along. But I can't now. Crack that lock, Jack. As quickly as you possibly can. Please."

"Ok. I'll get my team on it," he said. "We'll work all night if we have to."

She heard the excitement in his voice. The sweet perks of reciprocity. This was his chance for Michael's payback fuck, although he'd never mention it.

"Thank you. So much."

It was past the official cut-off time for FedEx pick-ups in the valley, so she assumed she'd have to drive quickly into Livingston. The guy on the phone took her urgency seriously—Katherine assumed she must have sounded differently from the usual Doll with a FedEx "emergency"—and he knew that the truck was running late with its drop offs, so he agreed to radio the driver. Katherine gave him Sophia's address.

By the time she had finally arrived at Sophia's, some of the "Sisters Who Sip" had already turned into the "Girls Who Guzzle."

Sophia scanned her. "Here's your glass. Would you prefer scotch?"

"No, wine is fine."

Katherine couldn't believe Sophia had each guest's initials etched into a wine glass. She handed her a golden linen cocktail napkin with "Sisters Who Sip" embroidered in white Edwardian Script. Ice sculptures of goddesses and grapes adorned the tables.

Sophia cocked an eyebrow to ask if there was anything Katherine needed to tell her, but Katherine shook her head.

"Well, you are just in time," Sophia said, not missing a beat in her party banter. "Marie's drinking is unprecedented."

"Marie's here? That's a shock."

"I think she needed the support of the sisterhood," Sophia said with a smirk, leading Katherine through the great room and toward the stairs. "Of course, the others are quite eager to show their compassion."

The party had drifted to one of Sophia's smaller downstairs rooms, where Marie was the center of attention. She sat on a couch, holding court with the twenty Dolls who variously sat and stood around her, clearly attending to everything she said without wanting to seem too obvious.

"You're all my best friends. My very, very, *very* best

friends." She was sloppy drunk, more than Marie ever let herself get in public. But there was something else Katherine had never seen on that plastic face of hers: a humble, almost pathetic, hunger for approval. "You know I'm a good person no matter what anyone says. Don't you?"

If she'd intended the last two words to sound rhetorical, she hadn't managed it.

"What's going on?" whispered Katherine to Alissa.

"I'm glad you're here. I really need to talk to you, Katherine—obviously not right now," Alissa whispered back. Then, in a louder voice Alissa continued, "What's going on, is that she's in deep, deep trouble and she wants us all to feel sorry for her."

"Not like we haven't heard her sob stories before," said Lyn. "She's always moaning about how she either can't keep an employee or can't keep a lover. Oh, wait. Those are the same thing, aren't they?"

Alissa and Lyn snickered.

Marie suddenly noticed Katherine. "You know I wouldn't do anything like that, don't you, Katherine?"

Katherine knelt in front of Marie and looked her right in her glazed eyes. "Marie, what do they say you've done?"

Marie closed her eyes and shook her head. Her oddly silent sobs made her shoulders bounce up and down like kids on a trampoline.

The wail seemed to explode from Marie. "I could never kill her! I could never kill anybody!"

The Dolls went quite still at that.

Marie clutched Katherine's hand and entreated her

with her red, wet eyes. "Of course I hated her. We all hated her." She looked around the room with sudden anger. "We did! You know we did! You all hated her!"

"Marie, has someone accused you of killing Stacey?"

"I would never, I could never, I couldn't ever," Marie wept, sinking back into the couch.

Katherine stood up. She whispered to Sophia, "I don't think I can stand any more of this."

"Why don't you go rest in the spare room at the top of the stairs? I've already had it made up for you," Sophia said. "On the very slim chance that she says anything interesting, I'll..."

"I would never kill her," Marie said again and wept. "Why would I? I didn't even have to."

Katherine turned at that. "Marie," she asked carefully. "What do you mean you didn't have to?"

Marie's eyes opened wide, "I'm not supposed to tell you."

Katherine walked back over and sat next to Marie, taking both her hands gently in her own. The other Dolls watched in suspense as if they were at a tight-wire exhibition. Maybe they were going to get a real answer, not the cocktail party version.

"It's okay, Marie," Katherine said softly. "You can tell me."

"Scott said I couldn't, couldn't tell anyone," she said.

"I'm sure he won't mind you telling me."

Marie pressed her lips together and shook her head.

Then Sophia said, "Where does Scott get off telling you what to do? He's probably off banging one of his sluts right this minute."

"That's right!" Marie yelled, instantly transformed into a living fury. "Where does that son of a bitch get off? I'll tell anyone I want!"

Katherine tossed Sophia an impressed glance. Sophia shrugged, knowing she was still the queen of manipulation.

"Why would I have killed Stacey when she was going away anyway?"

"Going away?" asked Katherine.

"Scott told me their 'relationship' was over. Stacey and Scott had been in a fight and she was running off to live the rest of her days on a tropical island with some billionaire! He promised me that soon I wasn't going to have to worry about her anymore."

"Who is this billionaire?"

"He didn't tell me that. We were having an argument and I threw that skank in his face and he told me she was leaving soon."

Katherine heard the voice of the woman at Kinkster in her head. *Says he's about to go off to some tropical paradise and take only his "loyal playthings."*

"Did Scott say *why* this billionaire was running off to an island?" Sophia asked.

"I don't feel well," said Marie.

"Did he say anything about when this was going to happen?" Katherine pressed.

"I don't feel well at all," whined Marie.

"Oh, for god's sake, Marie," Lyn said impatiently. "Just spill it."

Which Marie did. All over Sophia's carpet.

That broke the tension in the room. Katherine

stepped away from Marie and left her to the others. She put a hand to her forehead, trying to pull the pieces together.

"What can I do?" asked Sophia.

"I have to talk to Dan," said Katherine. "He needs to listen and not just operate on his Montana time."

"Stay with Marie and let me know if she lets anything else slip," Katherine said to Sophia. "Although I have a sense she's brought up everything she has in her, in more ways than one." As inviting as the guest room was at the moment, it would be a while before Katherine could relax.

"Call me if you need me, Katherine."

"I will. Oh, and one more thing. A FedEx truck will be here any time. Give them this." She opened her bag and pulled the small package out of her Birkin. "I'll text you the shipping address on my way out of the house. It has to go overnight, first delivery possible."

"What's..."

"I'll tell you all about it later, when I know."

CHAPTER FORTY-SEVEN

Dan and Nick sat at the Beanery drinking coffee after a late lunch. They both needed to recharge after time spent digging deeper into Scott's finances. Dan's back was to the wall. It was natural for him to survey the room, watch the front door and carry on a conversation.

"So, about that other stuff I found out," Dan started, "That S&M club over in Belgrade called Kinkster. That'd be Gallatin County. Not my jurisdiction. Michael took Katherine there, and she found out he was connected to a character named Pussywhip, who I've also got in my records. From my information she sounds like a hooker, but for some reason Katherine thinks she was Stacey Olsen and she was having an affair with her husband."

Nick chuckled. "Pussywhip? Seriously?"

"And she said Michael went by 'Polaris.' I don't know who this Pussywhip is or was, but I do know the Hawthorne's marriage sounds like a train wreck, and you know that's going to affect a woman's judgment."

"I obviously don't know her well, but Katherine doesn't seem like the type to use the cops to punish her husband," said Nick. "She's no Marie Stiles."

"She seems to believe that Michael is the perpetrator of the explosion. And that he's dangerous."

Nick took a swallow of his coffee and winced as if it

was horrible, but continued. "Looks like the deceased didn't miss any of the players around here. She must have been quite a girl."

"She could have been into kinky stuff, I guess," said Dan. "But Hawthorne, that surprises even me. He seems like such a wimp."

"Sometimes the wimps are the scariest ones."

"And Katherine has been scared," Dan said thoughtfully.

"In any case," said Nick, "I think we're going to learn more about this by questioning Scott Stiles about his finances than by exploring Michael Hawthorne's sex life."

"You think we have enough to confront him on?"

"Who? Oh. Stiles." Dan frowned in thought. "We can hit him with this Antelope Preservation thing and this Polaris Group..."

"Munch, not Polaris," grinned Nick.

Dan scowled. "Ridiculous names, both of them," he muttered. Then more forcefully, "I have a strong feeling we'll knock him off balance with those. He may let some things slip he didn't plan to."

"I say we do it soon."

"I say we do it this evening. Catch him before he has time to prepare."

"I need to get gas first," said Nick, digging for his wallet. "I can't get used to how fast you can empty a tank out here. Meet you at Stiles's place?"

"Good enough." He caught Nick's eye. He thought about telling him he'd done well with those ghost files. It felt right to be taking firm action finally, and it was Nick that made it possible. But there was no rush. The guy was probably getting more than enough compliments from the women in this place.

"One coffee to go, Janie," he said to the cashier.

CHAPTER FORTY-EIGHT

He was just about to leave the Beanery when Katherine called. He waved Nick on ahead as he took the call. They'd meet at Scott's place later, as planned.

"I have information for you. Where can I meet you in the next few minutes?"

"The next few minutes?"

"We need to meet in person."

He told her he was at the Beanery and said she could meet him there.

After another cup of coffee, he got sick of waiting inside, so he sat in his Durango and listened to the radio. He left a message for Nick saying he'd be a bit late and to hold off until he called him back.

She pulled up a moment later, hopped out, and came up to his window. Her smile was sweet.

"I've just been talking to a very drunk Marie Stiles. It seems her husband told her weeks ago that Stacey was scheduled to run off to a tropical island with an unnamed billionaire."

"What billionaire, what island?"

"I don't know what island, and I don't think she does either. But this means Marie had no reason to kill her...and neither did Scott."

"You could have something here." He wouldn't tell her what he was really thinking. *Fine euphemism for murder. Stacey's going to be sailing off to that big tropical island in the sky.* Sounded straight out of one of the romance novels his dispatcher read in the break room.

"Listen to me." She leaned into his window. Her face was turning red. "The billionaire is Michael. He's been predicting some kind of economic apocalypse and is getting ready to escape somewhere, apparently this island, with his 'chosen few.' He's probably doing something illegal to stockpile money. Stacey was supposed to go with him, but something happened. I think he was afraid she was going to report him, and he was desperate to prevent anything from blocking his escape. So he had her killed."

Dan did listen. "Ok. I'd like to hear more about this," he said. "I promise to take a look at that just as soon as we've wrapped up our investigation of Scott."

"No!" She was angry again. "You're chasing the wrong man. I'm certain Michael is the killer. He's desperate, convinced he's running out of time, and planning something huge right *now.*"

"Katherine, it's not exactly a solid lead. I'll get to it, I promise. But for right now, I've got to follow the trail in front of me."

"More people might *die* while you're chasing down that penny-ante blowhard!"

He was working hard to be sympathetic, but now was the time to shut down the nonsense. "Katherine, I know you're upset. But leave this to those of us with trained judgment."

"Sheriff," she said, "if your judgment includes losing every hair on your head because you used to fuck a pill-addicted psychotic, then maybe you need some more training."

She spun on her heel, swung into her car, slammed the door, and peeled out of the parking lot before Dan could react. Even then, his reaction wasn't much more than a great, hot, geyser of shame roaring up from deep inside him.

He backed the Durango out, very slowly because he could tell he wanted to stomp the gas. He thought he had gotten through to Katherine on their trail ride but these people had finally made him utterly, all-pervasively sick. If he couldn't chase them all out, at least he could knock down their kingpin.

He picked up his phone and called Nick. It was time to nail Scott Stiles.

★★★

Katherine had pulled off the road at the edge of Livingston. She was pissed and tired of the Sheriff placating her. She leaned her head against the steering wheel and closed her eyes. Sitting still for the first time in what seemed like forever, she felt a vast wave of fatigue sweeping over her.

From a great distance she heard her phone ring. For one sweet second she imagined that she was in her own bed and the phone was beeping on the nightstand and everything was normal, but then her eyes opened and she saw she was still in her car at the edge of the road in the fading light of the early evening.

It was Alissa. "Hey Katherine. Listen, I wanted to talk to you over at Sophia's. We never got to catch up about the stuff..."

"Hang on, Alissa, I have to ask you something. You remember Cody and Gram, your dryer guys that we saw at the rodeo?"

"Um...you think I'd forget?"

"They originally came to your house the same day Stacey died, wasn't it?"

"Yeah. I guess I was pretty freaked out by..."

"And did you tell me that they claimed to have helped a broken down FedEx truck?"

"Which is when I knew they must be handing me a line to excuse being so late. Everybody knows FedEx doesn't deliver on..."

"Thanks, Alissa. That's all I need for now."

"Okay, but Katherine, listen. Ever since what happened today with Marie, I've been thinking about something, and...well..."

"Well?"

"Maybe we could get together in person?"

Katherine exhaled sharply. Something in her gut told her this was about Brad. "Why don't you come over tomorrow? I'll still be at Sophia's. I have to go now."

She stared at the phone in her hand for several seconds before she clicked on 'Recents' and tapped Dan's name. It went to his voicemail.

"You said if I found one solid lead you'd follow it. Well, why don't you try looking into a FedEx truck on Club premises the morning of the blast?"

She hung up. Finding a suspect detail that he'd apparently missed felt good. Like kicking dirt in his face.

Her phone rang and rang and rang. It was Dan. Fuck him.

But she listened to his voicemail. "I'm sorry. Just give me a chance. I may be slower than what you think you need, but I'll get to it."

Whatever the fuck that was supposed to mean.

CHAPTER FORTY-NINE

Stiles sat behind his desk with his lawyer at his side, glaring stonily at them.

Dan asked, "Did you authorize the transfer of funds from loans which were backed by the equity in the Antelope Club without the board's knowledge?"

Stiles looked at his attorney, who nodded as if he were to proceed. "I have no idea what you're talking about." It was clear they'd rehearsed his answers.

"Did you authorize the investment of Antelope Club assets without prior approval of the board?"

Stiles spread his hands in a show of apology and gave them a phony smile. "I'm sorry, Sheriff. I just have no idea what you're talking about."

Dan held his gaze until Stiles's smile evaporated and a defensive anger started to build in his eyes. He was losing his cool but he noticed the lawyer giving him a worried look. The counsel opened his mouth as if to redirect the conversation, but Dan cut him off.

"What were the circumstances of the loan you took out from the Antelope Preservation Fund?"

Scott jerked. That one caught him totally off guard. He opened his mouth and shut it a couple of times before he finally said, "Never heard of it."

"Sorry, I didn't hear you," Dan said. "Your voice sounded kind of strangled."

"I said I've never heard of any Antelope Preservation

Fund."

Scott's lawyer was looking quizzically at his client, slightly apprehensive.

Dan read from his little notebook. "You received three hundred million dollars from Credit Luxembourg. But that money disappeared quickly, so you got a loan from the Antelope Preservation Fund, which you were paying usury interest on...quite the smart businessman."

Stiles shot Dan a look of murderous hatred.

Nick smiled and started in on his role as good cop, "Scott, it would help us a lot if you'd just walk us through what happened during those years," he said. "It could be we've got something wrong and you can straighten us out."

Scott said, "I'll straighten you out, all right, you fucking little Italian punk."

The lawyer leaned forward at that. "Gentlemen, I'm afraid my client has no more information to provide you."

"Maybe you can help us track down this Preservation Fund?" Nick asked with a smile. "Or, if not them, how about the Munch Group?"

Stiles flushed red. "Get the hell out of my office!" His voice was probably shriller than he would have liked.

Dan dipped his head as if he were about to say something he sincerely regretted. "Well, I'm awfully sorry to intrude, Mr. Stiles," he said with just a hint of folksy drawl. "But I'm investigating an arson and very likely a homicide. I may need to ask some more uncomfortable questions."

It was the lawyer, of course, who spoke next. "Are you accusing my client of involvement in this arson, Sheriff?"

"And are you counseling your client to impede the investigation of a fatal arson on Antelope Club property?"

"Oh, he wouldn't do that," said Nick. "The last thing Scott wants is for his board or investors to think he's covering up a scandal at the Club."

"Just who the fuck do you think you are? You were hired to help us, not stick your fucking nose where it doesn't belong!" Stiles yelled.

The lawyer raised a hand to shut him up. "Sheriff, unless you have some clear evidence linking my client to your case, I suggest you drop this line of inquiry."

"Well, well," said Dan.

It wasn't much of a comeback. Maybe he had overplayed his hand. They hadn't planned to go into Stacey's murder, since they had nothing there but a suspicion of a motive.

Then Dan said, "Although you know, Scott, I do wonder why you were telling people Ms. Olsen was going to disappear to a tropical island in the weeks before the incident."

Scott jerked to his feet as if a surge of electricity had been shot through his body. "Who told you that?"

The lawyer looked shocked. "Scott..."

"It's a lie! But who told you?"

"Scott!"

"It was Marie, wasn't it? That blubbering slob. She

doesn't know what she's talking about!"

Dan looked at his notebook as if he had to read it to get the details right. "I understand you said she was going off with a billionaire. Who were you referring to?"

Scott went pale, more pale than Dan ever thought he could get under his Big Sky tan. He just stared, looking terrified, and Dan had a sudden, strong intuition that it wasn't the long arm of the law Scott was afraid of.

The lawyer sprang to his feet and stepped in front of Scott as if to shield him from view. "Sheriff, you are going to have to leave this office now. And don't bother coming back unless you're armed with a warrant."

Dan rose very slowly. He looked at the lawyer, then he looked at Stiles. He gave Scott a little smile, letting the office lights reflect off his bald dome.

"I'm sure you'll be seeing us again," he said.

As soon as they were through the door, Nick asked, "What was that? And why didn't you tell me about the island before?"

Dan was scowling at his phone; a call had come in while they were in there. "Hang on a minute," he said. He listened to his voice mail as they walked to their cars. Dan shook his head in puzzlement and dropped the phone back in his pocket.

"Sorry about that," he said. "I didn't know any of it myself until after we parted company at the Beanery. Katherine heard it from Marie. Now let's go get a beer and figure out what's next."

Nick gestured at the phone. "Was that her?"

"What?"

"The voice mail. Sounded like Katherine."

"Just some nonsense." He threw open the door of his car and slid in.

"Seems like Katherine comes up with a lot of interesting nonsense lately."

Dan shook his head impatiently. "She was just babbling something about a FedEx truck on Club premises the day of the crime."

Nick looked at him. "So was there a FedEx truck on the premises the day of the crime?"

Dan slammed his door. "So what if there was? FedEx is always going in and out of that place. Those people can't wait for regular mail like the rest of us."

"Dan," Nick said. "The crime was on a Saturday, right? And if there's one thing I've learned about this rural place, it's that FedEx doesn't run here on Saturday."

Dan just looked straight ahead for a moment. Then very softly, he said, "Shit."

CHAPTER FIFTY

As the day wore on, she sat in the guest room with her laptop sipping green tea from Sophia's Wedgewood teacup. She had stayed in her yoga pants and didn't want to get up. The minute she decided to leave the bedroom, Sophia's full-time maid would come in and make up the guest bed with its eighteen silk and sequined satin pillows, and Katherine wanted the option to lie in bed longer.

She hadn't slept well that night, and every time she'd awakened she had clicked on "Track A Shipment" on the FedEx site. Belgrade, Memphis, JFK in the early morning. Then nothing until the phone call at 7:58 a.m., two minutes to ten in New York. Jack had received the flash drive. He was starting on it right away and would call her the instant he knew anything. Now the hours ticked by, and she resisted the urge to call.

For the last few hours she had been going through the financial news, looking for anything that might shed light on Michael's conviction that the world economy was about to collapse. There was nothing. The US economy was still stable. China was China. There were crises popping up like mushrooms in the Middle East, but nothing that pointed to a major calamity.

She called Jack. She couldn't help herself.

"We got through the lock easily enough, but the file itself is encrypted. All I know so far is that it's complex and Michael is good. I'm tearing at it and I've got my guys, some of the best hackers in the industry, on it."

"So, how much longer until you figure it out?"

"It may take a bit but we'll crack it, don't worry."

Don't worry. That almost made her laugh.

She went back into the financial pages, broadening her focus. She noticed one recent anomaly: market rises for gold, silver, platinum, diamonds, emeralds, rubies. There had been a recent rash of investor purchases across the globe, but no one could understand why yet. A legion of no-name companies in dozens of countries suddenly hungry for hard assets.

She remembered something Michael had said once: if the markets crashed and liquid, electronically traded assets suddenly lost their value, the only rich people left would be the ones who kept their money in metal and gems. It was classic Michael style to make purchases through countless quickly-formed companies in multiple countries. Could Michael alone be buying enough to drive whole markets up? What kind of money were we talking about here?

"Katherine, are you decent?" It was Sophia's voice from downstairs. "Alissa's here for you."

Alissa. Katherine had forgotten. Alissa, who never, ever suspected a thing. She was always full of chatter, but Katherine knew a bit of distraction wouldn't hurt her even though she was a bit nervous that it was about Brad. She left her room and walked downstairs to Sophia's kitchen.

Alissa wore a long black skirt with a tight black top and a golden serpent-head necklace that wound loosely around her neck like a lounging snake on a hot summer day. Apparently she was dressed to go somewhere. She had polished the look with a pair of glasses that soared entirely over the top.

"Alissa, those are fabulous," lied Katherine, knowing that Alissa expected and deserved a compliment. "I love the leopard." The creature was perched on top of the left frame of the lens with its tail dangling down along the nosepiece.

"The designer's from Sweden. I wore them out to dinner in Bozeman and this sweet man admired them, saying he was going right away to the Gallatin Mall to find a pair for his wife." She laughed, "Obviously the guy would never find them in Bozeman. I didn't have the nerve to tell him that I ordered them online and they cost about as much as a first-class ticket to New York."

Sophia poured them glasses of Pinot Grigio and then slipped away to leave the two alone.

"I really shouldn't be drinking anymore. I finished a bottle at home before I came. Why am I always telling you the truth? I think it's because you're the only one who listens to me."

Katherine tried to push back the guilt. "So, what did you want to tell me?"

Alissa was quiet for a while. After three long sips of wine she said, "Brad's taking me to Washington tonight."

"D.C. will be fun," Katherine said.

"I think he feels guilty for always leaving me in this place. Or maybe he thinks that I'm screwing someone else, who knows? But we're getting away together alone for once and I'm happy about that. Carmen is staying with Tyler for a few nights, thank god." She downed the rest of the wine in one gulp.

"Alissa..."

Suddenly Alissa was talking quickly. "Katherine, I'm sworn not to tell you this. Promise you'll not repeat this to anyone."

"Ok, I promise."

"You've been such a loyal friend to me, I mean you didn't tell anyone about the dryer guys and you've listened to me complain about Brad for so long, and I can tell you're going through something really awful with Michael. After you talked to Marie yesterday, the way you looked when she talked about Stacey's billionaire, I couldn't help thinking..."

When she wound down, Katherine asked, "Alissa, do you know something about Michael?"

"It's something Brad told me. I'm sorry, Katherine, I've wanted to tell you for so long, but Brad made it sound like it would be some kind of national calamity if I did. I bet he was just lying to me to shut me up."

"Just tell me."

Alissa took a deep breath and dove in. "Well, you know Brad is doing consulting work with the SEC. They're writing legislation and they think it's going to be passed quickly. They're going to do some kind of sting on high-frequency traders. I tried to memorize what he said. They're going to do something that will, hold on… 'minimize speed advantage.' Doesn't that mean stop fast trades?"

"Sounds close. That's not really a 'sting,' but it would certainly hurt Michael's business."

"More than that. Brad says the laws will be designed to put people like Michael out of business. Actually, he said specifically that. 'We're going to shut down that bastard Hawthorne and everyone like him.' He seems to have some kind of thing about Michael. He called him 'the most dangerous trader in the world.' That's 'trader' with a 'd,' not 'traitor' with…"

"I understand, Alissa."

"I'm sorry. I mean, I don't know if any of this will actually work. Michael's awfully smart, and between you and me, I don't think Brad is half the man his personal PR machine makes him out to be. But it could cause trouble for you, and I hope you know that's the last thing I would want."

Katherine only half listened as Alissa talked on. She had never seen Alissa for whom she really was. She'd always been Brad's young, trusting and stupid wife.

She looked at her over-the-top ensemble with her ridiculous leopard sunglasses and the gaudy snake necklace, but she realized she had been wrong about Alissa. And she'd been especially wrong to continue her relationship with Brad. Echoes of the Sheriff's words slipped into her thoughts, *honesty, integrity.* Here was Alissa trying to save her and Michael, and all this time she had been undermining Alissa's marriage. Maybe it had been somewhat justified years ago, but not anymore.

She had never considered Alissa her friend. She supposed she had always seen herself as above Alissa. In the beginning, she had thought of saving herself, saving her associates—but that was years back, before Alissa and Brad were even married. She'd simply continued sleeping with Brad when he traded up from the ice queen because she liked it. Having a secret, being wanted, keeping a bit of spice in her life after leaving the Street: that was what the relationship meant to her. Would Brad turn her in if she stopped seeing him? Would it really matter? Not one sub-prime architect had gone to jail and she doubted she'd be first. If Brad wanted to blow the whistle on what happened years ago, then so be it.

Katherine no longer wanted to be part of the reason for Alissa's unhappiness. What a shit she was. She had stolen a bit of Alissa's husband from her. She had never thought of it this way before, but it suddenly seemed obvious, and about as clear as the sky above and the river below.

And then she was trying to put herself in Michael's place. If he'd known the SEC was coming—and of course he'd have known—he'd have felt like a rat in a trap. He'd built an empire, and it was about to be undermined by the kinds of people he hated most, bureaucrats and old-school investors. And the ignorant general public he held in contempt. *The vast masses of have-nots.*

If he saw the end of his empire coming, what would he do? Cash in his chips and live in comfortable retirement? Go fishing with Scott Stiles?

No. Not Michael.

***

Sophia had come down the stairs. Alissa was decomposing. The excess wine had hit. They'd seen it many times before. Sophia made an excuse that she had to drive to town and drove Alissa home.

Before she could go any further, Katherine had to end it with Brad. She phoned him and he picked up, first ring.

"Can you meet me? It's important."

"I'm at the shooting range but I can leave now, baby, where?"

How she had let this go on for so long now made her nauseous. "The Grey Owl Fishing Access site. It'll be empty. It's freezing outside."

"Do I feel a sense of passion coming on?"

A sense of compassion, really.

Fifteen minutes later and she had to laugh when he slid in the car as if he were about to get a blowjob.

"Thanks for coming here so quickly."

All smiles. "Thanks for asking."

"Brad, this is different. More than I've ever asked of you."

"Go ahead, I'm yours."

"No you're not. You're Alissa's. I used to think she was just an idiot bimbo, but she's a good person. She cares about me and she loves you, and I can't do this anymore." Dan's words were there. She could see the mountains, the trees. She could sense the honesty that

Jean and the Wednesday Pine Riders stood for and although she would never be one of them, she had to change.

"She won't know. She never has."

"But that's the point, Brad, she does. She knows something's wrong because she drinks. And it starts with you not being totally hers. Look, you saved me. You saved my company. I owe you and if you want to tell the world what I did, then go ahead. You don't have to protect me anymore, but you do need to save your marriage and save your wife. Think about Tyler, too."

For once, Brad Fairbanks looked stumped.

"I'm surprised. Really surprised to hear this from you. I knew the sex was just sex or business as usual for you. I just never, ever would have guessed that you'd give a damn about Alissa."

"Well, do you love her?"

"Sure, I *love* her."

"Then we have to stop. If you think you have to turn me in, ok." Then with a smile, "You think after all these years they still care?"

Brad rolled his eyes. "I'm not turning you in."

"Well, I'm grateful for that, but I'll be even more grateful to hear that D.C. brings you two back together."

She wasn't going to bring up what Alissa had told her the SEC was planning on doing to Michael.

She had her own agenda.

CHAPTER FIFTY-ONE

He reviewed the Antelope Club's security guard's log for the day of the explosion while Nick sat in front of his desk drinking coffee.

"Most of the vehicles are residents, plus the usual flow of maintenance and gardening trucks. Their license plates are consistent with prior authorization and registration with the Club." He stopped. "Except this FedEx truck."

"On Saturday?"

"10:12 a.m. About an hour before the crime."

"Flip back to Friday," said Nick.

Dan scanned Friday's log. "FedEx was there," he said.

"See if it was the same license plate."

"Nope. Different."

Dan copied down the license plates and called over to the FedEx dispatch office in Belgrade. The Friday truck was one of their regulars, but the other wasn't on their list. Dan asked them to check other locations. After a long wait, the dispatcher told him that there was no record in the entire Montana fleet of a truck with that license number.

Nick said, "Now call the guard."

Dan held back his annoyance. He was the one to give orders. It wasn't worth the trouble to point out that he was already dialing Antelope Security. The guard who answered the phone tried to give him the runaround, told him he'd have to get authorization before he could check the photo records.

"I'm chasing a murderer," Dan barked. "Do you want to be the one who delayed me until it was too late?" Not very professional, but it felt good to knock somebody around.

After a long wait the guard came back on the phone and described what he saw in the photo from Saturday morning.

Dan summarized for Nick. "It was an International side-step van, basic issue. It could have been a clone. All they would have to have done is slap a FedEx decal on the side."

"Law enforcement goes undercover often enough using FedEx trucks. Why not our perp?"

"License plate starts with a 12. Hill County."

"That significant?"

"Prairie. Low population. Canadian border." Dan opened the Motor Vehicle Division database and punched in a search of the license number.

"Well?" Nick asked.

Dan entered the digits again, double-checking every number. "Nothing," he said.

"Nothing at all?"

"There is no such plate in Montana."

"A fake plate? Weird risk to take."

Dan didn't answer, just sat silently. This had to be the arsonists' vehicle, but what could he do with it? He'd put out a bulletin to the highway patrol, police, sheriffs and border guards to be on the alert for the plate, but he had little hope the perpetrators would have left it on the vehicle. They'd have to track down every van of that description registered in the state. But who said it was even registered in Montana?

He reached for the phone again. The one thing he had learned in his years of bumping up against Antelope Security was that they were as lazy as they were arrogant.

"I want you to open that photo record again. Read me the license straight off the picture."

A minute later he hung up.

"What?" Nick asked.

"Idiot wrote down a three instead of an eight." He pounded the new number into the system.

"Jackpot?"

"Registered to a company in Havre, HavRent LLC."

Nick leaned forward to look at the screen. "Havre. HavRent. You people in Montana are sure clever."

Dan exhaled, expelling the annoyance. The phone in the Hill County sheriff's office was already ringing. "Hey, Rob. Dan Bentley. I need you to look into something for me—immediately. I've got an International van connected to an arson and possible homicide down here. It's registered at someplace called HavRent."

"I know them," Rob said. "Vans, tractors, agricultural and construction equipment. Few ATVs too, I think. Place is out on Highway 2, west of town. Nice outfit, father and son. Been out there since, oh, maybe..."

"Rob," said Dan, "I need that van." He gave him the license, description, date in question, and his cell number. Then he added, "There's a time issue here."

"Count on me," Rob said.

Dan hung up. The room suddenly seemed unnaturally silent, the dusk gathering outside ominously dark. Now he could only wait, as the reins weren't in his hands.

CHAPTER FIFTY-TWO

It was three in the morning when the phone rang. Katherine remembered that line of Fitzgerald's: "In a real dark night of the soul, it's always three o'clock in the morning." Or five o'clock Eastern Time.

"We still don't have it all," Jack said. "But Katherine...I've been looking for what you suggested."

She had called him hours before with her suspicions, asking him to look for signs that the algorithm might contain market directives, especially sell-offs or anything else that might drive prices down.

"And?"

"I think you might be right. He may be launching a gigantic wave of sell-offs at absurdly low prices. But it also seems set to buy back the same assets and then immediately sell them again for even less."

"So it will look like prices are steadily dropping."

"But Katherine, listen to this...I think it's a worm. I don't think it's for selling off Michael's own assets, it's for triggering a drop in other people's values."

"Knocking over the dominoes," Katherine said.

"This could set off the biggest panic in decades— it could be like that flash crash back in 2010, but a hundred times worse."

"No, Jack. A lot worse. If you look at it, you'll see a perfect design to orchestrate the biggest panic in history."

"But why would he do that? Does he think he's going to be able to suck up a bunch of cheap assets this way? That's insane! This would crash the whole market!"

"The whole economy," Katherine said. "The whole global, credit-based, liquid-asset-driven economy."

"But why would he do that?"

"Because he can't have it his way anymore. Can you tell *when* this is going to happen?"

"I haven't found anything yet, but I'll look. Jesus, Katherine, what is he…"

"Find a launch time. I'll fill you in later."

Although soon enough she might not have to fill anyone in. It would be horrifically obvious that the world as they knew it was coming down like a house of cards: Michael wasn't predicting an economic collapse. He was creating one.

And now, when the SEC was about to put him in a harness, he turned the tables on them in the most sadistic way he knew. He might cage all mankind in a hellish world, including himself, but at least his hand would be on the end of the chain. He'd hold the riding crop. It was a global Kinkster.

What should she do? Who would believe her? She could imagine the whole world treating her like Dan Bentley, unless Jack could find something incontrovertible in that file. But Brad Fairbanks might listen.

She called Alissa; she wouldn't be calling Brad anymore. It went straight to voice mail. Probably lounging in her luxurious D.C. hotel room, enjoying sleeping in without a toddler to wake her at the crack of dawn.

Her phone rang. It was Jack.

"Katherine. I think I've found a timeline in here. If I'm right...he's launching today."

"Oh god."

"4:00 p.m. today, Eastern. Katherine, what do we do?"

"Call everyone you can think of," she said. "And pray they believe you."

"It sounds so insane..."

"I know. That's why I'm going to have to stop him myself."

"What? How?"

"Is there a way to shut this down if I get to his computers?"

"There could be. I don't know what stocks he's chosen yet, but they're probably in here. If not, there must be instructions in his main racks. I'll have my people see if they can write an algo to counteract this. But can you get to his computers?"

Four p.m. Eastern was two p.m. Mountain. She listened to the blowing wind outside. It was probably snowing. Terrible weather for flying. Plus, Michael had left on his copter yesterday, so it was probably still in Lolo. It would be seven hours to get to the Cave through the stretched-out highway, snow, and mountain roads.

"Do I have any choice?" she asked. She picked up the phone and awakened Jean.

"Sorry, Jean. I know it's early, very early."

"Oh that's ok, I have a surprise to tell you."

"Well, thank you, but it's got to wait. I need your help to get up to Michael's cave, his office. It's almost to the Idaho border, way up past Lolo, and I'm asking if you could drive me up there. Michael's about to do something horrible. I went there once, but do you know that area?"

"Sure do. I used to ride up there with the WPR. It was a while back but of course I remember. But why didn't you ask Dan, he's the one who should be going."

"Honestly Jean, I've tried, but he's still thinks it's because I have a bad marriage and he says he'll follow up, but who knows when that will be."

"I'll tell you more in the truck. It's a time issue. I've got to beat Michael to the punch, so to speak."

"You're at Sophia's, right? I'll be there in minutes."

★★★

Thursday morning. Dan awakened at 6:00 a.m., feeling as though he'd hardly slept. The first thing he did was call Hill County. HavRent wasn't answering yet and there was no telling when they would. Then he drank a whole pot of coffee to clear the cobwebs from his brain and drove to the office. Nick was supposed to be there in two hours, bringing all the ghost files his IT guy had cracked, so they could start putting together the case against Scott Stiles.

In the meantime, he would catch up on the rest of his business: disorderly drunks, houses broken into, a vicious dog up in Clyde Park. He was having a hard time keeping his mind on any of it. For a second he thought of calling Katherine to ask if there was anything else she could tell him about her husband's activities. Then he caught himself. No more letting Paradise Valley wives distort his priorities, remember?

He was going to do this right.

CHAPTER FIFTY-THREE

Ready to fire.

The optic cable, smooth and fast. The lasers firing like full bore. The crews on alert in his remote locations. The Lolo crew dismissed, all but the one mountain man left to guard the compound. The computers loaded and tested. The algos lined up in sequence. All he needed was the launch program.

It was beautiful to think about. That little bundle of code would send its commands to his racks, the pawn computers in New York, Shanghai, Singapore, Mumbai, and London, each of them adjacent to a major exchange so precise microseconds were not lost in electronic transmission. His two New York racks, one for NYSE and one for NASDAQ, would start a cascade in US markets soon before they closed, the best time for a panic. By the time the Asian markets opened they'd see a collapse already in progress in the US. Europe would simply be swept away by the tide.

"Buy when there's blood on the streets," Warren Buffett had said. That pompous ass Buffett, he thought he was the master investor of the world. He'd know the truth soon enough, as he watched Berkshire Hathaway's assets draining away. Buffett was really going to see blood on the streets this time, including his own. Michael's only regret was that he wouldn't be able to watch it firsthand. All he'd be able to see was the ocean lapping the white sand shore of his island paradise.

Once he'd launched the algo, the ball would be irreversibly rolling toward the cliff. To see it all come crashing down. Wasn't that the nightmare of every member of the Antelope Club—to find all the power, security, and money ripped away, leaving them exposed to the lowlifes they'd scorned?

It was time to update the launch algorithm. He'd been so preoccupied with all the hardware and logistical issues that he'd put that off until now. Just a few seconds of work, really. He'd copied the last version onto that flash drive. Which was where, now? Yes, in his jacket pocket, in his bag.

But no, it wasn't. The jacket was there, but not the drive. Not in the lining pocket either. It must have fallen out in the bag.

Except it wasn't there.

Michael paced around the spilled contents of the bag in the middle of his command room floor, trying to reconstruct when he'd seen the drive last. He'd been holding it in his hand when the Hellbitch burst into the room. That was the last he remembered.

Then it was still there, on the floor of his office at home. It had to be. Katherine wouldn't have noticed. If she had, she wouldn't have cared. There was no way Katherine could have picked it up. It was on the floor of his office. It had to be.

He could do without it, honestly. He had all the commands on his back up drive. Hell yes, he could forget the flash drive. Michael sat in front of his computers and copied, then updated the directives. Done.

There was nothing to worry about.

Once he'd launched the algo and set the ball rolling irreversibly toward the cliff, he could cruise back to the Antelope Club to pack up his personal treasures. There was his collection of pictures, to start with. He'd spent years tracking and culling those, and if internet commerce were to collapse they would be impossible to replace. Then there were those vintage violet wands he'd bought from a collector, ostensibly used in the notorious Toppkeller Club in Weimar Berlin. And his first edition of de Sade's *Justine*. And the precious treasure he kept in that one drawer, his battered Apple, his childhood computer.

Time to pull the trigger. As his hand began to touch the key to launch his algo, he paused. Once he pressed the key there was no turning back. His finger was the Enola Gay, like Tibbets, dropping "Little Boy" over Hiroshima, except the fallout would be another kind of devastation. He had created the moment history would never forget. He was in his own cyber-space oddity, Major Mike, like David Bowie's "Major Tom." Countdown…four, three, two, one. He screamed, "FIRE!" The screens flashed and the music he had programmed, "Coming Home," by Peter Schilling, was blasting. "Standing there alone the ship is waiting…drifting, falling, floating."

He felt the rush he had planned with precision. This was the euphoric high he wanted to savor. But thanks to the fucking Hellbitch, he had new plans.

"Get the Bell ready *now*. We're going back to the Valley in thirty minutes."

"Thirty minutes?" Rick's voice sounded like he'd been asleep. "I thought we were..."

"What part of 'now' don't you fucking understand? I've decided to do my packing early, that's all. Get it ready!"

That's right. It would be good to get the packing done early. One less thing to think about. And if he found the flash drive and could know for a fact that no one had gotten into his files, well, that was just a nice extra, wasn't it?

CHAPTER FIFTY-FOUR

She pounded on the bedroom door for what felt like an eternity before a barely awake Sophia threw it open.

"Sorry to wake you up, but I'm going up with Jean to Michael's compound. I wanted to tell you so someone knows where we're going."

"Slow down. It's dark outside. You're...what? What time is it?"

Katherine realized she'd never seen Sophia like this: no makeup, hair wild, eyes bleary and confused. For the first time she looked like a regular person.

"It's close to 5:00 a.m., I have to drive to Lolo. I want someone to know where we're going, in case something happens."

"You're crazy. Driving up there this time of year? Do you know how dangerous that is?"

"Jean's driving. We'll be safe."

She turned to go, but Sophia grabbed her arm. "Something's wrong. Tell me."

"It's too much to..."

"Michael's going to do something awful and you're trying to stop him."

"Yes. But there's no time for me to explain."

"There's time for me to grab my clothes, though."

"What...?"

"If I can go to that club I can certainly go up to the

Lolo Pass with you two. Does Jean know the way?"

"She says she does and has ridden her horse up there, plus Michael drove me to his compound once, a long time ago."

"Really, Jean and I will be fine."

"I don't know about Michael's big fancy hideout but I know those mountains. John likes his hiking and cross-country skiing to be super challenging. I need to get dressed. What am I going to wear? I'm sooo sick of all my outfits. Have you noticed that almost everything I own is black?"

Jean was sitting outside in her 1992 Ford F150 extended cab. That light blue and white truck probably had close to three hundred thousand miles on it, but she kept it in great shape. When she saw Sophia coming, too, she gave Katherine a questioning but stern look.

"She refuses to let us go alone," said Katherine.

"Hop in girls, we have a long drive ahead of us."

It was lighter outside than normal because the full moon was illuminating the endless landscape. It was what Katherine had heard hunters loved because they could see their prey.

Sophia rode in the back while putting on her clothes and applying makeup using her tiny mirror as Jean drove out of Paradise Valley. Sophia's idea of appropriate attire was a tight black top, a fur vest, and skinny, black rhinestone-studded jeans. Thank goodness John was in Indiana checking on his Flying Js. She sent him a text telling him where she was going. Had he been home he would have not liked the idea. She thought for a moment and sent a text telling Nick.

"It's John I love," she said quietly. "But Nick has pulled me out of more than one scary place in the past. I'm hedging my bets."

Jean looked at Katherine and rolled her eyes.

As much as Katherine hated the idea of dragging her friends into this insane mission, she couldn't deny that having them with her might be what she needed to see it through. Anxiety was twisting her stomach in knots, and even though Jean wasn't thrilled about Sophia, just the sound of Sophia's voice as the sun came up calmed her down.

"So, you said you'd explain this mission on the way," said Jean.

Jean's phone rang. "Who in the hell would call me now?"

"Mom. It's Will. Where are you? I brought over some parts for your truck. Didn't you see the ranch hand helping me last night? Where are you?"

"I'm on my way to LoLo."

"Ah shiiiit. What in the hell for?"

"What's wrong?"

"The four-wheel drive wasn't shifting easily into low. We thought we'd have it done for you before daylight. But the damn truck isn't here!"

"Will, I'll be just fine. I've known about the problem for a while now, I can get it into low. Don't worry about your mama."

"Why are you going to Lolo in this weather? Who are you with?"

"The weather is just fine around here. I'll let you know why we are taking this drive when I get back."

After Jean hung up with Will, she turned to Katherine. "So now, tell me *why* we're going to Lolo?"

"I've figured out the reason Michael has been acting so strangely, and to sum it up, it's global financial devastation. I should have told you sooner, but I had to be sure. You were right, Jean. It's about money, an enormous amount."

"I knew it, somehow her honesty took her away from me."

"I found Michael's flash drive with codes that will turn the world upside down. My guys in New York say I need to get to his Cave where his office is and try to stop him on his main computers."

She explained what Michael was going to do and what that would do to the world if they couldn't get to his Cave and find some way to stop him in time. Her voice was nearly cracking into sobs as she finished.

Sophia listened intently. "So, that's the important package I sent out. Clever, Katherine."

Their speed crept up. The endless mountains and then high-plains desert whipped past them. They roared past a few trucks, no other cars. Jean's hands were steady on the wheel, her eyes fixed straight ahead.

Katherine's phone rang. She looked in her hand bag and fumbled for it.

"I'm glad Jean's driving. Sometimes I wonder why you haven't been in more accidents," Sophia said, but the ringing had stopped before she found the phone.

"Very funny, Sophia. Jack Weber, it says." She dialed him back.

Jack answered on the first ring. "Thank god. I was afraid something had happened. How much longer until you're there?"

Katherine stared out the window into the vast Clark's Fork Valley. The Pintler Mountain Range framed the west and the Clark's Fork River graced Interstate 90. "Jean, is it still going to be at least a couple of hours?"

"At least," she replied.

"What do you have, Jack?"

"I think we know enough to try to reverse engineer that algo, but it's going to be close."

"Listen to me," said Katherine. "It's a simple fact of trading in the stock market. Once you identify which stocks Michael is targeting, you need to buy up what he's selling off, take the opposite position of his. Go long on all his short trades. That will stop his crash."

"It would take an exorbitant amount of capital to make any difference."

"We may not be able to stop the crash, but we can slow it down. Start by using all my vested interest in Stanford and Jones."

"That's a noble offer, Katherine, but it's not even close to enough."

"Then take over Stanford and Jones's direct market access. Use their funds. You've got to do whatever it takes, Jack."

"That could at least cost me my job. If not jail time."

"This isn't a time to worry about personal risks."

He laughed. "Are you sure you're Katherine Bailey Hawthorne?"

"Whatever it takes, Jack. And I've been thinking of what else he could do to amplify his panic. He'll have to back it in the media with a plausible reason for a gigantic panic, like a massive feed about China or North Korea launching some sort of doomsday war."

"I just happen to know a guy who wrote software to make tweets go viral, to retweet a message hundreds of thousands of times."

"Perfect! So get him to be ready to RT, 'counter tweet,' with enormous hits falsifying whatever media hysteria Michael's going to spread...if he takes that route."

"I like this world beater, the new Katherine," said Sophia.

"She does sound pretty powerful," said Jean.

"I was good in my day but I've never been a world beater. In my life I've only known one person who consistently conquered and beat the world. Who never failed at anything he took on."

Sophia didn't say a word. She knew exactly whom Katherine meant.

★★★

It wasn't on his desk. It wasn't on the floor. He moved the heavy desk to look behind it. Nothing. Then the file cabinet. Nothing. He turned the garbage can upside down. He emptied the drawers.

"Katherine?" he called. "Katherine!" He heard fear in his voice. He didn't like that. Fear was for the people he dominated. *"Katherine!"*

He hurried to the garage. Her car was there. Where the hell was she?

He could phone her. Tell her there was an emergency. She'd come and he'd seize her. Torture her until she told him where the flash drive was and what she knew.

She had it. She knew. She may not have cracked it, but she knew it mattered. And she knew people. No one half as smart as he was, but sometimes even a monkey could figure out how to open a lock.

"KATHERINE!"

That wasn't calling her, that was just rage. The last thing he could afford was to lose control.

Lolo. Why had he ever taken the Hellbitch to his compound? He should have kept everything secret from her, everything from the start.

He had to get back. He had programmed it to start whether or not she had the copy, but he had to lock himself in the command center and guard his machines personally until the final algo launched.

He called Rick. "We're going back to Lolo immediately."

"I'm just finishing my flight logs. Give me fifteen minutes."

Arrogance. Another one who didn't take Michael seriously enough.

"Rick." His voice was cold and steel-hard when he spoke again. That's the way he liked to hear it. "I never want to have to repeat an order to you. Ever again."

A pause.

"Yes, sir."

Back in control.

CHAPTER FIFTY-FIVE

"So, why do you suppose Michael, and not Scott, killed Stacey?" asked Jean.

Katherine thought for a while. They had left Missoula and the interstate behind and were climbing up US 12 into the mountains above the town of Lolo. The forest was dense, and thick huckleberry bushes grew beneath the conifers.

"I can guess. She followed the money trail and found out Scott was in debt to Michael. Got close to Michael to figure out what exactly he was doing. I like to think it's because she knew what he was planning and had the integrity to stand up to him."

Jean, with her eyes still on the road, just shook her head.

Katherine looked at the clock on the dashboard, eleven thirty. They still had a couple of hours before Michael's launch, but the remainder of the drive was going to be the challenge.

"Do you realize your jaw is clenched? Are you grinding your teeth?"

"Hand me my bag." Katherine needed her mouthpiece. "I like this new one better. See, it fits on my lower teeth instead of the upper. "

Sophia cringed. "Ugh… "

Jean took a curve quickly, banged on the steering wheel, bumping Sophia against the door.

"Sorry girls. I'm just plum mad."

The road was starting to wind more sharply. As they came around another turn, the tall peaks of granite skyscrapers came clear above the forested slopes.

The phone rang. Katherine answered and put it on speaker.

"Jack, can you hear me?" Katherine paused.

"They may be able to break the progression of the algorithm. But you have to get into Michael's controls."

"Ok, tell me exactly what I do when we get there."

Sophia looked at the screen. "Lost him."

"Shit!" yelled Katherine. "Try to bring him up on my laptop. It's back near your seat. I've got his email address in there. No never mind, just give it to me."

"You know I'm horrible with this stuff."

Katherine kept tapping the computer and the personal hotspot. "I've got it," she said. "Now send." Katherine punched the keys. "Nothing."

"Keep trying," said Sophia. "We have to get him back..." Her voice grew faint. The Tamarack pines were turning from green to yellow like a time-lapse effect. It began to snow harder.

Upward they climbed, low gears grinding, engine roaring, no one speaking. Katherine obsessively tracked the mileage markers at the side of the road, watching the numbers counting down, growing more anxious as they drew near the Idaho state line.

"Hmm, this snow blast makes it hard to see," said Jean. The truck slid to the left.

Katherine put a steadying hand on the wheel and

Jean brushed her off. "Keep going on the highway," said Katherine. "We've got to be getting close to the turn off."

The truck climbed again, until the silent forest suddenly vanished around them. They were above the timberline, among the peaks, although they could see little but the white void of the snowy sky.

"It's like there's nothing," said Sophia softly.

Jean pulled over into a turn out and stopped the truck and went outside.

"What's she doing?" asked Sophia.

"I imagine she's locking the wheels into four-wheel drive. I've seen her do it before. These older trucks aren't automatic like our cars."

It was taking Jean some time. The girls got out of the truck.

"Is there anything we can do to help?" asked Katherine.

"No, I've finally got it. Let's get going. Get back into the truck. We're set."

It seemed like they were floating, not driving through the thick snow. They came to a fork in the whitened road.

"I don't remember which way," sighed Katherine.

"I don't think we have any choice," said Jean. She nodded down the left fork. "That is so deep in snow I doubt we could make it through. We have to go right."

She rounded a bend as the downward grade increased. The Ford slid out of her control and hit a snow bank. She put it in reverse but the tires only spun. Forward, reverse, forward, but no movement.

They sat still for a moment. It was snowing hard and fiercely cold. Sophia checked the phones for a signal but there was nothing. Jean got out of her truck, pulled a shovel out of the back and began digging the snow out from under the cab.

CHAPTER FIFTY-SIX

"Bad weather is here again," said Nick.

"Uh-huh."

The Sheriff's phone rang. "Hi Dan, it's Will Larson. How ya' doin'?"

"Just fine. You?"

"I called because I'm not sure what's going on around here. My mom, who is always home in the mornings doing chores, is suddenly driving Katherine Hawthorne, her neighbor, and her friend, Sophia, to Lolo. This is totally out of character for her, so I wondered if you knew of anything strange going on up there. She told me she'd tell me about it when she returned. Which means to me, she doesn't know. This is not at *all* like her. Lolo at this time of year? *The Jean,* or not, it's out of character and dangerous. And I'm worried about her truck. I had just come over to work on it this morning."

"Haven't heard a word Will, but I hear you, strange. I'll let you know if I know anything more. Ok. Sure. Goodbye."

"Do you think it is snowing in the mountains?" asked Nick.

"I imagine it is," said Dan.

Nick was mercifully silent for a moment. Then he said, "Hope it doesn't get too bad for Katherine and Sophia."

Dan looked up at that. "That's just what Will Larson just called about, said it wasn't like his mom to take off so early."

"Hm? Oh, right. Didn't I tell you I got a text from Sophia this morning saying she, Katherine and Jean were driving up to Lolo Pass today?"

"What did Sophia tell you?"

Nick shrugged. "I assumed it was a Montana thing, tipping the search parties off before you vanish into the wilderness."

"No. Why are they going to Lolo?"

"She didn't say."

Dan looked out the window at the darkening clouds. "Katherine's husband owns some sort of compound up there in the peaks."

"Well, there you go."

The echoes of his last conversation with Katherine rang in Dan's ears. He grabbed his phone and dialed her. It went straight to voice mail.

"Katherine, this is Dan Bentley. I'd like you to call me right away." He felt as though there were more to say, but didn't know what it was. "Right away, please. Thanks." He hung up reluctantly.

He pounded Redial on the number he'd called four times that morning. "Rob, don't you have anything from HavRent yet?"

"Hey, Dan! Funny timing. I got a call from the father. He's back in cell phone range, heading up 87, and he says he'll look up that van once he's back at his office."

"Which is when?"

"Well, I didn't ask him that. I figured he meant sometime today, though."

Dan wanted to blow up but bit his tongue. "Did you tell him there's some urgency here? Give me his cell number and I'll call him myself."

"That's against protocol, Dan."

"Look, Rob, I've got no interest in pissing on your turf. I'd just like to have a conversation with the guy. Maybe I can take the whole hassle off your hands and let you get back to your job."

Rob didn't sound happy, but he gave Dan the number.

"Montana time," said Nick with a grin.

The guy answered on the first ring. Dan introduced himself, quickly described the van and gave him the license. "I'd really appreciate it if you could look that up the minute you can."

"Oh, hell, I don't need to look that up. That one's been out for a few weeks to the same people we were just running equipment to."

"That being who?"

"ZeroLT"

"OLT?" asked Dan.

"No they call it, Zero capital L, capital T."

"Where can I find them?"

"Don't know, honestly. I've got a couple phone numbers and an email address, but that's all they ever give us. They have a few different managers they send around to set things up."

"Give me whatever you've got," said Dan.

There was a long pause. "Really sorry, Sheriff,

but they've specifically asked us to never give their information out."

"This concerns a murder."

"I understand that, Sheriff. But this is my biggest customer. I wouldn't be in business if it weren't for them. Of course, if you had some kind of court order that I couldn't refuse, that would be different, but...a man's got to make a living."

Dan pushed him a few more times, but the guy wouldn't budge. He slammed the phone down. "Goddamn it," he said.

"You shouldn't have much trouble getting a warrant," said Nick.

"But it's going to take time. Damn it all!"

"We have to go up there in a chopper. Winds are bad and so is the snow, but I've flown through worse."

"Didn't know you were a pilot."

Dan grimaced as he called the Forest Service to see if the helicopter was free.

"It's here. Let's hustle, we need to make good time because the women have a good start on us and no telling what kind of trouble they're heading into-probably way more than the weather."

★★★

"Katherine and Sophia, you're going to have to get out and push this truck." Then she looked down at Sophia's feet. "Oh, damn, Sophia! Why did you wear heels to come up here?"

Sophia didn't respond but heard a gunshot. Then another. Before anyone could react, a huge hunter in military fatigues appeared at the truck. He had a savage air about him and looked as if he hadn't bathed in months. He was holding a freshly killed grouse.

He didn't see Jean on the other side of the truck.

Katherine was too scared to move. He banged the window with the barrel of his shotgun.

"Open up!"

The militiaman yanked on the car door. It was locked, but his brute force was equal to his size and the whole truck rocked.

Katherine shook her head. Then he swung his shotgun around to face them, and she rolled down the window.

"Do you know you're trespassin' on this here private property?" he barked.

Jean came around to face the mountain man. "Well, Well. I think you look somewhat familiar to me."

"Well, you don't to me, and you all is on my property."

"Aren't you Jimbo? Wasn't Ethel your Aunt?"

Katherine thought even up here in Lolo, this was Montana, everyone seemed to connect, either family or friends.

"So what if I am?"

"Well your Aunt Ethel was my Aunt Ida's good friend. They used to talk fondly about you."

Jean thought she saw a slight grin but then he pointed his gun again at Katherine in the truck.

"You a thinkin' this is a forest road?" he said, pointing his shotgun at Katherine.

"Look. Please. I'm trying to find my husband's

compound."

"Who's your husband?"

"Michael Hawthorne."

The man rose to his full height and stared down at her. "Get out, both of ya," he said. "All of you. Start walkin'."

"Do you know him? Where his compound is?" asked Katherine.

"I said, get out and start walkin'."

"Wait a minute now, Jimbo," said Jean.

"She can't," said Katherine. "She's got heels on."

"Then she can walk in her bare feet for all I care. Get out!"

"No," said Jean very slowly. "You don't know what's at stake."

"I know all I need to know. Her husband stole this land from my grand pappy when ol' Pop was too feeble to understand what he were selling."

"I'm sorry," said Katherine. "But please..."

"Your husband come through clearin' them trees like a viral cyclone of poison. He turned our land into his private utopia, flyin' in and out like he owns the world. His helo tears apart this here quiet. Then he's a thinkin' he can buy off our righteous anger by tossin' a few lousy jobs at us, just like the rest of his..."

"Please listen to me," said Jean. She was so calm. "We're not coming here to *visit* her husband. We're here to shut his operation down. And we need help."

"If she's his wife then you're all the same as he are."

"Maybe you could get our truck out of this snow and we could give you a ride," offered Sophia.

"Do I look like I need a ride?" he snapped.

"Sophia…" said Jean with a sigh.

"Look, we need a little help," said Jean.

Katherine noticed Sophia was now batting her eyes at Jimbo.

He looked at her, maybe liking a little more of what he saw. His face seemed to soften for a moment.

"All right. Fine. He looked at Jean. "What's your name, besides Aunt Ethel's friend's niece?"

"Jean," she said and stuck out her hand to shake his, but he moved her aside and motioned for her to get back in the driver's seat.

"When I get to the front of the truck I want you to put this motha into reverse and gun it." He paused as if she didn't understand what he was saying. "Do ya know what 'gun it' means? Step on the gas when I give it a shove."

"He really doesn't know who he's talking that way to," Jean laughed.

Katherine said, "I'm sorry. It's because you're with us."

"Jimbo has always been a little slow. Give him some time."

He trudged toward the front of the car.

"He thinks we're stupid," said Sophia with a laugh.

"It doesn't matter," said Jean. "We have one objective and now we have help."

The hunter put his shoulder on the hood and grill and used his mammoth legs to push. As the truck rolled back, Jean pressed the gas. The tires caught the road and the truck pulled free. He walked back to the side windows.

"Thanks so much," said Sophia, tilting her head with a smile.

"Yes, thank you," said Katherine. "My husband's about to do something terrible. We need to get to his compound, now."

The militiaman looked at Katherine then at Jean. First he said to Katherine, "You get in the back," and then to Jean, "Get out of that there seat. I'm drivin'."

Jean and Katherine did as he asked. The last thing they needed was to get trapped in a snow bank again, and this guy clearly knew what he was doing. Jean stepped out into the cold and hopped into the shotgun seat. Katherine jumped into the back. He heaved his weight into the driver's seat and tossed the dead grouse next to Katherine and Sophia. Its head flopped to the side.

"Ew," squealed Sophia.

"Quiet," he said.

Katherine tapped her iPhone. Twelve thirty. Only an hour and a half and she had no idea how far they were from the Cave now. The militiaman was eyeing her in the rearview mirror.

"You think you're gonna make a phone call with that smartie phone of yours? There ain't no signal up here."

"I was checking the time. We have to hurry."

They drove in silence for miles along a winding road that headed up to the top of a mountain.

Finally, Sophia spoke. "Where's your car?" she asked.

He snorted in contempt, then mimicked her in a high-pitched voice: "Where's your car?"

He finally pulled up to a bat-and-board shack nestled between two towering rocks, with smoke coming out of the chimney. He got out, grabbed his grouse. With his Remington twelve-gage pump in his other hand he said, "Get out and go inside."

"You don't understand," said Katherine urgently. "My husband is..."

"Quiet," said Jean.

He moved the gun so its muzzle nearly pointed at Katherine's head. "Inside."

Katherine and Sophia shared an anxious look and followed his orders. Jean followed.

The place was spartan and smelled like wild game frying. There was another man in military fatigues the same size as the first with similar looks. He had a long brown beard, and from the crudely made tattoos climbing up from under his collar and down from his jacket sleeves, Katherine wondered if he'd escaped from prison. She had never fully believed all the stories in the news about survivalists hiding in the mountains of Montana, dodging law enforcement for years, but now here they were, and she was at their mercy.

"So, what do we have here? You been down to the country club?" The other man thought he was funny.

"They was trespassin' on our land. This one's aunt was old Aunt Ethel's friend's niece and this one's Hawthorne's woman."

"They look pretty damn nice. Good work, bro!"

"I think I remember you also, you two are brothers.

You're...Mac. I remember way back going to your aunt's home. Didn't you guys build a tree house that looked like a fort in her big tree out back?"

"That'd be us. Glad to see ya," said Mac, as he switched focus to Sophia.

Sophia stepped back as he undressed her with his gaze. She tried to maintain her regal bearing, but Katherine could see beads of sweat beginning to form on her forehead.

Katherine forced herself not to think about anything but what she had to do. "Gentlemen. We need your help. I am trying to get to my husband's compound as quickly as possible because he's about to do something very bad."

"That's all he's ever did, as far as we know." Mac picked up a part of a deer leg out of the pan on the stove and took a bite.

"So, do you think you could help us take them down?"

The hunters looked at her with identical expressions of interest and skepticism.

"Why would you wanna to do that?"

"Because what he's about to do will bring down the world economy," she said. "And that will hurt every one of us."

The first brother sneered. "You think we need the world economy to survive?"

But the bearded one thought it over. "I don't suppose you have any proof of this."

Katherine looked questioningly at Sophia.

"I would if you had internet access."

He snorted.

"I know, that's absurd. But I..."

"I guess this place doesn't look very civilized to a lady like yourself," Mac said snidely. "I'm sure a woman like you could never think that us up here could ever be wired."

Katherine knew they were playing with her, testing her. She didn't have time for this. "Of course you are," she said, forcing a smile. "In fact, I think I've heard of you. You're freedom fighters, protecting our rights to liberty and arms. You're leaders up here, showing people how to keep the government off your trail. You guys are practically famous."

It was a gamble, pulled from a Reuter's story about militiamen in Lolo she had read.

"Maybe you *have* heard," Jimbo said at last. "I write a newsletter. Here, take a look." He placed a few dirty pamphlets in her hands. "Have thousands of readers. All of 'em sovereign citizens."

Katherine skimmed his newsletters and looked as impressed as she could. Most of them were about the "new world order," a conspiracy to rob every individual of his rights.

Jean brought Mac over to the corner of the room. "Do you have any horses here?"

"Sure we do. There's four of them. They're probably in the barn because of the snow."

"With all this fuss, would you mind if I took one up to Hawthorne's place? It's a matter of time, and by the time these three settle everything I can at least get there and do what I can with Hawthorne. He killed my niece. So I have my own reasons."

"Sure, Jean. I'm sorry. You have a gun?"

"Of course. Never go anywhere without packing. Which horse is the fastest?"

"Here, I'll bring you out there to the barn. Jitterbug's the gelding, I'd go with him."

"Girls, I'll see you up there," Jean nonchalantly announced.

"What!" said Sophia.

She waved away her concern and slipped out the cabin door. "Don't worry about me," she called back, leaving Sophia and Katherine stunned with another change in the plan.

Mac quickly helped Jean saddle up. "You know where it is? It's not far. Got a compass?"

"In my pocket," said Jean.

"It's magnetic north from here to a lodge pole pine. In about three miles you'll see an 'X' engraved in the tree. Turn left. Our friend Keith left here on his four-wheeler this morning so you may be able to track him. I think he's the only employee left. That's why your mission, besides him murdering your niece, makes hell of lot of sense to me. Tell 'em you've been friends with us since we were kids."

"Thanks Mac. Appreciate the help."

He watched as Jean looked at her compass, took off in a trot, and then a full gallop.

★★★

Katherine had been reading Jimbo's newspaper, trying to figure out a way to weave Michael's plan into Jimbo's theories, hoping it would light a fire and create a sense of urgency about the situation. "My god," Katherine said. "From what I can tell, my husband is about to bring exactly the new world order you're writing about here. He's attacking the world's financial grid, which will kill the private citizen and give the United Nations the excuse they've been waiting for to impose a dictatorship. The death of the free market will turn everyone but the elite into pawns with no rights."

"Prove it," said Jimbo.

His brother whipped a tarp off a table in the back of the shack. There sat a battered Dell computer, and when he clicked on the monitor she saw the Google home screen.

The connection was slow, and Katherine had to suppress an urge to scream as she waited for her Gmail to load. But there, at last, was a message from Jack from his Stanford and Jones account, frantic that she had disappeared on him and telling her that he and his crew were nearly finished with an algorithm to counter Michael's assault on the financial infrastructure. At the end of the message he told her they only had another hour. The email was twenty-eight minutes old.

"Thirty-two minutes from now," said Katherine, "American liberty will be assassinated. You've got to let me go."

Jimbo chuckled. "You ain't gettin' up there by car. Not in no thirty-two minutes and not in no thirty-two days."

Katherine could only stare at him.

Then he stood up and said, "I'm goin' to get them snowmobiles."

"Jean left on Jitterbug already."

Katherine exhaled. She suddenly felt dizzy and realized she hadn't taken a full breath since they'd entered the shack.

"You can't get on a snowmobile with the damned ridiculous things you're wearin'," Jimbo said to Sophia. "Put on these here pack boots."

Sophia cringed, took off her heels, and stepped into the heavy boots. The man opened a closet and threw them each a long, heavy camouflage coat. As they started to put them on he took a deep sniff and acted like he'd detected skunk.

"No, stop!" He raised and shook his arms. "Give 'em back!" He grabbed the coats.

Katherine wondered what kind of nut case he really was.

"I'll never kill another animal if you put 'em on with all the foo-foo stuff you're wearin'. Game will smell me for miles. I'm gonna reek like a perfume factory!" He went back into the closet and threw them each a scratchy, woolen blanket.

Sophia tried to flip it over her shoulder and wear it like a pashmina. She walked away. Katherine knew she was trying to find a mirror.

"This ain't no fuckin' fashion show," Mac said. "Come here. This here is the way you're gonna do it." He wrapped Katherine in the red blanket with the black stripe. He grabbed Sophia's green one and tucked it around her tightly. Then he pushed them both out the door.

Jimbo had the sleds waiting. "We're goin' to be haulin' ass," he said, "so get on and hold on!"

CHAPTER FIFTY-SEVEN

He could barely contain his fury. Fury at himself. He'd wasted precious time searching the house. He never should have gone back. He should have stayed in his compound every second until this was done and he should never have stopped taking the Xanax, he would have been able to think more calmly.

Fury at the Hellbitch. No matter what she'd done with the flash drive, she'd already thrown him off his stride. She's why he dropped it in the first place. She's why he'd felt the need to speed things up, going back to Kinkster to taunt him.

Updrafts and snow had slowed them down, stretched the flight to one hundred and thirty-two minutes and they still had the final climb to make. And now Rick was losing his nerve.

"Sir, the weather is deteriorating. Gusts over the pass are probably breaking forty miles an hour. We need to set down and let the worst of it move on. There's a landing pad at Lolo Hot Springs."

"We're not setting down anywhere except my compound," said Michael. His voice was as calm and cold as a glacier.

"We need to land and wait it out. Once the winds have died down we can cover the last leg in fifteen minutes. You'll be at the compound tonight, I'm positive."

"You know tonight is too late. Did you forget we're scheduled to fly to Costa Rica? I'll be at the compound fifteen minutes from now. Surely a man of your experience can fly us through a few gusts."

"It's precisely, sir, because of my experience, that I refuse to fly into this. With all due respect, I don't think you can imagine what bad weather conditions do to the control of a craft."

With all due respect. Arrogant prick.

Michael grabbed a rope off the floor of the helicopter. In one deft motion he looped it around Rick's throat and pulled it closed.

"What are you doing?" Rick yelled.

"Careful, Rick," Michael said with a smile. "Don't take your hands off the controls or we're both dead."

"What the *fuck* do you think you're *doing?*" Rick roared. "We're both dead if you don't get that fucking thing off my neck!"

"No, that's not right. You're going to fly us to the compound and set us down, or I'm going to take the controls away from you and do it myself."

"Sir, you could never land this thing in this wind!"

"Want to find out?" Michael asked, and he pulled the noose tighter.

"All right! All right! Fuck! Just stay calm and I'll take us in!"

Michael kept his hand on the noose the entire time Rick brought them over Highway 12, staying in the shelter of the cliff faces, and up the last thousand feet. The wind buffeted them and the snow cut their visibility, but soon enough Michael saw his compound ahead of them.

There was no sign of anyone. He should have known. All those fears the Hellbitch would crack his code and send someone after him were just last-minute jitters. Now he was almost sorry he had left the one big, stupid mountain man up there for security. He might come out when he heard the copter. He might complicate what had to happen next.

The helicopter pitched as it neared the pad. Rick wrestled it under control and brought it down with a bump. He cut the engine and sank back into his seat.

"All right," he exhaled. "You got your way, sir."

"Excellent job, Rick. You deserve a rest."

"Sir, with this kind of weather it's not the night to fly down to Central America. Now that we made it here we should let Gunner know. He has the jet in Missoula but that trip has to wait until the morning. For safety reasons I don't want to fly out of here before this storm is over."

"Oh, you won't," said Michael. And he tightened the noose.

Rick thrashed. He was bigger than Michael and greater in pure strength. But Michael had slipped behind his seat and taken the advantage in leverage. He pulled as tightly as he could, planted a knee in the back of Rick's seat, and hung on. Within a couple of minutes, it was over.

That was annoying, too. The first time he'd ever killed anyone with his bare hands, and he couldn't stop to savor it. He'd thought he could take his time with the first one, make it a special moment. But then wasn't the first time always a letdown? Maybe you just had to get it out of the way.

He called Gunner and said to be ready with the jet soon and not to bother to file a flight plan. He'd be there within the hour. He rolled Rick's lifeless body out of the helicopter.

CHAPTER FIFTY-EIGHT

As they flew through the pines and started to turn left, there was Jean galloping like wind and fire, more like a Kentucky Derby jockey with a cowgirl hat on, leaning forward, feet up in her stirrups, keeping him at a steady gallop. The horse heard the machines and she spun him around to the side to let the four wheelers pass. Katherine kept looking back and Jean was shockingly not far behind.

Katherine was hanging onto Jimbo's militiaman's jacket with one hand while holding her blanket with the other. At first she hadn't recognized the entrance to the Cave. She was looking at what she thought was a moss-covered wall when an earthen slab lifted up like a sod covered garage door and a huge man with a gun stepped through.

"Oh god," she gasped. "There's a guard."

"There sure is," the militiaman replied as he brought the four-wheeler to a halt. The man hoisted his gun and Katherine dove for cover, but he didn't shoot.

At which point the guard hollered, "Howdy, Jimbo! Howdy, Mac!" And he started walking down toward them, waving his automatic rifle in greeting.

"You know him?" Katherine asked.

"That's our friend Keith," Mac said with a grin. "Your husband's been hiring him off and on, never knowing he was financing us. Truth to tell, the only

387

reason I was willin' to believe your story was that Keith told us the bastard had fired everybody else and was actin' like somethin' big was about to happen."

Katherine shook her head. "Montana again," she said.

"You picked a good time to visit," Keith said as he came near them. "No one around but us. Now who are the females? "

Jean came up slowing to a walk and stopped.

"This is Jean," said Mac. "Her aunt and our Aunt used to be close friends."

"Well I'll be damned, that's Jitterbug!"

"Please," said Katherine. "I just need to get into Mr. Hawthorne's command area. Right away."

Keith turned an inquiring gaze toward Jimbo.

Jimbo replied, "Whatever her royal highness wants."

"I don't know," said Keith. "He pays me good wages."

"He's insane," retorted Katherine. "He's an evil psychotic, a sadist and willing to ruin the world because he can't have his way."

Keith nodded slowly. "And he's an elitist gasper, also."

"Which is what really matters, after all," muttered Sophia.

"Mac, take Jitterbug around back, out of the wind, so he can get some rest and cool down."

The big man turned without a word and walked back toward the entrance. Jean went in, Katherine and Sophia hesitated, until Jimbo pushed them forward. Apparently they were meant to follow.

Keith had led them silently through a maze of tunnels until they reached a room with its four walls lined with computer screens. Katherine stared at the screen in front of her, wondering what to do next.

Getting to this point had been almost bizarrely easy, as if God were parting the seas to let them through, but now she had hit a wall.

She looked at her phone. Five bars. Michael's compound was well wired. She dialed Jack.

Behind her, the big men turned as one and started back the way they came.

"You're not leaving us?" shrieked Sophia.

"We'd just as soon not be here when the owner comes home," said Jimbo. "Not that we're afraid, understand. But no free creature stays free by stickin' around with its foot in a trap."

"But what if we need you?" asked Sophia.

"Hush," said Jean.

"Always best not to need anyone, ma'am," said Keith, and they were gone.

"Katherine!" Jack yelled over the phone. "Where *are* you?"

"I'm in his command room," she said. "Now I hope to god you can tell me what to do."

"The first thing you've got to do is get me into his computer system," said Jack. "I think we may be able to negate his algo, but we've got to get it in there. And Katherine...we've got five minutes."

She put her phone on speaker. "The screen reads, 'Password required.' What now?"

"I...I don't know," Jack stammered. "There's nothing

in this code about his password...You need to think what password Michael would have used."

"Jack, there's got to be some way to hack this!"

"I'm sure, but it would take time. I'm betting this is a password he kept in memory, one that was never put down anywhere. What would he use?"

"His birthday?" questioned Sophia, leaning over the back of Katherine's chair.

"That's too obvious for Michael, but it's worth a try." Katherine typed it in. The screen changed, but not the way she wanted.

She read, "'Trespassing on BotDom domain is punishable by tight rope. Don't lose your balance!' It's flashing a winky-face icon. It's like the arrogant ass was expecting someone!"

"Just concentrate, Katherine. What would he use?"

"Maybe our Antelope Club member number..."

Nothing.

"Try it backwards," said Sophia.

Nothing.

"Jack, this is insane. It's probably something I don't even know about."

"You don't know that, Katherine. Think of what's important to him."

Important to Michael? Control. Violence. Sadism.

Katherine punched in KINKSTER. Nothing. She punched in POLARIS. Then PUSSYWHIP. Nothing. Nothing.

Then she paused. There was one other Kinkster nickname he had seemed awfully fond of. She typed it slowly, all in caps:

H E L L B I T C H. Hellbitch!

A long string of code suddenly filled the screen.

"We're in!" yelled Katherine.

He talked her through the process of getting Michael's computer online and dialing the Stanford and Jones servers.

Katherine noticed Jean in her peripheral vision going to check out another set of computer rooms.

"I've got it, Katherine. I'm seeing what you see. Now you have to get into his commands for the launch sequence." He recited a series of letters and numbers that she typed as quickly as she could. "The screen should be coming up now...It's all there...the stocks he's going to torpedo...we've just got to upload this reverse algo..."

"Jack, we're almost out of time!"

"I know, I know. I can send you the formula, but you're going to have to initiate it there. The whole system is set up to respond only to commands from *that* computer. Hang on..."

Katherine heard a noise behind her. It sounded like a grunt from Sophia, then a scuffle. She didn't dare look away from the screen.

"Jack, for god's sake..."

"It's nearly up. You just have to hit 'Enter' when I tell you, that's all."

"Jack..."

Then she felt the noose around her neck. It pulled her out of her seat. She couldn't breathe, the pain burned through her, but she blocked out all thoughts of everything but the Enter button.

"Now, Katherine!"

She stretched her finger toward the button, but the noose kept pulling her back. Her finger wouldn't reach. She strained desperately, but the noose pulled harder.

"Katherine! Hit Enter!"

"It's too late," hissed the voice in her ear. "Watch."

The algorithm on the screen flew into motion, numbers rolling past at ever increasing speed. The screens on the walls to both sides of her suddenly lit up with symbols Katherine recognized instantly: stock market reports.

"Katherine?" said Jack. He sounded lost. "Katherine...it's happened...it's happened..."

"And don't you feel privileged to have watched it from the front row, Jack?"

"Michael?"

"Who did you think?"

"Michael, where's Katherine?"

"Oh, she's right here, Jack. She's hearing everything you say. And she will for another minute or so."

Katherine struggled against Michael's grasp. She clawed at the noose and then reached back and tried to claw at him. It was no good. He had her trapped. She couldn't breathe. Her vision was closing down and her body was losing its strength. Darkness was coming. She could feel Michael's fingers shaking her neck while holding the noose.

"Do you even know *why* you're a Hellbitch? Do you? You stole my flash drive thinking you could stop me? You control nothing. You are nothing but a jailer guarding the prison of compromise, concealment, pretense, denial—everything I hated during those years of pretending, pretending to be mainstream, pretending to be your husband. You had these stupid wifely expectations, that I should fulfill the little role I was faking—Ha! You were too dense to see the real me, to understand that I'm something so much greater. That was the hell I was living in—and you're the bitch who held me trapped in it day after day, month after month. I even broke down, invited you to join me at Kinkster, but you couldn't even play a tiny, tiny bit. I'm sending you back straight to where the wicked are punished after death. Look at those screens. Beautiful! There will be nothing left and I'll own it all. I'll be…"

Jean walked into the room with her Glock pointed at Michael.

"Never killed anyone before, but now seems like the right time."

But Michael's grip wouldn't loosen. He clung like a snake to its prey, every ounce of strength and hatred in him channeled into his hands, into that noose.

Jean walked up to Michael slowly with her gun ready to fire. "Drop the rope."

As the darkness closed in, Katherine saw the stock prices on the screen plummeting further. She had the strange thought that the last thing she would be aware of in her life was an economic disaster. And her failure to stop it.

Jean took a shot purposely to just miss him and then went up to him and held the gun to his head. He loosened the rope.

It drove Katherine down hard into the keyboard. She felt the cut of the noose and pulled hard to remove it. It came free, and air tore painfully through her throat. Michael ran.

Jean saw the Sheriff who had come with Nick. They were moving in closely as Michael turned to run through another maze.

Katherine felt big hands on her shoulders, and a voice seemed to come from far away.

Jean said to Dan, "He's yours now." She dropped her gun as the Sheriff and Nick were on the chase for Michael.

Dan followed yelling as he ran, "Hope you're alright Katherine."

Then there were other sounds and voices that she struggled to make sense of. Nick and Dan were blocked right as a metal door shut before them. "Damn." They looked at the pad next to the door. There had to be a password for that, too. Dan turned on his heel to run back to Jean and Katherine, hoping they had any ideas for the passcode.

Katherine saw the screen. Her vision was blurry but she hit enter. She called out, as loudly as she could stand to, "Jack. I just hit enter and nothing is reversing. Do...what we said. Buy long... buy up all the stocks Michael sold."

"I've been doing it, Katherine," came Jack's voice. "All our assets, S&J's DMA and all their credit. I'm forcing long positions on everything he's shorting. But Katherine...it's too big..."

Dan came in and looked at Jean. "What's going on

here?"

"What *is* going on here?" said Jean. "I think Katherine tried her best to tell you. Michael killed my niece because she knew too much. Scott was stealing money and then getting loans from Michael, who as you are about to see, is planning to take down the world's financial economies. Katherine put the pieces together and here we are, stuck in this limbo. Now we have to hope Nick catches the bastard."

"I need a password for his thick metal doors," said Dan.

"Try HELLBITCH or POLARIS," said Katherine.

"Or 0LT, their truck," said Dan in a low tone as he began to run. "The FedEx truck that planted the bomb."

"Like Zero Latency Trading?" said Katherine loudly. "That would be Michael."

Dan made it back to Nick.

Katherine raised herself by the edge of the desk and leaned into the screen closely enough so that she could see the numbers. She could make out some of the numbers going briefly up, but then they started plateauing.

"Katherine, are you there?" called Jack.

"Keep buying," she gasped.

"Katherine, we're buying as fast as we can, but even with all our positions it's still hemorrhaging. What he's done is like an avalanche. The reverse algo missed the launch window when you couldn't press enter. Now we're trying to mop up a mess that keeps growing. Look at the screen!"

"You can't give up…"

"He has the media saying nuclear warheads are launching in North Korea, but my guy is reverse retweeting that one in a huge way. Doesn't make any difference, though. Katherine, I'm sorry…I don't know what else to do."

She watched as the numbers began dropping again, faster and faster.

Michael had won.

"We were so close," Jack said. "Just a few seconds earlier and we could have stopped it."

Katherine couldn't respond. She could only watch the numbers fall, watch the crash unfold.

"God," Jack said, "if we could only reach back in time, just a few minutes…"

"Jack."

"It's all evaporating, everything we own, everything we…"

"Jack. Shut up." Her mind was whirling, thoughts flashing into view and then vanishing again into the clouds still filling her brain. What Jack had said… going back in time…

"Yahoo!," she said under her breath. "Jack. What happened at Yahoo!. The glitch with the timestamps, trades executed on quotes that executed one hundred and ninety milliseconds into the future. They called them *fantaseconds*."

"Yes, of course I heard about it. But what does it matter?"

"We can't go back in time, but we can go *forward*. Yahoo! traded into the future. If we can do that too, slam our orders into the markets *ahead* of Michael's..."

"What good will that do?"

"Have faith in me, Jack. Mess with the time stamps. Replicate what happened at Yahoo!."

"I guess it's possible...but..."

"Jack," she yelled. "What *else* is there to do?"

"Okay, okay," he said. She could tell he was fighting panic. "Okay, I'm working on it."

Katherine closed her eyes, forcing herself to think clearly. "His whole game is based on setting off a downward trend and then amplifying the cascade. As prices drop, he makes them drop faster. If you alter the directive equations by fantaseconds, create a future that he never thought could exist, make his algos start hitting prices falling back—they might *flip*."

"Okay, hold on, hold on!" Jack's voice was nearly screeching.

"Jack, just forget everything and do it." Katherine's voice was very calm, a still point in the midst of the tornado. "Nothing exists but the work."

It was suddenly very quiet. Katherine stared at the screen, flashing like a strobe as an endless sequence of numbers rolled across it.

"Jack, are you there?"

Katherine heard nothing on the other end.

"Jack?"

"Katherine. I've done it, I've changed the time stamps, but you're going to have to enter the code. I'm sending it right now."

"Got it. It's here. Okay. Copying...and entering."

She watched the screen with the market prices.

They kept dropping.

"Nothing's happening," said Jack. "It's too much for us, Katherine."

Katherine eyes were frozen on the screen. Then, after a few seconds, she saw it; one set of prices moved up by three-quarters of a cent. She held her breath. It dropped again, then bounced up again. She scanned the screen. From one stock to another, the prices started jumping, huge leaps up followed instantly by deep, dizzying drops and skyrocketing rebounds.

"Look at it, Jack," she said.

"The numbers are going crazy," he said urgently. "The algos are crisscrossing, contradicting each other. It's all out of control."

"It's out of control," said Katherine, "but it's not a *crash* anymore."

They watched the careening figures in silence for another minute. Then Jack yelled, "Look at them, Katherine! Look at them!" He was screaming now. "Katherine...they're *stabilizing!*"

CHAPTER FIFTY-NINE

He had won. Beyond the mountains and the swirling snow, the financial infrastructure of the world was crashing down. He had executed the boldest, most brilliant, most financially devastating plan in the history of mankind. They had done everything they could to stop him, but he had beaten them. All they had succeeded in doing was making it harder for him to get away with it.

Escaping the Sheriff had been too easy. Of course he would be more concerned about the welfare of the Hellbitch. His PI had given a good chase and Michael barely had time to reach the console that closed all the doors in the compound. Now they all would have to get through one set of emergency doors after another, as Michael vanished into the flurries of white and made his way to the landing pad.

The Sheriff had landed his Montana Fish and Wildlife helicopter just twenty yards from Michael's chopper, but the idiot hadn't thought to disable his Bell. His escape was assured.

Now he just had to get his chopper to Missoula and he and Gunner would fly down to the island. He'd keep Gunner. It was too bad about Rick, really. Two pilots in the sky, like two engines, were better than one, but he was a numbers guy and flying was nothing but another formula. Michael was certain, license or not, he was a master pilot.

He swept snow from the cockpit windows with his hands, then jumped into the Bell and warmed his engines quickly. The winds were dropping now, the snow thinning so that he could see the cliffs and the gray skies. A perfect portal was opening for his escape. As he lifted to the hover, his landing gear stuck to the icy ground, threatening a rollover, but he guided the controls masterfully. He rose into the air and increased his speed.

He felt a sudden pitch to starboard, had to react quickly to adjust. He craned out to look down and see if something was dragging. It took him a moment to make sense of the strange object swinging on a rope from the bottom of his craft, but then he got it: the noose around Rick's neck had become tangled in the landing gear. Now he had one hundred and eighty pounds of dead weight swinging like a pendulum below him. It was nothing the Bell couldn't handle, but with the corpse whipping in the wind he'd have to steer more carefully. He looked down again to see if there was some easy way to dislodge it.

He saw a pine tree below him, but by the time he saw how the body was swinging toward it, he had no time to adjust. Rick's limp body smacked into the branches near the top of the tree and was caught. The rope pulled taut for an instant, unsteadying the craft. Michael increased acceleration and the rope snapped, but he couldn't control the pitch, and the Bell tilted into a steep angle.

Michael knew exactly what he had to do. Swing

the rudder against the pitch, increase rotor rpm, and stabilize. But his neurons couldn't fire quite fast enough, and before he could take control, the Bell was spinning off to the right.

Then he saw the granite cliff.

CHAPTER SIXTY

She heard the roar of a distant blast rolling through the corridors. She turned to look, but couldn't see anything past the doorway of the computer room. Then she saw Sophia, sitting on the floor with her back against the wall.

"So, did we win?" she asked.

"Depends how you look at it."

"Where are Dan and Nick, anyway?"

"I think once it dawned on them that you were busy saving the world he and Nick went looking for your husband," said Jean.

Katherine looked down the hallway they'd come through. She wanted to know what was happening outside, but she was also afraid to know.

Jack's voice came from the phone. He was hoarse from screaming. "Katherine, are you still there? Can you see the market numbers?"

Katherine's eyes couldn't focus on the screens. She leaned against the wall, feeling dizzy. The adrenaline was rushing out of her, leaving her empty and very aware of everything her body and emotions had been through. "You'll have to summarize for me, Jack."

"It's settling down," he sighed. "I think we've survived. Of course, the markets are in chaos and vulnerable to god knows what. We're going to need someone who really understands what happened to help us sort it out."

"Are you talking about me?"

"You'll have the resources," said Jack.

"How do you figure that?"

"I was just looking at the stocks we went long on in the middle of the crisis. It appears that you, I, and Stanford and Jones have just made a great deal of money."

Katherine shook her head. "Are you telling me that I actually profited from this?"

"A great investor profits from everything," Jack laughed. "You were always at the top, but now you're way ahead."

"I'll get back to you on my new philanthropic plans later," said Katherine. She turned and looked down the corridor again. Quietly, she added, "I have to find out what's happened to Michael."

Jean and Sophia supported her as she walked, slow and wobbly, through the corridors of the silent complex. Nick and Dan had shot their way through the thick doors, leaving them open to a cold wind that grew stronger as they drew near the front. At last they could see the gray sky through the dark square of the entrance. The silhouette of a man stepped suddenly in front of it.

"Sophia," he said. Nick walked quickly toward them. He tossed a quick smile at Jean and Katherine, but it was clear to her where his attention was focused. "Are you okay?"

She didn't answer, just accepted his outstretched arms and held him tightly.

He stepped back from the embrace, whipped a handkerchief from his pocket and started drying up the tears. His eyes devoured hers. "Just like old times, hmm?" he said softly.

"I suppose it's not the first time you've shown up just in time to save me," she said.

"I think you owe me something for that, don't you?"

"I do," she said. She gazed at him a moment longer, then she said, "Why don't you come over for dinner with John and me? I'll make you that Italian fish dish you used to love."

Nick flinched the tiniest bit. Then his smile widened and he chuckled. "I'm sure I'd have the time of my life," he said.

Dan stood at the edge of the stone terrace in front of the compound, looking across the gorge in front of them through binoculars. Jean and Katherine walked toward the edge, some distance from the Sheriff, and followed his gaze.

The smoky wreckage of a helicopter lay in the distant snow.

Katherine didn't have to ask who was inside it. The whole nightmare since Stacey's death was finally over. And so was her life with Michael.

The open space dream, the marriage to her Big Man of the Big Sky, had twisted and twisted and finally exploded until there was nothing left but a fiery corpse inside a blackened chopper. Money, power, greed, and lust had been turned to ashes almost as quickly as a flash of a BotDom trade. Death. As incomprehensible as the man she had once thought she'd loved.

She heard Dan's footsteps. He came up and stood next to her, putting his jacket around her shoulders. It was bitter cold. Snowy wind gusts felt like sand paper scraping her face.

"I'm sorry," he said. "Sorry for your loss. And I'm very sorry I didn't listen to you with more urgency."

"He killed Stacey because she watched Scott steal money from the Club and invest with Michael. Stacey got close to Michael to see what was truly going on."

She became embedded in her own thoughts. "I tried so hard to be the wife I thought I was supposed to be with Michael. But it was all a lie, a half-life."

"Maybe you need a different kind of life," Dan replied.

She looked at him.

She looked deeply into the big man with the big Stetson and the big hands but instead of seeing the dirt and grime and blood and slowness she saw the clarity of the mountains, the trees, the sky, the river and the moon. She paused as she felt it inside. "I'm wishing for the Montana way."

Jean came up to them both. "Now's not probably the time, Katherine, but to hell with it. What I wanted to tell you when you called so early in the morning, which now seems like days ago, is the WPR voted you in to become a fulltime member. They never told you, but they were watching how you handled your horse way back in March. New members were just voted in and now you're welcome on your own." Katherine hugged Jean and Dan took off his hat and tipped it in admiration.

EPILOGUE

Diana checked the golden Penn International reel, then the Black Bart Marlin Candy lures bobbing along through the water, forty feet away. They were out a couple of miles now. The water was deep but her thoughts weren't; all she wanted was to hook a big billfish. Too much, in fact. She knew how it worked mentally. She had to let the obsession go before it would happen.

She looked around her and smiled. She had her dreamboat at last, and it wasn't a man. Not that there were no men. A sixty-eight foot Merritt sport fisher with a nineteen and half foot beam, crewed by tanned and muscled poster boys as gorgeous as the vessel's fine teak wood work. Her mind drifted back to last night, in the cove, swimming naked in the warm waters, knowing they were watching her. It wasn't quite as thrilling as posing for Zig's photos. She missed that rush.

And then, as was usually the case when she started thinking about anything else, it struck. The rod bent and a moment later she saw the bill break from the water. She was in the seat, adrenaline pumping, fighting what felt like a monster of a fish with all her might.

"*Señorita Parker*," came a voice.

Fernando, her chef, brought up her iPad from

406

below. Why in the hell now? He was the best-looking one on the crew, and very good at making sure her nights on the vessel were as adventurous as the days, but he wasn't the brightest of the bunch. And he was definitely not a fisherman.

"¡No *ahora!*" she yelled. A spray of water covered the back of the boat. "Take it down. It'll get wet."

"*Si, si.*"

He vanished back down the stairs, hopefully to stay near his Wolf cook top.

This fight was harder than those from the last few days. Even with the monster of a sea vessel and an expert captain, she held on to the bent rod for what seemed like hours. Reeling up, then holding tightly as the thick line, compared to trout fishing, unspooled with great speed. The bill fish would sound, go deep below, then break from the waters and jump, coming down with a huge splash.

Maybe he would break off and escape, as she had done. But she would play it fairly, unlike Michael.

Stacey should have known when she raced down the trail to meet him at her home that his message was a trap; he wasn't changing his mind about his financial genocide and he wasn't giving back a cent of the millions Scott had invested with him. The Club's money. Michael thought Scott deserved to lose his money because of his greed. But Michael's greed was far worse.

She had gone directly to her barn, unsaddled her horse, taken off her boots and put on her clogs. As she had headed for the house she couldn't find her keys in her saddle horn bag. She had ended up unlocking the house and flipping on the lights remotely from her phone. She still shuddered when she thought of her intended demise.

She had known Michael was behind the deathly blow. She'd been lucky she kept a fireproof box of substantial cash buried on her property, just like her parents and her grandparents had done. As far back as she could remember, her family hadn't trusted banks. They couldn't have been more correct. And she'd known her old gardener would never talk. She'd given him more cash than his old Chevy truck was worth and she'd driven all the way to Minneapolis and purchased a new identity. Now Diana Parker was peacefully casting her dream.

The crew, apart from Fernando, was as excited as she was about the huge marlin. When it finally came close to the boat, they asked if she wanted it. They should have known by now that a photo would suffice. *"Dejo vivir. Viva y dejo vivir!"*

Let it live. Live and let live. Let them all live. Another day of raging, beautiful life.

Fernando brought back her iPad. Why did he fucking think she wanted to look at her iPad?

"¿Usted quiere musica differente?"

No, she didn't want different music. The music she'd programmed into the boat's sound system was fine. She took it from him. In some ways she hated her iPad, but she still hadn't broken her old habits: her homepage was still the business news. Before she could toss it aside, she saw the headline.

HFT KING MICHAEL HAWTHORNE DEAD IN HELICOPTER CRASH

The details were fragmentary still. He had flown his helicopter into a cliff near his compound at Lolo Pass, that was clear. But there were also reports that he had murdered one person and assaulted at least one other. And somehow he may have been partly responsible for a disruption of the world's financial markets the same day.

So it was done. She felt a surprising moment of sorrow, and then the vast relief of her greatest fears flowing out of her. He would not be hunting her, intent on pulling off what he'd barely missed last time, and she could now rescue what he intended to destroy. Michael, believing she was dead, had forgotten she was also a founder of his island bank with full authority, which meant control. She could now complete her vision. She would convert his massive amounts of emeralds, diamonds, and gold back to liquid currency.

The Antelope Club would soon notice the infusion of their lost capital. And native Montanans, those who had lost their livelihoods because they no longer could work or hunt on land that had become the private domain of the overly privileged, would be getting assistance through designated funds from The Montana Treasure Foundation. Soon there would be a large anonymous donation to The Nature Conservancy and Trout Unlimited, to preserve, purchase and protect resources for *public* use. And the mortgage foundation that Katherine had founded with

Jack would have a major donator, thanks to Michael. Now Michael would be posthumously supporting the minions he sought to destroy.

She scanned the articles until she found the next piece she was looking for. "Hawthorne is now reportedly being connected to the recent arson-bombing of a home in Livingston, Montana. The home's resident, Antelope Club CFO Stacey Olsen, has not been found and is presumed dead."

Let her stay dead, then. And let Diana Parker live.

"Hold it here," she said to the captain. "I need to soak up some sunshine while it lasts."

She ran her fingers through her thick blonde mane and straightened out her bikini bottom. She asked for a towel and a glass of champagne and made her way to the smooth bow of the boat.

Raising her glass to the sun descending toward the sea she murmured. "*Viva y deja vivir.*"

Made in United States
Troutdale, OR
04/06/2024

18981967R00257